THE TEXANS

Time can dim the star of many a man, but not these *hombres* whose legacy will burn brightly in the western sky forever

THE BEST OF THE WEST

Traditional American fiction is alive in these pages filled with the fabled men of the time when this land was new

Other Western Anthologies
Edited by Bill Pronzini and Martin H. Greenberg:

TREASURY OF CIVIL WAR STORIES

THE WESTERN HALL OF FAME: *An Anthology of Classic Western Stories Selected by the Western Writers of America*

THE BEST WESTERN STORIES OF STEVE FRAZEE

THE LAWMEN*

THE OUTLAWS*

SECOND REEL WEST

THE COWBOYS*

THE WARRIORS*

THE THIRD REEL WEST

THE RAILROADERS*

THE STEAMBOATERS*

THE CATTLEMEN*

THE HORSE SOLDIERS*

THE GUNFIGHTERS*

*Published by Fawcett Books

THE TEXANS

Edited by
Bill Pronzini and
Martin H. Greenberg

FAWCETT GOLD MEDAL · NEW YORK

Acknowledgments

"The Ranger," by Zane Grey. Copyright 1929 by Curtis Publishing Company. Copyright renewed © 1957 by Lina Elise Grey; Copyright renewal to Zane Grey, Inc., © 1958. Reprinted by permission of Zane Grey, Inc.

"One More River to Cross," by William R. Cox. Copyright © 1966 by William R. Cox. Reprinted by permission of the author.

"The Beast and Sergeant Gilhooley," by Wayne Barton. Copyright © 1979 by Wayne Barton; first published in *Far West*, Summer 1979, Wright Publishing Company, Box 2260, Costa Mesa, CA 92626. Reprinted by permission of the author.

"Trail Song," by Bennett Foster. Copyright 1950 by the Curtis Publishing Company. Reprinted by permission of the Scott Meredith Literary Agency, Inc., 845 Third Avenue, New York, NY 10022.

"King Fisher's Road," by Clay Fisher. Copyright © 1978 by Clay Fisher. From *Nine Lives West* by Clay Fisher. Reprinted by permission of the author.

"The Last Indian Fight in Kerr County," by Elmer Kelton. Copyright © 1982 by The Western Writers of America, Inc. Reprinted by permission of the author.

Contents

Introduction

The Texans is the first volume in a new series of Western fiction anthologies. It contains stories not only set in the Lone Star State, but that fictionally recreate the many aspects of its colorful and exciting history—stories written primarily by authors past and present who have lived within its boundaries.

The eleven tales in these pages are told through the eyes of ranchers, cowboys, peace officers, Kiowa and Comanche Indians, soldiers, drifters, outlaws, gamblers, homesteaders, men involved in the transportation industry, a very special lady known as Lou, and many more. In them you'll visit such cities as Austin, San Antonio, Brownsville, Nacogdoches; you'll cross the Rio Grande river, ride with the Texas Rangers, travel the Goodnight-Loving Trail, traverse vast cattle ranges, venture into the Texas Panhandle and the red Caprock land; and you'll meet such historical figures as Sam Houston, Jim Bowie, King Fisher, and such legendary characters as Pecos Bill.

Subsequent volumes in the series will take you to California, Arizona, New Mexico, Montana, Wyoming, and other Western states large and small. In each book you'll find short Western fiction at its most entertaining and historically accurate, by such major writers as Zane Grey, Owen Wister, Mark Twain, Jack Schaefer, Dorothy M. Johnson, Louis L'Amour, Elmore Leonard, Loren D. Estleman, and Elmer Kelton.

We hope you enjoy this first leg of our fictional journey through the Old West, and all those that will follow.

—Bill Pronzini and
Martin H. Greenberg

1

A dentist who turned to the writing of stories of the American West at age thirty-two, Zane Grey became a legend in his own time—and the bestselling Western writer of all-time, with more than ten million copies sold before the advent of the paperback era. Among his sixty books are such classics as Riders of the Purple Sage *(1912),* The U.P. Trail *(1918),* The Vanishing American *(1925),* Arizona Ames *(1932), and* Western Union *(1939). A staggering total of 108 silent and sound films have been made from Grey's novels and shorter works. Although much of his fiction is set in Arizona, he wrote expertly about other areas of the Western frontier—nowhere better about the Lone Star State than in the border tale featuring Texas Ranger Vaughn Medill, which follows.*

The Ranger

★★★★★★★★★★★★★★★

Zane Grey

1

PERIODICALLY of late, especially after some bloody affray or other, Vaughn Medill, ranger of Texas, suffered from spells of depression and longing for a ranch and wife and children. The fact that few rangers ever attained these cherished possessions did not detract from their appeal. At such times the long service to his great state, which owed so much to the rangers, was apt to lose its importance.

Vaughn sat in the shade of the adobe house, on the bank of the slow-eddying, muddy Rio Grande, outside the town of Brownsville. He was alone at this ranger headquarters for the very good reason that his chief, Captain Allerton, and two comrades were laid up in the hospital. Vaughn, with his usual notorious luck, had come out of the Cutter rustling fight without a scratch.

He had needed a few days off, to go alone into the mountains and there get rid of the sickness killing always engendered in him. No wonder he got red in the face and swore when some admiring tourist asked him how many men he had killed. Vaughn had been long in the service. Like other Texas youths he had enlisted in this famous and unique state constabulary before he was twenty, and he refused to count the years he had served. He had the stature of the born Texan. And the lined, weathered face, the resolute lips, grim except when he smiled, and the narrowed eyes of cool gray, and the tinge of white over his temples did not begin to tell the truth about his age.

Vaughn watched the yellow river that separated his state from Mexico. He had reason to hate that strip of dirty water and the hot mosquito and cactus land beyond. Like as not, this very day or tomorrow he would have to go across and arrest some renegade native or fetch back a stolen calf or shoot it out with Quinola and his band, who were known to be on American soil again. Vaughn shared in common with all Texans a supreme contempt for people who were so unfortunate as to live south of the border. His father had been a soldier in both Texas wars, and Vaughn had inherited his conviction that all Mexicans were his natural enemies. He knew this was not really true. Villa was an old acquaintance, and he had listed among men to whom he owed his life, Martiniano, one of the greatest of the Texas *vaqueros*.

Brooding never got Vaughn anywhere, except into deeper melancholy. This drowsy summer day he got in very deep indeed, so deep that he began to mourn over the several girls he might—at least he believed he might—have married. It all seemed so long ago, when he was on fire with the ranger spirit and would not have sacrificed any girl to the agony of waiting for her ranger to come home—knowing that some day he would never come again. Since then sentimental affairs of the heart had been few and far between; and the very latest, dating to this very hour, concerned Roseta, daughter of Uvaldo, foreman for the big Glover ranch just down the river.

Uvaldo was a Mexican of quality, claiming descent from the Spanish soldier of that name. He had an American wife, owned many head of stock, and in fact was partner with Glover in several cattle deals. The black-eyed Roseta, his daughter, had been born on the American side of the river, and had shared advantages of school and contact, seldom the lot of most señoritas.

Vaughn ruminated over these few facts as the excuse for his infatuation. For a Texas ranger to fall in love with an ordinary Mexican girl was unthinkable. To be sure, it had happened, but it was something not to think about. Roseta, however, was extraordinary. She was pretty, and slight of stature—so slight that Vaughn felt ludicrous, despite his bliss, while dancing with her. If he had stretched out his long arm and she had walked under it, he would have had to lower his hand considerably to touch her glossy black head. She was roguish and coquettish, yet had the pride of her Spanish forebearers. Lastly she was young, rich, the belle of Las Animas, and the despair of cowboy and *vaquero* alike.

When Vaughn had descended to the depths of his brooding he discovered, as he had many times before, that there were but slight grounds for any hopes which he may have had of winning the beautiful Roseta. The sweetness of a haunting dream was all that could be his. Only this time it seemed to hurt more. He should not have let himself in for such a catastrophe. But as he groaned in spirit and bewailed his lonely state, he could not help recalling Roseta's smiles, her favors of dances when scores of admirers were thronging after her, and the way she would single him out on those occasions. *"Un señor grande,"* she had called him, and likewise "handsome gringo," and once, with mystery and fire in her sloe-black eyes, "You Texas ranger—you bloody gunman—killer of Mexicans!"

Flirt Roseta was, of course, and doubly dangerous by reason of her mixed blood, her Spanish lineage, and her American upbringing. Uvaldo had been quoted as saying he would never let his daughter marry across the Rio Grande. Some rich rancher's son would have her hand bestowed upon him; maybe young Glover would be the lucky one. It was madness for Vaughn even to have dreamed of winning her. Yet there still abided that much youth in him.

Sounds of wheels and hoofs interrupted the ranger's reverie. He listened. A buggy had stopped out in front. Vaughn got up and looked round the corner of the house. It was significant that he instinctively stepped out sideways, his right hand low where the heavy gun sheath hung. A ranger never presented his full front to possible bullets; it was a trick of old hands in the service.

Someone was helping a man out of the buggy. Presently Vaughn recognized Colville, a ranger comrade, who came in assisted, limping, and with his arm in a sling.

"How are you, Bill?" asked Vaughn solicitously, as he helped the driver lead Colville into the large whitewashed room.

"All right—fine, in fact, only a—little light-headed," panted the other. "Lost a sight of blood."

"You look it. Reckon you'd have done better to stay at the hospital."

"Medill, there ain't half enough rangers to go—round," replied Colville. "Cap Allerton is hurt bad—but he'll recover. An' he thought so long as I could wag I'd better come back to headquarters."

"Ahuh. What's up, Bill?" asked the ranger quietly. He really did not need to ask.

"Shore I don't know. Somethin' to do with Quinela," replied Colville. "Help me out of my coat. It's hot an' dusty. . . . Fetch me a cold drink."

"Bill, you should have stayed in town if it's ice you want," said Vaughn as he filled a dipper from the water bucket. "Haven't I run this shebang many a time?"

"Medill, you're slated for a run across the Rio—if I don't miss my guess."

"Hell you say! Alone?"

"How else, unless the rest of our outfit rides in from the Brazos. . . . Anyway, don't they call you the 'lone star ranger'? Haw! Haw!"

"Shore you don't have a hunch what's up?" inquired Vaughn again.

"Honest I don't. Allerton had to wait for more information. Then he'll send instructions. But we know Quinela was hangin' round, with some deviltry afoot."

"Bill, that bandit outfit is plumb bold these days," said Vaughn reflectively. "I wonder now."

"We're all guessin'. But Allerton swears Quinela is daid set on revenge. Lopez was some relation, we heah from Mexicans on this side. An' when we busted up Lopez' gang, we riled Quinela. He's laid that to you, Vaughn.''

"Nonsense," blurted out Vaughn. "Quinela has another raid on hand, or some other thievery job of his own."

"But didn't you kill Lopez?" asked Colville.

"I shore didn't," declared Vaughn testily. "Reckon I was there when it happened, but Lord! I wasn't the only ranger."

"Wal, you've got the name of it an' that's jist as bad. Not that it makes much difference. You're used to bein' laid for. But I reckon Cap wanted to tip you off."

"Ahuh . . . Say, Bill," continued Vaughn, dropping his head. "I'm shore tired of this ranger game."

"My Gawd, who ain't! But, Vaughn, *you* couldn't lay down on Captain Allerton right now."

"No. But I've a notion to resign when he gets well an' the boys come back from the Brazos."

"An' that'd be all right, Vaughn, although we'd hate to lose you," returned Colville earnestly. "We all know—in fact everybody who has followed the ranger service knows you should have been a captain long ago. But them pig-headed officials at Houston! Vaughn, your gun record—the very name an' skill that make you a great ranger—have operated against you there."

"Reckon so. But I never wanted particularly to be a captain—leastways of late years," replied Vaughn moodily. "I'm just tired of bein' eternally on my guard. Lookin' to be shot at from every corner or bush! Think what an awful thing it was—when I near killed one of my good friends—all because he came suddenlike out of a door, pullin' at his handkerchief!"

"It's the price we pay. Texas could never have been settled at all but for the buffalo hunters first, an' then us rangers. We don't get much credit, Vaughn. But we know someday our service will be appreciated. . . . In your case everythin' is magnified. Suppose you did quit the service? Wouldn't you still stand most the same risk? Wouldn't you need to be on your guard, sleepin' an' wakin'?"

"Wal, I suppose so, for a time. But somehow I'd be relieved."

"Vaughn, the men who are lookin' for you now will always be lookin', until they're daid."

"Shore. But, Bill, that class of men don't live long on the Texas border."

"Hell! Look at Wes Hardin', Kingfisher, Poggin—gunmen that took a long time to kill. An' look at Cortina, at Quinela—an' Villa. . . . Nope, I reckon it's the obscure relations an' friends of men you've shot that you have most to fear. An' you never know who an' where they are. It's my belief you'd be shore of longer life by stickin' to the rangers."

"Couldn't I get married an' go way off somewhere?" asked Vaughn belligerently.

Colville whistled in surprise, and then laughed. "Ahuh? So that's the lay of the land? A gal!—Wal, if the Texas ranger service is to suffer, let it be for that one cause."

Toward evening a messenger brought a letter from Captain Allerton, with the information that a drove of horses had been driven across the river west of Brownsville, at Rock Ford. They were in charge of Mexicans and presumably had been stolen from some ranch inland. The raid could be laid to Quinela, though there was no proof of it. It bore his brand. Medill's instructions were to take the rangers and recover the horses.

"Reckon Cap thinks the boys have got back from the Brazos or he's had word they're comin'," commented Colville. "Wish I was able to ride. We wouldn't wait."

Vaughn scanned the short letter again and then filed it away among a stack of others.

"Strange business this ranger service," he said ponderingly. "Horses stolen—fetch them back! Cattle raid—recover stock! Drunken cowboy shootin' up the town—arrest him! Bandits looted the San Tone stage—fetch them in! Little Tom, Dick, or Harry lost—find him! Farmer murdered—string up the murderer!"

"Wal, come to think about it, you're right," replied Colville. "But the rangers have been doin' it for thirty or forty years. You cain't help havin' pride in the service, Medill. Half the job's done when these hombres find a ranger's on the trail. That's reputation. But I'm bound to admit the thing is strange an' shore couldn't happen nowhere else but in Texas."

"Reckon I'd better ride up to Rock Ford an' have a look at that trail."

"Wal, I'd wait till mawnin'. Mebbe the boys will come in. An' there's no sense in ridin' it twice."

The following morning after breakfast Vaughn went out to the alfalfa pasture to fetch in his horse. Next to his gun a ranger's horse was his most valuable asset. Indeed a horse often saved a ranger's life when a gun could not. Star was a big-boned chestnut, not handsome except in regard to his size, but for speed and endurance Vaughn had never owned his like. They had been on some hard jaunts together. Vaughn fetched Star into the shed and saddled him.

Presently Vaughn heard Colville shout, and upon hurrying out he saw a horseman ride furiously away from the house. Colville stood in the door waving.

Vaughn soon reached him. "Who was that feller?"

"Glover's man, Uvaldo. You know him."

"Uvaldo!" exclaimed Vaughn, startled. "He shore was in a hurry. What'd he want?"

"Captain Allerton, an' in fact all the rangers in Texas. I told Uvaldo I'd send you down pronto. He wouldn't wait. Shore was mighty excited."

"What's wrong with him?"

"His gal is gone."

"Gone!"

"Shore. He cain't say whether she eloped or was kidnapped. But it's a job for you, old man. Haw! Haw!"

"Yes, it would be—if she eloped," replied Vaughn constrainedly. "An' I reckon not a bit funny, Bill."

"Wal, hop to it," replied Colville, turning to go into the house.

Vaughn mounted his horse and spurred him into the road.

2

VAUGHN'S personal opinion, before he arrived at Glover's ranch, was that Roseta Uvaldo had eloped, and probably with a cowboy or some *vaquero* with whom her father had forbidden her to associate. In some aspects Roseta resembled the vain daughter of a proud don; in the main, she was American bred and educated. But she had that strain of blood which might well have burned secretly to break the bonds of conventionality. Uvaldo, himself, had been a *vaquero* in his youth. Any Texan could have guessed this seeing Uvaldo ride a horse.

There was much excitement in the Uvaldo household. Vaughn could not get any clue out of the weeping kin folks, except that Roseta had slept in her bed, and had risen early to take her morning horseback ride. All Mexicans were of a highly excitable temperament, and Uvaldo was no exception. Vaughn could not get much out of him. Roseta had not been permitted to ride off the ranch, which was something that surprised Vaughn. She was not allowed to go anywhere unaccompanied. This certainly was a departure from the freedom accorded Texan girls; nevertheless any girl of good sense would give the river a wide berth.

"Did she ride out alone?" asked Vaughn, in his slow Spanish, thinking he could get at Uvaldo better in his own tongue.

"Yes, señor. Pedro saddled her horse. No one else saw her."

"What time this morning?"

"Before sunrise."

Vaughn questioned the lean, dark *vaquero* about what clothes the girl was wearing and how she had looked and acted. The answer was that Roseta had dressed in *vaquero* garb, looked very pretty and full of the devil. Vaughn reflected that this was quite easy to believe. Next he questioned the stable boys and other *vaqueros* about the place. Then he rode out to the Glover ranch house and got hold of some of the cowboys, and lastly young Glover himself. Nothing further was elicited from them, except that this same thing had happened before. Vaughn hurried back to Uvaldo's house.

He had been a ranger for fifteen years and that meant a vast experience in Texas border life. It had become a part of his business to look through people. Not often was Vaughn deceived when he put a query and bent his gaze upon a man. Women, of course, were different. Uvaldo himself was the only one here who roused a doubt in Vaughn's mind. This Americanized Mexican had a terrible fear which he did not realize that he was betraying. Vaughn conceived the impression that Uvaldo had an enemy and he had only to ask him if he knew Quinela to get on the track of something. Uvaldo was probably lying when he professed fear that Roseta had eloped.

"You think she ran off with a cowboy or some young feller from town?" inquired Vaughn.

"No, señor. With a *vaquero* or a peon," came the amazing reply.

Vaughn gave up here, seeing he was losing time.

"Pedro, show me Roseta's horse tracks," he requested.

"Señor, I will give you ten thousand dollars if you bring my daughter back—alive," said Uvaldo.

"Rangers don't accept money for their services," replied Vaughn briefly, further mystified by the Mexican's intimation that Roseta might be in danger of foul play. "I'll fetch her back—one way or another—unless she has eloped. If she's gotten married I can do nothin'."

Pedro showed the ranger the small hoof tracks made by Roseta's horse. He studied them a few moments, and then, motioning those following him to stay back, he led his own horse and walked out of the courtyard, down the lane, through the open gate, and into the field.

Every boy born on the open range of vast Texas had been a horse tracker from the time he could walk. Vaughn was a past master at this cowboy art, long before he joined the rangers, and years of man-hunting had perfected it. He could read a fugitive's mind by the tracks he left in dust or sand.

He rode across Glover's broad acres, through the pecans, to where the ranch bordered on the desert. Roseta had not been bent on an aimless morning ride.

Under a clump of trees someone had waited for her. Here Vaughn dismounted to study tracks. A mettlesome horse had been tethered to one tree. In the dust were imprints of a riding boot, not the kind left by cowboy or *vaquero*. Heel and toe were broad. He found the butt of a cigarette smoked that morning. Roseta's clandestine friend was not a Mexican, much less a peon or *vaquero*. There were signs that he probably had waited there on other mornings.

Vaughn got back on his horse, strengthened in the elopement theory, though not yet wholly convinced. Maybe Roseta was just having a lark. Maybe she had a lover Uvaldo would have none of. This idea grew as Vaughn saw where the horses had walked close together, so their riders could hold hands. Perhaps more! Vaughn's silly hope oozed out and died. And he swore at his own ridiculous, vain dreams. It was all right for him to be young enough to have an infatuation for Roseta Uvaldo, but to have entertained a dream of winning her was laughable. He laughed, though mirthlessly. And jealous pangs consumed him. What an adorable, fiery creature she was! Some lucky dog from Brownsville had won her. Mingled with Vaughn's romantic feelings was one of relief.

"Reckon I'd better get back to rangerin' instead of moonin'," he thought grimly.

The tracks led in a roundabout way through the mesquite to the river trail. This was two miles or more from the line of the Glover ranch. The trail was broad and lined by trees. It was a lonely and unfrequented place for lovers to ride. Roseta and her companion still were walking their horses. On this beautiful trail, which invited a gallop or at least a canter, only lovemaking could account for the leisurely gait. Also the risk! Whoever Roseta's lover might be, he was either a fool or plain fearless. Vaughn swore lustily as the tracks led on and on, deeper into the timber that bordered the Rio Grande.

Suddenly Vaughn drew up sharply, with an exclamation. Then he slid out of his saddle, to bend over a marked change in the tracks he was trailing. Both horses had reared, to come down hard on forehoofs, and then jump sideways.

"By God! A holdup!" grunted Vaughn in sudden concern.

Sandal tracks in the dust! A native bandit had been hiding behind a thicket in ambush. Vaughn swiftly tracked the horses off the trail, to an open glade on the bank, where hoof tracks of other horses joined them and likewise boot tracks. Vaughn did not need to see that these new marks had been made by Mexican boots.

Roseta had either been led into a trap by the man she had met or they had both been ambushed by three Mexicans. It was a common thing along the border for Mexican marauders to kidnap Mexican girls. The instances of abduction of American girls had been few and far between, though Vaughn remembered several over the years whom he had helped to rescue. They had been pretty sorry creatures, and one was even demented. Roseta being the daughter of the rich Uvaldo, would be held for ransom and therefore she might escape the usual horrible treatment. Vaughn's sincere and honest love for Roseta made him at once annoyed with her heedless act, jealous of the unknown who had kept tryst with her, and fearful of her possible fate.

"Three hours start on me," he muttered, consulting his watch. "Reckon I can come up on them before dark."

The ranger followed the broad, fresh trail that wound down through timber and brush to the river bottom. A border of arrow weed stretched out across a sand bar. All at once he halted stockstill, then moved as if to dismount. But it was not necessary. He could read from the saddle another story in the sand and this one was one of tragedy. A round depression in the sand and one spot of reddish color, obviously blood, on the slender white stalk of arrow weed, a heavy furrow, and then a path as though made by a dragged body through the green to the river—these easily-read signs added a sinister note to the abduction of Roseta Uvaldo. In Vaughn's estimation it cleared Roseta's comrade of all complicity, except that of heedless risk. And the affair began to savor somewhat of Quinela's work. The ranger wondered whether Quinela, the mere mention of whose name had brought a look of terror into Uvaldo's eyes when Vaughn had spoken to him, might not be a greater menace than the Americans believed. If so, then God help Roseta!

Vaughn took time enough to dismount and trail the path through the weeds where the murderers had dragged the body. They had been bold and careless. Vaughn picked up a cigarette case, a glove, and a watch, and he made sure that by the latter he could identify Roseta's companion on this fatal ride. A point of gravel led out to a deep current in the river, to which the body had been consigned. It might be several days and many miles below where the Rio Grande would give up its dead.

The exigencies of the case prevented Vaughn from going back after food and canteen. Many a time had he been caught in the same predicament. He had only his horse, a gun, and a belt full of cartridges. But they were sufficient for the job that lay ahead of him.

Hurrying back to Star he led him along the trail to the point where the Mexicans had gone into the river. The Rio was treacherous with quicksand, but it was always safe to follow Mexicans, provided one could imitate them. Vaughn spurred his horse across the oozy sand, and made deep water just in the nick of time. The swift current, however, was nothing for the powerful Star to breast. Vaughn emerged at precisely the point where the Mexicans had climbed out, but to help Star he threw himself forward, and catching some arrow weeds, hauled himself up the steep bank. Star floundered out and plunged up to solid ground.

The ranger mounted again and took the trail without any concern of being ambushed. Three Mexicans bent on a desperate deal of this sort would not hang back on the trail to wait for pursuers. Once up on the level mesquite land it was plain that they had traveled at a brisk trot. Vaughn loped Star along the well-defined tracks of five horses. At this gait he felt sure that he was covering two miles while they were traveling one. He calculated that they should be about fifteen miles ahead of him, unless rough country had slowed them, and that by early afternoon he ought to be close on their heels. If their trail had worked down the river toward Rock Ford he might have connected these three riders with the marauders mentioned in Captain Allerton's letter. But it led straight south of the Rio Grande and showed that the kidnapers had a definite destination in mind.

Vaughn rode for two hours before he began to climb out of the level river valley. Then he struck rocky hills covered with cactus and separated by dry gorges. There was no difficulty in following the trail, but he had to proceed more slowly. He did not intend that Roseta Uvaldo should be forced to spend a night in the clutches of these desperadoes. Toward noon the sun grew hot and Vaughn began to suffer from thirst. Star was soaked with sweat, but showed no sign of distress.

He came presently to a shady spot where it was evident that the abductors had halted, probably to eat and rest. The remains of a small fire showed in a circle of stones. Vaughn got off to put his hand on the mesquite ashes. They were still hot. This meant something, though not a great deal. Mesquite wood burned slowly and the ashes retained heat for a long while. Vaughn also examined horse tracks so fresh that no particle of dust had yet blown into them. Two hours behind, perhaps a little more or less!

He resumed the pursuit, making good time everywhere, at a swift lope on all possible stretches.

There was a sameness to the brushy growth and barren hills and rocky dry ravines, though the country was growing rougher. He had not been through this section before. He crossed no trails. And he noted that the tracks of the Mexicans gradually were heading from south to west. Sooner or later they were bound to join the well-known Rock Ford trail. Vaughn was concerned about this. Should he push Star to the limit until he knew he was close behind the abductors? It would not do to let them see or hear him. If he could surprise them the thing would be easy. While he revolved these details of the problem in his mind he kept traveling full speed along the trail.

He passed an Indian corn field, and then a hut of adobe and brush. The tracks he was hounding kept straight on, and led off the desert into a road, not, however, the Rock Ford road. Vaughn here urged Star to his best speed, and a half hour later he was turning into a well-defined trail. He did not need to get off to see that no horses but the five he was tracking had passed this point since morning. Moreover, it was plain that they were not many miles ahead.

Vaughn rode on awhile at a full gallop, then turning off the trail, he kept Star to that same ground-eating gait in a long detour. Once he crossed a stream bed, up which there would be water somewhere. Then he met the trail again, finding to his disappointment and chagrin that the tracks indicated that the riders had passed. He had hoped to head off the desperadoes and lie in wait for them here.

Mid-afternoon was on him. He decided not to force the issue at once. There was no ranch or village within half a night's ride of this spot. About sunset the Mexicans would halt to rest and eat. They would build a fire.

Vaughn rode down into a rock defile where he found a much-needed drink for himself and Star. He did not relish the winding trail ahead. It kept to the gorge. It was shady and cool, but afforded too many places where he might be ambushed. Still, there was no choice; he had to go on. He had no concern for himself that the three hombres would ambush him. But if they fell in with another band of cutthroats! It was Roseta of whom he was thinking.

Vaughn approached a rocky wall. He was inured to danger. And his ranger luck was proverbial. As he turned the corner of the rock wall he found himself facing a line of men with leveled rifles.

"Hands up, gringo ranger!"

3

VAUGHN was as much surprised by the command given in English as by this totally unexpected encounter with a dozen or more Mexicans. He knew the type all too well. These were Quinela's bandits.

Vaughn raised his hands. Why this gang leader was holding him up instead of shooting on sight was beyond Vaughn's ken. The Mexicans began to jabber like a lot of angry monkeys. If ever Vaughn expected death it was at that moment. He had about decided to pull his gun and shoot it out with them, and finish as many a ranger had before him. But a shrill authoritative voice deterred him. Then a swarthy little man, lean-faced, and beady-eyed, stepped out between the threatening rifles and Vaughn. He silenced the shrill chatter of his men.

"It's the gringo ranger, Texas Medill," he shouted in Spanish. "It's the man who killed Lopez. Don't shoot. Quinela will pay much gold for him alive. Quinela will strip off the soles of his feet and drive him with hot irons to walk on the choya."

"But it's the dreaded gun ranger, señor," protested a one-eyed bandit. "The only safe way is to shoot his cursed heart out here."

"We had our orders to draw this ranger across the river," returned the leader harshly. "Quinela knew his man and the hour. The Uvaldo girl brought him. And here we have him—alive! . . . Garcia, it'd cost your life to shoot this ranger."

"But I warn you, Juan, he is not alone," returned Garcia. "He is but a leader of many rangers. Best kill him quick and hurry on. I have told you already that plenty gringo *vaqueros* are on the trail. We have many horses. We cannot travel fast. Night is coming. Best kill Texas Medill."

"No, Garcia. We obey orders," returned Juan harshly. "We take him alive to Quinela."

Vaughn surveyed the motley group with speculative eyes. He could kill six of them at least, and with Star charging and the poor marksmanship of native bandits, he might break through. Coldly Vaughn weighed the chances. They were a hundred to one that he would not escape. Yet he had taken such chances before. But these men had Roseta, and while there was life there was always some hope. With a tremendous effort of will he forced aside the deadly impulse and applied his wits to the situation.

The swarthy Juan turned to cover Vaughn with a cocked gun. Vaughn read doubt and fear in the beady eyes. He knew Mexicans. If they did not kill him at once there was hope. At a significant motion Vaughn carefully shifted a long leg and stepped face front, hands high, out of the saddle.

Juan addressed him in Spanish.

"No savvy, señor," replied the ranger.

"You speak Spanish?" repeated the questioner in English.

"Very little. I understand some of your Mexican lingo."

"You trailed Manuel alone?"

"Who's Manuel?"

"My *vaquero*. He brought Señorita Uvaldo across the river."

"After murdering her companion. Yes, I trailed him and two other men, I reckon. Five horses. The Uvaldo girl rode one. The fifth horse belonged to her companion."

"Ha! Did Manuel kill?" exclaimed the Mexican, and it was quite certain that this was news to him.

"Yes. You have murder as well as kidnaping to answer for."

The Mexican cursed under his breath.

"Where are your rangers?" he went on.

"They got back from the Brazos last night with news of your raid," said Vaughn glibly. "And this morning they joined the cowboys who were trailing the horses you stole."

Vaughn realized then that somewhere there had been a mix-up in Quinela's plans. The one concerning the kidnaping of Roseta Uvaldo and Vaughn's taking the trail had worked out well. But Juan's dark, corded face, his volley of unintelligible maledictions directed at his men betrayed a hitch somewhere.

Again Vaughn felt the urge to draw and fight it out. What
crazy fiery-headed fools these tattered marauders were! Juan
had lowered his gun to heap abuse on Garcia. That luckless
individual turned green of face. Some of the others still held
leveled rifles on Vaughn, but they were looking at their leader
and his lieutenant. Vaughn saw a fair chance to get away, and
his gun hand itched. A heavy-booming Colt—Juan and Garcia dead—a couple of shots at those other outlaws—that would
have stampeded them. But Vaughn as yet had caught no
glimpse of Roseta. He put the grim, cold impulse behind him.

The harangue went on, ending only when Garcia had been
cursed into sullen agreement.

"I'll take them to Quinela," cried Juan shrilly, and began
shouting orders.

Vaughn's gun belt was removed. His hands were tied behind his back. He was forced upon one of the Mexicans'
horses and his feet were roped to the stirrups. Juan appropriated his gun belt, which he put on with the Mexican's love
of vainglory, and then mounted Star. The horse did not like
the exchange of riders, and there followed immediate evidence of the cruel iron hand of the outlaw. Vaughn's blood
leaped, and he veiled his eyes lest someone see his savage
urge to kill. When he raised his head, two of the squat, mot-
ley-garbed, and wide-sombreroed Mexicans were riding by,
and the second led a horse upon which sat Roseta Uvaldo.

She was bound to the saddle, but her hands were free. She
turned her face to Vaughn. With what concern and longing
did he gaze at it! Vaughn needed only to see it flash white
toward him, to meet the look of gratitude in her dark eyes,
to realize that Roseta was still unharmed. She held her small
proud head high. Her spirit was unbroken. For the rest, what
mattered the dusty disheveled hair, the mud-spattered and
dust-covered *vaquero* riding garb she wore? Vaughn flashed
her a look that brought the blood to her pale cheeks.

Juan prodded Vaughn in the back. "Ride, gringo." Then
he gave Garcia a last harsh command. As Vaughn's horse
followed that of Roseta and her two guards into the brook,
there rose a clattering, jabbering melee among the Mexicans
left behind. It ended in a receding roar of pounding hoofs.

The brook was shallow and ran swiftly over gravel and
rocks. Vaughn saw at once that Juan meant to hide his trail.

An hour after the cavalcade would have passed a given point here, no obvious trace would show. The swift water would have cleared as well as have filled the hoof tracks with sand.

"Juan, you were wise to desert your gang of horse thieves," said Vaughn coolly. "There's a hard-ridin' outfit on their trail. And some, if not all of them, will be dead before sundown."

"*Quien sabe?* But it's sure Texas Medill will be walking choya on bare-skinned feet *mañana*," replied the Mexican bandit chief.

Vaughn pondered. Quinela's rendezvous, then, was not many hours distant. Travel such as this, up a rocky gorge, was necessarily slow. Probably this brook would not afford more than a few miles of going. Then Juan would head out on to the desert and try in other ways to hide his tracks. As far as Vaughn was concerned, whether he hid them or not made no difference. The cowboys and rangers in pursuit were but fabrications of Vaughn's to deceive the Mexicans. He knew how to work on their primitive feelings. But Vaughn poignantly realized the peril of the situation and the brevity of the time left him.

"Juan, you've got my gun," said Vaughn, his keen mind working. "You say I'll be dead in less than twenty-four hours. What's it worth to untie my hands so I can ride in comfort?"

"Señor, if you have money on you it will be mine anyway," replied the Mexican.

"I haven't any money with me. But I've got my checkbook that shows a balance of some thousands of dollars in an El Paso bank," replied Vaughn, and he turned round.

The bandit showed his gleaming white teeth in derision. "What's that to me?"

"Some thousands in gold, Juan. You can get it easily. News of my death will not get across the border very soon. I'll give you a check and a letter, which you can take to El Paso, or send by messenger."

"How much gold, Señor?" Juan asked.

"Over three thousand."

"Señor, you would bribe me into a trap. No. Juan loves the glitter and clink of your American gold, but he is no fool."

"Nothing of the sort. I'm trying to buy a little comfort in my last hours. And possibly a little kindness to the señorita there. It's worth a chance. You can send a messenger. What do you care if he shouldn't come back? You don't lose anythin'."

"No gringo can be trusted, much less Texas Medill of the rangers," replied the Mexican.

"Sure. But take a look at my checkbook. You know figures when you see them."

Juan rode abreast of Vaughn, impelled by curiosity. His beady eyes glittered.

"Inside vest pocket," directed Vaughn. "Don't drop the pencil."

The Mexican procured the checkbook and opened it. "Señor, I know your bank," he said, vain of his ability to read, which to judge by his laborious task was limited.

"Ahuh. Well, how much balance have I left?" asked Vaughn.

"Three thousand, four hundred."

"Good. Now, Juan, you may as well get that money. I've nobody to leave it to. I'll buy a little comfort for myself— and kindness to the señorita."

"How much kindness, señor?" asked the Mexican craftily.

"That you keep your men from handlin' her rough—and soon as the ransom is paid send her back safe."

"Señor, the first I have seen to. The second is not mine to grant. Quinela will demand ransom—yes—but never will he send the señorita back."

"But I—thought—"

"Quinela was wronged by Uvaldo."

Vaughn whistled at this astounding revelation. He had divined correctly the fear Uvaldo had revealed. The situation then for Roseta was vastly more critical. Death would be merciful compared to the fate the half-breed peon Quinela would deal her. Vaughn cudgeled his brains in desperation. Why had he not shot it out with these yellow desperadoes? But rage could not further Roseta's cause.

Meanwhile the horses splashed and clattered over the rocks in single file up the narrowing gorge. The steep walls were giving way to brushy slopes that let the hot sun down. Roseta looked back at Vaughn with appeal and trust—and something more in her dark eyes that tortured him.

Vaughn did not have the courage to meet her gaze, except for the fleeting moment. It was only natural that his spirits should be at a low ebb. Never in his long ranger service had he encountered such a desperate situation. More than once he had faced what seemed inevitable death, where there had seemed to be not the slightest chance to escape. Vaughn was not of a temper to give up completely. He would watch for a break till the very last second. For Roseta, however, he endured agonies. He had looked at the mutilated bodies of more than one girl victim of these bandits.

When at length the gully narrowed to a mere crack in the hill, and the water failed, Juan ordered his guards to climb a steep brush slope. There was no sign of any trail. If this brook, which they had waded to its source, led away from the road to Rock Ford, it would take days before rangers or cowboys could possibly run across it. Juan was a fox.

The slope was not easy to climb. Both Mexicans got off their horses to lead Roseta's. If Vaughn had not been tied on his saddle he would have fallen off. Eventually they reached the top, to enter a thick growth of mesquite and cactus. And before long they broke out into a trail, running, as near as Vaughn could make out, at right angles to the road and river trail. Probably it did not cross either one. Certainly the Mexicans trotted east along it as if they had little to fear from anyone traveling it.

Presently a peon came in sight astride a mustang, and leading a burro. He got by the two guards, though they crowded him into the brush. But Juan halted him, and got off Star to see what was in the pack on the burro. With an exclamation of great satisfaction he pulled out what appeared to Vaughn to be a jug or demijohn covered with wickerwork. Juan pulled out the stopper and smelled the contents.

"*Canyu!*" he said, and his white teeth gleamed. He took a drink, then smacked his lips. When the guards, who had stopped to watch, made a move to dismount he cursed them vociferously. Sullenly they slid back into their saddles. Juan stuffed the demijohn into the right saddlebag of Vaughn's saddle. Here the peon protested in a mixed dialect that Vaughn could not translate. But the meaning was obvious. Juan kicked the ragged peon's sandaled foot, and ordered him on, with a significant touch of Vaughn's big gun, which he wore so pompously. The peon lost no time riding off. Juan remounted, and directed the cavalcade to move forward.

Vaughn turned as his horse started, and again he encountered Roseta's dark intent eyes. They seemed telepathic this time, as well as filled with unutterable promise. She had read Vaughn's thought. If there were anything that had dominance in the Mexican's nature it was the cactus liquor, *canyu*. Ordinarily he was volatile, unstable as water, flint one moment and wax the next. But with the burn of *canyu* in his throat he had the substance of mist.

Vaughn felt the lift and pound of his heavy heart. He had prayed for the luck of the ranger, and lo! a peon had ridden up, packing *canyu*.

4

Canyu was a distillation made from the maguey cactus, a plant similar to the century plant. The peon brewed it. But in lieu of the brew, natives often cut into the heart of a plant and sucked the juice. Vaughn had once seen a Mexican sprawled in the middle of a huge maguey, his head buried deep in the heart of it and his legs hanging limp. Upon examination he appeared to be drunk, but it developed that he was dead.

This liquor was potential fire. The lack of it made the peons surly: the possession of it made them gay. One drink changed their mental and physical world. Juan whistled after the first drink: after the second he began to sing "La Paloma." His two guards cast greedy, mean looks backward.

Almost at once the fairly brisk pace of travel that had been maintained slowed perceptibly. Vaughn began to feel more sanguine. He believed that he might be able to break the thongs that bound his wrists. As he had prayed for his ranger luck so he now prayed for anything to delay these Mexicans on the trail.

The leader Juan either wanted the *canyu* for himself or was too crafty to share it with his two men; probably both. With all three of them, the center of attention had ceased to be in Uvaldo's girl and the hated gringo ranger. It lay in that demijohn in Star's saddlebag. If a devil lurked in this white liquor for them, there was likewise for the prisoners a watching angel.

The afternoon was not far enough advanced for the sun to begin losing its heat. Shade along the trail was most inviting and welcome, but it was scarce. Huge pipelike masses of organ cactus began to vary the monotonous scenery. Vaughn saw deer, rabbits, road runners, and butcherbirds. The country was uninhabited and this trail an unfrequented one which certainly must branch into one of the several main traveled trails. Vaughn hoped the end of it still lay many miles off.

The way led into a shady rocky glen. As of one accord the horses halted, without, so far as Vaughn could see, any move or word from their riders. This was proof that the two guards in the lead had ceased to ride with the sole idea in mind of keeping to a steady gait. Vaughn drew a deep breath, as if to control his nervous feeling of suspense. No man could foretell the variety of effects of *canyu* on another, but certain it must be that something would happen soon.

Juan had mellowed considerably. A subtle change had occurred in his disposition, though he was still the watchful leader. Vaughn felt that he was now in even more peril from this Mexican than before the advent of the *canyu*. This, however, would not last long. He could only bide his time, watch and think. His luck had begun to take over. He divined it, trusted it with mounting hope.

The two guards turned their horses across the trail, blocking Roseta's horse, while Vaughn's came up alongside. If he could have stretched out his hand he could have touched Roseta. Many a time he had been thrilled and bewildered in her presence, not to say stricken speechless, but he had never felt as he did now. Roseta contrived to touch his bound foot with her stirrup, and the deliberate move made Vaughn tremble. Still he did not yet look directly down at her.

The actions of the three Mexicans were as clear to Vaughn as crystal. If he had seen one fight among Mexicans over *canyu*, he had seen a hundred. First the older of the two guards leisurely got off his horse. His wide straw sombrero hid his face, except for a peaked, yellow chin, scantily covered with black whiskers. His clothes hung in rags, and a cartridge belt was slung loosely over his left shoulder. He had left his rifle in its saddle sheath, and his only weapon was a bone-handled machete stuck in a scabbard attached to his belt.

"Juan, we are thirsty and have no water," he said. And his comrade, sitting sideways in his saddle, nodded in agreement.

"Gonzalez, one drink and no more," returned Juan, and lifted out the demijohn.

With eager cry the man tipped it to his lips. And he gulped steadily until Juan jerked it away. Then the other Mexican tumbled off his horse and eagerly besought Juan for a drink, if only one precious drop. Juan complied, but this time he did not let go of the demijohn.

Vaughn felt a touch—a gentle pressure on his knee. Roseta had laid her gloved hand there. Then he had to avert his gaze from the Mexicans.

"Oh, Vaughn, I *knew* you would come to save me," she whispered. "But they have caught you. . . . For God's sake, do something."

"Roseta, I reckon I can't do much, at this sitting," replied Vaughn, smiling down at her. "Are you—all right?"

"Yes, except I'm tired and my legs ache. I was frightened badly before you happened along. But now—it's terrible. . . . Vaughn, they are taking us to Quinela. He is a monster. My father told me so. . . . If you can't save me you must kill me."

"I shall save you, Roseta," he whispered low, committing himself on the altar of the luck that had never failed him. The glance she gave him then made his blood run throbbing through his veins. And he thanked the fates, since he loved her and had been given this incredible opportunity, that it had fallen to his lot to become a ranger.

Her eyes held his and there was no doubt about the warm pressure of her hand on his knee. But even during this sweet stolen moment, Vaughn had tried to attend to the argument between the three Mexicans. He heard their mingled voices, all high-pitched and angry. In another moment they would be leaping at each others' throats like dogs. Vaughn was endeavoring to think of some encouraging word for Roseta, but the ranger was replaced for the moment by the man who was revealing his heart in a long look into the small pale face, with its red, quivering lips and great dark eyes uplifted, filled with blind faith.

The sound of struggling, the trample of hoofs, a shrill cry

of "Santa Maria!" and a sodden blow preceded the startling crash of a gun.

As Vaughn's horse plunged he saw Roseta's mount rear into the brush with its rider screaming, and Star lunged out of a cloud of blue smoke. A moment later Vaughn found himself tearing down the trail. He was helpless, but he squeezed the scared horse with his knees and kept calling, "Whoa there—whoa boy!"

Not for a hundred rods or more did the animal slow up. It relieved Vaughn to hear a clatter of hoofs behind him, and he turned to see Juan tearing after him in pursuit. Presently he turned out into the brush, and getting ahead of Vaughn, turned into the trail again to stop the ranger's horse. Juan proceeded to beat the horse over the head until it almost unseated Vaughn.

"Hold on, man," shouted Vaughn. "It wasn't his fault or mine. Why don't you untie my hands—if you want your nag held in?"

Juan jerked the heaving horse out of the brush and onto the trail, finally leading him back toward the scene of the shooting. But before they reached it Vaughn saw one of the guards coming with Roseta and a riderless horse. Juan grunted his satisfaction, and let them pass without a word.

Roseta seemed less disturbed and shaken than Vaughn had feared she would be. Her dilated eyes, as she passed, said as plainly as any words could have done that they now had one less enemy to contend with.

The journey was resumed. Vaughn drew a deep breath and endeavored to arrange his thoughts. The sun was still only halfway down toward the western horizon. There were hours of daylight yet! And he had an ally more deadly than bullets, more subtle than any man's wit, sharper than the tooth of a serpent.

Perhaps a quarter of an hour later, Vaughn, turning his head ever so slightly, saw, out of the corner of his eye, Juan take another drink of *canyu*. And it was a good stiff one. Vaughn thrilled as he contained himself. Presently Juan's latest act would be as if it had never been. *Canyu* was an annihilation of the past.

"Juan, I'll fall off this horse pronto," began Vaughn.

"Very good, señor. Fall off," replied Juan amiably.

"But my feet are tied to the stirrups. This horse of yours is skittish. He'll bolt and drag my brains out. If you want to take me alive to Quinela, so that he may have a fiesta while I walk choya, you'd better not let me fall off."

"S. Ranger, if you fall you fall. How can I prevent it?"

"I am so damned uncomfortable with my hands tied back this way. I cain't sit straight. I'm cramped. Be a good fellow, Juan, and untie my hands."

"S. Texas Medill, if you are uncomfortable now, what will you be when you tread the fiery cactus on your naked feet?"

"But that will be short. No man lives such torture long, does he, Juan?"

"The choya kills quickly, señor."

"Juan, have you thought about the gold lying in the El Paso bank? Gold that can be yours for the ride. It will be long before my death is reported across the river. You have plenty of time to get to El Paso with my check and a letter. I can write it on a sheet of paper out of my notebook. Surely you have a friend or acquaintance in El Paso or Juarez who can identify you at the bank as Juan—whatever your name is."

"Yes, señor, I have. And my name is Juan Mendoz."

"Have you thought about what you could do with three thousand dollars? Not Mexican pesos, but real gringo gold!"

"I have not thought, señor, because I do not like to give in to dreams."

"Juan, listen. You are a fool. I know I am as good as daid. What have I been a ranger all these years for? And it's worth this gold to me to be free of this miserable cramp—and to feel that I have tried to buy some little kindness for the señorita there. She is part Mexican, Juan. She has Mexican blood in her. Don't forget that. . . . Well, you are not betraying Quinela. And you will be rich. You will have my horse and saddle, if you are wise enough to keep Quinela from seeing them. You will buy silver spurs—with the long Spanish rowels. You will have jingling gold in your pocket. You will buy a *vaquero*'s sombrero. And then think of your *chata*—your sweetheart, Juan. . . . Ah, I knew it. You have a *chata*. Think of what you can buy her. A Spanish mantilla, and a golden cross, and silver-buckled shoes for her little feet. Think how she will love you for that! . . . Then, Juan, best of all, you can go far south of the border—buy a hacienda, horses, and cattle, and live there happily with your *chata*. You will only get killed in Quinela's service—for a few dirty pesos. . . . You will raise mescal on your hacienda, and brew your own *canyu*. . . . All for so little, Juan!''

"Señor not only has gold in a bank but gold on his tongue. . . . It is indeed little you ask and little I risk.''

Juan rode abreast of Vaughn and felt in his pockets for the checkbook and pencil, which he had neglected to return. Vaughn made of his face a grateful mask. This Mexican had become approachable, as Vaughn had known *canyu* would make him, but he was not yet under its influence to an extent which justified undue risk. Still, Vaughn decided, if the bandit freed his hands and gave him the slightest chance, he would jerk Juan out of that saddle. Vaughn did not lose sight of the fact that his feet would still be tied. He calculated exactly what he would do in case Juan's craftiness no longer possessed him. As the Mexican stopped his horse and reined in Vaughn's, the girl happened to turn round, as she often did, and she saw them. Vaughn caught a flash of big eyes and a white little face as Roseta vanished round a turn in the trail. Vaughn was glad for two things, that she had seen him stop and that she and her guard would be unable to see what was taking place.

All through these anxious moments of suspense Juan appeared to be studying the checkbook. If he could read English, it surely was only a few familiar words. The thought leaped to Vaughn's mind to write a note to the banker quite different from what he had intended. Most assuredly, if the El Paso banker ever saw that note Vaughn would be dead; and it was quite within the realm of possibility that it might fall into his hands.

"Señor, you may sign me the gold in your El Paso bank,'' said Juan, at length.

"Fine. You're a sensible man, Juan. But I cain't hold a pencil with my teeth.''

The Mexican laughed. He was more amiable. Another hour and another few drinks of *canyu* would make him maudlin, devoid of quick wit or keen sight. A more favorable chance might befall Vaughn, and it might be wiser to wait. Surely on the ride ahead there would come a moment when he could act with lightning and deadly swiftness. But it would take iron will to hold his burning intent within bounds.

Juan kicked the horse Vaughn bestrode and moved him across the trail so that Vaughn's back was turned.

"There, señor," said the Mexican, and his lean dark hand slipped book and pencil into Vaughn's vest pocket.

The cunning beggar, thought Vaughn, in sickening disappointment. He had hoped Juan would free his bonds and then hand over the book. But Vaughn's ranger luck had not caught up with him yet.

He felt the Mexican tugging at the thongs around his wrists. They were tight—a fact to which Vaughn surely could attest. He heard him mutter a curse. Also he heard the short expulsion of breath—almost a pant—that betrayed the influence of the *canyu*.

"Juan, do you blame me for wanting those rawhides off my wrists?" asked Vaughn.

"Señor Medill is strong. It is nothing," returned the Mexican.

Suddenly the painful tension on Vaughn's wrists relaxed. He felt the thongs fall.

"*Muchas gracias*, señor!" he exclaimed. "Ahhh! . . . That feels good."

Vaughn brought his hands round in front to rub each swollen and discolored wrist. But all the time he was gathering his forces, like a tiger about to leap. Had the critical moment arrived?

"Juan, that was a little job to make a man rich—now wasn't it?" went on Vaughn pleasantly. And leisurely, but with every muscle taut, he turned to face the Mexican.

5

THE bandit was out of reach of Vaughn's eager hands. He sat back in the saddle with an expression of interest on his swarthy face. The ranger could not be sure, but he would have gambled that Juan did not suspect his deadly intentions. Star was a mettlesome animal, but Vaughn did not like the Mexican's horse, to which he sat bound, and there were several feet between them. If Vaughn had been free to leap he might have, probably would have, done so.

He swallowed his eagerness and began to rub his wrists again. Presently he removed the pencil and book from his pocket. It was not mere pretense that made it something of an effort to write out a check for Juan Mendoz for the three thousand and odd dollars that represented his balance in the El Paso bank.

"There, Juan. May some gringo treat your *chata* someday as you treat Señorita Uvaldo," said Vaughn, handing the check over to the Mexican.

"*Gracias,* señor," replied Juan, his black eyes upon the bit of colored paper. "Uvaldo's daughter then is your *chata*?"

"Yes. And I'll leave a curse upon you if she is mistreated."

"Ranger, I had my orders from Quinela. You would not have asked more."

"What has Quinela against Uvaldo?" asked Vaughn.

"They were *vaqueros* together years ago. But I don't know the reason for Quinela's hate. It is great and just. . . . Now, señor, the letter to your banker."

Vaughn tore a leaf out of his bankbook. On second thought he decided to write the letter in the bankbook, which would serve in itself to identify him. In case this letter ever was presented at the bank in El Paso he wanted it to mean something. Then it occurred to Vaughn to try out the Mexican. So he wrote a few lines.

"Read that, Juan," he said, handing over the book.

The man scanned the lines, which might as well have been written in Greek.

"Texas Medill does not write as well as he shoots," said Juan.

"Let me have the book. I can do better. I forgot something."

Receiving it back Vaughn tore out the page and wrote another.

Dear Mr. Jarvis:
    If you ever see these lines you will know that I have been murdered by Quinela. Have the bearer arrested and wire to Captain Allerton, of the Rangers, at Brownsville.

At this moment I am a prisoner of Juan Mendoz, lieutenant of Quinela. Miss Roseta Uvaldo is also a prisoner. She will be held for ransom and revenge. The place is in the hills somewhere east and south of Rock Ford trail.

MEDILL

Vaughn reading aloud to the Mexican improvised a letter which identified him, and cunningly made mention of the gold.

"Juan, isn't that better?" he said, as he handed the book back. "You'll do well not to show this to Quinela or anyone else. Go yourself *at once* to El Paso."

As Vaughn had expected, the Mexican did not scan the letter. Placing the check in the bankbook, he deposited it in an inside pocket of his tattered coat. Then without a word he drove Vaughn's horse forward on the trail, and following close behind soon came up with Roseta and her guard.

The girl looked back. Vaughn contrived, without making it obvious, to show her that his hands were free. A look of radiance crossed her wan face. The exertion and suspense had begun to tell markedly. Her form sagged in the saddle.

Juan appeared bent on making up for lost time, as he drove the horses forward at a trot. But this did not last long. Vaughn, looking at the ground, saw the black shadow of the Mexican as he raised the demijohn to his mouth to drink. What a sinister shadow! It forced Vaughn to think of what now should be his method of procedure. Sooner or later he was going to get his hand on his gun, which stuck out back of Juan's hip and hung down in its holster. That moment, when it came, would see the end of his captor. But Vaughn remembered how the horse he bestrode had bolted at the previous gunshot. He would risk more, shooting from the back of this horse than at the hands of the other Mexican. Vaughn's feet were tied in the stirrups with the rope passing underneath the horse. If he were thrown sideways out of the saddle it would be a perilous and very probably a fatal accident. He decided that at the critical time he would grip the horse with his legs so tightly that he could not be dislodged, and at that moment decide what to do about the other Mexican.

After Juan had a second drink, Vaughn slowly slackened

the gait of his horse until Juan's mount came up to his horse's flank. Vaughn was careful to keep to the right of the trail. One glance at the Mexican's eyes sent a gush of hot blood over Vaughn. The effect of the *canyu* had been slow on this tough little man, but at last it was working.

"Juan, I'm powerful thirsty," said Vaughn.

"Señor, we come to water hole bime-by," replied the Mexican thickly.

"But won't you spare me a nip of *canyu*?"

"Our mescal drink is bad for gringos."

"I'll risk it, Juan. Just a nip. You're a good fellow and I like you. I'll tell Quinela how you had to fight your men back there, when they wanted to kill me. I'll tell him Garcia provoked you. . . . Juan, you can see I may do you a turn."

Juan came up alongside Vaughn and halted. Vaughn reined his horse head and head with Juan's. The Mexican was sweating; his under lip hung a little; he sat loosely in his saddle. His eyes had lost their beady light and appeared to have filmed over.

Juan waited till the man ahead had turned another twist in the trail with Roseta. Then he lifted the obviously lightened demijohn from the saddlebag and extended it to Vaughn.

"A drop—señor," he said.

Vaughn pretended to drink. The hot stuff was like vitriol on his lips. He returned the jug, making a great show of the effect of the *canyu*, when as a matter of cold fact he was calculating distances. Almost he yielded to the temptation to lean and sweep a long arm forward. But a ranger could not afford to make mistakes. If Juan's horse had been a little closer! Vaughn expelled deeply his bated breath.

"Ah-h! Great stuff, Juan!" he exclaimed, and relaxed again.

They rode on, and Juan either forgot to drop behind or did not think it needful. The trail was wide enough for two horses. Soon Roseta's bright red scarf burned against the gray-green brush again. She was looking back. So was her Mexican escort. And their horses were walking. Juan did not appear to take note of their slower progress. He long had passed the faculty for making minute observations. Presently he would take another swallow of *canyu*.

Vaughn began to talk, to express more gratitude to Juan,

to dwell with flowery language on the effect of good drink—of which *canyu* was the sweetest and most potent in the world—of its power to make fatigue as if it were not, to alleviate pain and grief, to render the dreary desert of mesquite and stone a region of color and beauty and melody—even to resign a doomed ranger to his fate.

"Aye, señor—*canyu* is the blessed Virgin's gift to the peon," said Juan, and emphasized this tribute by having another generous drink.

They rode on. Vaughn asked only for another mile or two of lonely trail, free of interruption.

"How far, Juan?" asked Vaughn. "I cannot ride much farther with my feet tied under this horse."

"Till sunset—señor—which will be your last," replied the Mexican.

The sun was still high above the pipes of organ cactus. Two hours and more above the horizon! Juan could still speak intelligibly. It was in his lax figure and his sweating face, especially in the protruding eyeballs, that he betrayed the effect of the contents of the demijohn. After the physical letdown would come the mental slackening. That had already begun, for Juan was no longer alert.

They rode on, and Vaughn made a motion to Roseta that she must not turn to look back. Perhaps she interpreted it to mean more than it did, for she immediately began to engage her guard in conversation—something Vaughn had observed she had not done before. Soon the Mexican dropped back until his horse was walking beside Roseta's. He was a peon, and a heavy drink of *canyu* had addled the craft in his wits. Vaughn saw him bend down and loosen the rope that bound Roseta's left foot to the stirrup. Juan did not see this significant action. His gaze was fixed to the trail. He was singing:

"Ay, mía querida chata."

Roseta's guard took a long look back. Evidently Juan's posture struck him apprehensively, yet did not wholly overcome the interest that Roseta had suddenly taken in him. When he gave her a playful pat she returned it. He caught her hand. Roseta did not pull very hard to release it, and she gave him another saucy little slap. He was reaching for her when they passed out of Vaughn's sight round a turn in the green-bordered trail.

Vaughn gradually and almost imperceptibly guided his

horse closer to Juan. At that moment a dog could be heard barking in the distance. It did not make any difference to Vaughn, except to accentuate what had always been true—he had no time to lose.

"Juan, the curse of *canyu* is that once you taste it you must have more—or die," said Vaughn.

"It is—so—señor," replied the Mexican.

"You have plenty left. Will you let me have one more little drink. . . . My last drink of *canyu*, Juan! . . . I didn't tell you, but it has been my ruin. My father was a rich rancher. He disowned me because of my evil habits. That's how I became a ranger."

"Take it, señor. Your last drink," said Juan.

Vaughn braced every nerve and fiber of his being. He leaned a little. His left hand went out—leisurely. But his eyes flashed like cold steel over the unsuspecting Mexican. Then, with the speed of a striking snake, his hand snatched the bone-handled gun from its sheath. Vaughn pulled the trigger. The hammer fell upon an empty chamber.

Juan turned. The gun crashed. *"Dios!"* he screamed in a strangled death cry.

The leaps of the horses were not quicker than Vaughn. He lunged to catch the Mexican—to keep him upright in the saddle. "Hold, Star!" he called sternly. 'Hold!''

Star came down. But the other horse plunged and dragged him up the trail. Vaughn had his gun hand fast on the cantle and his other holding Juan upright. But for this grasp the frantic horse would have unseated him.

It was the ranger's job to manage both horses and look out for the other Mexican. He appeared on the trail riding fast, his carbine held high.

Vaughn let go of Juan and got the gun in his right hand. With the other then he grasped the Mexican's coat and held him straight on the saddle. He drooped himself over his pommel, to make it appear he had been the one shot. Meanwhile, he increased his iron leg grip on the horse he straddled. Star had halted and was being dragged.

The other Mexican came at a gallop, yelling. When he got within twenty paces. Vaughn straightened up and shot him through the heart. He threw the carbine from him and pitching out of his saddle, went thudding to the ground. His horse bumped hard into the one Vaughn rode, and that was fortunate, for it checked the animal's first mad leap. In the melee that followed Juan fell off Star to be trampled under frantic hoofs. Vaughn hauled with all his might on the bridle. But he could not hold the horse and he feared that he would break the bridle. Bursting through the brush the horse ran wildly. What with his erratic flight and the low branches of mesquite, Vaughn had a hard job sticking on his back. Presently he got the horse under control and back onto the trail.

Some few rods down he saw Roseta, safe in her saddle, her head bowed with her hands covering her face. At sight of her Vaughn snapped out of the cold horror that had enveloped him.

"Roseta, it's all right. We're safe," he called eagerly as he reached her side.

"Oh, Vaughn!" she cried, lifting her convulsed and blanched face. "I knew you'd—kill them. . . . But, my God—how awful!"

"Brace up," he said sharply.

Then he got out his clasp knife and in a few slashes freed his feet from the stirrups. He leaped off the horse. His feet felt numb, as they had felt once when frozen.

Then he cut the ropes which bound Roseta's right foot to her stirrup. She swayed out of the saddle into his arms. Her eyes closed.

"It's no time to faint," he said sternly, carrying her off the trail, to set her on her feet.

"I—I won't," she whispered, her eyes opening, strained and dilated. "But hold me—just a moment."

Vaughn folded her in his arms, and the moment she asked was so sweet and precious that it almost overcame the will of a ranger in a desperate plight.

"Roseta—we're free, but not yet safe," he replied. "We're close to a hacienda—perhaps where Quinela is waiting. . . . Come now. We must get out of here."

Half carrying her, Vaughn hurried through the brush along the trail. The moment she could stand alone he whispered, "Wait here." And he ran onto the trail. He still held his gun. Star stood waiting, his head up. Both other horses had disappeared. Vaughn looked up and down the trail. Star whinnied. Vaughn hurried to bend over Juan. The Mexican lay on his face. Vaughn unbuckled the gun belt Juan had appropriated from him, and put it on. Next he secured his bankbook. Then he sheathed his gun. He grasped the bridle of Star and led him off the trail into the mesquite, back to where Roseta stood. She seemed all right now, only pale. But Vaughn avoided her eyes. The thing to do was to get away and not let sentiment deter him one instant. He mounted Star.

"Come, Roseta," he said. "Up behind me."

He swung her up and settled her in the saddle.

"There. Put your arms around me. Hold tight, for we're going to ride."

When she had complied, he grasped her left arm. At the same moment he heard voices up the trail and the rapid clipclop of hoofs. Roseta heard them, too. Vaughn felt her tremble.

"Don't fear, Roseta. Just you hang on. Here's where Star shines," whispered Vaughn, and guiding the nervous horse into the trail, he let him have a loose rein. Star did not need the shrill cries of the peons to spur him into action.

6

As the fleeing ranger sighted the peons, a babel of shrill voices arose. But no shots! In half a dozen jumps Star was going swift as the wind and in a moment a bend of the trail hid him from any possible marksman. Vaughn's concern for the girl behind him gradually eased.

At the end of a long straight stretch he looked back again. If *vaqueros* were riding in pursuit the situation would be serious. Not even Star could run away from a well-mounted cowboy of the Mexican haciendas. To his intense relief there was not one in sight. Nevertheless, he did not check Star.

"False alarm, Roseta," he said, craning his neck so he could see her face, pressed cheek against his shoulder. He was most marvelously aware of her close presence, but the realization did not impede him or Star in the least. She could ride. She had no stirrups, yet she kept her seat in the saddle.

"Let 'em come," she said, smiling up at him. Her face was pale, but it was not fear that he read in her eyes. It was fight.

Vaughn laughed in sheer surprise. He had not expected that, and it gave him such a thrill as he had never felt in his life before. He let go of Roseta's arm and took her hand where it clung to his coat. And he squeezed it with far more than reassurance. The answering pressure was unmistakable. A singular elation mounted in Vaughn's heart.

It did not, however, quite render him heedless. As Star turned a corner in the trail, Vaughn's keen glance saw that it was completely blocked by the same motley crew of big-sombreroed Mexicans and horses from which he had been separated not so long before that day.

"Hold tight!" he cried warningly to Roseta, as he swerved Star to the left. He drew his gun and fired two quick shots. He did not need to see that they took effect, for a wild cry rose, followed by angry yells.

Star beat the answering rifle shots into the brush. Vaughn heard the sing and twang of the bullets. Crashings through the mesquites behind, added to the gunshots and lent wings to Star. This was a familiar situation to the great horse. Then for Vaughn it became a strenuous job to ride him, and a doubly fearful one, owing to Roseta. She clung like a broom to the speeding horse. Vaughn, after sheathing his gun, had to let go of her, for he needed one hand for the bridle and the other to ward off the whipping brush. Star made no allowance for that precious part of his burden at Vaughn's back, and he crashed through every opening between mesquites that presented itself. Vaughn dodged and ducked, but he never bent low enough for a branch to strike Roseta.

At every open spot in the mesquite, or long aisle between the cacti, Vaughn looked back to see if any of his pursuers were in sight. There was none, but he heard a horse pounding not far behind and to the right. And again he heard another on the other side. Holding the reins in his teeth Vaughn re-loaded the gun. To be ready for snap shots he took advantage of every opportunity to peer on each side and behind him. But Star appeared gradually to be outdistancing his pursuers. The desert grew more open with a level gravel floor. Here Vaughn urged Star to his limit.

It became a dead run then, with the horse choosing the way. Vaughn risked less now from the stinging mesquite branches. The green wall flashed by on each side. He did not look back. While Star was at his best Vaughn wanted to get far enough ahead to slow down and save the horse. In an hour it would be dusk—too late for even a *vaquero* to track him until daylight had come again.

Roseta stuck like a leech, and the ranger had to add admiration to his other feelings toward her. Vaughn put his hand back to grasp and steady her. It did not take much time for the powerful strides of the horse to cover the miles. Finally Vaughn pulled him into a gallop and then into a lope.

"*Chata*, are you all right?" he asked, afraid to look back, after using that romantic epithet.

"Yes. But I can't—hold on—much longer," she panted. "If they catch us—shoot me first."

"Roseta, they will never catch us now," he promised.

"But—if they do—promise me," she entreated.

"I promise they'll never take us alive. But, child, keep up your nerve. It'll be sunset soon—and then dark. We'll get away sure."

"Vaughn, I'm not frightened. Only—I hate those people— and I mustn't fall—into their hands again. It means worse— than death."

"Hush! Save your breath," he replied, and wrapping a long arm backward round her slender waist he held her tight. "Come, Star, cut loose," he called, and dug the horse's flank with a heel.

Again they raced across the desert, this time in less of a straight line, though still to the north. The dry wind made tears dim Vaughn's eyes. He kept to open lanes and patches to avoid being struck by branches. And he spared Star only when he heard the animal's heaves of distress. Star was not easy to break from that headlong flight, but at length Vaughn got him down to a nervous walk. Then he let Roseta slip back into the saddle. His arm was numb from the long strain.

"We're—far ahead," he panted. "They'll trail—us till dark." He peered back across the yellow and green desert, slowly darkening in the sunset. "But we're safe—thank Gawd."

"Oh, what a glorious ride!" cried Roseta between breaths. "I felt that—even with death so close. . . . Vaughn, I'm such a little—fool. I longed—for excitement. Oh, I'm well punished. . . . But for you—"

"Save your breath, honey. We may need to run again. After dark you can rest and talk."

She said no more. Vaughn walked Star until the horse had regained his wind, and then urged him into a lope, which was his easiest gait.

The sun sank red in the west; twilight stole under the mesquite and the *pale verde*; dusk came upon its heels; the heat tempered and there was a slight breeze. When the stars came out Vaughn took his direction from them, and pushed on for several miles. A crescent moon, silver and slender, came up over the desert.

Young as it was, it helped brighten the open patches and the swales. Vaughn halted the tireless horse in a spot where a patch of grass caught the moonlight.

"We'll rest a bit," he said, sliding off, but still holding on to the girl. "Come."

She just fell off into his arms, and when he let her feet down she leaned against him. "Oh, Vaughn!" He held her a moment, sorely tempted. But he might take her weakness for something else.

"Can you stand? . . . You'd better walk around a little," he said.

"My legs are dead."

"I want to go back a few steps and listen. The night is still. I could hear horses at a long distance."

"Don't go far," she entreated him.

Vaughn went back where he could not hear the heaving, blowing horse, and turned his keen ear to the breeze. It blew gently from the south. Only a very faint rustle of leaves disturbed the desert silence. He held his breath and listened intensely. There was no sound! Even if he were trailed by a hound of a *vaquero* he was still far ahead. All he required now was a little rest for Star. He could carry the girl. On the way back across the open he tried to find the tracks Star had left. A man could trail them, but only on foot. Vaughn's last stern doubt took wing and vanished. He returned to Roseta.

"No sound. It is as I expected. Night has saved us," he said.

"Night and *canyu*. Oh, I watched you, ranger man."

"You helped, Roseta. That Mexican who led your horse was suspicious. But when you looked at him—he forgot. Small wonder . . . Have you stretched your legs?"

"I tried. I walked some, then flopped here. . . . Oh, I want to rest and sleep."

"I don't know about your sleeping, but you can rest riding" he replied, and removing his coat folded it around the pommel of his saddle, making a flat seat there. Star was munching the grass. He was already fit for another race. Vaughn saw to the cinches, and then mounted again, and folded the sleeves of his coat up over the pommel. "Give me your hand. . . . Put your foot in the stirrup. Now." He caught her and lifted her in front of him, and settling her comfortably upon the improvised seat, he put his left arm around her. Many a wounded comrade had he packed this way. "How is—that?" he asked unsteadily.

"It's very nice," she replied, her dark eyes looking inscrutable in the moonlight. And she relaxed against his arm and shoulder.

Vaughn headed Star north at a brisk walk. He could not be more than six hours from the river in a straight line. Canyons and rough going might deter him. But even so he could make the Rio Grande before dawn. Then and then only did he surrender to the astonishing presence of Roseta Uvaldo, to the indubitable fact that he had saved her, and then to thoughts wild and whirling of the future. He gazed down upon the oval face so balanced in the moonlight, into the staring black eyes whose look might mean anything.

"Vaughn, was it that guard or you—who called me *chata*?" she asked, dreamily.

"It was I—who dared," he replied huskily.

"Dared! Then you were not just carried away—for the moment?"

"No, Roseta. . . . I confess I was as—as bold as that poor devil."

"Vaughn, do you know what *chata* means?" she asked gravely.

"It is the name a *vaquero* has for his sweetheart."

"You mean it, señor?" she asked, imperiously.

"Lord help me, Roseta, I did, and I do. . . . I've loved you long."

"But you never told me!" she exclaimed, with wonder and reproach. "Why?"

"What hope had I? A poor ranger. Texas Medill! . . .
Didn't you call me 'killer of Mexicans'? "

"I reckon I did. And it is because you *are* that I'm alive
to thank God for it. . . . Vaughn, I always liked you, respected you as one of Texas' great rangers—feared you, too.
I never knew my real feelings. . . . But I—I love you *now*."

The night wore on, with the moon going down, weird and
coldly bright against the dark vaulted sky. Roseta lay asleep in
Vaughn's arm. For hours he had gazed, after peering ahead and
behind, always vigilant, always the ranger, on that wan face
against his shoulder. The silent moonlit night, the lonely ride,
the ghostly forms of cactus were real, though Vaughn never
trusted his senses there. This was only the dream of the ranger.
Yet the sweet fire of Roseta's kisses still lingered on his lips.

At length he changed her again from his right arm back to
his left. And she awakened, but not fully. In all the years of
his ranger service, so much of which he lived over on this
ride, there had been nothing to compare with this. For his
reward had been exalting. His longings had received magnificent fulfillment. His duty had not been to selfish and unap-
preciative officials, but to a great state—to its people—to the
native soil upon which he had been born. And that hard duty,
so poorly recompensed, so bloody and harrowing at times,
had by some enchantment bestowed upon one ranger at least
a beautiful girl of the border, frankly and honestly Texan, yet
part Spanish, retaining something of the fire and spirit of the
Dons who had once called Texas their domain.

In the gray of dawn, Vaughn lifted Roseta down from the
weary horse upon the south bank of the Rio Grande.

"We are here, Roseta," he said gladly. "It will soon be
light enough to ford the river. Star came out just below
Brownsville. There's a horse, Roseta! He shall never be risked
again. . . . In an hour you will be home."

"Home? Oh, how good! . . . But what shall I say,
Vaughn?" she replied, evidently awakening to the facts of
her predicament.

"Dear, who was the feller you ran—rode off with yesterday
mawnin'?" he asked.

"Didn't I tell you?" And she laughed. "It happened to be

Elmer Wade—*that* morning. . . . Oh, he was the unlucky one.
The bandits beat him with quirts, dragged him off his horse.
Then they led me away and I didn't see him again.''

Vaughn had no desire to acquaint her then with the tragic
fate that had overtaken that young man.

''You were not—elopin'?''

''*Vaughn!* It was only fun.''

''Uvaldo thinks you eloped. He was wild. He raved.''

''The devil he did!'' exclaimed Roseta rebelliously.
''Vaughn, what did *you* think?''

''Dearest, I—I was only concerned with trackin' you,'' he
replied, and even in the gray gloom of the dawn those big
dark eyes made his heart beat faster.

''Vaughn, I have peon blood in me,'' she said, and she
might have been a princess for the pride with which she con-
fessed it. ''My father always feared I'd run true to the Indian.
Are you afraid of your *chata*?''

''No, darlin'.''

''Then I shall punish Uvaldo. . . . I shall elope.''

''Roseta!'' cried Vaughn.

''Listen.'' She put her arms around his neck, and that was
a long reach for her. ''Will you give up the ranger service?
I—I couldn't bear it, Vaughn. You have earned release from
the service all Texans are so proud of.''

''Yes, Roseta. I'll resign,'' he replied with boyish, eager
shyness. ''I've some money—enough to buy a ranch.''

''Far from the border?'' she entreated.

''Yes, far. I know just the valley—way north, under the
Llano Estacado. . . . But, Roseta, I shall have to pack a gun—
till I'm forgotten.''

''Very well, I'll not be afraid—way north,'' she replied.
Then her sweet gravity changed to mischief. ''We will punish
Father. Vaughn, we'll elope right now! We'll cross the river—
get married—and drive out home to breakfast. . . . How Dad
will rave! But he would have me elope, though he'd never
guess I'd choose a ranger.''

Vaughn swung her up on Star, and leaned close to peer up
at her, to find one more assurance of the joy that had befallen
him. He was not conscious of asking, when she bent her head
to bestow kisses upon his lips.

The tall tale is a time-honored tradition, in and out of Western fiction; and so are such wild and woolly characters as Paul Bunyan and that great Texas cowboy, Pecos Bill. Short-story writer William C. White's amusing account of Pecos Bill, Panhandle Pete, and a four-footed, long-haired howling animal named Baby among the arroyos of West Texas is the tall tale at its most delightful.

Pecos Bill and the Willful Coyote

★★★★★★★★★★★★★★★★

William C. White

THE great legendary cowboy of Texas, Pecos Bill, used to sing of himself,

> *Oh, I'm wild and woolly*
> *And full of fleas,*
> *Ain't never been curried*
> *Below the knees*
>
> *I'm a wild she-wolf*
> *From Bitter Creek*
> *And it's my night*
> *To h-o-w-l!*

No one of the many stories tells precisely what happened to him at the end of his career. They don't tell because no one knows except Panhandle Pete who was there and he wouldn't talk until just recently.

Here, for the first time, is Pete's story.

There were a lot of things Pecos Bill used to like, Pete says, and liquor and women and the smell of sagebrush and the way the prairie looked in spring and shooting and riding and singing and the taste of beef broiled over a little outdoor fire were just a few of the things he liked. But I guess what he liked best was hunting coyotes. Ever since he'd been a small boy he'd chased coyotes, trapped coyotes, shot coyotes, thrown rocks at coyotes, and run them ragged on foot until they dropped, with their tongues hanging out. "They're smart animals," Bill always said. "It's a test of a man's intelligence to outthink 'em."

As Bill got older and his wind wasn't so good any more, he had to give up chasing coyotes, that is, until Baby came along.

I was with him the night he ran into Baby and I'll never forget it. We were riding along forty miles south of El Paso on as nice a night as I ever saw. The stars were out and it was bright. There was even a piece of moon. That was what made it so funny. We were riding along and Bill was singing cheerfully,

> Beat the drums lowly and play your fifes slowly,
> Play the dead march as you drag me along.
> Take me to the graveyard and lay a sod o'er me.
> For I'm a poor cowboy and I know I done wrong.

Pecos Bill always sang that song when he was feeling extra happy.

All of a sudden he says, "That's funny!"

"What's funny?"

"There, on that ridge, that thunderstorm coming up."

I looked and saw a black cloud coming up all right, but the stars and the moon were still shining.

"Never saw a thunderstorm on a starbright night," Bill said. "I'd call that almost a first-class miracle."

Something flashed on the ridge and Bill said, "It's lightning all right." We rode on faster. Bill stopped sudden. "That's funny!"

"What's funny?"

"Did you hear any thunder after that lightning?"

"Nope." I said that because I didn't hear any thunder and we were close enough to the storm to hear it if there was any thunder. "Nope, I didn't hear any."

"Look! Lightning again and no thunder!" Bill shook his head. "I believe in miracles but only one a time. A thunderstorm so close with lightning and no thunder, that's almost a first-class miracle."

We rode closer and suddenly we heard a sound. I guess you'd call it laughter but it was child's laughter and a woman's laughter and a waterfall's laughter, mixed with a horse's neigh and the noise of a tin can full of pebbles, and the roar of a lot of cowboys howling at a joke. It sounded like "Hayheehaw! Haiharhoo! Hearhoiheh!" and ended with "Huh, huh, huh!" delicate, like a skeptical baby.

"A laughing thunderstorm," Bill said, angry, "would be a third miracle. Hell, that's a coyote and the lightning is his eyes flashing!"

The black cloud raised a head and we could see right enough it was a coyote and the biggest one I ever saw and no one ever saw a bigger one. It was easy to tell it was a female because she walked dainty. She was so big she'd have to lie on her side and bend her neck out of shape to nibble at sagebrush. She must have heard us for the next thing she came at us, just like a thunderstorm that got up on its heels and began chasing you. She went by in such a rush, the air around was chilly for the next half hour. Bill didn't have a chance to draw his gun and fire. All he said was "Oh, Baby!"

That's how Baby got her name!

"Baby!" Bill repeated.

Somewhere, off in the distance, in the next county or maybe over in New Mexico we heard the "Hayheehaw" and so on and then the final "Huh, huh, huh!"

Bill was awful thoughtful for a while. "I'm going to hunt that baby and get her if it's the last thing I do. Baby! There's a coyote's coyote!"

Me and Bill hunted Baby all that year and all the next and the year after that and the year after that, too. Maybe there were even more years but those are all I remember. It was a long time.

Hunting Baby wasn't hard. She was always obliging and willing to hang around and be hunted. We chased her over most of Texas. When we couldn't find her on dark nights she'd let out that laugh of hers, particularly the "Huh, huh,

huh" part, and off we'd go. Other times her eyes would flash in the distance and there we'd go again. Sometimes that fooled us—more than fifty times we saw flashes like that and went off hell for leather and found that what we were chasing on the horizon was really a thunderstorm or a twister. Of course, when it thundered, then we knew it wasn't Baby. Half the times Baby'd have been lying low, watching us make fools of ourselves. As we turned back soaking wet we'd hear her "Huh, huh, huh!" off in the other direction. Other times we could get on her trail by waiting till she went to a water hole. She had a thirst like a desert and could drink a hole dry with the noise of a rusty pump. Some nights when we thought we'd lost her, her tracks would help us. They were always deep round holes and you couldn't miss 'em. It's getting off my story, but it was those tracks that helped develop West Texas—they were so deep they caught a lot of rain water and held it through dry spells and the grass grew thick around 'em. A lot of cattlemen today still use those tracks for water holes.

It wasn't hunting Baby that was tough, it was bagging her. In five years Pecos Bill must have had a thousand shots at her, from all distances from a hundred feet to a mile, and he shot at her with lead and iron and silver and a couple of times with a shotgun full of scrap iron. Nothing took any effect. Sometimes the stuff we fired hit Baby's sides and bounced back at us. Once we had to hide under a *mesquite* thicket for an hour while it rained railroad scrap all around us. As a six-inch piece of steel rail hit Bill on the neck he said, "We just won't try that one again. It's like being hunted by a coyote and shot at."

Other times when Baby was feeling frisky she didn't bother to bounce bullets back at us. She just timed the shot so that as it came to her she leaped up in the air and the bullets went right under her. Then she'd land with a smack you could hear a long way off and sometimes the earth would crack under her. Half the *arroyos*, those little canyons, in West Texas is from where Baby landed after those jumps. She'd have probably started up a couple of earthquakes in any country not so tough as West Texas.

"That Baby!" Bill would say, after missing her once again.

He sounded awful proud. "She's just willful! Plumb will-ful!"

I guess it got to be a game with Baby because no matter what we tried to do, her laugh never changed or got angry or snarly. Some nights when Bill didn't feel like going out after her, Baby'd hang around and there was a kind of disappoint-ment in her laugh, like a kid you promised ice cream for supper he didn't get.

I know it got to be a game with Bill and I never saw him so happy. Of course, from time to time we'd take a job to get enough money to try out some new scheme Bill had thought up for getting Baby. That was all he did think about, night after night. He figured out all kinds of baits and snares and devices but none of 'em worked. He figured out every kind of trap. After Baby picked up one of 'em and heaved it in the air with her hind foot and it landed on Bill and me and kept us pinned down for five days, we gave up traps. Even that didn't make Bill sore. He laughed and shook his head. "That Baby! She's smart." That was the way he was talking about her. Sometimes when he saw Baby running in the moonlight he'd say, "Look at the way that moonlight shines her gray fur! I bet you never saw anything prettier." And when she'd run fast, Bill'd say, "I bet that's the fastest animule there is!" The way he'd talk, you might have thought Bill was raising a child to show off at the State Fair.

One idea Bill had almost did get Baby. The idea was to chase her into the middle of Randall County, which we did, and then to run barbed wire right around the boundaries of the county, which we did. We used all the barbed wire in West Texas doing it and we strung it right. When we got done, stringing it over trees and poles and houses, I never saw such a mess of barbed wire. There wasn't a hole in it big enough for a rattlesnake to crawl through and we ran it so high that not even Baby could jump over it. There we had Baby penned up right and all we had to do now was to wait until she got too weak to move. That wouldn't take too long because we'd been having a drought and the water holes were as dry as sun-bleached bones. And Baby was always thirsty.

We must have waited outside that barbed wire a couple of weeks and all the time Bill kept saying, "We got her this time all right, we got her! She won't be willful no more!"

And Bill would jump around excited like a colt in a loco patch. "When man matches his intelligence with animules," Bill would say, "man must win. That's natchural!" Every night we heard Baby crying inside there behind the wire like she was trying to find a way out and getting madder and madder. The more she cried the more Bill grinned and yelled, "We got her this time!"

Then one night when we were watching, there was a new sound behind the wire, a soft "Plop, plop, plop!"

"What's that mean?" Bill asked, nervous. "Sounds like she was throwing mudpies." Then he guessed it. "Baby's digging, that's what it is. She's trying to dig her way out and she's throwing up dirt!" He looked half proud as he said, "I knew she'd figure out something to do." He looked half mad as he said, "That won't get her nowhere. We'll surround the fence and when her head shows we'll wallop her."

So Bill called out all the people from Potter, Armstrong, Swisher, and Deaf Smith counties, the ones around Randall. They were glad to stand watch because they're always glad to take a crack at anyone or anything coming from Randall county.

Three days and three nights we waited and the "Plop, plop, plop" continued but it got fainter and fainter as Baby dug deeper. "This time we got her sure," Bill said. He patrolled the fence day and night with a paddle made from a wagon tongue.

About midnight we heard a new kind of noise. It began as a hiss and turned into a roar and the earth shook and half the people around the fence ran like hell. The roar got louder and right then I felt rain in my face. It felt like rain, it was wet, but when I got some on my hand it had a funny smell.

In the midst of the loud roaring we heard a funny noise. It was "Hayheehaw," and the rest of it and then "Huh, huh, huh!" It sounded awful frightened, but it wasn't coming from back of the fence, it was coming from somewhere behind us.

"That's Baby!" Bill started to jump. "And she's out, she's gotten out!" I never saw a man so mad but he wasn't so mad he couldn't say, "She's that smart, that Baby."

It was beginning to rain even harder. "How'd she get out?"

"Blew out," Bill said. "That's not rain, it's oil. It's got

the same smell as the stuff I used to rub on my stiff joints. She dug to hit a pocket and a gusher blew her out.''

Way off in the distance, running like a breeze toward Mexico, we heard Baby. "That scared her," Bill said, rueful. "She ought to know I didn't mean to have it happen like that. She's scared. She won't come back."

His laugh was awful faint. "She must be over the Rio Grande by now."

Bill nodded, "I didn't think she'd take it like that." He sounded all choked up and he went to his horse and rode off like mad toward Amarillo.

It took me four days to find him. When I caught up with him he was in Amarillo at the Unweaned Calf bar. He wasn't alone, either. Somewhere he'd picked up a girl whose name was Kankakee Katie. I ain't much for women myself—I never learned how to tell a good one from a bad one and I've never been sure there's any real difference. Katie was a big blonde and from the way she was lapping up *pulque*, a pretty fair forager. She was confronting Bill and that was what mattered. I heard he'd been crying for three days when he got to town. Now he sat gloomy like and all he'd say was "Baby!"

"Who's this Baby you're muling over?" Katie asked him. He just shook his head.

"I never heard a man make as much fuss over me," Katie said, like it annoyed her.

Bill just says "Baby," dreamy like.

"It's awful bad manners," Katie said, "to keep grieving over one lady when you're in the company of another."

"Baby was no lady," Bill said.

"What was she, a hell cat?"

Bill shook his head. "A coyote!"

"That's no way to talk about her," Katie said, like she had to defend her sex. "What was she, blonde or brunette?"

"Gray," Bill said, "gray like early morning. Baby!"

Katie lapped up some more *pulque*. "I think you're loco but I tell you, I could go for a man who'd say 'Katie' the way you say 'Baby.' "

Bill reached for the bottle and began to cry at the same time and when he cries it's like the first freshets coming down an *arroyo* in spring.

"Katie," I said, "he's really upset about a coyote." I told

her about Baby and how Bill was afraid she was gone for good.

"He's grieving like that over a four-footed long-haired howling animal?" I didn't know whether Katie was going to laugh or upset the table. She didn't do either. She began to cry. "I never thought I'd meet such a tenderhearted person in all my life. Bill reminds me of my mother—she was tenderhearted like that, too." And she cried as hard as Bill.

Bill blinked and smiled at me. "Pete, here's what I need—sympathy and a chance to forget Baby." As he pounded his fist on the table, the walls of the Unweaned Calf shook and the barkeep looked scared. "Katie, if you'll have me, I'm yours. How's for marrying me and lighting out and we'll get a little ranch and raise cattle?"

Katie didn't know whether she was being kidded or not. Then she hit the table with her fist and the walls shook even harder and down to the floor dropped a little guy who was standing at the bar but not holding on tight. "Pardner," Katie said. "I heard about marriage and I always wanted to try it. It's a deal!" She stopped crying and dried her eyes on her shirtwaist sleeve. "We'll get a ranch house and we'll paper the walls with the pages of a mail-order catalogue and make everything snug." Then she looked worried. "Nope, it's only a dream."

Bill's face got black. "When I make a promise it's a promise."

Katie shook her head. "What about Baby? I know men better than anything in the world except maybe women. Sooner or later you'll get the old hankering to go after Baby and then not even a good woman's love or a forty-foot fence could hold you."

"I told you I was through with Baby," Bill roared and he made such a noise the little guy at the bar hit the floor again.

"A man's a man and a woman's a fool for forgetting it," Katie said, almost ready to cry again. "I just can't risk having my heart broken over a coyote." She finished off the bottle of *pulque*. "Nope, we'll stay friends, Bill, and I'll be a sister to you."

"I'll be consternated!" Bill yelled. "I believe you're jealous of Baby!"

"A lady has a right to her feelings, such as she feels,"

Katie said, wiping her eyes on her shirtwaist sleeve. "I'll tell you what to do, Bill. I ain't going to have no coyote come between us. You bring me Baby's hide and I'll marry you."

Bill just sat back in his chair.

"Besides, it'd be convenient to have," Katie said. "If Baby's as big as you say, we could use the hide for a parlor rug and have some lap over in the dining room and what's left we could stuff chinks with."

"I can't do that," Bill said promptly. "I've been trying for years with no luck."

"You don't sound like you even wanted to get it," Katie said with a pout.

"Sure, I want to get it, but how?"

"You talk like you're glad a coyote's smarter than Pecos Bill."

"That's enough." Bill banged the table and half the bottles on the bar fell down. "It's a bargain, I'll get it."

"Right now?"

"Right now!"

"Then I'll go off and hunt up a wedding dress and some shoes," Katie said. "You bring the hide back here and we'll have the hottest wedding there ever was in Amarillo." She headed for the door, like a barn being carried off in a spring flood.

Bill didn't say anything for quite a while. He picked up the *pulque* bottle and found it was empty. He asked, "Got any ideas, Pete?"

"About Katie?" I shook my head.

"About getting Baby. I can't let the little woman down."

He stood up and started to the bar. "Let's have a drink and start thinking."

When Bill asked the barkeep for *pulque* the barkeep shook his head. "You finished the last bottle. I haven't got a drop."

"Then gimme whiskey."

"On top of *pulque*?" The barkeep looked astonished and the little man beside the bar fell to the floor and lay there.

"What's wrong with that?" Bill asked, getting hot.

"You mix my drinks like that, they'll take the hide off you." But the barkeep poured out whiskey. "However, it's your hide."

Bill swung around like he was boiling mad. "What did you say?"

"I said if you mix my drinks they'll take the hide off you—!"

"Yeep!" Bill brought a fist down on the bar and cracked the top plank. "We got it!" He slugged down the whiskey. "We got it!"

I thought he was crazy. "Got what?"

He pounded me on the back and I bounced toward the front door. "Hurry out, Pete, and get two big water tanks!"

Well, I came back to the bar with the tanks and when I got there Bill had every bottle off the shelves and he was opening them so fast the popping of corks sounded like gunfire. From somewhere he had got fifty gallons of *pulque* and that went into the tanks first. Then he poured in all the whiskey in the place.

He was awful enthusiastic. "We'll mix up a drink for Baby that'll take her hide off sure. There's been a drought in this Dust Bowl and we'll pick up a good dry water hole, fill it up with this mixture, and see what Baby does."

In the tanks went twenty gallons of rum, three cases of bourbon, seven bottles of gin, and a bottle of soda water. The barkeep came up from the cellar with another armful of bottles. One of them had a funny shape.

"What's that?" Bill asked.

"Something called 'Cream dess Violets.' A salesman gave it to me."

"Put it in!"

"Here's Liquor dess Peaches."

"Put it in!"

In went cherry brandy, a bottle of bitters, and a gallon of Dago red. Bill didn't look satisfied. "Got anything else in bottles?"

The barkeep who was baldheaded handed over a flask of hair tonic.

Bill stuck his finger in the soup and licked it. "Tastes pretty nearly right. What else you got?"

The barkeep offered a bottle of catsup and that went in.

Again Bill sampled the results. "Almost right? Got anything else in a bottle?"

"Some perfume called Eau d'Amour I was saving for my wife."

"Put it in!"

Bill stuck his finger in once more. "That's perfect! It ought to take the hide off a cactus!"

Three teams of horses and ten men and the biggest dray in the county drew the tanks out to the water hole that Bill had decided to use. He had to hope the odor would attract Baby, wherever she was. The mixture from one tank went into the hole with a splash and the odor it gave off knocked seven men to the ground. I felt a little dizzy myself but Bill was too excited to notice anything. Twenty-one lizards who lived around that hole ran to it, took one small drink, and twenty of them lay on their backs with their toes turned up. The twenty-first just vanished in a small explosion.

After the men revived, they started to move the second tank to the hole but Bill stopped them. "Hold it! Baby may not come here before this stuff dries up and we'd better save the other tank for another night. We never could mix this drink again the same way."

With the hole half filled we drove off a piece and waited. We waited a long while and we tried to keep Bill quiet but he was pretty nervous. Most of the time he said, "I hope she comes." Sometimes he said, "This is a dirty trick to play on Baby!" Even from a mile away the water hole smelled like an old barroom on Sunday morning. Bill walked up and down saying, "I wonder where Baby is, I wonder what Katie's doing, I wonder if Baby is coming, I wonder if Katie is getting ready," until he sounded all mixed up, as if he was expecting Katie to turn up at the water hole while Baby got ready for a wedding.

Every so often there would be little explosions at the water hole and Bill said, "That must be jackrabbits coming in for a drink! Boy, if only Baby'd come."

Then we heard a funny noise off in the distance, the noise of a rush of a big wind. Bill knew what it was and he yelled, "It's Baby! She's sniffing!" A minute later, over the horizon, came the black shadow that was Baby, running full speed. She came so fast that she had to stop herself at the water hole by braking with her front feet and threw up a sandstorm that blacked out El Paso three days later. We were too excited to pay any attention.

We saw the shadow stand by the hole and we watched Baby lower her head. We heard one more sniff, like a tornado taking a deep breath, and there was an explosion and a roar that knocked us flat. Bill stood up first. "That got her!" He began jumping. "That got her!" And he started to the hole with all of us running like mad.

Bill beat us all there and when we caught up to him he said, "I'm consternated! Look at this!" There lay Baby's hide, thick, gray, tangled and matted, but there was nothing of Baby inside it. Bill didn't know what to do or think. He just stood scratching his head. "I didn't think it would work as good as that." He shook his head. "Well, I got her at last!" His voice sounded funny. Then he said, "Load as much of the hide as you can on the wagon and drag the rest. We'll get back to town and see Katie."

We put a lot of the hide on the wagon and it was piled up like a hayrick. On the way back to town, Bill remembered the unused tank of the mixture. "I'm going to bottle and sell it," he said. "It'll be a wonderful thing for knocking off warts and freckles."

We pulled up in front of the Unweaned Calf and Bill yelled, "Hey, Katie!" He was feeling pretty good again. "Hey, Katie, come out and see what I got!"

A flock of barflies rushed out but no Katie, and Bill began to grumble. "Look at the trouble you go to, just for a woman and then she's off primping herself and too busy to come look." He decided to wait for her and invited everyone in for a drink. By this time fifty guys were going up and down the street boasting how they caught the coyote by putting whiskey on her tail.

The barkeep had renewed his stock from somewhere and Bill ordered drinks all around. After twenty minutes he began to yell, "Hey, Katie!"

The barkeep gave him a funny look. "You mean that blonde you were talking to yesterday?"

"Yeah, what about her?"

"Last night a cowhand comes in with a couple hundred dollars and said he was going up to San Antone. Katie said she always wanted to see San Antone so she goes with him. They left about midnight!"

Well, Bill stowed the hide and the tank of mixture away in a shed and he said, "Let's get out of this country, Pete." We went over to New Mexico for a time, punching cattle, but it wasn't the same Bill. He was thoughtful and silent and he never sang any more. He never talked about Baby, either. Then we drifted back to El Paso again and got a job at the One Legged M Ranch. Bill worked hard but his heart wasn't in his work. At night he used to leave our shack and go out and sit somewhere by himself and he got sore if I offered to go along. When he did talk, he was pretty gloomy. "I'm getting old," he'd say. "I think we ought to go out to California for our last days. That's where rich Texans and poor Texicans go before they die. They sit in the sun, I heard, and eat oranges."

Once he said, "I done wrong killing Baby. I shouldn'ta done it. I was so happy when she was around to chase, I didn't know how happy I was."

I couldn't get him interested in roping or riding or liquor or shooting. As for women, when the sister of the owner of the One Legged M came for a visit Bill ran off and hid in the hills for a week.

He came back with a funny look on his face and he wouldn't talk. But that night he said, "Come along with me."

We walked a mile from the ranch buildings. Bill said mysteriously, "Hear anything?"

All I heard was a lot of crickets and maybe a lizard in the grass. I asked, "Where?"

"Over there, back of that hill."

I listened again and I heard a cow in heat and a horse neighing. "I don't hear nothing special."

Bill wasn't even listening to me. He was grinning like a kid. "I can hear her, coming nearer." He shook his head. "She sounds mighty lonesome tonight, mighty lonesome." He repeated, "So lonesome, that 'Huh, huh, huh!' "

I knew who he was talking about. I just chewed on a piece of grass and said nothing.

"You sure you don't hear nothing?" Bill asked.

"I got a cold." I tried to hide what I was thinking about Bill. "I don't hear nothing so good."

The next day I found Bill in the bunkhouse packing his kit. "I'm going back to Amarillo," he said and he wouldn't explain why. "I just got an idea, that's all."

He did explain on the way back. "Baby's still hanging around waiting for me, Pete. I know it." He glared at me. "You think I'm crazy."

I shook my head mighty quick. "Different people hear different things."

"The reason we can't see her is because she has no hide," Bill said, like he'd thought it out. "Did you ever see a coyote without a hide?"

"Nope, I never did."

"No one ever did and that proves it. If a coyote's going to be seen he just has to have a hide!"

We rode on quite a spell and I didn't have a word to say.

Then Bill said, "When we get to Amarillo, I'm going after Baby."

I almost fell off my horse and it wasn't the horse's fault. "How will you do that?"

Bill didn't say. We came into town and he went to the shed where he stored all the stuff after he got Baby's hide. It was still there but except to pat it once, he wasn't interested in it. He went right to the tank of mixture and pounded it.

It sounded as empty as a dry well.

"It's gone and I can't even mix it again," Bill said, and he sounded heartbroken. "I figured that maybe if I drank some of it, it'd put me in the same shape as Baby. Then I could have gone after her."

I just shook my head. I couldn't say a word.

Bill began to fuss around the tank. With the top off, he lowered himself inside. Then I heard him yell, "Get a cup, Pete! There's just a little bit left here."

I got him a cup and he fished up one cupful and even for that he had to scrape bottom. When he came from the tank he was grinning from earlobe to earlobe. I was pretty worried but I figured he knew what he was doing.

"You going to drink this now?"

"No, sir," Bill said with a lot of pride. "I'm going to drink it fit and proper." And with that he began to sing

Oh, I'm wild and woolly
And full of fleas,
Ain't never been curried
Below the knees!

I tried to argue with him all the way to the Unweaned Calf but his mind was made up. He just kept singing. He told the barkeep, "This time I brought my own liquor."

The barkeep looked suspicious. "How about a chaser?"

"I hope I'll never need a chaser," Bill said, with a pleasant laugh. He looked around the room and saw about twenty people. "Come on folks, gather round and I'll show you something you can tell your grandchildren." He raised the cup but I was feeling too bad to watch close.

Before he tastes it he sings

Take me to the graveyard and lay a sod o'er me,
For I'm a poor cowboy and I know I done wrong!

When I heard that I knew he was extra happy again.

"Pete!" he said to me. "You've been a good friend. When you find someone like Baby, don't treat her bad!"

Then he takes a good long swig from the cup.

There's a sort of flash and explosion, not loud but gentle like and when I look up, Bill's gone. Completely gone and not a sign of him! Then, and the men who were in the Unweaned Calf at that moment will swear to it, drunk or sober, we heard a gentle fluttering sound. Down from the ceiling like falling leaves came the clothes Bill had been wearing, his shirt, his hat, his pants, his boots, and the hand-carved belt he was so proud of. For a second they stood by themselves, just as if Bill was inside 'em, then they collapsed to the floor.

And that was the end of Pecos Bill, as far as anyone knew.

I hung around town for a couple of days but I was awful lonesome so I went back to my job at the One Legged M, feeling like a lost calf. I worked extra hard by day so I'd be good and tired at nights but even then I couldn't sleep.

One night I got up and walked out to where Bill and me used to sit. I was there in the quiet and I just couldn't forget

Bill. The only noise I heard was a couple of lizards in the grass.

Now, I ain't going to swear to this because I never heard it again but as I was sitting there that night a wind came up sudden and it got real cold. The grass began to move or I thought it did. And right behind me I heard "Hayheehaw!" and so on and then "Huh, huh, huh!" Maybe it could have been the wind in the trees but there weren't any trees and anyway, where did that sudden wind come from? A minute later I swear I heard Bill's voice, as happy as if he was chasing along behind, doing what he liked to do most in all this world.

But I couldn't see a thing.

I would even think that I had dreamed it except that the next morning Bert Simmons who owns the One Legged M called us outside and we followed him behind the barn. The ground there used to be as level and smooth as a piece of harness strap but this morning there was a brand new *arroyo*, fifty feet deep and running for a quarter mile, just like a big crack in the earth. It was the sort or crack we used to see when Bill and me shot and Baby jumped in the air to duck and then landed hard.

Well, I'm sure that wasn't the finish of the whole thing although I never again heard a sound like Baby or saw any traces. But I've been reading in the newspapers about those California earthquakes and I remember what Bill used to say about wanting to finish his days in California. No one knows what causes those earthquakes, I hear, but I got my own ideas ever since I heard that California was a sort of soft place, nowhere near as tough as West Texas and a whole lot more brittle.

Born in North Carolina at the beginning of the Civil War, O. Henry (William Sydney Porter) moved to Texas in 1882 and lived there for the next fifteen years. He knew his adopted state well and wrote about it with gusto. Many of his delightful "surprises" have Texas settings, and several of these are included in his 1904 collection, Heart of the West; *among them are "The Higher Abdication" (which has a San Antonio area setting) and such other classics as "The Reformation of Calliope" and "The Caballero's Way." The latter story introduced that memorable character, the Cisco Kid, who was destined to undergo a surprising metamorphosis from desperado in O. Henry's story to dashing "Robin Hood of the Old West" in the 1950s TV series starring Duncan Renaldo and Leo Carrillo.*

The Higher Abdication

★★★★★★★★★★★★★★★

O. Henry

CURLY the tramp sidled toward the free-lunch counter. He caught a fleeting glance from the bartender's eye, and stood still, trying to look like a businessman who had just dined at the Menger and was waiting for a friend who had promised to pick him up in his motor car. Curly's histrionic powers were equal to the impersonation; but his makeup was wanting.

The bartender rounded the bar in a casual way, looking up at the ceiling as though he was pondering some intricate problem of kalsomining, and then fell upon Curly so suddenly that the roadster had no excuses ready. Irresistibly, but so composedly that it seemed almost absentmindedness on his part, the dispenser of drinks pushed Curly to the swinging doors and kicked him out, with a nonchalance that almost amounted to sadness. That was the way of the Southwest.

Curly arose from the gutter leisurely. He felt no anger or resentment toward his ejector. Fifteen years of tramphood spent out of the twenty-two years of his life had hardened the fibers of his spirit. The slings and arrows of outrageous fortune fell blunted from the buckler of his armoured pride. With especial resignation did he suffer contumely and injury at the hands of bartenders. Naturally, they were his enemies; and unnaturally, they were often his friends. He had to take his chances with them. But he had not yet learned to estimate these cool, languid, Southwestern knights of the bungstarter, who had the manners of an Earl of Pawtucket, and who, when they disapproved of your presence, moved you with the silence and despatch of a chess automaton advancing a pawn.

Curly stood for a few moments in the narrow, mesquite-paved street. San Antonio puzzled and disturbed him. Three days he had been a nonpaying guest of the town, having dropped off there from a box car of an I. & G. N. freight, because Greaser Johnny had told him in Des Moines that the Alamo City was manna fallen, gathered, cooked, and served free with cream and sugar. Curly had found the tip partly a good one. There was hospitality in plenty of a careless, liberal, irregular sort. But the town itself was a weight upon his spirits after his experience with the rushing, businesslike, systematized cities of the North and East. Here he was often flung a dollar, but too frequently a good-natured kick would follow it. Once a band of hilarious cowboys had roped him on Military Plaza and dragged him across the black soil until no respectable rag-bag would have stood sponsor for his clothes. The winding, doubling streets, leading nowhere, bewildered him. And then there was a little river, crooked as a pot-hook, that crawled through the middle of the town, crossed by a hundred little bridges so nearly alike that they got on Curly's nerves. And the last bartender wore a number nine shoe.

The saloon stood on a corner. The hour was eight o'clock. Homefarers and outgoers jostled Curly on the narrow stone sidewalk. Between the buildings to his left he looked down a cleft that proclaimed itself another thoroughfare. The alley was dark except for one patch of light. Where there was light there were sure to be human beings. Where there were human beings after nightfall in San Antonio there might be food, and there was sure to be drink. So Curly headed for the light.

The illumination came from Schwegel's Café. On the sidewalk in front of it Curly picked up an old envelope. It might have contained a check for a million. It was empty; but the wanderer read the address, "Mr. Otto Schwegel," and the name of the town and state. The postmark was Detroit.

Curly entered the saloon. And now in the light it could be perceived that he bore the stamp of many years of vagabondage. He had none of the tidiness of the calculating and shrewd professional tramp. His wardrobe represented the cast-off specimens of half a dozen fashions and eras. Two factories had combined their efforts in providing shoes for his feet. As you gazed at him there passed through your mind vague impressions of mummies, wax figures, Russian exiles, and men lost on desert islands. His face was covered almost to his eyes with a curly brown beard that he kept trimmed short with a pocket-knife, and that had furnished him with his *nom de route*. Light-blue eyes, full of sullenness, fear, cunning, impudence, and fawning, witnessed the stress that had been laid upon his soul.

The saloon was small, and in its atmosphere the odors of meat and drink struggled for the ascendency. The pig and the cabbage wrestled with hydrogen and oxygen. Behind the bar Schwegel labored with an assistant whose epidermal pores showed no signs of being obstructed. Hot wienerwurst and sauerkraut were being served to purchasers of beer. Curly shuffled to the end of the bar, coughed hollowly, and told Schwegel that he was a Detroit cabinet-maker out of a job.

It followed as the night the day that he got his schooner and lunch.

"Was you acquainted maybe mit Heinrich Strauss in Detroit?" asked Schwegel.

"Did I know Heinrich Strauss?" repeated Curly, affectionately. "Why, say, 'Bo, I wish I had a dollar for every game of pinochle me and Heine has played on Sunday afternoons."

More beer and a second plate of steaming food was set before the diplomat. And then Curly, knowing to a fluiddrachm how far a "con" game would go, shuffled out into the unpromising street.

And now he began to perceive the inconveniences of this stony Southern town. There was none of the outdoor gaiety and brilliancy and music that provided distraction even to the poorest in the cities of the North. Here, even so early, the gloomy, rock-walled houses were closed and barred against the murky dampness of the night. The streets were mere fissures through which flowed gray wreaths of river mist. As he walked he heard laughter and the chink of coin and chips behind darkened windows, and music coming from every chink of wood and stone. But the diversions were selfish; the day of popular pastimes had not yet come to San Antonio.

But at length Curly, as he strayed, turned the sharp angle of another lost street and came upon a rollicking band of stockmen from the outlying ranches celebrating in the open in front of an ancient wooden hotel. One great roisterer from the sheep country who had just instigated a movement toward the bar, swept Curly in like a stray goat with the rest of his flock. The princes of kine and wool hailed him as a new zoological discovery, and unroariously strove to preserve him in the diluted alcohol of their compliments and regards.

An hour afterward Curly staggered from the hotel barroom dismissed by his fickle friends, whose interest in him had subsided as quickly as it had risen. Full-stoked with alcoholic fuel and cargoed with food, the only question remaining to disturb him was that of shelter and bed.

A drizzling, cold Texas rain had begun to fall—an endless, lazy, unintermittent downfall that lowered the spirits of men and raised a reluctant steam from the warm stones of the streets and houses. Thus comes the "norther" dousing gentle spring and amiable autumn with the chilling salutes and adieux of coming and departing winter.

Curly followed his nose down the first tortuous street into which his irresponsible feet conducted him. At the lower end of it, on the bank of the serpentine stream, he perceived an open gate in a cemented rock wall. Inside he saw camp fires and a row of low wooden sheds built against three sides of the enclosing wall. He entered the enclosure. Under the sheds many horses were champing at their oats and corn. Many wagons and buckboards stood about with their teams' harness thrown carelessly upon the shafts and doubletrees. Curly recognized the place as a wagon-yard, such as is provided by merchants for their out-of-town friends and customers. No one was in sight. No doubt the drivers of those wagons were scattered about the town "seeing the elephant and hearing the owl." In their haste to become patrons of the town's dispensaries of mirth and good cheer the last ones to depart must have left the great wooden gate swinging open.

Curly had satisfied the hunger of an anaconda and the thirst of a camel, so he was neither in the mood nor the condition of an explorer. He zigzagged his way to the first wagon that his eyesight distinguished in the semi-darkness under the shed. It was a two-horse wagon with a top of white canvas. The wagon was half filled with loose piles of wool sacks, two or three great bundles of gray blankets, and a number of bales, bundles, and boxes. A reasoning eye would have estimated the load at once as ranch supplies, bound on the morrow for some outlying hacienda. But to the drowsy intelligence of Curly they represented only warmth and softness and protection against the cold humidity of the night. After several unlucky efforts, at last he conquered gravity so far as to climb over a wheel and pitch forward upon the best and warmest bed he had fallen upon in many a day. Then he became instinctively a burrowing animal, and dug his way like a prairie-dog down among the sacks and blankets, hiding himself from the cold air as snug and safe as a bear in his den. For three nights sleep had visited Curly only in broken and shivering doses. So now, when Morpheus condescended to pay him a call, Curly got such a stranglehold on the mythological old gentleman that it was a wonder that anyone else in the whole world got a wink of sleep that night.

Six cowpunchers of the Cibolo Ranch were waiting around the door of the ranch store. Their ponies cropped grass nearby, tied in the Texas fashion—which is not tied at all. Their bridle reins had been dropped to the earth, which is a more effectual way of securing them (such is the power of habit and imagination) than you could devise out of a half-inch rope and a live-oak tree.

These guardians of the cow lounged about, each with a brown cigarette paper in his hand, and gently but unceasingly cursed Sam Revell, the storekeeper. Sam stood in the door, snapping the red elastic bands on his pink madras shirtsleeves and looking down affectionately at the only pair of tan shoes within a forty-mile radius. His offense had been serious, and he was divided between humble apology and admiration for the beauty of his raiment. He had allowed the ranch stock of "smoking" to become exhausted.

"I thought sure there was another case of it under the counter, boys," he explained. "But it happened to be catterdges."

"You've sure got a case of happenedicitis," said Poky Rodgers, fence rider of the Largo Verde *potrero*. "Somebody ought to happen to give you a knock on the head with the butt end of a quirt. I've rode in nine miles for some tobacco; and it don't appear natural and seemly that you ought to be allowed to live."

"The boys was smokin' cut plug and dried mesquite leaves mixed when I left," sighed Mustang Taylor, horse wrangler of the Three Elm camp. "They'll be lookin' for me back by nine. They'll be settin' up, with their papers ready to roll a whiff of the real thing before bedtime. And I've got to tell 'em that this pink-eyed, sheep-headed, sulphur-footed, shirt-waisted son of a calico broncho, Sam Revell, hasn't got no tobacco on hand."

Gregorio Falcon, Mexican vaquero and best thrower of the rope on the Cibolo, pushed his heavy, silver-embroidered straw sombrero back upon his thicket of jet black curls, and scraped the bottoms of his pockets for a few crumbs of the precious weed.

"Ah, Don Samuel," he said, reproachfully, but with his touch of Castilian manners, "escuse me. Dthey say dthe jack-rabbeet and dthe sheep have dthe most leetle *sesos*—how you call dthem—brain-es? Ah don' believe dthat, Don Samuel—escuse me. Ah dthink people w'at don' keep esmokin' to-bacco, dthey—bot you weel escuse me, Don Samuel."

"Now, what's the use of chewin' the rag, boys," said the untroubled Sam, stooping over to rub the toes of his shoes with a red-and-yellow handkerchief. "Ranse took the order for some more smokin' to San Antone with him Tuesday. Pancho rode Ranse's hoss back yesterday; and Ranse is goin' to drive the wagon back himself. There wa'n't much of a load—just some woolsacks and blankets and nails and canned peaches and a few things we was out of. I look for Ranse to roll in today sure. He's an early starter and a hell-to-split driver, and he ought to be here not far from sundown.''

"What plugs is he drivin'?" asked Mustang Taylor, with a smack of hope in his tones.

"The buckboard grays," said Sam.

"I'll wait a spell, then," said the wrangler. "Them plugs eat up a trail like a road-runner swallowin' a whip snake. And you may bust me open a can of green-gage plums, Sam, while I'm waitin' for somethin' better."

"Open me some yellow clings," ordered Poky Rodgers. "I'll wait, too."

The tobaccoless punchers arranged themselves comfortably on the steps of the store. Inside Sam chopped open with a hatchet the tops of the cans of fruit.

The store, a big, white wooden building like a barn, stood fifty yards from the ranch-house. Beyond it were the horse corrals; and still farther the wool sheds and the brush-topped shearing pens—for the Rancho Cibolo raised both cattle and sheep. Behind the store, at a little distance, were the grass-thatched *jacals* of the Mexicans who bestowed their allegiance upon the Cibolo.

The ranch-house was composed of four large rooms, with plastered adobe wall, and a two-room wooden ell. A twenty-feet-wide "gallery" circumvented the structure. It was set in a grove of immense live-oaks and water-elms near a lake—a long, not very wide, and tremendously deep lake in which at nightfall, great gars leaped to the surface and plunged with the noise of hippopotamuses frolicking at their bath. From the trees hung garlands and massive pendants of the melancholy gray moss of the South. Indeed, the Cibolo ranch-house seemed more of the South than of the West. It looked as if old "Kiowa" Truesdell might have brought it with him from the lowlands of Mississippi when he came to Texas with his rifle in the hollow of his arm in '55.

But, though he did not bring the family mansion, Truesdell did bring something in the way of a family inheritance that was more lasting than brick or stone. He brought one end of the Truesdell-Curtis family feud. And when a Curtis bought the Rancho de los Olmos, sixteen miles from the Cibolo, there were lively times on the pear flats and in the chaparral thickets off the Southwest. In those days Truesdell cleaned the brush of many a wolf and tiger cat and Mexican lion; and one or two Curtises fell heirs to notches on his rifle stock. Also he buried a brother with a Curtis bullet in him on the bank of the lake at Cibolo. And then the Kiowa Indians made their last raid upon the ranches between the Frio and the Rio Grande, and Truesdell at the head of his rangers rid the earth of them to the last brave, earning his sobriquet. Then came prosperity in the form of waxing herds and broadening lands. And then old age and bitterness, when he sat, with his great mane of hair as white as the Spanish-dagger blossoms and his fierce, pale-blue eyes, on the shaded gallery at Cibolo, growling like the pumas that he had slain. He snapped his fingers at old age; the bitter taste to life did not come from that. The cup that stuck at his lips was that his only son Ransom wanted to marry a Curtis, the last youthful survivor of the other end of the feud.

For a while the only sounds to be heard at the store were the rattling of the tin spoons and the gurgling intake of the juicy fruits by the cowpunchers, the stamping of the grazing ponies, and the singing of a doleful song by Sam as he contentedly brushed his stiff auburn hair for the twentieth time that day before a crinkly mirror.

From the door of the store could be seen the irregular, sloping stretch of prairie to the south, with its reaches of light-green, billowy mesquite flats in the lower places, and its rises crowned with nearly black masses of short chaparral. Through the mesquite flat wound the ranch road that, five miles away, flowed into the old government trail to San Antonio. The sun was so low that the gentlest elevation cast its gray shadow miles into the green-gold sea of sunshine.

That evening ears were quicker than eyes.

The Mexican held up a tawny finger to still the scraping of tin against tin.

"One waggeen," said he, "cross dthe Arroyo Hondo. Ah hear dthe wheel. Verree rockee place, dthe Hondo."

"You've got good ears, Gregorio," said Mustang Taylor. "I never heard nothin' but the song-bird in the bush and the zephyr skallyhootin' across the peaceful dell."

In ten minutes Taylor remarked: "I see the dust of a wagon risin' right above the fur end of the flat."

"You have verree good eyes, señor," said Gregorio, smiling.

Two miles away they saw a faint cloud dimming the green ripples of the mesquites. In twenty minutes they heard the clatter of the horses' hoofs: in five minutes more the gray plugs dashed out of the thicket, whickering for oats and drawing the light wagon behind them like a toy.

From the *jacals* came a cry of: *"El Amo! El Amo!"* Four Mexican youths raced to unharness the grays. The cowpunchers gave a yell of greeting and delight.

Ranse Truesdell, driving, threw the reins to the ground and laughed.

"It's under the wagon sheet, boys," he said. "I know what you're waiting for. If Sam lets it run out again, we'll use them yellow shoes of his for a target. There's two cases. Pull 'em out and light up. I know you all want a smoke."

After striking dry country Ranse had removed the wagon sheet from the bows and thrown it over the goods in the wagon. Six pair of hasty hands dragged it off and grabbed beneath the sacks and blankets for the cases of tobacco.

Long Collins, tobacco messenger from the San Gabriel outfit, who rode with the longest stirrups west of the Mississippi, delved with an arm like the tongue of a wagon. He caught something harder than a blanket and pulled out a fearful thing—a shapeless, muddy bunch of leather tied together with wire and twine. From its ragged end, like the head and claws of a disturbed turtle, protruded human toes.

"Who-ee!" yelled Long Collins. "Ranse, are you a-packin' around of corpuses? Here's a—howlin' grasshoppers!"

Up from his long slumber popped Curly, like some vile worm from its burrow. He clawed his way out and sat blinking like a disreputable, drunken owl. His face was as bluish-red and puffed and seamed and crosslined as the cheapest round steak of the butcher. His eyes were swollen slits; his nose a pickled beet; his hair would have made the wildest thatch of a Jack-in-the-box look like the satin poll of a Cléo de Mérode. The rest of him was scarecrow done to the life.

Ranse jumped down from his seat and looked at his strange cargo with wide-open eyes.

"Here, you maverick, what are you doing in my wagon? How did you get in there?"

The punchers gathered around in delight. For the time they had forgotten tobacco.

Curly look around him slowly in every direction. He snarled like a Scotch terrier through his ragged beard.

"Where is this?" he rasped through his parched throat. "It's a damn farm in an old field. What'd you bring me here for—say? Did I say I wanted to come here? What are you Reubs rubberin' at—hey? G'wan or I'll punch some of yer faces."

"Drag him out, Collins," said Ranse.

Curly took a slide and felt the ground rise up and collide with his shoulder blades. He got up and sat on the steps of the store shivering from outraged nerves, hugging his knees and sneering. Taylor lifted out a case of tobacco and wrenched off its top. Six cigarettes began to glow, bringing peace and forgiveness to Sam.

"How'd you come in my wagon?" repeated Ranse, this time in a voice that drew a reply.

Curly recognized the tone. He had heard it used by freight brakemen and large persons in blue carrying clubs.

"Me?" he growled. "Oh, was you talkin' to me? Why, I was on my way to the Menger, but my valet had forgot to pack my pajamas. So I crawled into that wagon in the wagon-yard—see? I never told you to bring me out to this bloomin' farm—see?"

"What is it, Mustang?" Poky Rodgers, almost forgetting to smoke in his ecstasy. "What do it live on?"

"It's a galliwampus, Poky," said Mustang. "It's the thing that hollers 'willi-wallo' up in ellum trees in the low grounds of nights. I don't know if it bites."

"No, it ain't, Mustang," volunteered Long Collins. "Them galliwampuses has fins on their backs, and eighteen toes. This here is a hicklesnifter. It lives under the ground and eats cherries. Don't stand so close to it. It wipes out villages with one stroke of its prehensile tail."

Sam, the cosmopolite, who called bartenders in San Antone by their first name, stood in the door. He was a better zoologist.

"Well, ain't that a Willie for your whiskers?" he commented. "Where'd you dig up the hobo, Ranse? Goin' to make an auditorium for inbreviates out of the ranch?"

"Say," said Curly, from whose panoplied breast all shafts of wit fell blunted. "Any of you kiddin' guys got a drink on you? Have your fun. Say, I've been hittin' the stuff till I don't know straight up."

He turned to Ranse. "Say, you shanghaied me on your d—d old prairie schooner—did I tell you to drive me to a farm? I want a drink. I'm goin' all to little pieces. What's doin'?"

Ranse saw that the tramp's nerves were racking him. He despatched one of the Mexican boys to the ranch-house for a glass of whisky. Curly gulped it down; and into his eyes came a brief, grateful glow—as human as the expression in the eye of a faithful setter dog.

"Thanky, boss," he said, quietly.

"You're thirty miles from a railroad, and forty miles from a saloon," said Ranse.

Curly fell back weakly against the steps.

"Since you are here," continued the ranchman, "come along with me. We can't turn you out on the prairie. A rabbit might tear you to pieces."

He conducted Curly to a large shed where the ranch vehicles were kept. There he spread out a canvas cot and brought blankets.

"I don't suppose you can sleep," said Ranse, "since you've been pounding your ear for twenty-four hours. But you can camp here till morning. I'll have Pedro fetch you up some grub."

"Sleep!" said Curly. "I can sleep a week. Say, sport, have you got a coffin nail on you?"

Fifty miles had Ransom Truesdell driven that day. And yet this is what he did.

Old "Kiowa" Truesdell sat in his great wicker chair reading by the light of an immense oil lamp. Ranse laid a bundle of newspapers fresh from town at his elbow.

"Back, Ranse?" said the old man, looking up.

"Son," old "Kiowa" continued, "I've been thinking all day about a certain matter that we have talked about. I want you to tell me again. I've lived for you. I've fought wolves and Indians and worse white men to protect you. You never had any mother that you can remember. I've taught you to shoot straight, ride hard, and live clean. Later on I've worked to pile up dollars that'll be yours. You'll be a rich man, Ranse, when my chunk goes out. I've made you. I've licked you into shape like a leopard cat licks its cubs. You don't belong to yourself—you've got to be a Truesdell first. Now, is there to be any more nonsense about this Curtis girl?''

''I'll tell you once more,'' said Ranse, slowly. ''As I am a Truesdell and as you are my father, I'll never marry a Curtis.''

''Good boy,'' said old ''Kiowa.'' ''You'd better go get some supper.''

Ranse went to the kitchen at the rear of the house. Pedro, the Mexican cook, sprang up to bring the food he was keeping warm in the stove.

''Just a cup of coffee, Pedro,'' he said, and drank it standing. And then:

''There's a tramp on a cot in the wagon-shed. Take him something to eat. Better make it enough for two.''

Ranse walked out toward the *jacals*. A boy came running.

''Manuel, can you catch Vaminos, in the little pasture, for me?''

''Why not, señor? I saw him near the *puerta* but two hours past. He bears a drag-rope.''

''Get him and saddle him as quick as you can.''

''Prontito, señor.''

Soon, mounted on Vaminos, Ranse leaned in the saddle, pressed with his knees, and galloped eastward past the store, where sat Sam trying his guitar in the moonlight.

Vaminos shall have a word—Vaminos the good dun horse. The Mexicans, who have a hundred names for the colors of a horse, called him *gruyo*. He was a mouse-colored, slate-colored, flea-bitten roan-dun, if you can conceive it. Down his back from his mane to his tail went a line of black. He would live forever; and surveyors have not laid off as many miles in the world as he could travel in a day.

Eight miles east of the Cibolo ranch-house Ranse loosened the pressure of his knees, and Vaminos stopped under a big ratama tree. The yellow ratama blossoms showered fragrance that would have undone the roses of France. The moon made the earth a great concave bowl with a crystal sky for a lid. In glade five jackrabbits leaped and played together like kittens. Eight miles farther east shone a faint star that appeared to have dropped below the horizon. Night riders, who often steered their course by it, knew it to be the light in the Rancho de los Olmos.

In ten minutes Yenna Curtis galloped to the tree on her sorrel pony Dancer. The two leaned and clasped hands heartily.

"I ought to have ridden nearer your home," said Ranse. "But you never will let me."

Yenna laughed. And in the soft light you could see her strong white teeth and fearless eyes. No sentimentality there, in spite of the moonlight, the odor of the ratamas, and the admirable figure of Ranse Truesdell, the lover. But she was there, eight miles from her home, to meet him.

"How often have I told you, Ranse," she said, "that I am your half-way girl? Always half-way."

"Well?" said Ranse, with a question in his tones.

"I did," said Yenna, with almost a sigh. "I told him after dinner when I thought he would be in a good humor. Did you ever wake up a lion, Ranse, with the mistaken idea that he would be a kitten? He almost tore the ranch to pieces. It's all up. I love my daddy, Ranse, and I'm afraid—I'm afraid of him, too. He ordered me to promise that I'd never marry a Truesdell. I promised. That's all. What luck did you have?"

"The same," said Ranse, slowly. "I promised him that his son would never marry a Curtis. Somehow I couldn't go against him. He's mighty old. I'm sorry, Yenna."

The girl leaned in her saddle and laid one hand on Ranse's, on the horn of his saddle.

"I never thought I'd like you better for giving me up," she said ardently, "but I do. I must ride back now, Ranse. I slipped out of the house and saddled Dancer myself. Good-night, neighbor."

"Good-night," said Ranse. "Ride carefully over them badger holes."

They wheeled and rode away in opposite directions. Yenna turned in her saddle and called clearly:

"Don't forget I'm your half-way girl, Ranse."

"Damn all family feuds and inherited scraps," muttered

Ranse vindictively to the breeze as he rode back to the Cibolo.

Ranse turned his horse into the small pasture and went to
his own room. He opened the lowest drawer of an old bureau
to get out the packet of letters that Yenna had written him
one summer when she had gone to Mississippi for a visit.
The drawer stuck, and he yanked at it savagely—as a man
will. It came out of the bureau, and bruised both his shins—
as a drawer will. An old, folded yellow letter without an
envelope fell from somewhere—probable from where it had
lodged in one of the upper drawers. Ranse took it to the lamp
and read it curiously.

Then he took his hat and walked to one of the Mexican
jacals.

"Tia Juana," he said, "I would like to talk with you a
while."

An old, old Mexican woman, white-haired and wonder-
fully wrinkled, rose from a stool.

"Sit down," said Ranse, removing his hat and taking the
one chair in the *jacal*. "Who am I, Tia Juana?" he asked,
speaking Spanish.

"Don Ransom, our good friend and employer. Why do
you ask?" answered the old woman wonderingly.

"Tia Juana, who am I?" he repeated, with his stern eyes
looking into hers.

A frightened look came in the old woman's face. She fumbled with her black shawl.

"Who am I, Tia Juana?" said Ranse once more.

"Thirty-two years I have lived on the Rancho Cibolo,"
said Tia Juana. "I thought to be buried under the coma mott
beyond the garden before these things should be known. Close
the door, Don Ransom, and I will speak. I see in your face
that you know."

An hour Ranse spent behind Tia Juana's closed door. As
he was on his way back to the house Curly called to him from
the wagon-shed.

The tramp sat on his cot, swinging his feet and smoking.

"Say, sport," he grumbled. "This is no way to treat a
man after kidnappin' him. I went up to the store and borrowed a razor from that fresh guy and had a shave. But that
ain't all a man needs. Say—can't you loosen up for about

three fingers more of that booze? I never asked you to bring me to your d—d farm.''

''Stand up out here in the light,'' said Ranse, looking at him closely.

Curly got up sullenly and took a step or two.

His face, now shaven smooth, seemed transformed. His hair had been combed, and it fell back from the right side of his forehead with a peculiar wave. The moonlight charitably softened the ravages of drink; and his aquiline, well-shaped nose and small, square cleft chin almost gave distinction to his looks.

Ranse sat on the foot of the cot and looked at him curiously.

''Where did you come from—have you got any home or folks anywhere?''

''Me? Why, I'm a dook,'' said Curly. ''I'm Sir Reginald—oh, cheese it. No; I don't know anything about my ancestors. I've been a tramp ever since I can remember. Say, old pal, are you going to set 'em up again tonight or not?''

''You answer my questions and maybe I will. How did you come to be a tramp?''

''Me?'' answered Curly. ''Why, I adopted that profession when I was an infant. Case of had to. First thing I can remember, I belonged to a big, lazy hobo called Beefsteak Charley. He sent me around to houses to beg. I wasn't hardly big enough to reach the latch of a gate.''

''Did he ever tell you how he got you?'' asked Ranse.

''Once when he was sober he said he bought me for an old six-shooter and six bits from a band of drunken Mexican sheep-shearers. But what's the diff? That's all I know.''

''All right,'' said Ranse. ''I reckon you're a maverick for certain. I'm going to put the Rancho Cibolo brand on you. I'll start you to work in one of the camps tomorrow.''

''Work!'' sniffed Curly, disdainfully. ''What do you take me for? Do you think I'd chase cows, and hop-skip-and-jump around after crazy sheep like that pink and yellow guy at the store says these Reubs do? Forget it.''

''Oh, you'll like it when you get used to it,'' said Ranse. ''Yes, I'll send you up one more drink by Pedro. I think you'll make a first-class cowpuncher before I get through with you.''

"Me?" said Curly. "I pity the cows you set me to chaperon. They can go chase themselves. Don't forget my nightcap, please, boss."

Ranse paid a visit to the store before going to the house. Sam Revell was taking off his tan shoes regretfully and preparing for bed.

"Any of the boys from the San Gabriel camp riding in early in the morning?" asked Ranse.

"Long Collins," said Sam briefly. "For the mail."

"Tell him," said Ranse, "to take that tramp out to camp with him and keep him till I get there."

Curly was sitting on his blankets in the San Gabriel camp cursing talentedly when Ranse Truesdell rode up and dismounted on the next afternoon. The cowpunchers were ignoring the stray. He was grimy with dust and black dirt. His clothes were making their last stand in favor of the conventions.

Ranse went up to Buck Rabb, the camp boss, and spoke briefly.

"He's a plumb buzzard," said Buck. "He won't work, and he's the low-downest passel of inhumanity I ever see. I didn't know what you wanted done with him, Ranse, so I just let him set. That seems to suit him. He's been condemned to death by the boys a dozen times, but I told 'em maybe you was savin' him for torture."

Ranse took off his coat.

"I've got a hard job before me, Buck, I reckon, but it has to be done. I've got to make a man out of that thing. That's what I've come to camp for."

He went up to Curly.

"Brother," he said, "don't you think if you had a bath it would allow you to take a seat in the company of your fellowman with less injustice to the atmosphere."

"Run away, farmer," said Curly, sardonically. "Willie will send for nursey when he feels like having his tub."

The *charco*, or water hole, was twelve yards away. Ranse took one of Curly's ankles and dragged him like a sack of potatoes to the brink. Then with the strength and sleight of a hammer-thrower he hurled the offending member of society far into the lake.

Curly crawled out and up the bank spluttering like a porpoise.

Ranse met him with a piece of soap and a coarse towel in his hands.

"Go to the other end of the lake and use this," he said. "Buck will give you some dry clothes at the wagon."

The tramp obeyed without protest. By the time supper was ready he had returned to camp. He was hardly to be recognized in his new blue shirt and brown duck clothes. Ranse observed him out of the corner of his eye.

"Lordy, I hope he ain't a coward," he was saying to himself. "I hope he won't turn out to be a coward."

His doubts were soon allayed. Curly walked straight to where he stood. His light-blue eyes were blazing.

"Now I'm clean," he said meaningly, "maybe you'll talk to me. Think you've got a picnic here, do you? You clodhoppers think you can run over a man because you know he can't get away. All right. Now, what do you think of that?"

Curly planted a stinging slap against Ranse's left cheek. The print of his hand stood out a dull red against the tan.

Ranse smiled happily.

The cowpunchers talk to this day of the battle that followed.

Somewhere in his restless tour of the cities Curly had acquired the art of self-defense. The ranchman was equipped only with the splendid strength and equilibrium of perfect health and the endurance conferred by decent living. The two attributes nearly matched. There were no formal rounds. At last the fiber of the clean liver prevailed. The last time Curly went down from one of the ranchman's awkward but powerful blows he remained on the grass, but looking up with an unquenched eye.

Ranse went to the water barrel and washed the red from a cut on his chin in the stream from the faucet.

On his face was a grin of satisfaction.

Much benefit might accrue to educators and moralists if they could know the details of the curriculum of reclamation through which Ranse put his waif during the month that he spent in the San Gabriel camp. The ranchman had no fine theories to work out—perhaps his whole stock of pedagogy embraced only a knowledge of horse-breaking and a belief in heredity.

The cowpunchers saw that their boss was trying to make a man out of the strange animal that he had sent among them; and they tacitly organized themselves into a faculty of assistants. But their system was their own.

Curly's first lesson stuck. He became on friendly and then on intimate terms with soap and water. And the thing that pleased Ranse most was that his "subject" held his ground at each successive higher step. But the steps were sometimes far apart.

Once he got at the quart bottle of whisky kept secretly in the grub tent for rattlesnake bites, and spent sixteen hours on the grass, magnificently drunk. But when he staggered to his feet his first move was to find his soap and towel and start for the *charco*. And once, when a treat came from the ranch in the form of a basket of fresh tomatoes and young onions, Curly devoured the entire consignment before the punchers reached the camp at supper time.

And then the punchers punished him in their own way. For three days they did not speak to him, except to reply to his own questions or remarks. And they spoke with absolute and unfailing politeness. They played tricks on one another; they pounded one another hurtfully and affectionately; they heaped upon one another's heads friendly curses and obloquy; but they were polite to Curly. He saw it, and it stung him as much as Ranse hoped it would.

Then came a night that brought a cold, wet norther. Wilson, the youngest of the outfit, had lain in camp two days, ill with a fever. When Joe got up at daylight to begin breakfast he found Curly sitting asleep against a wheel of the grub wagon with only a saddle blanket around him, while Curly's blankets were stretched over Wilson to protect him from the rain and wind.

Three nights after that Curly rolled himself in his blanket and went to sleep. Then the other punchers rose up softly and began to make preparations. Ranse saw Long Collins tie a rope to the horn of a saddle. Others were getting out their six-shooters.

"Boys," said Ranse, "I'm much obliged. I was hoping you would. But I didn't like to ask."

Half a dozen six-shooters began to pop—awful yells rent the air—Long Collins galloped wildly across Curly's bed, dragging the saddle after him. That was merely their way of gently awakening their victim. Then they hazed him for an hour, carefully and ridiculously, after the code of cow camps. Whenever he uttered protest they held him stretched over a roll of blankets and thrashed him woefully with a pair of leather leggings.

And all this meant that Curly had won his spurs, that he was receiving the puncher's accolade. Nevermore would they be polite to him. But he would be their "pardner" and stirrup-brother, foot to foot.

When the fooling was ended all hands made a raid on Joe's big coffee-pot by the fire for a Java nightcap. Ranse watched the new knight carefully to see if he understood and was worthy. Curly limped with his cup of coffee to a log and sat upon it. Long Collins followed and sat by his side. Buck Rabb went and sat at the other. Curly—grinned.

And then Ranse furnished Curly with mounts and saddle and equipment, and turned him over to Buck Rabb, instructing him to finish the job.

Three weeks later Ranse rode from the ranch into Rabb's camp, which was then in Snake Valley. The boys were saddling for the day's ride. He sought out Long Collins among them.

"How about the bronco?" he asked.

Long Collins grinned.

"Reach out your hand, Ranse Truesdell," he said, "and you'll touch him. And you can shake his'n, too, if you like, for he's plumb white and there's none better in no camp."

Ranse looked again at the clear-faced, bronzed, smiling cowpuncher who stood at Collins's side. Could that be Curly? He held out his hand, and Curly grasped it with the muscles of a bronco-buster.

"I want you at the ranch," said Ranse.

"All right, sport," said Curly, heartily. "But I want to come back again. Say, pal, this is a dandy farm. And I don't want any better fun than hustlin' cows with this bunch of guys. They're all to the merry merry."

At the Cibolo ranch-house they dismounted. Ranse bade

Curly wait at the door of the living room. He walked inside.
Old "Kiowa" Truesdell was reading at a table.

"Good-morning, Mr. Truesdell," said Ranse.

The old man turned his white head quickly.

"How is this?" he began. "Why do you call me 'Mr.—'?"

When he looked at Ranse's face he stopped, and the hand
that held his newspaper shook slightly.

"Boy," he said slowly, "how did you find it out?"

"It's all right," said Ranse, with a smile. "I made Tia
Juana tell me. It was kind of by accident, but it's all right."

"You've been like a son to me," said old "Kiowa," trem-
bling.

"Tia Juana told me all about it," said Ranse. "She told
me how you adopted me when I was knee-high to a puddle
duck out of a wagon train of prospectors that was bound
West. And she told me how the kid—your own kid, you
know—got lost or was run away with. And she said it was
the same day that the sheep-shearers got on a bender and left
the ranch."

"Our boy strayed from the house when he was two years
old," said the old man. "And then along came these emi-
grant wagons with a youngster they didn't want; and we took
you. I never intended you to know, Ranse. We never heard
of our boy again."

"He's right outside, unless I'm mighty mistaken," said
Ranse, opening the door and beckoning.

Curly walked in.

No one could have doubted. The old man and the young
had the same sweep of hair, the same nose, chin, line of face,
and prominent light-blue eyes.

Old "Kiowa" rose eagerly.

Curly looked about the room curiously. A puzzled expression came over his face. He pointed to the wall opposite.

"Where's the tick-tock?" he asked, absent-mindedly.

"The clock," cried old "Kiowa" loudly. "The eight-day
clock used to stand there. Why—"

He turned to Ranse, but Ranse was not there.

Already a hundred yards away, Vaminos, the good flea-
bitten dun, was bearing him eastward like a racer through
dust and chaparral towards the Rancho de los Olmos.

*Twice recipient of a Western Writers of America Spur Award—
for Best Historical Novel of 1958,* Short Cut to Red River;
*and for Best Short Story of 1959, "Grandfather Out of the
Past"—Noel M. Loomis specialized in off-trail, sometimes
grim stories of the Old West. "When the Children Cry for
Meat" is one such story, set in the Texas Panhandle in the
1840s and featuring a band of Kiowa Indians and their half-
Comanche chief, Ikämosa. Loomis's other novels include* Rim
of the Caprock *(1952),* Buscadero *(1953),* The Twilighters
(1955), and Ferguson's Ferry *(1962).*

When the Children Cry for Meat

★★★★★★★★★★★★★★

Noel M. Loomis

I N the spring of 1844, Ikämosa's small band of Kiowa Indians was encamped under the east edge of the Caprock
in the Texas Panhandle, hopefully awaiting the warmth of a
spring already long overdue. Old Ansote, the Kiowa historian, painting his crude symbols on the buffalo hide that bore
the Kiowa calendar, had named February "the month the
children cried for meat." Doheñte, the ambitious war leader
of the band, was restlessly predicting a dry summer with no
game at all, and loudly saying that something drastic had to
be done. But Ikämosa, the half-Comanche chief of the band,
was keeping his concern to himself, hoping to avoid panic,
but at the same time worried by a report brought by a Wichita
Indian from beyond the Gañta P'a, the Double Mountain
Fork, that the buffalo had not yet begun to move north because the grass was not turning green.

The Wichita had been in their camp only a short time, and
Ikämosa was the only one who could talk his language, so

when he relayed the message to the band, he softened it a little to give himself time for thought. The next morning, sitting cross-legged before a small fire of mesquite-roots, he pretended to be absorbed in preparations to attach an iron arrow-point to a scrapped hackberry shaft. He would have preferred a young dogwood shoot, for hackberry required much straightening, but there were few young shoots of anything within range of two days on horseback.

He sensed movement at one side, and then out of the corner of his black eyes he watched T'ene-badaí, Bird Appearing, his third wife, glide down the path toward the creek with their child on her back. T'ene-badaí had hardly sixteen summers, but Ikämosa observed for the first time that her shoulders were thin, and he wondered if she had some mysterious, hidden illness of women. His other two wives had seemed to get along fairly well on the scanty food of the last several months.

He made another turn with the sinew, and Doheñte, No Moccasins, the war leader, came up, nodded gravely, and sat down with considerable ceremony, legs crossed and his heavily beaded leggings, that he had obtained from an American trader, very prominent. He wore his black hair in a long braid down one side, and now his shrewd black eyes in his broad wolf-face stared for an instant at Ikämosa, then darted to T'ene-badaí, who had paused at the chinaberry tree to shake the sand out of her moccasins. There was a question in his eyes that Ikämosa did not understand, but he went ahead with his wrapping. Doheñte, turning his attention to the fire, observed, "Our wives have trouble finding enough snakes and tortoises to keep from starving."

"It is true," said Ikämosa, involuntarily looking toward T'ene-badaí, who was on her knees with her hands in the water. He pulled his thoughts back to Doheñte. He puffed slowly on the pipe and then handed it to the war leader; this was an informal smoke, and it was not necessary to observe the ritual. He glanced at Doheñte's long braid; it was whispered that Doheñte had married his fourth wife just to get her hair to add to his own.

"I have not found game," Ikämosa admitted, "because I thought that any day the buffalo would be here, that it was not necessary to look very far." He gazed up at the great,

forbidding, purple-and-brown palisade that to all Plains Indians meant the Pasañgya, the Edge Prairie, the Llano Estacado. ''Even the mustangs and the antelope have not
appeared.''

''The grass on the Pasañgya does not grow without water,'' Doheñte pointed out. ''And this winter we have had
much cold but little snow.''

Ikämosa took the pipe back. ''True,'' he said.

''Without grass,'' Doheñte went on, ''there will be few
prairie-dogs and fewer rabbits, and coyotes will go to other
parts of the country. Deer and antelope and buffalo will not
be here, and the bears will migrate. There will not even be
ta-kiadl—prairie chickens.''

That was sarcasm, for the Kiowas did not like any kind of
fowl, and Ikämosa grunted.

Doheñte seemed intent on driving home the dismal fore-
cast: ''It does not seem that there will be anything to eat this
summer but skunks and horned toads.''

Ikämosa shuddered. Skunks were always bad medicine, and
he said thoughtfully, ''Unless we move the band to another
place.''

''Where could we go?'' Doheñte demanded.

Ikämosa was silent. This valley along the Tóñ-zo-gódal
P'a, the Swift Water River where the Tehaneko had been mas-
sacred three years before, had been an ideal camping-place
for many years.

''If it is bad here, it will be bad everywhere,'' said Doheñte.

Ikämosa tried to sort out the truths from Doheñte's insistent words. Doheñte was a year older, and Ikämosa, seeing
the hostility in Doheñte's eyes, knew for the first time that
Doheñte was a good war leader, but when he was not on the
trail he was a constant troublemaker. But Ikämosa restrained
his tongue, and watched T'ene-badaí come back up the trail
with a rawhide container filled with water. She glanced at
him briefly, and he thought there was a hunger in her eyes,
but he could not read them further, for she looked at the
ground again, and bent far over as she trudged up the incline
to her tent.

Ikämosa turned suddenly and caught Doheñte's beady eyes
on T'ene-badaí's back as she disappeared into the tipi.

Doheñte said, "Your third wife has grown into a woman."

"Yes," Ikämosa said shortly, and his tone forbade Doheñte's pursuit of the subject, for Doheñte's interest in women was well known.

Doheñte pointed at the brass kettle with the stem of the pipe. "Your father did not have such a convenience as that, but ate his meat raw, or singed a little on the coals."

"For my taste," said Ikämosa thoughtfully, "it was better meat, cooked that way. Boiled meat has little flavor."

Doheñte's eyes dropped, and he picked up the former conversation: "Nevertheless, you have found items like that brass kettle very useful."

"It is worth nothing empty," said Ikämosa.

"It need not be empty," said Doheñte, extending his pipe.

Ikämosa took the pipe and looked at the fire. "I do not know how you expect to put food in it when there is none to be had," he said.

Doheñte watched Ikämosa sharply. "Man-henk'ia—the Hañpóko known as No Arm, from Bent's Fort," he said, "is building a trading-post on the P'o P'a—Beaver Creek. He sends word to all Indians to trade there with him, and promises to have flour, cornmeal, dried meat, sugar, salt, tobacco, and coffee. Tobacco—not willow-bark!" he said scornfully. "And coffee!" he exclaimed. "I have not had real coffee all winter—nothing but roasted acorns from the Gañta P'a."

"Nor have I," said Ikämosa, choosing his words carefully. "But we agreed when we formed this band that we would not trade with the Hañpóko, the Americans, except for powder and balls."

"It is true," said Doheñte, "but I cannot bear to see my wives and children go hungry. I hear their sobbing in the night."

Or, rather, thought Ikämosa, *you are thinking of hot coffee in that well-padded stomach.*

He put aside the thought of hot coffee, for it made his own stomach growl. He said, "We have had no meat for weeks—nothing but a few wild potatoes that my women found up under the Caprock—and those hardly made one kettleful."

"Then it is agreed," said Doheñte, rising. "We shall go to Man-kenk'ia. The women and children will be glad!"

But Ikämosa did not stir. "We have nothing to trade—no white iron, no yellow iron, no hides or skins."

"Man-henk'ia will trust us until winter."

"And charge us three prices. It is an old trick of the Hañ-póko."

"It is their way," said Doheñte, "and beggars cannot be choosers."

"We are not beggars," Ikämosa said levelly, and knocked the ashes out of his pipe against the rock. "It means our women will work for him next fall and winter, preparing skins. It means that we shall have to get still more flour and coffee from him, and vermilion and beads and ribbons, and brass kettles. . . ." He stood up. "And then Man-henk'ia will own us because he will own all our work for years to come."

"You cannot object to food," said Doheñte.

"If we get it this way. I don't like the things that come with it," Ikämosa said stubbornly. "The Kiowas have always been free to come and go. Sometimes we have been hungry, but we have depended on our own efforts to get food—and we have always gotten it."

"New things, good things, brought to our country—"

Ikämosa stood up. "New things, good things are no better because we can reach across a counter and take them—especially when we shall have to work for months to pay for them. The men had it right," he said. "The Hañpóko come among us with things we do not need, and make us want them, and then make us work to buy them."

"Man-henk'ia is there when the buffalo are not," Doheñte observed shrewdly.

"It is true," said Ikämosa. "And always with his hand out, and always with invisible bands like ropes of deer-sinew that tie us to him and his mud tipi."

Doheñte said shrewdly, "Your wives' parents will think badly of you if you do not provide for them when it is as easy as this."

Ikämosa looked at him. "In a matter like this, I will make my own decision. The parents are not involved."

Doheñte did not seem discouraged, and Ikämosa wondered what he was holding back. He wondered too why Doheñte was so insistent. "Rather than trade our wives' work and eventually their bodies to Man-henk'ia," Ikämosa said, "we can send scouts in all directions to find game, and then move to the place where it is."

Doheñte's eyes took on a strange glint. "Then you refuse?" he asked.

"I think there is a better way," said Ikämosa.

Doheñte said casually, "Some predicted you would say that."

"You have discussed it, then?"

Doheñte shrugged. "A little."

"How do the others feel?"

Doheñte seemed studiously absorbed in the fire. "Some said that because your mother was a Comanche slave, you would not care whether the Kiowas starve or not."

Ikämosa drew a sudden deep breath. "I was raised a Kiowa," he said, "but I have never lost the Comanche's love of coming and going as he wishes."

"But of course I told them," said Doheñte, "that since your father was a Kiowa chief, and since you were raised a Kiowa, of course you are interested in nothing but the welfare of the band."

Ikämosa moistened his dry lips.

Doheñte glanced at T'ene-badaí's tipi. "How will your wives feel when other wives have ribbons and beads, and they have none?"

Ikämosa said, flatly, "You came here to force a showdown. That is plain. You will start campaigning against me now, and one of us will have to leave the band. You had that in mind when you walked up here." For a moment his annoyance got the better of him. "Leave my fire or I will throw you in it," he said.

Doheñte's black eyes glinted. "Perhaps they were right—perhaps you are more Comanche than Kiowa." He turned and walked away.

Ikämosa watched his horny feet send out little spats of dust as he walked away. For some reason, Doheñte had his mind set on trading with Man-henk'ia, and Ikämosa knew that he would talk to every warrior in the tribe—and perhaps even to the women—to convince them that it was best.

Ikämosa heard a soft step behind him, and turned to look at T'ene-badaí. She met his eyes briefly and stepped to the kettle. "I found a frog," she said, and dropped it into the simmering water.

He shuddered. Frogs were worse than snakes.

"It is food," she said, "and your flesh hangs like wet rags on your big bones."

He put out a hand to stop her as she started to leave.

"You are not happy with me," he said.

For the first time in weeks, she looked at him squarely. "You have never made me unhappy," she said.

He frowned. "Your eyes have been downcast for a long time."

"Perhaps."

"Do you want to go back to your parents?"

She eyed him levelly. "I am a woman now. I would not go back to my father's tipi."

He said slowly, "You might have come to me against your will."

She was scornful. "You forget that my father is the son of a Zép-ko-éte, and he never sold any of his daughters unless they wanted to go."

Yes, he remembered now. And he remembered also that he and she had stood together many evenings beyond the firelight; he remembered her laughing black eyes, and how she had grown to womanhood at his very touch. Yes, he remembered. "But what has happened now?" he asked.

She said softly, her eyes on the ground: "I knew that you and I were right for each other, and I was glad, but I did not know or think . . . I was too inexperienced to realize that your other wives would not allow us to have each other."

It hit him with staggering force that he had taken it for granted that his other wives would be kind to her, but that he had not given it a second thought—and the joy had fled from her eyes.

"I do not complain," she said. "This is the way of the Kiowas."

He realized he could not complain either. He remembered the quiet, delightfully sweet days of their first week, away from the band, up near the Caprock; early summer evenings whose caressingly mild breezes had wafted over them the sweet fragrance of mesquite blossoms while they talked and while they loved. Then they had come back with the band,

and T'ene-badaí had been installed in her own tipi, but he realized now that his other wives, Dämätána and Agabia, had begun to make demands on him, and presently he had once again been drawn into the affairs of the band and into the circle of his own family, while T'ene-badaí had been pushed further and further into the background. He knew too, as he looked at her honest eyes, that he had brought his first two wives to take care of his tipi and his medicine and his honors—and they had been well satisfied; but he had taken T'ene-badaí because there had been something in her eyes especially for him. He had never admitted that to anybody, for it would have been unmanly, but he was keenly aware of it now, and it did not seem entirely reprehensible to him.

He heard the voices of his other two wives coming across the village from their parents' home, and it struck him for a moment that they sounded like a flock of hen-turkeys. But he put the thought behind him. They had been wives in all that he had asked of them; perhaps they had no more capacity to be wives. Perhaps, he thought for a fleeting second, they were not even women yet, whereas T'ene-badaí, hardly more than half the age of Dämätána, had grown into a woman before his eyes.

He was glad that T'ene-badaí also heard the voices of the older women, lowered her eyes, and went back to her tipi. A moment later, as he was sitting down before the fire preparing to make the deer-hoof glue to fasten the feathers on the arrow, he heard their baby wail plaintively, and he knew that T'ene-badaí was trying to nurse it from her pitifully thin breasts that held hardly more than enough milk to wet its lips. And for a moment his heart went out to them both, and he felt heavily on his shoulders the burden of their hunger.

Then his other wives were there and swept past him without noticing him and without speaking to him. Their voices rose as they discussed the new trading-post of Man-henk'ia, and obviously they were excited about it.

He sat there for a while, hearing the low wail of T'ene-badaí's baby. Finally it bothered him so that he went to the tipi and stood for a moment until his eyes became accustomed to the darkness and he could make out T'ene-badaí with the child in her arms.

He suddenly felt an uncontrollable hunger for her, but her

eyes were down, and the exquisite poignancy of his desire settled into a dull, throbbing thing confused with a great many other feelings that he could not sort out.

One thing was clear, however. "I will get meat for you," he said.

She looked up at last, and there was no hostility in her eyes. "Do not do anything you do not want to do," she said.

He turned away in time to see Bäo, the wrinkled father of Dämätána and Agabia, walk up to his fire.

They went through the formalities, and then Bäo said, "Doheñte reports you are opposed to our getting supplies from Man-henk'ia."

Ikämosa nodded, his eyes on Bäo's.

"Both my daughters are in favor," said Bäo.

Ikämosa said, "I thought they would be."

"There is no use being stubborn," Bäo went on. "If the Hañpóko is willing to furnish us things on credit, why should we not accept them?"

Ikämosa looked at him, but made no attempt to answer.

"What else can you do?" Bäo demanded.

"I can find meat," said Ikämosa.

"The band will not follow you."

"That is something we do not know."

"Doheñte will not follow you."

Ikämosa nodded. He had expected that. "And you?" he asked.

Bäo hesitated, then said, "If my daughters want to go with you—but they too must eat."

"I have noticed," said Ikämosa, "that their shoulders are well filled out." It occurred to him then that they might secretly have been getting food from the Hañpóko, but it was a disloyal thought and he put it out of his mind. "If they are attracted to the Hañpóko," he said slowly, "it is because of beads and ribbons."

"A woman is entitled to pretty things, isn't she?"

"She is," said Ikämosa, realizing with a pang that T'enebadaí had had very few pretty things. "But it is a question whether she should trade her birthright for them."

Old Bäo's black eyes looked from a wrinkled face. "Are you, then, opposed to Man-henk'ia?"

"I do not think it wise."

Bäo said, "There will be a meeting tonight, at which all
the warriors will have a chance to talk, and the decision will
be made."

Ikämosa nodded. He had just caught a whiff of the cooking
frog, and it smelled good. Old Bäo also smelled it, and looked
into the kettle with distaste. "Is this what you are providing
your family to eat . . . this . . . this *kadlei-kyadlei*?" he
asked.

Ikämosa did not answer, did not nod, and presently old
Bäo went away. Then Ikämosa fished the frog out of the simmering water and took it to T'ene-badaí.

"I cannot," she said. "You have a big body, and it needs
much more food than mine."

For a moment her eyes were soft, and he was touched. His
hand rested lightly on her shoulder. "Then eat it for the milk
it will produce," he said, and left it with her.

⸱ It was the greatest meeting ever held by Ikämosa's band.
All forty-two of his warriors were there, sitting in the first
rows around the fire. Ikämosa took his usual place at the head
of the circle. The women were sitting scattered behind the
men, and beyond, half in darkness, the children were playing,
some running, occasionally shouting or shrieking. Ikämosa
got settled, feeling the hostility against him, and took his
time starting the pipe while Doheñte sprinkled sage on the
fire as a purifying incense.

Ikämosa dipped the pipe toward the four corners of the
compass, and blew out puffs of smoke for the sun and the
earth and the moon. Then he passed the pipe to old Bäo, who
went through approximately the same routine before handing
the pipe to Doheñte. It would be some time before the pipe
would get all the way around and they could begin the talk,
so Ikämosa looked for his wives. He saw Dämätána and Agabia sitting with their mothers. He looked for T'ene-badaí, but
could not find her. She was not with her parents, and he could
not see her anywhere within the light of the fire. He wondered
where she was and what she was doing.

Presently Doheñte started the talk about Man-henk'ia the
Hañpóko. Ikämosa pointed out their original agreement, but
Doheñte said that Man-henk'ia had been known to them a
long time and had been a friend. Bäo echoed Doheñte's ar-
guments, and then, one at a time, the other warriors spoke

on the matter, each one taking up time according to his importance in the tribe.

It was after midnight before each one had spoken. By that time it was clear that they were united against Ikämosa. Dohente had done his work well, for not a single voice was raised against the thought of dependence on the trading-post for their future supplies.

After the last man had finished, Ikämosa filled and lit the pipe again—the fragrant willow-bark—and went through the same ritual, and then started it around the circle. He had to have time to think, to decide whether he should accede to the wishes of the others, or whether he would adhere to the long-standing rule—the precept of his father. It was not an easy decision. His own feelings were strong, but they were all he had to support him against the combined opinions of the band. Eventually he had to speak, to say his thoughts, to act as chief. He put the pipe down and fixed his gaze on the fire, asking for guidance from his medicine, for wisdom to know the best course, for strength to follow it.

"The majority—in fact, every one here except me—wants to trade with Man-henk'ia," he said, "and it would be a stubborn chief who would not listen to the wishes of the people."

Old Bäo smiled thinly, and Dohente had a satisfied smirk on his bronze face, but Ikämosa ignored them, for the only thing that mattered was the right decision. "It is against my judgment," he said, "but it may, after all, be the best decision." He sat up straighter, listening, and on the night wind he heard it again: the faint wail of his and T'ene-badaí's child.

Old Bäo heard it, too, and was quick to take advantage of it. "Your own child needs milk," he said, "but there cannot be milk without food."

But Ikämosa was thinking of something else: of T'ene-badaí, who was not sitting with any of them, not even with her own mother. The shocking thought came to him that perhaps T'ene-badaí, hungering for food and for the bright ornaments of the Hañpóko, had already left the camp, and left their baby behind. It blinded him for a moment, and he closed his eyes until the shock passed. Then he opened his eyes and reached again for the pipe. He made the usual salutations, but when he finished, he put the pipe back on the stone to indicate he had come to a decision, that there would be no further talk.

He looked up and saw old Bäo's shrewd eyes on him, saw Doheñte's cynical face, and suddenly knew what Doheñte's interest was: special favors from the trader. He looked around the circle, searching each face in turn. The older ones were harder to read; the very young ones were difficult to interpret, but he saw many whose motivations were plain: acquiescence to the wishes of their wives, an easier life, and perhaps, in some, a little avarice—a hope that they could somehow get more than somebody else.

"The Hañpóko are as numerous as the leaves on a *qua-hei peip*—a mesquite bush," said old Bäo. "It is bound to come sooner or later."

Ikämosa drew a deep breath. "I am not going to give in to it." He looked straight at Doheñte. "I am not going with you. My family and I will go to look for *kadl-hia*—buffalo. If the buffalo will not come to us, we will go to them."

Old Bäo glared at him, outraged. Doheñte's thin lips were drawn up in a smirk. There was utter silence for a moment.

"The Tonkawas will be after you," said Doheñte. "They will take your wives and eat your children."

Ikämosa knew that Doheñte was merely putting on face, that he would be glad to get rid of Ikämosa, because, with Ikämosa gone, Doheñte, who was leading this move, would be elected chief. Ikämosa thought to himself: *This band will turn into coffee-coolers sitting around the post—little better than beggars.*

"I can fight the Tonkawas," he said aloud, "and I am not afraid." He knew what Doheñte had been saying against him, and he threw it in their faces, honoring the memory of his mother at the same time: "I am half Comanche. I am not afraid."

There was a moment of silence, and old Bäo said finally, "Your wives will not go with you."

"My wives will go where I go."

"Your first two wives are my daughters," said Bäo, slowly. "They will not go."

Ikämosa concealed his hurt. So they had already decided. Turning his head slowly, he looked at Dämätána and Agabia, sitting near their father's tipi. They stared at him without

change of expression, without any evidence of friendliness—
and he knew, as he turned back, that they too were against
him, that the ribbons and beads of Man-henk'ia were more
important to them than the privilege of coming and going as
they wished; that the ease of making a trip to the trading-post
and returning with food that would not have to be paid for
until next winter was more important to them than anything
else. He felt also that if those two, who had had the best of
his efforts, were ready to desert him, then T'ene-badaí also
would go with the band, for she had far less of material possessions than they had.

It frightened him for a moment, and he wondered if he had
spoken hastily. He looked at the warriors around him—at
Dohente, who was so determined to have his way; at Ansote
the historian, who had said nothing, but who was getting old
himself and perhaps foresaw an easier life where a man would
not have to mount and ride whenever game was in sight or
food was scarce; at the ancient Giákaíte, who could no longer
ride or hunt and whose eyes were too dim for him even to
make arrows, and who had nothing to look forward to under
normal circumstances except perhaps, one day in the coming
summer, being left in the middle of the Pasañgya with a bag
of mesquite meal, to die of starvation; at Set-dayáite, who
still had many horses and six wives—one from each of the
families of influence; at Pa-tepte, who was half Mexican and
who had a nagging wife; at Mápódal, Split Nose, the father
of T'ene-badaí, who also was old and hoping to avoid the
common end; at all the others whose impassive, uncompro-
mising stares told him their feelings. The power of the tribal
opinion was frightening, massive, smothering, and he began
to weaken. Then he looked at Dohente's horny feet, and for
the first time he understood Dohente, whose lifelong refusal
to wear moccasins had been a defiance of tribal customs. For
the first time, Ikämosa understood that that defiance had not
been for a good purpose, but rather to attract attention.

He felt the tribal pulse-beat in his wrists, and he fought to
throw it off. Suddenly, in pure Comanche fashion, he resented being forced. He straightened up and looked at them
all. "If you want to be coffee-coolers—to sit around the trader's post and drink his coffee and pretend to be wise and
agreeable when he is selling you things you don't need for

things you haven't got, it is a great thing. But tomorrow some other trader will build a post a little closer—perhaps on the Iyúgua P'a, and maybe he will have alcohol, and you will have become dependent on his goods, and you will go there for them, and while you are there you will taste the alcohol, and you will lose control of your senses—and when you wake up, like the Tonkawas, you will have drunk up all your skins for the next winter, and then you will not have any left to buy the beads and the ribbons that your wives now want.'' He looked at them, sitting around him so impassively, and suddenly, for a moment, he was angry. ''But maybe,'' he shouted, ''you will not any longer need those beads and ribbons, because maybe in your drunkenness you will have killed your wives and left their bones unburied.'' He stopped for a moment to cool off.

Old Bäo must have been a little uncertain, for he offered a last defense: ''You are not like us anyway. You are half Comanche.''

''Yes, I am half Comanche,'' said Ikämosa, ''and I am not afraid to go alone.'' He spoke to Ansote across the fire. ''I respect your age and position as historian, but you can look a long way back, and you must know that I speak the truth. It may well be that the Hañpóko with their many-shooting guns are the reason for the buffalo's being absent. I do not know. It may be that the Hañpóko with their barrels of food have prayed away the rain so that we should be forced to trade with them. I do not know. It may be that the Hañpóko with their beads and their ribbons have made our wives dissatisfied so that we shall be forced to promise our next year's skins to keep our wives from complaining. I do not know. But I do know this!'' He paused and looked around the circle, till finally his gaze stopped on Doheñte. ''I know that every time we use something the Hañpóko sells, we create a hunger for it, and we have to go back and get more of it—and I know that we can get those things nowhere else, and so after a while we don't like to go too far away, and the game gets still more scarce, and then we are the slaves of those who have the goods we do not need.''

Of them all, only Ansote seemed alarmed. The rest had been well prepared by Doheñte. But Ansote muttered, ''It is a mistake.''

"The price of doing right," Ikämosa said, "is always ten times as high when a man has to fight his own people. When they are not sure, they want to force everybody else to do the same, so they will all be in the same fix. The price is high," he repeated, "but I am going to pay it. I shall go today—within an hour, when the sky turns light in the east. If I must go alone, I will go alone."

He stood up and waited for an answer, but there was none. "I am going to find the buffalo," he said. "When I do, I will send word. By that time, some of you may have found out what it is like to belong to the Hañpóko, and you may want to live like men again." He strode from the fire, sad at their short-sightedness, but weighed down with uncertainty in spite of his brave words. He had lost everything: his wives and children, his band, his chieftainship. He was alone, and it was a terrible feeling.

He reached his fire and saw the brass kettle still in place. But his tipi was down—down and packed upon his horses. He felt a glad rush of exaltation, for T'ene-badaí was waiting, her baby on her back. She was going with him, and that was enough for the moment, because his heart was oppressed over the hostility of the tribe, and the frightening realization that he was leaving the band and going to an unknown place.

They set out in silence, and no one came to watch them leave. He went ahead, leading his four horses, and T'ene-badaí walked behind, her eyes on the ground, her mule following her. He led the way to the south, and they camped that night near a gyppy spring that he would not allow her to drink from. He saw her eyes on him once, but he was still too full of hurt and uncertainty to speak to her.

They went on the next day into a wildly broken country of steep hills, many scattered rocks, and dense underbrush; they camped that night without water and without food. They continued south on the third day, and the country got worse for traveling; they found water but no game. On the fourth day it was the same. On the fifth day he knew from T'ene-badaí's ashen face that she could not go much farther. On that day they found honey in a hollow pecan tree, and he realized that they were lost, and perhaps in Tonkawa country.

He had been so depressed by the knowledge that he had been rejected by his people for being steadfast in his principles that he had hardly looked at T'ene-badaí for the first two days. Then the heaviness had begun to wear off, replaced by the dire need for water, and then by the steady, day-after-day absence of game, the constant, growing hunger pains, and the harsh knowledge that their plight was desperate.

He made the small fire that night in silence. He watched his wife nurse their child at dry breasts, and heard its tiny wail of hunger during the night.

On the sixth morning he was awake at dawn, and perhaps, he thought, he was about to die of starvation, for a great deal of the hurt and the fear and the uncertainty were gone, and in their place had come a feeling of peace. He thought of T'ene-badaí then, and looked over at her and found her eyes wide, watching his. He said, "They never did let you have enough to eat, did they?"

She shrugged. "It was their way," she said.

He knew. Envy and jealousy were common among Indian women, and he should have watched. "I. . . ."

She glanced past his shoulder, and her eyes widened. She whispered in a very low voice, "There is a *kadl-hia* in the valley, half a mile down."

He froze for an instant, then looked. Buffalo! His mind added up all the factors in a flash. His buffalo horse, the *takoñ*, the black-eared horse, was grazing with the mule ridden by T'ene-badaí. Ikämosa slid silently out of his bed, put his killing knife in the waistband of his breechclout, slipped over to the grazing animals like a shadow in the early morning, and stood up when the horse was between him and the buffalo. Careful not to disturb the horse, he slid on it without a bridle. She was somehow beside him, soundless, and put his lance in his hand. In the dim light he touched her face and let his fingers stay there for a moment. He looked down at her thin face, and realized his own weakness, and closed his eyes for a moment to implore his power for strength and skill and courage. Then he urged the horse forward at a walk, keeping low on its side opposite the buffalo, his leg hooked over the horse's withers, his eyes watching the *kadl-hia* from under the horse's neck.

The buffalo was a big one—an old bull, cast out by the younger bulls, and therefore it had been feeding alone and was in good shape. The horse went steadily closer. The bull looked up, its black, curved horns silhouetted against the eastern sky; then, not seeing Ikämosa, it went back to grazing.

The horse was almost alongside before the buffalo got Ikämosa's scent and whirled. The horse had expected that, and dodged backward to evade the horns. Then it swung around the buffalo and came up behind at a hard gallop. Ikämosa yelled as the buffalo straightened out; he wanted it to run. It became confused, and did run, and the *takoñ* drew alongside, its hooves pounding in the soft grass. But fifty yards ahead was a thick growth of chaparral, and if the buffalo could make it, the horse would not be able to follow.

Ikämosa pounded the horse with his left hand as it drew up on the buffalo's right side; then he leaned far over and drove the point of the lance with all his might into the soft spot behind the shoulder-blade. The lance went deep, through the lungs and somewhere near the heart.

The buffalo staggered, then regained its balance, wheeled to the left, and pounded up the valley, the long lance bobbing from its back.

Ikämosa stopped the horse and watched the buffalo go. If chased, the animal would stay on its feet for hours, even though the lance should be in a vital spot; but if not followed, it would surely die—if the lance should be in a vital spot. Ikämosa looked up and saw T'ene-badaí a short distance away, watching.

The lance got caught off-balance and snapped in two. Then the bull turned in a half-circle and came back down the valley, running like a red-eyed demon. Blood was streaming from its mouth, but its head was still in normal position. It went past without seeing him, and Ikämosa wheeled the *takoñ* and went after it, now uncertain of his catch. If the buffalo should be so crazed as to run for a long time, the horse would not be able to keep it in sight; the *takoñ*, now in fair shape because it had not been ridden, might run for two or three hours, but no more. There was no doubt that the bull was crazy with fear and pain—such an animal was the hardest to kill.

Ikämosa drew his knife as the *takoñ* pulled up on the left side this time. The buffalo swerved and ran with new speed, and suddenly Ikämosa's fear of losing the meat came over him, and he felt momentarily faint; then the *takoñ* was alongside once more, and Ikämosa leaned far over and began to cut at the buffalo like a man possessed. He went in through the soft spot ahead of its hip-bone, and the sharp knife worked fast while the bull seemed not to feel the pain in its already crazed brain.

Ikämosa dug deep with the knife, slashed here and there furiously; he put both hands in the hole and came up with a steaming kidney. He slid off the horse, for he knew the bull could not go far now, and he stared at the hot, bloody kidney for a moment while the old hunger went over him like a weakening pain. For one moment he held the kidney aloft to show his power that he was appreciative of its help; then he buried his face in the kidney and bit out a huge chunk of steaming meat and swallowed it whole. He trembled and took a second bite, and then remembered his wife. She was coming on the mule, and he ran to her and handed her the kidney without a word.

The buffalo was slowing down; it would stop, he felt sure, by the time it reached the stream. He did not want to alarm it and inspire it to renewed efforts, so he stayed for a moment, watching it, while he and T'ene-badaí finished the hot kidney. They washed in the creek, and he went after the bull, which by now was on its knees, its head pendulous, its chin whiskers brushing the earth.

Four buzzards were overhead, and a coyote was standing in the edge of the chaparral, but Ikämosa cut the buffalo's throat, and presently they had it skinned and the meat piled on the hide. T'ene-badaí went back for horses, and they took the meat to camp. By that time, they were ravishingly hungry, and ate again: hump ribs and leaf fat—all raw. They had a fire going, and began to make racks out of willow branches to dry the meat. Then they were hungry, and ate again.

They ate and worked all day and into the night. They ate cooked tongue, raw liver, small intestines. Before it was over, they had eaten twenty pounds of meat apiece—and for the first time in months their stomachs were full. Already the meat had produced milk in T'ene-badaí's small body, and her brown breasts, once shrunken, now were full and ripe, and the baby nursed eagerly, and, when it had finished, no longer cried.

Toward the second dawn they had all the meat on racks; it would take another day and night to dry it, and one of them would have to stay awake to keep the animals away. But in the meantime they would eat fresh meat until they could hold no more. Ikämosa looked at T'ene-badaí across the fire. Her eyes were open, and he recognized the age-old question in them.

But something worried him. "You could have stayed with the band," he said, "and you would have been sure."

She smiled in the soft West Texas dawn. "I told my father to sell me to you because I wanted to be your wife."

"Wouldn't you rather," he asked, "be sure of food every day?"

"If we are hungry today, we will have food tomorrow," she said. "I am not afraid when I am with you."

He saw the question again in her eyes, and he got up and went around the fire. She was on her feet to meet him, and he took her hungrily but gently into his arms.

William R. Cox has been delighting fans of the Western story since he began writing for the pulp magazines in the 1930s. In addition to hundreds of short stories, he has published such tophand novels as Comanche Moon *(1959),* Moon of Cobre *(1969),* Jack O'Diamonds *(1972), and the recent Fawcett series featuring gambler and lawman Cemetery Jones:* Cemetery Jones *(1985),* Cemetery Jones and the Maverick Kid *(1986),* Cemetery Jones and the Dancing Guns *(1987). "One More River to Cross" is vintage Cox—an evocative tale of Nacogdoches and environs during the days of Sam Houston.*

One More River to Cross

★★★★★★★★★★★★★★★

William R. Cox

THE crowd jeered as the tall, erect old man lifted his strong chin and climbed into the carriage. His friend looked at the glowering crowd, began to speak, then shrugged and clucked to the bay horse, picking up the lines, heading toward the Houston Manse.

"A terrible decision," said Sam Houston. "Texas is lost."

Henry Lee Morgan gently checked the restive bay. "Always a Rubicon since Caesar wrote his memoirs. It turns a man's mind backwards."

"I can only think of the future, of the Texans who will die, of the women who will suffer, of the children who will have to pay."

Morgan was silent for a moment. His friend was seventy, he had made his stand against Secession and lost, sadness draped the huge frame so that once out of sight of the multitude the wide shoulders sagged.

Morgan said deliberately, "There is always a time of decision. Do you know why I am here, amigo?"

"To stand by me, as always, since San Jacinto."

"But how did I come to San Jacinto? You never heard the story. Do you mind Rab Rock?"

The thundering brow furrowed, then cleared and a small smile hovered on the mobile lips. "Ah, the wild man."

"Wild as a desert stallion. Ignorant as a Mexican goat. Brave as a cougar. I met him in Nacogdoches. That was in eighteen and thirty-six and I was new come from Georgia."

The old soldier-statesman relaxed, listening. He needed respite and Henry Lee Morgan was a noted teller of Texas tales.

Nacogdoches, you remember it, a filthy town filled with spies, couriers, rascals, murderers, all bearing their own rumors of war and devastation, almost none believing that Santa Ana could be defeated, that Cos would not follow to lay waste the land of the settlers. I met Bowie there, in the days when he had stopped drinking whiskey and was about to join the command at San Antonio de Bexar. He was a dour creature, unsure, defeated by the loss of his beloved wife and children, torn by the fact of his sworn oath of allegiance to Mexico, yet determined to be in the fight.

Irritated by his talk, I went looking for a certain young lady named Janet Drew. She was from Philadelphia and her aged, drunken father had taken up land southward, below the Llano. They were traveling in a coach, mind you, with only a small driver named Saunders, intending to make their way through that country without escort. She was a sweet, brave girl.

I knew little more than did she, but even the greenest pea had heard that Big Nose was out with a band of cutthroat Comanches. The stories they told about this renegade were blood-curdling but true. Women were his special pleasure, the Comanches being full-blooded men, unlike many of the other tribes.

I told myself this was none of my business, but there had been something about Janet Drew, something a young man from Savannah could cling to, a frankness, an honesty lacking in the lady from whom he had run away. The war between Texas and Mexico meant little to me, it was there, I could join it any time. I fretted about the girl and her footless father who had been an army man and thought he was competent to make his way any place under the sun. Colonel Drew had long since given in to John Barleycorn, but like so many, he was not aware of this. He confused his dreams with reality.

I could not find the girl. In my search, I came to a cantina run by one Pancho Arregiera, a man of no conscience and no loyalty. It was a low-ceilinged dive, full of smoke and bad odors, but I was weary. I sat against the wall at a table and a bold slattern brought me whiskey, taking another bottle to a nearby table. It was then I first beheld Rab Rock.

He had an enormous, shaggy head, you remember. His eyes were wide-spaced and his mouth was bold and gentle at once. He was six feet four in his buckskin and carried only the knife he had been given by Bowie, eschewing a pistol, in which he did not believe. Two of his men were with him, Hacker and Sancho.

Hacker was small and bony, a product of New York slums, a ferrety man with quick hands. Sancho was part Yaqui, with the smoothest olive skin and the largest of brown doe eyes. They were drinking heavily, all three of them, as two empty bottles testified. Rab reached out as the girl served the whiskey and slapped her hard enough to hurt, but the girl laughed on a shrill note and waited for more. He was that way with women, they fell flat for him.

After a few moments four men came into the Cantina. They wore serapes but it was evident they were heavily armed. By happenstance they were in my line of vision but behind Rab and his companions. The leader had a scar which split his right cheek, the others were mongrels. They sat down without removing floppy woolen hats which partially concealed their faces.

Rab Rock was saying in his loud voice, "Fella got in trouble here t'other day. His lawyer told him to get out, he didn't have no chance. Fella says, 'Where'll I go? I'm in Texas now.' "

His companions roared approval. Hacker was wanted for murder in New York, Sancho was an escapee from a Mexican jail. Rab—well, Rab had broken every law in a dozen states with his violence and original ideas of justice. They had lived off the country for several years at this time, they and the mulatto, French.

"Country full o' rascals," Hacker said in his flat accent. "War and damnation. Big Nose and Santa Ana. It's a grand place, Texas."

"Here's to Sam'l Houston," Rab cried, tilting his mug. "Here's to us'ns."

It was then the scar-faced man dropped his serape and leaped at Rab's back. He had a long knife in one hand and a pistol in the other. The pistol misfired.

I was wearing a cap and ball weapon which I had primed at Bowie's suggestion before going about this town. Scar-face was directly in front of me. Without conscious thought, I shot him through the head.

The other three assassins were already in action. They were men who knew their business, coming in low with their sharp blades, slashing upward, hoping to cripple their victims, then finish the job at will. But Rab Rock was out of his chair, facing them.

Those awful hands of Rab's reached out and took two of the attackers by the napes of their necks. He brought them together like cymbals. He shook them and turned them around and banged them again. Then his Bowie was flashing and blood ran.

The other man found himself between Hacker and Sancho. He lost his nerve and tried to run. Hacker merely laughed as Sancho threw his knife so that it stuck neatly between the shoulder blades.

Rab turned the leader over with his toe and said, "I swan, it's old Diablo. He never did get over that business on the Llano."

"He's over it now," said Hacker.

They were all looking at me. My hands were shaking—I had never killed before. I sat there, staring back at them, a skinny young fellow from Savannah.

Rab said, "Now look at him, will you? Saved my life, he did."

"Señor, gracias," Sancho said, bowing, showing even white teeth, his eyes mocking. "It would have been but a shame to waste this newly opened bottle."

They brought the whiskey to my table. They did not so

much as glance at those who came to lug away the corpses. They were merry and they were curious and they were cool, as though they had merely swatted three houseflies, and I the fourth.

It is a time like this when whiskey is welcome. In an hour I was no longer shaking in my boots. I was drunk, but I had no qualms, no fear. I remember telling them of my search for Janet Drew, and I fear it must have been a dramatic story. Possibly I shed some tears. At any rate, Rab got it into his head that I had lost my lady love and was therefore devastated.

And since one good turn deserved another, always, in Rab's lexicon, I found myself with allies. They were not exactly the men I would have chosen. In fact, the next morning I was again scared stiff when I found myself in a lice-infested room with the three of them and French.

But you must know about French. He was bigger than Rab and handsomer. He was one half Creole and one half Negro, and he was sleeping beside me when I awakened.

And I was lately from Georgia.

While I was watching him, gap-mouthed, he opened his eyes. They were brown-green, slanting, almost oriental. He recognized the situation at once. He smiled reassuringly, the most wonderful and natural smile in the world.

He said, "You saved Rab's life. Since Rab long ago rescued me from worse than death, there is a bond between us." He extended his hand.

Do you remember French's hands? They should have been modeled by a great sculptor. They were long and lean and the fingers tapered. He had been educated as a doctor in order to save time and money on the plantation of his father. I have often wondered about that man, who had produced this magnificent creature and then had used him, beaten him, almost broken him before Rab came into the bayous on one of his crazy expeditions to provide the means of escape. A medical man, purportedly a gentleman, a wealthy man with every advantage—how could he do it? What manner of beast was in him? What were his nightmares?

I shook French's hand and was better for it. No one who ever knew him could forget him. Brief as was our acquaintance, he stands out even above Rab Rock in my recollections of that time. He was able to put me, a prejudiced Southron, at my ease.

We managed to wash up that morning in dirty water, we managed to eat, we managed to gather on the street opposite the livery stable. Nacogdoches was a beehive of seething disorder, but we seemed to be waiting for someone or something. There had been pick-me-ups, you understand, a sort of hard cider in which they poured a bit of liquor. Nothing was clear excepting that Rab Rock had a huge hatred for Big Nose and was determined to carry me southward on the trail of the coach and Janet Drew in hopes he might encounter the redskin chieftain. At the moment this seemed quite normal and correct. My horse was saddled, my warbag packed, I had an extra supply of ammunition to fit both dueling pistols and the hunting rifle from home.

It was then Bowie found us and took me apart. "Do you know who you are associating with?" he demanded. "Do you know these are the most dangerous outlaws in Texas?"

"I don't see that the law is attempting to take them into custody," I responded. I did not care for the Bowie of Nacogdoches, a cantankerous, bitter man.

"Only because we are at war. They are guerrillas, Morgan. They prey on pack trains, they raid towns, they kill and rape and pillage whenever the mood is upon them. Rab Rock refuses to join our army. They are out for themselves—first, last and all the time."

I answered, "And so, my dear Bowie, is everyone I have ever met this side of Savannah. And about ninety percent of the people back there in Georgia."

"Then you are not for us?"

"For whom?"

"For Texas."

"And who is Texas?"

He looked at me in that canny way he had. He said, "You are newly arrived, of course. Well, go your way. But remember I have warned you about Rab Rock and his men."

Yet when I rejoined the group, Rab waved to Bowie and yelled, "See you later, Jim."

And Bowie made a gesture and said, "San Antonio, if you change your mind."

And then Peter Decker arrived. He was a deaf mute, it developed, a lank man with blond hair worn long on his shoulders. He seemed uneasy in even such a small town as this one, and I learned he had been a man of the mountains since early in the century, until he made some mistake with the Indians and they turned against him and drove him out.

Rab and he exchanged signs, then Rab said, "Your lady is gone down the Llano. Big Nose is in that part of the country. We better get goin'."

We all mounted. Their horse flesh was superb—they'd stolen nothing but the best. My own gray was weathered and had bottom, as I had found on my journey into Texas. We headed out of town, going south on that trail, which is now gone and forgotten as the Llano has altered its course and its shape in the years since. But you mind the road; it was along the river on the eastern bank and the settlers broadened it with their wagons and their cattle and sheep and the bare feet of their children when that part of East Texas was settled.

We rode two abreast, with Rab and Hacker in front, French and me behind them. Sancho was the rear guard. Peter went ahead and we did not see him. He was roving, swift as a ghost, searching out the countryside, even fording the river, which was swollen out of season. The Llano was blue and not very wide, but deep except at certain places which Peter well knew. It had a way of twisting through the land between its low, wooded banks. There was a murmurous sound to it in those days when it was wild and untamed. It was a small river, but a good one. It was a river which fed the countryside, and the land was productive, all that land in that country in that time.

We were a weird-looking crew, armed to the teeth, each of us from a different background and, in truth, a cross section of Texas in '36. French wanted to talk.

"If you'll excuse me, Mr. Morgan, I don't get to talk to gentry very often. Truth is, I try not to engage them in conversation. It is better not to."

"I have had my fill of the gentry," I told him.

"Yes. I can guess." His handsome features were heavy with thought. "It is about Rab."

"A remarkable man."

"Indeed. Remarkable. The things we have done, sir, would

seem impossible. Just the few of us. We have slain more
Indians than I can remember. We have taken what we wanted
in this wild country. We lost a few men, from time to time,
but the five of us have survived and prospered. Rab carries
enough gold in his saddlebag to buy half the blustering pol-
iticians in Nacogdoches.''

"In the jungle the strong survive."

"We have done as we wish. However, sir, we are all young.
What of tomorrow?''

"There will be laws. Mexican laws or Texas laws. There
will be men to enforce them.''

"Precisely. And Rab should be a leader. He is a giant. His
heart is pure." French's eyes flashed, he came alive when he
spoke of his hero. "Do you know that Hacker was tubercular,
dying, when we picked him up? Sancho was captive of the
Comanches, we rescued him. Peter was a broken man, the
torture he had endured nigh finished him, he was afraid of
his own shadow. Rab restored them.''

"With the aid of your medical knowledge.''

French pushed away his contribution with a wave of his
hand. "Where would I have been had not Rab come to the
bayous? No, sir, you must believe me, Rab is worth saving.
Rab could make you a country here, in this wilderness. Rab
could dam this river and create a kingdom of his own.''

"But he will not," I suggested. "It is not in him to do
such a thing.''

"You could talk to him. He likes you. We could join Bowie,
fight the Mexicans. Bowie would use us as scouts, he has
agreed. When the war in over, we would be respected men,
not feared outlaws." Tears of earnestness were in French's
eyes.

I could not help saying, "In a slave state.''

French smiled. "Slavery will exist only so long as sensible
men do not examine it. Are you, for instance, in favor of
slavery?''

"No," I admitted. "But what about you, your future?''

"Can you believe Rab would let anyone attempt to harm
me?" French laughed freely, then sobered. "No, it is Rab
who must be considered. If he volunteers, if he joins the
Texas army, he will become a legend in the land. If we con-

tinue in our present way, we will be killed, one by one, and our names will be anathema.''

It was curious to hear this ex-slave speak in such terms, but he had, you see, been educated, and in learning to read, he had assembled his own philosophy. His analysis was perfectly correct, although at the time I was too young to thoroughly appreciate it.

I said, ''French, I'm sorry, but I know nothing of the politics of this war. It seems very uneven. Houston has no army, not a real army. There will be thousands upon thousands of Mexican soldiery in Texas within the month. I should be careful about advising anyone.''

''Mexican soldiers are indentured,'' said French. ''That means they are slaves. Do you believe a slave will fight well for his masters?''

''I just don't know,'' I said. ''I'll think about it.''

''Speak to him when he is not with the drink,'' French urged. ''You will find him a true man.''

''I will talk to him,'' I promised.

We made camp early, before dark. I was puzzled at this and somewhat anxious about the girl. Peter had been tracking but was not in view. Sancho came up to report that no one followed, ate cheese and bread, drank from a goatskin of wine and vanished. Rab only sipped at the harsh native liquid, sitting cross-legged, towering, straight-backed, wiping his lips, then smiling at me. French slid apart and Hacker slept, his hatchet face on a curved, thin arm as the sun sank behind the blue, shimmering river.

Rab said, ''It's a fine land, now ain't it? Tennessee's hills were never like this.''

''I didn't know you were a southerner,'' I said.

''Am I?'' He laughed then. ''The way you say it, like it was a proud thing, I sure ain't. What I was, I was a bound boy to a man named Fisher, a German fella. He whupped me every night. There was a sturdy kitchen chair. One night I hit him and then I hit him again. And again.'' He was happy at the memory. ''All the starvin' and the beatings went up in smoke. There he lay, his neck broke. He looked beautiful to me.''

''And you came to Texas.''

''In time, I came to Texas.'' He was sober and his aspect

altered in a strange way. "You are an educated man. I reckon you agree with French."

"In what way?"

"French says I have no pattern. Must a man have a way planned? Must he live by rote?"

I was comfortable, being all of twenty-four years of age. "I can't say. For myself, I had none, until I met the girl, Janet Drew." I was amazed at myself for speaking so. "When we met in St. Louis, something seemed to be born, then to grow a little. It is a strange development. I was running from a woman, from family, from some dead, dull past which bore in upon me. It occurs to me that all of us here are somewhat alike, Rab Rock."

"All running." He nodded. This seemed to please him. "Yet come together strong and ready. Texas is good, a good place."

"But you won't fight for Texas," I said, remembering French's plea.

"No. We're not men for that. We may kill more Mexicans than Bowie's entire company. But we'll not join an army. We ain't the kind for it."

"But I understand Bowie would make scouts of you . . ." I broke off, embarrassed, but he only smiled again, looking off toward French, nodding.

He said, "You don't ken William Barrett Travis. Bowie goes to join him at San Antonio. 'Colonel' Travis, if you please, and on the ground first. And Sam Houston didn't make Bowie a general, only a colonel like Travis. Oh, no, sir. Not for Rab Rock. Nothing the like of that for me and my boys."

"But what do you want?"

He considered with care, spoke slowly. "I want a place where me and my boys can have a house. A big house, with women in it. And good horses in the stable and dogs for huntin'. I want all to share and share alike." He paused, then went on artlessly, " 'Course I got to be boss, because they will start argifyin' among themselves and Hacker gets notions and Sancho . . . Well, they need a boss. But I want us all to be even. 'Specially French. That's the way it's got to be."

"How are you going to attain all this?"

"Take it. When we find it, we'll just take it. Then we'll hold it and damn anybody tries to get it away from us."

"What about government? There has to be government in a country."

"We'll be part of the government," Rab promised him. "You got enough land, enough money, you can be in any government. You oughta know that."

And I did, I knew that. This man was illiterate but he had a grasp on things as they were and are and always will be. French was looking at me, shaking his head, but there was no more to say on that subject.

Rab went on, "You take French, now. I got to look out for him. Why, he's saved more lives than we've taken."

It was remarkable the way he dealt with life and death, impartially, since the two are inseparable. His respect and love for French went into it; I suppose, they had been closer than brothers for years.

"He'll be the doctor for the people around us," Rab said, dreaming his dream aloud now, unashamed. "We'll start a whole new way down here, wherever we settle. Texas? It's been good to us, but only because we was able to grab and hold on. So long as we got French, we'll be all right."

There was no mistaking the ring of those last words. The man meant every syllable. Whatever his wild, improbable goal, it was wrapped up in the person of the remarkable mulatto with the physician's hands. I knew better than to pursue the matter further.

"Tell me about Big Nose," I said.

"No good for his own people, no good for anybody. I been after him a long time, now. One of the things we got to do is kill him."

Peter came suddenly into the twilight, standing, leaning a little toward Rab, gesticulating with nimble hands. French came closer and watched, then exhaled sharply, which seemed to awaken Hacker.

Rab stood up and put his fingers to his lips and whistled. Then he turned to me, his face kindly. "We're a little late. Big Nose hit the coach."

My blood turned gelid, I sat staring at him, unable to ask the question for fear of the answer.

Rab said, "Killed the coachman. The old father won't last

long, they got him alive after he shot a couple of 'em. We got to go and get the girl.''

"Get her away from them? Can we do it?" My heart began to beat again.

"There's twenty of 'em," Rab said. "We better be on the way."

I had heard plenty about the Comanches. The thought of the girl in their hands was pure horror. I was twenty-four and even then little more than a boy. I do not remember getting to my horse, I only remember Rab ordering me to ride with him. The others all knew what to do; I was a neophyte, half scared, half murderous, riding like the wind down that grassy trail alongside the Llano.

Soon enough Peter stopped us with a sign. We had come up to the coach, which was on its side. The horses had been slain first, and then the driver, who was skewered to the ground by a long spear and otherwise resembled a gory pincushion. Rab yanked out one of the arrows and examined it by the light of a tiny flame provided by Hacker's flint and steel.

"Big Nose, all right. His marking."

Peter was already showing the way the Indians had gone, toward the south, along the river. Rab looked concerned and Sancho came in and shrugged, speaking rapid Spanish which I did not then understand. French sucked in his breath and they all looked dubiously at me, excepting Rab, who spoke in level accents.

"This here Big Nose, he's a canny savage. They is only one high point of land in this here country. It's a bluff over the river, with rocks down below, where the water runs swift and deep. They call it Lopez Leap. That's where the Injuns went to make their camp."

Hacker said, "They'll have scouts down the side of the hill. There ain't no use tryin' to get up there."

Sancho lifted one shoulder and said, "The girl, she is gone goose, no? We will lose our hair for nothing, I think."

But Rab still looked at me in the darkness; I could feel his glance, and French did not stir. "The river, what about the river?"

"I was raised on the Savannah. We might float a raft," I told him. "I can't ask you to do it, you know."

French said quickly, "I know about rafts."

Hacker and Sancho waited until Rab spoke. I think they already knew his decision; they merely stated their own positions, then let him tell them the way it had to be.

Rab said, "Wasn't no river in the hills. I can't swim."

"Me neither," said Hacker.

French said, "You can go by land, with Peter. We'll scale the bluff and create a surprise diversion. Perhaps you could come in, that is, if Peter can account for the scouts."

"Sancho and Peter can snake in better than me," said Rab. "That puts three on the land side and three on the river. I like it better that way."

"But if you can't swim," I began, then stopped, realizing that no one went against Rab's decision. I added lamely, I fear, "I wouldn't want to endanger you in the river."

"Reckon I can take care of myself if I have to," he said. "Now, about that there raft."

There was a tall cypress which had fallen in a storm. The long knife of Mr. Bowie had many uses, and now it became a machete, cutting branches away. Sancho came with long grasses of amazing toughness, and we had ropes with which to entwine the limbs we so hastily hacked to proper length. There is a trick to this, which at that time I knew very well, but it was arduous labor. We were sweating and the moon was high, if faint behind clouds, when we were finished and the raft on the riverside, ready to be launched. Hacker threw himself down and snorted.

"I don't like it, Rab. It's kinky."

"Sure, it is," agreed the leader cheerfully. "Ain't it always been? You just go ahead with the boys."

Hacker looked at me. "You come along and he goes all the way. Too bad you don't know what it means, Mister." He turned and followed Peter and Sancho, who merely waved as they melted into the shadows.

"I do know," I told Rab. "There's no reason for you to do it."

"No reason? I been after Big Nose for two long years," he said. "He's got an old man to torture and a girl; it's a time to tackle him."

"But the odds are against us. He has high gun on us. There are twenty to our six. And won't they kill the captives as soon as we attack?"

"They might try to kill 'em. They may not get the chance. If we don't get on with it, howsomever, them people won't have any show, now, will they?"

He turned toward the raft, a shaky vessel in the current which was running. He hesitated just a fraction of a second then, but French steadied the clumsy craft while we scrambled aboard with our rifles and pistols and knives very much in the way, and clung to the cross-ties which held the logs together. French slipped alongside us like a huge eel, and we were off.

It was a rough voyage. French and I had skinned poles with which we fended us off floating timber and several large rocks. The moon continued to play tricks in the most fickle manner, now revealing danger, now shrouding us in blackness by hiding behind heavy, scudding clouds. A young man has few fears for his own safety, particularly in crises of physical danger, but I was terribly afraid for Janet. Possibly this fright gave me strength, for we were able to accommodate ourselves to the turbulent river to the place where we could see the bluff rising above us, harsh against the lowering sky.

There were no words between us as we hauled and pulled, now deliberately aiming for the jagged rocks, not knowing any other means of going ashore. Rab lay at full length, his jaw set. The Llano began to rage beneath us as French and I poked with the poles until our arms nearly fell out of the sockets.

Then, an accident of fate, there was a protruding branch, growing from an underwater brush, heavy and strong. Rab seized it. We ran to help him, dropping our poles. The moon threw us a glimmer of light and we threshed and strove—and were out of the current and floating in a pool of still water.

In a moment we were ashore and checking our powder. Rab inhaled deeply and showed us a wide, carefree grin.

"Never been so scared in my life. We got lucky, didn't we? It'll be all right now. Luck's with us."

French shook his head. "Could be we used up our good luck. Could be there's bad ahead. Let's go cautious, Rab, real cautious."

"Cautious never wins," said Rab. He looked up at the cliff towering above us. "Betcha there's a way up yonder if we look right sharp."

We were a hundred paces from the river when he found it. Now we were speaking in whispers, already in the mood of skulking attack. Rab did not speak, he merely indicated with a fierce gesture that there was a path leading upward. It wound into what now became darkness as the moon went under, irregular footholds in the steep sides of the bluff, certainly not designed by man, a freak of nature. It might end halfway, but Rab believed in his luck and we began the ascent, he first, then myself, the greenhorn, then French.

If they thought of the danger of a dislodged rock rattling down to give our presence away, I never knew it. The night had turned quite cold, but I was sweating. And then, after we had climbed interminably, the moon again came swishing from behind the woolly clouds.

We hung there like three ants upon a stalk of grass, helpless. But Rab looked up, still grinning, and saw the way. His hand touched my shoulder and we turned our stares skyward. The next bank of puffy, gray, billowing vapor swam slowly toward the leering moon.

It was then that everything went wrong. There were shots above us and wild yells. Without hesitation, despite the moonlight, Rab began climbing, reckless now of any consequence. Behind me French pushed, so that I must needs follow the leader. My hands were torn on the sharp edges of stone, but we kept going, unthinking of anything but possible disaster.

The shots continued and the sound of howling savage grew with it. We had reached the last yards of the ascent and had come over the top when portentous silence fell. We lay prone, our eyes fixed upon the scene.

The Indian fires were high. Stakes had been driven into the earth. The old man, Colonel Gray, was tied to one, hanging in his bonds, bleeding, his beard upon his chest. The other, nearer one, Janet was attached to by leather thongs, held upright by them, her head fixed so that she must see everything that went on.

You know the Comanches, like the Kiowas, their cruelty is their amusement, their only reason for mirth. They had been torturing the Colonel, of course, when the trouble began with Peter and Sancho and Hacker. They had almost been caught between us. We did not know then nor ever what went wrong. We only know that somehow the ambuscade from the other side had failed and that our men were discovered too soon.

Hacker was down on his knees. A huge Indian had sunk a tomahawk into his skull. Sancho was struggling with two captors. Peter was prone, his head in the farthest corner of the fire, unmoving. A brave was hauling him out, brandishing a small scalping knife.

There were four or five dead redskins lying about. We three lay there a moment, estimating the chances. French breathed, "No good. The luck ran out."

"They'll be slaves," Rab warned. "The girl and Sancho. You know what will happen to them."

French breathed the word again, "Slaves," and was silent. He knew too well the import.

Rab said, "The guns first. Ready?"

We remained in our prone positions, drawing beads as Rab muttered, "You take the right. I've got Big Nose. French— the left."

It was like a scene from Dante's *Inferno*. Even as I triggered my overloaded fowling piece, I had no sense of killing people. These were not people, they were figures in an awful pageant.

We had little enough against them. Three shots from long guns, three pistols. It was point-blank, however, and we did have the element of surprise, as Rab well recognized. We drew our long knives and screamed, rushing toward them.

By the grace of God, our shots took some effect. Rab missed Big Nose, but his bullet caught the Indian who was scalping Peter. We also had the advantage of temperament. Indians will fight at their choice, but were always inclined to flinch upon continued pressure. We struck them.

My own part was small. I hacked at a brave reeking of sweat and fear and he went down. I saw a squaw making for Janet with blade in hand, and without conscious volition I cut her throat. I slashed Janet loose with the razor edge of the Bowie and yelled to her to get away, to hide.

From that angle I could see Rab and French. It was an awesome sight.

Rab had found Big Nose. The Indian was huge, an animal of a man. Rab was holding his left wrist as he cut him with the point of the knife. French was killing with the unbelievable agility and strength of a born warrior. The Indians, recovering, seized lances, anything that came to hand. There was a ring around the two of them, pushing and mauling. I came laterally upon it, dancing around, hitting at naked red spines.

Then a shot rang out. I heard Rab's wild yell and out of the corner of my eye saw an Indian with an old musket. I took after him, but he ran into the darkness toward the river.

I turned back and Rab sent two Comanches reeling, their bodies scarlet with blood. I tried to get to him and fell ignominiously over a dead body.

When I sat up, it was all over. There wasn't an Indian in sight, except those who were unable to run. Big Nose lay dead at Rab's feet.

But Rab was the only one of us standing. His face was wet with sweat, his great arms, blood-stained, hung loose at his sides. His strange eyes were sunken in his head.

French lay at full length. I rushed to him, but the bullet from the musket had gone through his heart. Rab did not even bend his head toward his dead friend.

"He was right," he rumbled in his throat. "The luck ran out."

Sancho was alive. He stumbled toward us, holding his right arm in his left hand. The others were dead. Janet came from the rocks, creeping, weeping. I held her and she was shivering as though with ague.

I said, "I'm sorry, Rab," words as futile as the babbling of the Llano, which now could be heard below us.

"It was the luck, the damnable luck." He turned to Sancho to ask what had happened, what went wrong.

Sancho pitched forward. There was a horrible hole in his back. He was dead when he hit earth.

"All gone," said Rab. "All the boys."

An Indian dying well, as they sometimes did, keened on a high note and thrust from the ground with a spear. Rab took hold of the shaft, reversed it, and without changing his bemused expression, skewered the attacker to the ground. He moved slowly, among them, then, head bowed, preoccupied, making sure all were dead.

It was then I realized why we had so quickly prevailed.

Peter's count had been correct; there were twenty Comanches. But possibly half of them were squaws. They all held weapons, or there was a knife or a hatchet nearby their bodies, yet they were females and not fit to cope with such as Rab or French. A baby squawled from afar and Rab went to it with as much abstraction as though it were an infant wolf, and I took Janet away from the scene. She could endure no more.

We made a rude camp and then Rab and I built up the fires, for there was no time nor energy for burial here. I tried to say something for the fallen men of our party, but knew Rab was not listening as the flames leaped higher and higher and we had to turn away. He sat with us through that night while we slept.

In the morning he had drawn a map upon a piece of bark. With infinite detail he showed us how to follow the river, how to branch off and come safely to the property which was now in Janet's name. He went over it several times to make sure we innocents understood.

Janet said at last, "But surely you'll come with us? You could share it with us. We want you to have half of everything. We have funds to build and stock the ranch and hire workers. You could be our partner. You won't refuse us?"

I interjected, "We need you, Rab."

He almost smiled. "It's right good of you all."

"Without your men this life is ended for you," I insisted. "Why not make a new one, with us?"

"Aye, ended," he agreed. "French is dead." He looked at the morning sun, squinted, shook his head. "One favor is all I ask of you. When the story is told, make it plain that my boys were not seeking booty. We raided, we stole. We killed. But this last hooraw, it wasn't for loot."

"It was for me," cried Janet. "I'll always know it."

"Mebbe. Mebbe not. We was after Big Nose. We was after a fight. We was always like that." He pondered. "Thank ye kindly, but just say it wasn't for loot."

He got up, shook himself and stared down at the river. He said, "I'm goin' across."

"But, Rab, we do need you," I said. "Can't you see us down there, then make up your mind?"

"Ain't got much of a mind to make up. I been fightin' and

brawlin' for me. Me and mine. Now I reckon it's got to be played out another way."

"What do you mean?"

"Texas," he said, grinning without mirth. "Across that river to the west is San Antone. Bowie's there. I figure to join him."

He made a polite, awkward little bow and started for the place where we had come up to the bluff. His shoulders had been bowed, but now he straightened and was jaunty, turning, bowing, waving. "Adios, amigos. Go make a place for me, just in case. Mebbe I'll come see you all one day."

Then he was gone out of sight, down the rocky side of the bluff, toward the river, the way we had come. I often wondered how he got across and where, since he couldn't swim.

The carriage turned into the path leading to the Houston manse. The two ladies on the veranda arose and started forward.

Sam Houston said, "We know he crossed, all right."

"That we know."

"And you did not cross, but later came to battle." Sam Houston's wide mouth relapsed into a smile. "What you are telling me is, we never know what lies the other side of the Rubicon. Each crossing brings its own answer, eventually."

"I think you are right about Texas in 1861," said Morgan. "But somehow, Texas will survive."

Houston nodded. He clambered down with his head high.

Morgan went to greet the small woman with large eyes, holding her close.

"Janet," he said. "It's going to be all right. Sam forded his river."

Camels in Texas? Yes, indeed—thanks to the U.S. War Department in 1850s, as Wayne Barton relates in this rollicking tale of an "invasion" of the beasts into the 8th Infantry at Fort Davis. Barton, a Midland, Texas, chemical engineer who writes Western fiction as an avocation, received a WWA Best Short Story Spur in 1980 for "One Man's Code." His novels include Ride Down the Wind *(1981) and* Return to Phantom Hill *(1983).*

The Beast and Sergeant Gilhooley

★★★★★★★★★★★★★★

Wayne Barton

I N the fall of 1854, by the grace of God and the genius of the War Department, there came six companies of the 8th Infantry to Fort Davis, Texas, to fight the Indians. Now, the Indians—Comanche and Apache at that time, with maybe a Kiowa now and then—had some four horses to the man, and more as fast as they could steal them from before a plow or beneath a cavalryman. By the time the infantry could march a company of troops and a battery of jackass artillery out to try conclusions, the Indians were likely eighty miles away and laughing among themselves.

Perceiving the problem, the War Department moved again in its mysterious way. Thus it was that four troops of the U.S. Dragoons were sent to even up the game. And thus it was that I, Terence Rafferty, first came to know that God-forsaken land.

I was at that time a sergeant in G Troop, as fine a body of men as ever touched saddle leather, though inclined to rowdiness at times. That is, I was a sergeant until I struck the acquaintance of one Gilhooley, a sergeant of the 8th Infantry. His head it was I struck, when he was moved to remark that

116

Dragoons were the most shiftless and spineless louts yet unhanged. We remonstrated, whereupon the colonel, a most unsympathetic man, reduced us both to ranks and gave us a month of walking post.

"This be your doing, Gilhooley," I raged at him many a time as we trekked about in full packs. "And when I'm sergeant again, you'll sweat for it."

"Sergeant, indeed!" he replied. "And if I can't get back my stripes ahead of a lily-livered nag-nurse, I'll take my retirement and grow potatoes!"

Indeed, it seemed he might be right, for while we passed the time with such pleasantries, Chief Alsate of the Apache came down to negotiate a peace. While the negotiating was at its height, the chief's men perfidiously ran off twenty of G Troop's horses. An unfortunate incident it was, and cruelly misconstrued.

" 'Twas not my understanding they meant us all to be infantry," Gilhooley said, and I was hard put to find any answer save that he was a wide-mouthed, ring-tailed ape.

Now, all bad things end, and by token, I at last returned to duty. In truth, I was needed, for we had but two hundred troopers to patrol the stretch from the great sand dunes to the Rio Bravo. I was of course a private, my stripes having gone to Liam Gillespie, a fine lad, though lacking in experience.

The troop kept busy for the better part of a month, chasing to places the Apache had been, but always too late to catch a glimpse of him. Uncommonly frustrating it was, and never a thought had I for Gilhooley until we returned to the fort. Then I found that the War Department had stretched forth its hand again, and my revenge had been all a man could wish.

We came around a bend in the road, and the horses shied tremendously, and there was Gilhooley, clinging to the lead rope of the most wicked-looking beast that ever I saw.

"And what might be scaring our horses?" Liam sang out. " 'Tis an infantry louse, boys!"

" 'Tis a camel, you ignorant scut," said Gilhooley. "Guinevere, by name. Sent by the generals for a beast of burden, and a fine, sweet-tempered creature she is." With that, he reached up to fetch her a pat on the neck, and the camel snorted through her nose and bit him on the arm.

Ah, but those days are a happy memory to me yet. The

War Department had sent fifty of the vile creatures, along with a dozen Arabic drivers and an officer that understood drivers and camels and all, so he said. It did my heart good to sit on the barracks stoop of an evening and watch the 8th struggle with the brutes. A camel has no fit place to carry a pack, along with a fixed determination not to carry it anyplace, and the profanity was wonderful to hear.

My job was soon cut short, however. Training ended and field operations began, and there was my name listed to ride escort for the first camel train.

We moved out in early morning, and a strange caravan we were. There were twenty laden camels, and twenty pack mules by way of comparison, all snorting and braying and showing they cared not a bit for the company they were keeping. The drivers were men from the 8th, commanded by a captain, and the officer that understood camels rode ahead. And round about the whole Noah's ark rode myself and Liam Gillespie and ten more men from G Troop.

I found time to pass a word with Gilhooley. It wasn't easy, for my old troop horse had never a thought around a camel but to turn and run as far as might be from the sight. 'Twas a natural reaction, making him smarter, mayhap, than the Secretary of War.

"Maybe we'll find these monsters good to eat," I greeted Gilhooley. " 'Tis plain they're good for nothing else."

Gilhooley puffed his pipe and smiled. "I'll wager you a month's pay," said he, "that Gwinny will be carrying her load when horse nor mule can move another step." And he reached to pat her neck again, while she kicked out sideways and caught him on the rump.

"Done!" I said. "But beware that beast, or you'll not live to pay me."

"That I will not." And he picked up his pipe he had dropped and resumed hauling on the lead rope.

There was much betting of that sort, with the infantrymen all backing their strange charges. And indeed, the camels stalked through the furnace heat of the desert with never a stumble. We'd hardly been out a day when one of the mules gave out, and the camels took up its load along with their own.

"You'll see," Gilhooley cackled. "At the end, they'll carry you and your horses, too."

When we stopped to boil coffee, the officer of camels came back to tell the captain what a glorious success the experiment was. The captain was agreeing left and right when one of the camels rose, shrugged off her pack politely, and ambled over to pass the time of day with the troop horses.

They bolted as if the devil had come among them with his fiery pitchfork, kicking coffee and cavalrymen to the winds in their flight. Two or three came near to stepping on the officers, and a hard task we had rounding them up again. Consequently, the captain wasn't in too bright a mood a little later, when the lead camel kicked her driver once or twice, then settled on her knees to go to sleep.

"What ails this infernal thing?" the captain yelled. "Get her on her feet, you men! Here, wait! Hold those animals!"

For the other camels, seeing what a good idea it was, had followed suit, grunting and snorting among themselves and wishing they'd thought of it sooner. The captain leveled a finger at the officer of camels.

"Lieutenant, these things are your charge. Find out what's wrong and get them moving."

The lieutenant prodded and poked awhile, earning a lot of bad camel language and a bite on the leg. Finally, he came to his conclusion.

"It's their feet," said he.

"What's that supposed to mean?"

"They're footsore from crossing these rocks. I don't think they can go on."

Now, a camel, instead of having a hoof like an honest beast, has pads like a cat's to let him walk on sand. The rocky trail had cut those pads cruelly. Indeed, it was a wonder the camels had stood it so long before declaring their holiday.

We milled around for a time, the officers considering the best way to get back to camp. They'd not decided, when a galloper from E Troop came tearing along the trial and reined in before us.

"Thank God I've found you!" he cried. "The Indians are attacking the stage stop at Stadman's Wells."

We had taken care to lead our zoo to a place where we wouldn't be observed. The Indian rides horses and eats mules, and heaven alone knows what he might make of camels. Now we were nigh on fifty miles from Stadman's Wells. Our captain swore at length, then called for Liam.

"What am I to do, with sixty men and twenty soft-shod camels! Gillespie, take your squad and ride to the rescue. We'll push on behind as best we can."

"Well enough, sir!" Liam grinned. Off we pounded at the forced march, dragging an extra mount to carry our water. 'Twas a long, dry crossing, and we'd no time to waste with mules. Our march took us through the night and into the dawn, and there in the dawn the Apache ambushed us.

We'd come into a canyon, and the Indians were waiting in the rocks above. I was riding drag on the column with a youngster named Reid. When he heard the first shots, he made to spur ahead. But I saw an Apache swoop down to cut out our pack horse, and I grabbed Reid's bridle.

"Do you ride for the 8th," I said. "Tell them we're down without water. If they come in haste, they may find us yet alive."

"Aye, sergeant." And he was away at the gallop. I shook my old Springfield free and came into the fight. Liam had the squad on foot behind some rocks, safe enough for the moment. As soon as I might, I told him about the water.

"Ah, that puts another face on it," he said. "The Indians can starve us out, and a long wait we'll have for the 8th."

In truth, there seemed little that the infantry could do. The captain had not mules enough to mount his whole force, nor could he afford to split it. 'Twas a long day we spent in the broiling sun, trading shots while our canteens ran dry.

Nor was it better when darkness came. The Apaches crept close to our lines, shouting and shooting to keep us awake. At last, they built a great fire down the canyon, and we could hear them chanting around it. About four in the morning, they commenced screeching and screaming as though all that came before was play. Then there was a dead and awful silence.

That brought us awake as no sound could have, and we strained our eyes in the dark. From the Indian camp came the groan of a thing in mortal agony.

"It's the devil himself," someone whispered, and I felt my own flesh crawl. The groan came again, closer to us.

"Beware, boys," cried Liam. " 'Tis some heathen trick."

"Hold your fire, ye ninnies!"

The shout came from the air a good eight feet over my head, and I fairly jumped out of my skin. But I knew that voice.

"My faith," I gasped. "It's Gilhooley!"

"Himself."

Someone thought to strike a light. It flamed up, and there was Gilhooley, reclining on Guinevere's back for all the world like the Queen of Sheba. He spoke to the beast, which moaned like a lost soul and humped to her knees. Her sides were draped with water bags.

"And how do you find yourselves?" Gilhooley inquired politely. Liam gaped at him like a hooked trout.

"Man, the Indians!"

"Indians?" said Gilhooley. "Well, yes, there was a few. From the way they ran when we charged down on them, 'tis likely they'd never seen a camel before."

He heaved a sigh and slid to the ground, rubbing his back.

"Ah, but I'll never speak ill of the Dragoons again. 'Twas a rare treat, breaking the little darling to the saddle."

"But how?" Liam demanded, still disbelieving his eyes. "Yesterday, she could walk hardly a step."

Trooper Blaine, quicker than the rest of us, bent to look at Gwinny's feet. "Boots!" He sat back and howled with laughter. "Doughfeet that she is, she's wearing boots."

And so she was. Cut out a bit to fit her foot, but sound infantry boots all the same, and laced up well about the ankle.

"No joking, now," Gilhooley warned. " 'Tis not polite to mock the beast as saved your mangy hides."

He spoke the truth, but still it was hard to ride out in the morning. Gilhooley took the point, his camel stepping out like a princess in ballet slippers, while we panted in the dust. The 8th greeted us warmly, you may be sure, and at the last Gilhooley got back his stripes, with my month's pay and a medal to boot, for his daring rescue.

And there's the part of the whole business as sticks in my craw. He deserved his stripes, mayhap, and the matter of the wager could be argued. But as for the medal, 'tis plain it should have gone to Guinevere.

Himself a cowhand and rancher, Bennett Foster was an expert as well as entertaining chronicler of life on the great cattle ranges of the Southwest. For more than twenty years, beginning in the mid-1930s, he contributed regularly to the Western pulps and to such slick magazines as The Saturday Evening Post *(where "Trail Song" first appeared) and* Collier's. *Outstanding among his nearly twenty novels are* Seven Slash Range *(1936),* Badlands *(1938),* Owl-Hoot Trail *(1940), and* Winter Quarters *(1942).*

Trail Song

★★★★★★★★★★★★★★

Bennet Foster

> *Come along boys and listen to my tale,*
> *I'll tell you of my troubles on the old*
> *Chisholm Trail,*
> *Co-ma ti yi you-pe, you-pe ya, you-pe ya,*
> *Co-ma ti yi you-pe, you-pe ya.*

CHISHOLM Trail, Western Trail, any trail—it made no difference to Dan McKee. Dan couldn't recollect the day he was too young to follow after cattle; he couldn't recall the time he wasn't with a wagon.

Dan thought he was someplace around twenty-one or -two; he didn't know for sure. He reckoned his folks were dead, but he wasn't certain. Once he rode clear to East Texas to see some people named McKee but it turned out they were no kin. Dan's idea was to stand on his own feet and look the boss and every other straight in the eye. He wasn't the only kithless, kinless man in Texas.

In the spring of '82 Dan went north with Sam Cashmole's trail outfit. When Dan hired on in Sanantone he and the boss had a talk.

"I figure," Cashmole said, "that any man who can't put enough strays in the herd to make three times his wages ain't worth his salt. That's the way I figure."

"That used to be so," Dan said, "but there's a trail cutter at Doan's Crossing and another up by the Nations. You can't take no strays through them. They pare a herd down to its road brand."

"I know that," Cashmole agreed, "but we ain't goin' by Doans or the Nations. We're goin' north of Fort Sumner and through Trinchera Pass over the old Goodnight route. There's lots of little *ranchos* that way and them Mexicans never had nerve enough to cut a herd. Unless we have real bad luck we ought to do all right. Want to gamble?"

"I reckon," Dan agreed.

Cashmole's trail crew received their cattle in Kendall county. They burned the Hackamore road brand across the noses of the big, many-colored steers, and when the count had been agreed on and a settlement made, the men who had tendered the cattle gave them a full day's help to start. After that it was up to the trail outfit. They went northwest through the mesquite and every night for the first week double guards were put around the cattle and half the remuda was hobbled and guarded, too. Then, with the steers shaken down to trailing, they entered a more open country and precautions were relaxed.

Dan McKee and Church Fynas rode the points. The two of them spread their bed together and stood last guard together. In the morning, when the cattle left the bedground, Dan and Church were on hand to drift them in the right direction. On the drive, they bent the leaders according to Cashmole's orders, and when native cattle tried to join up, it was Dan and Church who loped out and threw them off. Behind those two the others rode in swing and drag, pinching the herd down to size, sacking up the corners, bringing up the rear. The cook drove the wagon, off to right or left as the wind indicated, keeping out of the dust, and the horse wrangler brought the remuda along. There were twelve men, a hundred horses, two thousand cattle and a wagon moving across the plains and for a while they were scrupulously honest.

The wrangler kid got homesick.

"When I get home," the wrangler said, "I'm goin' to sleep a month. My maw's got the best feather beds in Texas and I'm goin' to lay down on about two of 'em an' get up when I'm ready."

"You're gettin' the idea, kid," said Dan McKee. "Trail hands learn to do their sleepin' in the winter."

"An' this water," the wrangler kid continued, "ain't fit to drink. Nothin' but alkali. I had the belly cramps all day. Down home we got a spring and a spring-house where maw keeps the milk and butter. The water's just as sweet!"

Supper was long done and the fire was dying. The first guard men were circling the cattle and Sam Cashmole had ridden out to prowl around the herd and see how it was resting. Church Fynas sat up on his bed.

"My folks have got a spring-house on their place," Church said. "We put the buttermilk there to cool after we've churned. There ain't nothin' better than fresh, cold buttermilk with little specks of butter floatin' in it."

Across the fire Ben Sparn and Steve Youngalls paused in their pitch game. "We had a dug well," Steve said. "Thirty foot deep and the water cold as ice. I could have used some of that today."

"Branch water." Ben Sparn spoke thoughtfully. "A creek run right through our place. Us kids swum in it."

"We'll drink water out of cow tracks this trip," said Dan McKee, "and like it, too. This water ain't so bad."

"Eggs," said the wrangler kid, his thoughts passing from drink to food. "I ain't ate a egg in I don't know when. Maw used to fry me half a dozen and dish 'em up with home cured ham."

"Come out of it, kid!" Dan ordered. "Do you want to get the cook down on you? You hired out for a tough hand; if you're homesick, why did you take the job?"

"Blamed if I know," the wrangler kid answered, his candid eyes on Dan. "Wasn't you ever homesick?"

"I guess not," said Dan, and laughed.

Next night, fifteen miles along the way, Dan McKee sat down beside the wrangler kid. "Get the cook to give you some soda an' mix it with tallow," he advised. "Take a little of that and this alkali water won't gripe you so bad. Whereabouts do you live, kid?"

"Up by New Braunfels. We got a farm."

"Tell me about it." Dan rolled a cigarette and smoked and listened while the wrangler kid talked.

Last night I was on guard and the leaders broke the ranks,
I hit my horse down the shoulders and I spurred him in
   the flanks!
The wind began to blow and the rain began to fall,
Hit looked, by grab, like we was goin' to lose 'em all!

North of Yellowhouse, a brisk and businesslike man, carrying authority for the CV and other brands, met the Hackamore herd. Sam Cashmole made him welcome, fed him at the wagon, and proffered a horse. The stranger needed no horse for he led a spare and, after dinner, worked the herd, bunched and held for his convenience. The trail cutter was complimentary when he had finished.

"As clean a bunch as I've worked this year," he announced. "You must of been extra careful, Cashmole."

"We've tried to be," Sam Cashmole answered piously. "Better stay the night with us."

The trail cutter spoke his thanks but refused the offer. When he was gone, Cashmole addressed the crew. "Tomorrow," he said, "we'll be out of Goodnight's country. I wouldn't want to start anything with that old man around. Two-three days and we'll be across the line. After that you can turn loose your wolf."

Next day the route led straight west and so for two days following, then curved north again. Now, when native cattle appeared, curious and eager to join the marching ranks of steers, Dan and Church rode out as usual. Some they drove off, but others—cattle that offered contrast in neither size nor sex—they added to the herd. Not many; just a few. Any trail herd was bound to collect some strays and if Sam Cashmole's Hackamores arrived at market with more than ordinary—why then, who would question them?

"Just don't be greedy, boys," Cashmole advised. "There ain't no use in bein' reckless."

The Hackamore herd passed well north of Fort Sumner and, reaching the Pecos, followed up the stream. Then, leaving the river, they entered upon a broad and grass-grown plain, flanked on either side by broken country. So far the march had been uneventful, the steers handling like well drilled troops; but now, daily, storm clouds appeared to north and west and were eyed apprehensively.

"Makin' big," Dan McKee stated. "It wouldn't surprise me none if the boss didn't call a rain guard tonight."

Sam Cashmole called the rain guard, splitting the crew in half. As part of the second guard, Dan and Church turned in but not to sleep. They watched lightning flicker along the horizon and heard the thunder roll. Big raindrops splatted down, the wind blew steadily and, suddenly, the rain was a torrent.

"Here's hell!" Dan shouted above the wind. "Come on!"

They fought their way to their night horses, mounted and started to the cattle. Before they reached the herd, they knew that it was moving.

A figure loomed up beside Dan and Ben Sparn's voice came to him. "They ain't runnin'. They just got up an' walked away. We couldn't hold 'em."

"Stay with 'em!" Dan called and, turning with the wind, went with the cattle. He was ahead of them; he planned to stay ahead.

Toward morning, the rain thinned, then ceased. The dawn crept over the hills like a dripping veil. As the light grew, Dan saw that he was in broken country, and when the sun came up, a clean and new-washed world lay all about him. He stopped his night horse on a ridge and took his bearings.

Behind him the flats showed in the sun, dotted here and there with clumps of cattle; to right and left the ridges fell away and before him was a valley. A stream ran down it to the east, limpid and silvery between cottonwoods, a hay meadow glistened with its wetness and there were other fields, smaller and planted in rows. From a house, hidden by rising land, a thread of smoke rose up and, down below apiece, were six big steers.

Dan McKee was wet and cold but did not notice his discomfort. He drank it in, the fields, the stream, the rolling, grass-grown ridges. Here, so his cowman's eyes remarked, was cattle land. Hay from the vega to feed the winter horses, breaks and cedars for protection and grass over all outdoors. He rode on down.

The house with the smoking chimney was in a fold of
ground. There were cottonwoods for shade, a well with curb
and pulley, a monstrous woodpile and a set of pole corrals.
As Dan arrived a man stepped out and a woman peered from
the door. A boy came from the pens toward the woodpile and
Dan drew rein, speaking his greeting gravely and in Spanish.
He was, he said, looking for cattle that had drifted during the
night.

The grizzled man listened, nodding his head in understanding. He had seen a few cattle, doubtless his visitor had
seen them too. Coffee was ready and an invitation was issued.
Dan got down and tied his horse; the boy had carried in an
armload of wood and the scent of frying meat was almost
more than a hungry man could bear. Dan gave his name and
the grizzled man shook hands and tipped his hat politely. He
was Blas Aragon, he said and, shivering in the cold and damp,
Dan followed him.

The house was adobe, its walls full two feet thick. A girl,
kneeling at the hearth, sprang up as the men entered. Blas
spoke the introductions naming his wife, Duvina, his daughter, Filepita, his son, Jaime. Coffee steamed in a cup, the
meat was crisp fried steak and there were hot tortillas. Filepita—'' 'Fia'' her brother called her—waited on Dan McKee.
Her hair was black as a midnight sky, long lashes shielded
her dark eyes, her cheeks were flushed, her mouth was a full-
lipped, red-ripe menace. About eighteen, Dan judged. It was
hard to tell.

'Fia had a question. Had Senor McKee seen a steer, a gray
steer, three years old, branded with a Spanish A and with
white horns, black tipped?

Dan shook his head and Blas Aragon laughed. The steer
was 'Fia's pet, he said, she had raised it from a calf after the
cow died. El Topo, the mole, she called the steer.

"He will eat tortillas from my hand," 'Fia added, "ta-
males, too, the husks and all. *Por favor, Senor*, if you see El
Topo will you drive him back? He stays about the house.
Sometimes he wanders, but never before has he stayed away
so long."

Gravely, Dan promised that should he see El Topo he would
turn him back. Then, having spoken thanks for food and
warmth, he mounted and rode. On the slope he collected the

six steers, all Hackamores and, farther on among the ridges, found eight head more. Driving these, he reached the flats and met Church Fynas with another drive.

"I got a dozen," Church reported. "We were ahead of 'em, Dan. I think we got the ones that went the farthest."

"I think you're right," Dan agreed. "What's that you got?" He pointed to a gray steer, its white horns black tipped.

"That's a stray." Church grinned all across his beard-stubbled face. "Got a little Spanish A on him and not another mark. Ain't he a dandy? Looks like a mouse."

"More like a mole." Dan returned Church's grin. "El Topo. Let's take 'em on. We got to change horses and work them little pockets out."

They took their drive on. To north and south they saw other cattle and west of them was a band of horses.

"The kid's got the remuda anyhow," Church said. "He didn't lose 'em. Looks like he was headed for the wagon."

By mid-morning the Hackamore crew had help in gathering their scattered steers. A man named Linder, accompanied by four riders, arrived at the wagon. Cross VL was Linder's brand and he ran on the flats, between the broken countries. Steadily, on fresh horses, the Hackamores and Cross VLs pushed cattle into a herd. By evening time Sam Cashmole estimated that he had most of his steers.

"And some of your stuff, too, of course," he said to Linder. "We'll make a circle in the morning, then work the herd and get yours out. We got some strays with us, naturally, but we know them." He looked at Linder narrowly.

"I ain't interested in nothin' but Cross VLs," Linder announced. "What strays you got are your business. I wouldn't mind if you picked up every cow in the Trementina."

"The Trementina?" Dan McKee queried.

"The country over east," Linder said, impatiently. "Nothin' but Mexicans. Them and me don't get along too good."

"Have they been stealin' from you?" Cashmole asked.

"I just moved in here," Linder answered, "an' they ain't had a chance. I rode over there an' told 'em if I had any trouble I wouldn't send for no sheriff." His face was grim. "Closest sheriff's at Raton anyhow an' that's a hundred miles. I told 'em . . ."

Dan McKee turned away. It was an old story he had heard before. Little men held down a country; then somebody—somebody bigger and tougher than they were—brought in cattle. Dan knew how the story ended. Linder would run his bluff and after a time the breaks as well as the flat would be Cross VL.

That night, when Dan took his guard, the man he relieved spoke a warming. "There's a gray steer hangin' out on the east side of the herd. I had to turn him back four times. Better look out for him."

"I will," Dan promised.

> Stray in the herd and the boss said to kill it,
> So I shot him in the rump with the handle of a skillet.

The herd was worked next morning. Before noon, Linder declared himself satisfied and the Hackamores moved on. That night, when they bedded, El Topo took station at the south side of the herd and Church Fynas, noticing this, pitched a loop over the steer's head and tied him to a bush.

"You were just a little too anxious last night," Church said. "I'll tie you till we're out of your country."

At two o'clock, taking the last guard, Dan saw El Topo standing there with the rope around his neck. El Topo was looking south.

As the Hackamores moved on north the gray steer became one of the characters of the herd. He was gentle as a dog and had no fear of men, either on foot or horseback. Once, when wagon and herd were close, the steer wandered over and begged so plainly that the cook passed out a piece of bacon rind. El Topo chewed and slobbered rolling his eyes in ecstasy, and after that the first guard always roped him and tied him up. If they didn't he would haunt the wagon for a while and then drift unobtrusively southward until caught and driven back.

"That gray steer," Church said, "is sure a homelover. He's in the drags all day and every night he's on the south side, lookin' back. He's homesick, I guess."

"Yes," said Dan, "he's homesick. I've been noticin'."

"You talk like you was sorry for him," the wrangler commented. "Wasn't you ribbin' me about bein' homesick a while back? Didn't you ask me why I'd hired on if I was home-sick?'' With time the kid wrangler had grown bolder.

"You're a man," Dan said. "You could make up your own mind. El Topo never had a choice; we just brought him along."

That was the way Dan thought about it. El Topo had been given no choice and Dan felt sorry for the steer. And there was another way he felt; a way he could not describe. On last guard, in the lonesome morning hours, Dan saw El Topo yearning for the south and, as he rode his slow circle about the herd, it seemed to Dan that he could see the valley, too. There was the limpid stream between the cottonwoods, the rain-jeweled meadow, sparkling in the morning sun, the thread of smoke from the hidden house. Sometimes it seemed to Dan that he could smell the coffee and the frying meat, could hear the grave and courteous voice of Blas Aragon; could see 'Fia's eyes, anxious and dark beneath dark lashes, and her red lips forming a request.

Por favor, Senor . . .

Then, when he looked at El Topo, Dan McKee felt like a dog, a sneaking, sheep killing dog.

The Hackamore trail herd crossed the Ratons and, two days north of Trinchera pass, Ben Sparn's horse fell with him. Ben had to ride the wagon for a while and Dan took his place on first guard. Steve Youngalls, also on first guard, roped El Topo and staked him out. Dan, circling the cattle, saw the gray steer and stopped. El Topo was looking off to-ward the south through the dusk and, after a long minute, Dan rode up, removed the stake rope and coiled it. He went on and, meeting Steve, passed over the coil.

"You won't need this," Dan said gruffly.

Continuing his circle, Dan came to the spot where the gray steer had been. El Topo was gone and, the next morning, Dan spoke to Church.

"I turned El Topo loose last night," he announced awk-wardly. "Seemed like he wanted to go home extra bad."

Church Fynas was Dan's friend. "Oh?" Church said.

"Yes," said Dan. "I'll settle with you for the steer when Sam pays off. An' Church—I'd just as soon you didn't say nothin' about it to the wrangler."

We hit Caldwell and we hit her on the fly,
We bedded down the cattle on a hill close by.

Sam Cashmole sold out in Pueblo. All the cattle, Hacka-mores and strays, too, went to one buyer, a man who supplied beef to the mines. Sam sold the wagon, the wagon mules and the remuda, making a clean sweep, and then paid off his hands. Each man had three months' wages coming as well as a prorata share in the strays and, with money in their pockets, they went to town. There were baths to take, shaves and haircuts to acquire; their clothing was worn out and, besides these necessities, Pueblo offered liquor, gambling, and women. Dan and Church walked into the first saloon.

"I want to pay you for that gray steer," Dan said. "Sam got thirty-six dollars a round for the cattle. Here's what I owe you."

Church took the money, knowing better than to offer objection. "I wonder if that steer got home," he said. "Be kind of funny to find out, wouldn't it?"

"Yes, it would," Dan agreed and then, "You know, Church—I think I'll go an' see."

"Ride back all that ways?" Church was incredulous. "You're crazy, Dan. We're goin' home on the cars."

Steve Youngalls, Ben Sparn, and the kid wrangler came into the saloon. They were gaudy in cheap new suits, their faces shown from close and recent shaving, they were feeling their liquor. They hailed Dan and Church boisterously, decreeing drinks for all.

"Where's Dan?" the kid wrangler demanded after a time. "I want to buy him a drink. Where is he? He was here a minute ago."

I'm on my best horse an' I'm goin' at a run,
I'm the quickest shootin' cowboy that ever pulled a gun!

Dan McKee rode south on a horse bought in Pueblo. He led a pack horse and his eyes were fixed on the horizon beyond which lay the Ratons. He rode eagerly, covering in hours those distances which had taken days on the drive north, and when he was below Trinchera pass he looked at every cow-track, wondering if El Topo had made it.

Nearing the end of the trail, Dan slowed down. He reached the flats below the Trementina in mid-afternoon and could have completed his journey before sunset but an odd fancy held him. He wanted to crown the ridge and again in the morning sun look down upon the valley. Dan made camp, boiled coffee, and waited.

With false dawn he was up and saddling. When the morning wind blew chill, he entered the broken country and, as the sun came up, stopped on the ridge. The Trementina spread before him, the rolling grass-land, the limpid stream, its cottonwoods yellow now that frost had come, the hay vega, still green, the little fields. Dan saw a thread of smoke against the eastern sky and rode on down.

A gray steer stood by the well at Blas Aragon's house. El Topo! Dan reined in and the steer looked at him inquiringly. Blas came to the door; there was recognition in his eyes and he spoke a greeting, bidding Dan dismount. Jaime came and led the horses away as Blas and Dan walked to the house. At the door, Blas paused and stepped aside.

"¡Pas!" he said. *"Mi casa es suyo."*

It was an old word, spoken in courtesy. "Enter. My house is yours." Dan went in. Duvina was pouring coffee and 'Fia sprang up from beside the hearth. It was just as Dan remembered.

He spoke to Duvina. To 'Fia he said, "Your pet came home."

"Two weeks ago," 'Fia answered.

Jaime came in. He had put the horses in the pen, he said. Blas seated his guest and food was brought.

All the way south Dan McKee had ridden in anticipation, eager and expectant, of what he did not know. On the ridge, in the sunrise, it had bubbled in him, rising like heady wine. Now, when fulfillment should have come, the buoyancy was gone. Why, Dan wondered. Why?

He looked about him and in blank eyes read the answer. On his first visit he had been a stranger but he was welcome. Now he was not a stranger but the welcome was gone. That was why. Blas might say, "My house is yours," Jaime might care for the horses, Duvina might cook, and 'Fia place food at his hand but these things were obligations to a guest. They did not want him. Why? Because of El Topo? Dan did not know.

The meal ended and Dan gave thanks for the food and arose. Outside the house there was a bench and above it, from the roof, thrifty Duvina had hung long curls of squash and melon to sun-dry. Dan sat on the bench and rolled a cigarette but his host refused tobacco; talk also. To Dan's conversational gambits Blas replied in monosyllables, closing each opening. The wind freed leaves from the cottonwoods and they fell in a golden shower. Dan McKee ground out his cigarette and stood up. He was, he said, just passing through; he was grateful and now he would ride on. Blas murmured polite and insincere objections and Dan went to the corrals.

Jaime had unsaddled and unpacked. Dan caught his bed horse and packed; he caught the other horse and saddled. He was a fool, he told himself; he didn't know what had brought him back to this country or what he had expected to find. Whatever it was, he surely hadn't found it. Anyhow he had his horses and his saddle and his bed; he had money in his pocket and a gun on his hip and what more did a man need? Or want, either? Dan tied his latigo with a final jerk.

Horses stopped, hidden from him by the house, and he heard men talking. Collecting reins and leap rope, Dan started for the gate. The voices lifted in anger and he let the horses go. When Dan rounded the corner of the house he saw Linder, a Cross VL rider that he recognized, and Blas Aragon.

"I told you I'd be over after that steer!" Linder's voice was loud and his face was red. "That's a Hackamore stray. I seen it when we helped 'em gather cattle!"

Any pretext, any little thing, seized on and magnified to make trouble. That was the way it was done. Bully and quarrel, push and shove, kill sometimes; crowd the other man and drive him out. Dan remembered Linder's words to Sam Cashmole. This was a chapter in the same old story and—relief flooded Dan—it was an explanation as well. The Aragons didn't know about El Topo; their coldness to Dan had been a reflection from their difficulties with the Cross VL. Dan had stepped into the backwash of resentment that Linder had aroused; it wasn't Dan the Aragons disliked, it was all *gringos*.

Blas stood with his back toward the house, facing the Cross

VL men. He wasn't giving an inch; he didn't act a bit scared. Dan moved along the wall, getting into position. It was the same old story but this time there would be an added entry. Linder nor the rider nor Blas saw him arrive.

"Hello, Linder," Dan said.

He leaned against the wall, negligent, lounging, his thumb tucked into his belt, the picture of a man at ease. His voice was soft but his eyes were not, and from the way he stood and the way he looked, plain as plain, Dan was siding Blas Aragon. Three faces turned toward him and everybody stood still and kept still.

"Up kind of early, ain't you?" Dan continued.

Linder grunted like a man hit low. "Hello, McKee."

Dan pushed off from the wall. "That steer you're talkin' about belongs to Aragon," he said. "We picked it up by mistake. I've come a considerable out of my way to see that it got home. It's the girl's pet."

"Well," Linder said awkwardly, "I didn't know that. I was just tryin' to do you fellers a favor." Confronted by one of his own breed, a tougher member of the clan, Linder backed down.

The time to crowd a man was when you had him running. Dan moved up beside Blas. "It looks to me," he drawled, "like maybe you was tryin' to steal a steer. That's how it looks to me." Linder had come to start trouble; Dan dumped trouble in his lap and waited.

Now was the time. It started now or not at all. Dan watched Linder and saw no trouble there. Linder looked away. He was going to take it and Dan gave him a way out.

"Of course a man can be mistaken," he said.

"That's right." Linder spoke quickly with relief. "Anybody can make a mistake. I didn't know about the steer."

"But you know now," Dan said. "Was there anything you wanted to tell Aragon? He don't talk English much. Maybe I could tell him for you."

"No," Linder answered. "No, there wasn't. We got to be goin'. Come on, Pete."

The Cross VL men rode upvalley, climbed a ridge and were gone. Dan moved, turning toward the corrals. Blas caught his arm, protesting, stopping him.

"No! You are not to go! I will not let you go!"

'Fia and Jaime came from the house. From the door Duvina urged her husband to bring their guest. 'Fia caught Dan's hand and held it and El Topo, loafing around the corner of the house, stopped and lifted his nose toward a dangling strip of melon.

"*¡Por favor!*" Blas said, his voice warm and urgent. "*¡Pase! ¡Pase, amigo!*"

Dan looked at Blas, reading the friendship written on his face. He looked at Duvina and in her eyes there was a welcome and a pleading. They needed him. Blas and Duvina needed Dan McKee. Dan realized their need and knew its cause. While Dan McKee dwelt in the Trementina it was safe, secure from Linder and all his kind. While Dan McKee was there the waters of the stream would flow undisturbed, the sun would shine, the rain would fall and, through sunshine, wind and rain, Blas and Duvina, 'Fia and Jaime, would move in peace and unafraid. And why? Because of Dan McKee.

Dan looked at 'Fia, 'Fia with night-black hair and eyes that were quickly hidden by long lashes and, suddenly, it was there again, the eager, buoyant effervescence that lifted up his heart. Why?

El Topo stretched his neck, pulled down a strip of melon and stood munching it, the yellow rind dangling from his mouth. He looked for all the world like some big, overgrown boy, enjoying stolen sweets. Like a boy, Dan laughed, not at El Topo but at the answer to his question. El Topo had come home to stay—and so had Dan McKee!

With my knees in the saddle and my seat in the sky,
I'll quit punchin' cows in the sweet bye an' bye.
Co-ma ti yi you-pe you-pe ya.

Two highly respected names in contemporary Western literature are Will Henry and Clay Fisher; both are pseudonyms of Henry Wilson Allen, who has won more Spur Awards from the Western Writers of America—four—than any other writer. These include two Best Historical Novel Spurs, for From Where the Sun Now Stands *(1960) and* Gates of the Mountains *(1963); and a pair for Best Short Story: ''Isley's Stranger'' (1962) and ''The Tallest Indian in Toltepec'' (1965). ''King Fisher's Road,'' about the Texas legend, King Fisher, is Henry/Fisher/Allen's usual superb blend of fiction and historical fact.*

King Fisher's Road

★★★★★★★★★★★★★★★★

Clay Fisher

I CAME into Kearney on the afternoon stage. It was four hours late, pretty bad even for the American Mail Company. When I got down in front of the division office it was ten minutes of six P.M. Even so, no one had gone home yet. American Mail paid for twelve hours work and got it.

I stood a moment, unwrapping a fresh cigar and wondering anew why they had sent for me. The assignment was to open a new stage route between San Antonio and Uvalde, Texas, that I knew. But opening new routes was not exactly the way in which I earned my company keep, and so my curiosity mounted.

Going into the office I nodded at two clerks I knew, but they kept their eyes to their accounts. Aha, I thought, I've been let out at last. The poor fellows are embarrassed by what they know and what I am about to find out. Well, no man lasts forever. The hand is quicker than the eye, they say, and in my business it had better be. Apparently, though, some diligent employee had reported to the division super that I was coming down with a hard case of slowing up. How this rumor had taken wing interested

136

me. To my knowledge I hadn't turned down any private invitation to compete, nor come out second in any public performance of my work. This should have reassured me, but it did not. The truth was that of a given cold morning or after too many hours in the saddle I was a whisper less quick than an eye wink these latter days. But who had found me out, and how? That was the matter of interest.

Giving the cowardly clerks a good eyeing, I went on past their desks and stopped at the one to the rear of the office. This one bore a sign which read, "EVERETT D. STONE, SUPERINTENDENT," an accurate statement, if superfluous. Anyone would know Stone was a superintendent. He was too fat for a working man, and not worried enough. Presently he was frowning, though, and I took it he was not happy with the report he was studying. That seemed reasonable. It was a thick report and had a telegram pinned to it, and telegrams are always trouble. I stood by a polite bit, then scuffed my boots.

"Hello," I said, "somebody here send for a road opener?"

Stone looked up sort of flustered. He put the report quickly under some other papers, taking off his glasses and then acting real surprised to see me there.

"Harry, boy! Harry Roebuck!" he said, getting up and placing me a chair. "Sit down, sit down—"

I gave him a pretty well wrung-out nod, took the seat and said, "Well, Mr. Stone, who turned me in?"

He just looked at me, beaming.

"Harry, you old coyote," he said, "how have you been?"

"I've been right fine," I said, "but I got an idea I'm not going to stay that way."

He gave me the eye and said, "Um, yes, let's see here now," and began ruffling through some old waybills on his desk. "Cuss it all, I had that file right in front of me."

I gave him the eye back and reached over and pulled the report out from under the other papers.

"Yes, sir," I said. "Could this possibly be it, Mr. Stone?"

He took the report, looking it over as though it had just come off the key.

"Why so it is! I tell you, Harry, my eyesight is going bad."

"Mine isn't," I told him. "Mind reading me that telegram you got pinned on top? It looks to bear the same date as the one you sent me."

He gave me one more look and surrendered.

"First let me go back a ways," he said. "Do you remember Bunker Johnson?"

"Why don't you ask me if I remember my mother? You know I remember Bunk. He broke me in on this job." I watched him close now. "Don't tell me," I said, "that something has happened to old Bunk."

Stone put up his hands.

"Now wait, get the whole story. We called you here to go down to Texas and supervise the opening of a new stage route into Uvalde. Am I right?"

"As summer rain. And that brings up another point. Why me?"

"That," nodded Stone, "brings us right back to Bunk Johnson. We put him on the job and he couldn't handle it."

"Bunk couldn't handle a route opening? Must be some route. He's one of the best men you've got."

"He was one of the best," Stone said, handing over the telegram. "Read this."

I held the telegram up to the sunset light. It read: JOHNSON KILLED GUNFIGHT J. K. FISHER UVALDE THIS DATE. SIGNED. WESTCOTT.

I gave it back to Stone.

"Who's Westcott?" I asked.

"Our Uvalde office manager."

"That leaves us with J. K. Fisher."

"Yes. Ever hear of him, Harry?"

"Not till now. Should I have?"

Stone nodded grimly, voice tight.

"Try 'King Fisher,' " he said.

"*Him,*" I answered, "I've heard of. Go ahead."

Stone laid it out for me them. Fisher had announced to all Texas that he was closing the Uvalde road to through traffic. Specifically he had warned American Mail they were not going to run their new stage line over it. Moreover, he had run the Uvalde manager out of town and back to San Antonio. He had then planted a sign squarely in the middle of the road proclaiming it was his road and that the rest of the world could take the other. When the company sent Bunk Johnson, their senior shotgun guard, over from the Dallas office to make certain the first stage went through to Uvalde on schedule, Fisher ambushed the stage at his sign in the road, forced Bunk, an older man no longer in his prime as a gunman, to draw, then shot him off the seat box of the stage and left him dying in the dirt of the Uvalde road. It was here that they had sent for Harry Roebuck and the question now was, would Roebuck take the job or wouldn't he? Roebuck being me, and me seeing no place to hide in the division office, I threw in.

I still had a question or two of my own, however.

"I don't get it," I frowned. "Why would Fisher want that road closed? What's he got against American Mail? It don't make sense."

Stone wagged his head, held up his hands again.

"It makes sense, Harry," he said. "Hard, dirty sense. By now, most folks know the law had a habit of following American Mail west. We move into a town and trouble moves out. Fisher knows that, too, and trouble is his business. He's a hell-raiser and a rustler and is making money with his left hand faster than his right can spend it. Uvalde's his town and unless we get that new run through, it's going to stay his town. If he can buffalo American Mail, who's going to stop him?"

"Well, for one thing, what's holding up the Texas Rangers?"

"They're not on our payroll, Harry. You are."

"That's a handy way of looking at it—for the Texas Rangers," I said. "But it suits me. I'll take the job. When do I leave?"

Fool questions never go long begging for blunt answers and this one was no more than decently out of my mouth than a train whistled sharply down at the depot. Stone pulled out his watch.

"That's the 6:05 for San Antone," he said. "How soon you want to leave?"

I wasn't going to let him run any cold bluffs on me. I pulled out my own watch.

"6:01," I said. "Good a time as any to go to Texas and kill a man."

Stone looked at me a little hard.

"How's that, Harry?" he said.

"It's what you want done, isn't it, Mr. Stone?" I answered him.

"Now, Harry, I didn't say that!"

"No, we never do *say it*, Mr. Stone. But somehow it always manages to come out that way, doesn't it?"

I started for the door but Stone caught up to me.

"I know it's a rough job, Harry," he said. "You don't have to take it."

"No," I said, "and I don't have to take the company's money, either, but I've developed some soft habits doing so all these years, and eating is one of the worst."

"Now see here, Harry," he came back at me, "there's no call for you to take such a hard-nose attitude. American Mail will always have some kind of a job for you."

"Thank you," I said, "but some kind of a job is not my kind of a job." The train tooted again just then and I started out the door once more.

"Harry," said Stone anxiously, "be careful!"

"Thank you," I repeated, "I never got hurt running for a train yet," and that it is the way we left it.

It was seven hundred miles from the division office to San Antonio. The 6:05 was a makeup train of two mail cars, one chair car and thirty-three cattle car empties to be dropped at Fort Worth. Naturally we did not establish any new line records. I had plenty of time to think, which I didn't need at all. I had known when I left the office why American Mail had sent for me, and what my job was—or rather what it was meant to be— to go down to Texas and kill King Fisher, one of the two fastest guns alive. I didn't blame the company for the order, as a man with a reputation like King's doesn't leave either the law, or legitimate business folks, much of any other approach. But I had a hunch about young King Fisher and I intended to play it through. Providing, that is, I could get somebody to play it with me. In that direction my first move was almost straight across the street from the depot in San Antonio, and I made it as soon as I lighted down there the next evening.

Angling through the dust away from the depot, I squinted through the twilight to make sure my friends were still doing business in Bexar County and sure enough they were. The oil lamp hung from the front roof eave had just been lit and its rays showed me the sign hadn't changed a dot or a comma." HDQTRS. TEXAS RANGERS, CO. A," it read, which was a good thing, for I required—required?—I had to have—the approval of my hunch by the Rangers before trying it on King Fisher. Also I might need their active backing, and they were pretty fair country gun-fighters or, for that matter, city gutter-fighters, and what I had in mind for King was a sort of combination of John Wesley Hardin and the Marquis of Queensbury set to Texas rules.

Luckily, I caught Captain Randolph in a sinking spell and he not only approved my idea for dealing with the one-man war in Uvalde County but said that any further aid the Rangers could furnish me, I had only to name it. They had tried several of their own hunches on King Fisher and his Uvalde crowd without what you might call a crowning success anywhere along the line. My underhanded approach sounded just right to them and they graciously gave me the green light to go ahead and run its track into Uvalde—if I could.

My first need was for a good night's sleep, which I got for a dollar and a half at the Unicorn Hotel. I had quite a few visitors during the night but it takes more than a couple of hundred playful bites to keep a really tired man awake. Besides, everybody has to make his living the best way he can in this life, and I never did grudge an honest bedbug his pint of my blood.

Sunrise next morning I was hitting along the main road west out of San Antonio in a two-horse rig rented from the Alamo Livery & Prairie Hay Company, across from the firehouse and down the street from the Ranger headquarters building. That's the old firehouse, on the corner of the square, not the one they have now.

It was a fine morning, my team full of ginger and even me feeling like I might live. My purpose, of course, was not to study the Texas daybreak but to feel out the party of the second part. When you go up against a gunfighter of King Fisher's reputation you have got to call it a war. And in a war the first thing you do is scout the enemy lines. For me, I had to see that reported sign of King Fisher's with my own eyes and, if possible, get a close-up look at the famous young man who had put it there, before deciding precisely how to open my campaign to get American Mail's first stage into Uvalde on time and as advertised.

Presently, I struck a county road coming in from the side. The turn-off sign read, "UVALDE, 55 MI.," and I set myself for the long drive. About four that afternoon, coming around a sharp bend made blind by heavy mesquite, oak and catclaw thorn trees, I very nearly had to burn off the hide on my team's hocks, hauling them up. The rig slid sideways, decided not to tip over, settled down in a cloud of red Texas real estate. I dug the grit out of my eyes and shook my head three to five times, but it would not go away. There it stood planted right square in the middle of the wagon ruts of the Uvalde road, and what it said was as to-the-point as a sat-on pin.

THIS IS KING FISHER'S ROAD
TAKE THE OTHER

I got down from the rig, still shaking my head, and walked over for a closer study of the sign. Looking at it, I had to grin.

There it was sure enough, the sign which was to become a legend, along with the wild youngster who put it there. How could you help grinning at that kind of brass? Planting a split-board sign in the middle of a public thoroughfare and expecting folks to take it seriously? It was one too many for an old hand like me, and I stepped up to work it loose and throw it aside, still chuckling over the pure gall it had taken to put it there. But that was what fooled so many people about King Fisher. And what made him different. Deadly different. He did have that lighthearted sense of humor and playful good clean fun.

I had no more than put my hands to the sign, than a string of gunshots set in from immediately uproad. The first one took off my hat and knocked it skittering through the air. The following ones kept it going on the same jumpy course. I froze right where I was, hands still on the sign. But I did move my eyes enough to see who was working the artillery.

What I saw would have made a man break his gin bottle.

He was a young fellow, twenty-odd. Tall, dark-skinned, soot-black hair, Mexican handlebar mustache, eyes like obsidian chips, and dressed as no gunman of reputation before him, or since.

Starting at the top he wore a Chihuahua sombrero, snow-white, with a gold Aztec snake for a hatband. Next came a gold-embroidered soft buckskin jacket, a red silk waist-sash and—it's hard to believe even retelling it—chaps made out of Bengal tiger skins! After the chaps, the fact his boots were grass green leather with yellow dragons sewed in eight rows of pale petunia stitching couldn't shine. Neither could his spurs being hung with little silver bells which actually chimed when he walked. Nothing could hope to touch those cat-hair pants, not even the brace of ivory-handled Colts with which he was chasing my hat. But the way he was using those Colts was two other things again. He didn't miss that hat with a one of the twelve shots he threw at it, and he fired right- and left-handed, alternately, from horseback! He jumped that hat around like it was a tin can and him firing a .22 pumpkin roller from the shoulder. And he was only getting started.

When the hat hit the ground following his last shot, the gunman got down off his horse and walked slowly past me. Reaching the fallen hat, he reloaded one shell into his right-hand gun and pointed the gun at the hat. Then, turning away as though he couldn't bear to watch himself do it, he shot that poor wounded hat. Having put it out of its misery, he removed his own sombrero and held it to his chest while he bowed his head in respect. Then he turned to me and said with genuine commisery, "It's done for, poor thing. I'll give it a proper burying for you, mister."

Well, I looked him over and answered back: "Thank you. I reckon you would do as much for me, too, providing I asked for it."

"Let's say, providing you keep on asking for it, Mr. Roebuck," he said with a nice smile.

I looked at him sideways.

"You seem pretty well acquainted with me, friend," I said. "Who are you?"

The young fellow stepped back and looked down at himself as though to see if maybe he had forgotten to put on his pants, or something. But seeing the tiger skin chaps, red silk bellyband and all the rest of it was in place, he glanced back up at me sort of hurt like and said in a most gentle and courteous voice, "Now, Mr. Roebuck, that wasn't too kindly of you. Take another careful look and see if you can't do better. Squint hard, now, it's bound to come to you."

I nodded, more to myself than to him.

I knew who he was all right and he knew that I did. There just weren't that many gunfighters wearing tiger chaps and white Mexican sombreros running loose in West Texas that spring. I was looking at the one and only, the original and no substitute— Mr. J. K. Fisher, of Uvalde.

The latter, waiting politely, said at last,

"Well, Mr. Roebuck?"

"Well, Mr. Fisher," I countered.

He shrugged.

"I'd say it was your move. What would you say?"

"I'd agree."

"What do you aim to do with it?"

"Go buy me a new hat."

He liked that. He broke into his sudden, sunny smile.

"You know, Mr. Roebuck, it's too bad you're working for American Mail. I got an idea we could get along right fine riding for the same side. What you think?"

"I got that idea, too, King," I told him carefully. "Otherwise, I wouldn't have taken on this job of opening up your road for the company."

Now the smile turned frostbit, chilling the voice along with it.

"Nobody's opening up my road, Mr. Roebuck. Not you, not American Mail, not nobody." He frowned in honest dismay, pointing to his sign. "Can't you *read*?"

"Sure," I said quickly. "But can you?"

That worried him. He knew I wasn't getting smart with him, and his frown deepened.

"What you mean?" he said.

For answer I gave him the paper which I had had the Rangers draw up for me.

"Open it up, King," I urged him, "and read it."

He hesitated, wanting to look inside and see what it said. He sensed it was something out of the ordinary, something to do with him and with why I was there for American Mail. But in the end his natural outlaw suspicion was too strong for him. He shoved the paper back at me, shaking his head.

"You read it," he said. "On your way back to San Antone. You'll have lots of time for you're getting started right now."

"Don't be a fool, Fisher," I said, taking the paper. "At least read it—see what it says."

"Mr. Roebuck," he replied, "you get back in that rig and you wheel it around and you light out and don't you slow down till you're shut of Uvalde County, hear?"

"That your final offer, King?"

"It is unless you want to wind up where that other American Mail fellow did."

"You mean Bunker Johnson?"

"Whatever his name was."

"Whatever his name was, eh?" He had said it offhandedly and now caught the anger in my slow repeat of his words. At once his attitude changed.

"Listen, Mr. Roebuck," he said, "there wasn't time for getting any names. I asked this fellow to turn around and go back easy and nice as you can ask a man to do anything. He drew on me, left me no choice."

I shook my head, still seething inside.

"No choice, King?" I asked. "You sure you wanted a choice? I just tried to give you one all wrote up in black and white." I tapped the paper in my hand. "You wouldn't even look at it. No, you didn't want my choice and I don't think you wanted Bunk Johnson's. Now you listen to me, boy, and you listen good. You're going to get another kind of a choice now—from me personally. I'm ordering that stage you shot Bunk Johnson off of sent back through to Uvalde. When she comes, she'll be bringing you that other choice, *sabe*?"

"No *sabe*," he said. "Try it again."

"I'll be on that stage," I told him, "right where Bunk Johnson was."

"Then you'll wind up in the dirt where he did."

"That's the chance I'm taking, King. The one you're taking is something else again."

"Such as?"

"Such as the difference between me and Bunk Johnson."

I had turned and headed for the rig with the statement, but he called softly after me.

"What difference is that, Mr. Roebuck?"

I wheeled on him, flashing the draw. The old Colt bucked and roared to the thunder of five shots blending. King Fisher's white hat jumped off his head and kept right on jumping through the air behind him, exactly as had mine earlier. As it landed in a chaparral thicket, I holstered the .44 Special and said just as quietly as I could.

"That difference, Mr. Fisher. Good day, sir."

I gave him a nod as short as a bobcat's tail and climbed into the rig. Backing the horses, I swung them about, heading them for San Antonio. King Fisher had to jump to avoid being run down. The last I saw of him he was standing in the dust peering off after me and shaking his head as though to say what a damned shame it was American Mail didn't know when it was licked.

Personally, I sort of agreed with him.

That night I spent in Castroville, a cowtown halfway between San Antonio and Uvalde. My idea was to spare myself the extra miles on the stage out of San Antonio next morning, while at the same time hoping to pick up some interim information on the enemy in the Castroville cantinas. I caught a mail rider going east and gave him a note for Captain Randolph and one for Charley Mertens in our San Antonio office requesting that he roll the Uvalde stage as planned, seeing that it picked me up here in Castroville not later than high noon. That done, I waited for midnight, time for the native telegraph to start clicking in from Uvalde and for local tongues to get sloshy enough to repeat what came off the key from King Fisher's town.

I had my news by one A.M.

Word was that another damnfool American Mail agent had collared King and challenged him on his own terms and trade—as a gunfighter. Over in Uvalde the populace was waiting and wagering on the outcome. For American Mail money was mighty scarce. King was swaggering the main stem of his hometown good-naturedly offering to lay ten for one on himself and getting no takers. The synthesis of opinion in Uvalde was that if the Texas Rangers couldn't pin back King Fisher's ears, no mealy-nose American Mail detective was going to do it. As for King, he was telling his fellow Uvaldans that if they wanted to see how fast a four-horse stagecoach could get turned around in the middle of a thirty-foot county road, they need only show up out by his sign late next afternoon. Last I heard, going to bed, was that Uvalde was planning to take King up on his invitation, whole-sale. It figured to be the biggest turnout in West Texas since Captain Jack Coffee Hays whipped the Mexicans at Salado.

Next morning the stage rolled in Castroville at 11:36 A.M. After a twenty-minute rest to water the teams, I took over on the box, relieving the regular driver. I noticed that on my way out of town several of the locals took off their hats and held them to their left breasts as I passed by. It gave me a nice feeling to know I wasn't without friends, even though a stranger.

I wasn't fooling myself any about King Fisher, however. His hand wasn't going to be holding a hat. But where I wasn't fooling myself about him, I was hoping I had fooled him about me. I had led him to think he had me in the same corner he had old Bunk Johnson, making me come at him with a gun in my hand.

Yet I had no intention of playing the game to those rules. A man doesn't get old in this business giving away advantages to young gunfighters. I didn't mean to give one ounce of edge to King Fisher. All's fair in love and war, I figured, and what young King and I had to settle between us wasn't precisely a love affair. And I didn't let my conscience slow me up any, either. I wasn't five minutes off regular schedule—four P.M.—rounding that mesquite bend just shy of King's sign.

Well, I don't think Grant got a bigger cheer for taking Vicksburg than I did for taking that last turn on two wheels. That crowd was happier to see me than Sitting Bull was to see Custer, and for the same reasons. Still a man had to admit it was a thrill seeing that many good folks collected in one piece so far out in the sagebrush, and in such a high, fine humor, too.

The atmosphere at that road sign of King Fisher's was that of a small-time Manassas. As the citizens of our national Capital turned out to watch the boys in blue rout Johnny Reb at the Battle of Bull Run, so the voting populace of Uvalde had come along to watch King Fisher and the American Mail detective shoot it out. I could tell with one look, coming around that bend, that I was being given less chance than Lee at Cemetery Ridge. That piebald collection of saddle horses, buggies, buckboards, surreys, Studebakers and Conestogas coagulated there in the boondocks was one hundred and ten percent in favor of their man. When they sighted me down the road and let out that yell, I don't think you could have sold a chance on American Mail for six hundred dollars, Union.

And King didn't keep them waiting.

Mounting up immediately, he swung his flashy paint into a high lope, skidded him up, short, ten feet the Uvalde side of his sign. On my side of the sign, maybe fifty feet—no, closer to seventy—I was doing the same with my four-horse hitch and big old highside Abbott & Downing coach. It got that quiet you couldn't hear a baby cry nor an old man hawk to spit. I mean that multitude didn't let out a peep.

In the stillness, King slid from his saddle, stepped clear of his horse. I wrapped my lines, set the brake, eased down off the driver's box, moved out to one side of the coach. There we were, the two champions, one of the law and the other of disorder, come to a halt facing each other at a distance of maybe sixty feet—just a deliberate shade outside good gunfighting range.

The crowd sucked in and took a tighter hold on its breath. All eyes were on King Fisher and he knew it. He took one step toward me and spoke up frosty.

"All right, Mr. Roebuck, let's start the walk-up. You make it as close as you want. Cut loose when you're ready."

He started toward me again but I held up both hands real quick.

"Hold it, King," I said, "That's close enough."

He grinned and made a little box.

"Age before youth and beauty, Mr. Roebuck. Make your move."

I returned the grin as best I could.

"I'm going to, King," I told him, "but not the way you think."

His grin was well gone now.

"Pull your gun, Mr. Roebuck—"

I shook my head, still holding up my hands.

"The only thing I'm going to pull, King, is the buckle on my gun belt. You shoot me while I'm doing that and you got a whole townful of readymade witnesses right behind you."

"Yeah," he said, "but you're forgetting one thing, Mr. Roebuck. They're friendly witnesses."

"All right," I answered him, "let's try it this way: you cut down on me while I'm dropping my buscadero rig and you'll get your own belt punched six extra holes before your gun clears leather. You don't believe it, *you* take a look behind *me*. Maybe you can't read but you can damn sure count. So count."

The crowd got pin-still as King looked past me to the stagecoach. I saw his eyes go wide, and knew why.

The old Abbott & Downing had sprouted rifle-snouts. She was bristling steel barrels like a stirred-up quill pig. From beneath the canvas luggage cover of the roof decking two hard-looking riflemen held their Winchesters on a line with King Fisher's belt buckle. From the two forward and two rear window curtains of each side, below, peered four more earnest marksmen, their carbines pinned to the same target. Their total number was six, their reputations certain, their identity undeniable. They were the gentlemen in the white hats—the Texas Rangers.

King Fisher gave them, and me, a look of black disgust. He showed no fear of the Rangers but did include an expression of great disappointment in Harry Roebuck.

"It's a pretty lowdown trick, Mr. Roebuck," he said. "But what does it prove?"

"It proves you've got a lot to learn about life, King," I told him. "And, personally, I think you're man enough to learn your first lesson right here."

"What have you got to teach me, Mr. Roebuck? How to be a liar like you?"

"I didn't lie to you, boy," I said. "But maybe you did to me."

"Now what you mean by that?"

"I said I'd come back alone on the driver's box of that stage, just like Bunk Johnson came. I did it."

"Yeah, with six Rangers hid out behind your back!"

"Well, King, it looks like you brought along a few friends too."

"It isn't the same. You know it isn't. You lied to me, Mr. Roebuck."

I looked him in the eye, answering quietly.

"Well, boy, if I didn't keep my word, let's see if you can keep yours."

I unbuckled my gun belt and let it slide to the ground. The crowd from Uvalde pulled in behind King, the Rangers got out of the stage and moved up behind me. I armed out of my coat, started unbuttoning my shirt.

"You said," I went on, "that if I came back on that driver's box where Bunk Johnson was, you would put me right where you put him, in the dirt of this road."

I dropped my shirt and my voice with it.

"Let's see you do it, King. Like a man, without your guns."

He studied me through the longest five seconds on record, then slipped off his gun belt, slid his vaquero shirt off his head and put up his hands. Soundlessly, under that hot Texas sun, we began circling.

What followed was the wildest bare-knuckle fight ever staged south of Chicago, with the six referees wearing white hats and Winchesters and the audience all armed and ready to cut loose with anything from a .22 derringer to a sawed-off shotgun if it didn't like the decision. But it would be unkind to detail that battle. King Fisher didn't have a chance. I beat him very nearly blind and when it was all over he was down in the dirt and all done. I was about as bad off but I was still on my feet. The cheering of the crowd had fallen off as though somebody had stuck its collective head in a bucket of swamp water. The Rangers moved silently in on King Fisher and the folks from his hometown moved silently away from him. Within five minutes the last of them was started back toward Uvalde. Groggily, King watched them go, leaving him alone with his enemies, a chastened, humbled man. When two of the Rangers had helped him to his feet, he turned to me.

"Well, Mr. Roebuck," he acknowledged unhappily, "it looks as though you were right. Your word is better than mine. What is the next stage of the ambush? Back to San Antone with the Rangers?"

I shook my head soberly.

"No, King, the Rangers didn't come along to arrest you. They were just here to see we had a fair fight and to make sure, to their own satisfaction, that you couldn't read. I told them you acted like you couldn't, but I reckon they'd feel better about it if you showed them your ownself. Here."

I handed him the same paper I had tried to get him to read before, and this time he took it. After a puzzled look at all of us, he unfolded it and began frowning his way through what it said. Pretty quick, he looked back up.

"Why, I don't believe it," he said. "This here is a deputy sheriff's appointment for Uvalde County in my name. It's writ right there, 'J. K. Fisher,' plain as fresh paint."

"That's right, King." I smiled. "She's all yours, courtesy of the Texas Rangers. You see, they agreed with me that you'd make a better live deputy than a dead outlaw. They got Governor Marvin to go along with them on my idea and he added one of his own. There's a full executive amnesty from the state of Texas goes with that star Captain Randolph, yonder, is fishing out of his vest pocket."

I bobbed my head toward the Ranger captain standing off to our left. King looked over at him and Randolph stepped toward him holding out the emblem. King kind of straightened up.

"I guess that makes it my move, don't it?" he said.

"I'd say it did," I replied. "What you aim to do with it?"

He looked at me dead serious and said, "Same thing you did when I asked you that question, Mr. Roebuck."

I returned his look, puzzled.

"How's that, King?" I said.

"Go get me a new hat." He grinned. "Care to come along?"

"Oh, I dunno. What kind you going to get?" I played it sober-sided now but it didn't slow him a wink.

"Well, something appropriate to my new standing in the community, I should think," he said. He moved to Randolph and took the star from him, pinning it carelessly upside down on his Mexican shirt, which he had gotten back into while we talked. Then, easing back over to me, he went on as though nothing had interrupted his statement. "Whatever kind of a hat they're recommending for wet-eared deputy sheriffs in West Texas this spring."

I had to hand him back his grin now, and something else as well. Reaching down, I got his gun belt out of the road and reached it over to him.

"Hang it on, Sheriff," I said. "I got an American Mail Company passenger run needs guarding into Uvalde."

King belted on his gun and, while I was getting into my shirt, picked mine up from the dirt and handed it to me with a bow and a sweep of his arm toward the coach.

"After you, sir—"

Straightening up he put his hand over his heart.

"The welfare of American Mail is the civic responsibility of every decent law-abiding resident of Uvalde County. I am deeply affected by this opportunity to make sure the sons of bitches understand it."

He watched me pass him by, headed for the stage, then gave his gun belt a determined hitch and started after me. The Rangers caught up his horse, tied him to the luggage boot, climbed aboard and waved the "all set" sign. I swung up to the box, followed by King Fisher. Reaching under the seat, King pulled out the regular guard's shotgun, barred it across his knees.

"All right," he said, "let's go."

I whistled up the teams. Slapping them smartly with the lines, I kicked off the brake and yelled, "Hee-yahh! Hee-yahh!" They hit into their collars and the stage began to roll. The minute it did, King made an excited motion toward the road in front of us and hollered out, "Hold on!"

I slammed the brakes back on and hauled up the teams. King jumped down and ran off up the road. Pretty soon he was back lugging his uprooted sign. Climbing back up with me, he stowed it under the roof-deck tarp, picked the shotgun up again and nodded to me.

"You never can tell, Mr. Roebuck. I might want to go back in business for myself someday."

I gave him the eye, shook up the teams, got the coach to rolling again. Half an hour later she was parked in front of American Mail's new office in Uvalde and the adventure of King Fisher's road was closed.

As for King, he did go back in business for himself some years later, and was killed in an ambush with Ben Thompson in the Vaudeville, a theater-saloon in San Antonio, in March of 1884.

They say King Fisher never had a chance, but I know better. I gave him one and it was a good one. Yet he didn't end any different from all the other wild guns before and after him. When the bullet with his name on it came along, he was there.

In the fifties and early sixties, Will C. Brown (C.S. Boyles) wrote as admirably of the frontier years in his home state as any author then producing popular Western fiction. Testimony to this fact is "Red Sand," a first-rate story of the Caprock country at the end of the Civil War, as well as such novels as The Border Jumpers *(1955), the paperback edition of which was voted Dell's best Western novel of the year, and* The Nameless Breed *(1960), which was the recipient of a WWA Best Novel Spur.*

Red Sand

★★★★★★★★★★★★★★

Will C. Brown

WHEN the late northers hit with early spring on the red Caprock land in time of drought, the country violently came apart and as much parched soil seemed to be in the air as on the earth. All the maverick vastness then dissolved into a surging ink dust that covered every living thing almost to strangulation. Red sand whipped men's faces and clogged their eyes and nostrils. The wind, the constant, yammering wind, battered the walls of lonely nester houses, and pried into every crevice to lay its gritty hand. And if a man was weak, not made for it, the red grit could grind itself into his reason, as well as into his clothes, his teeth, and his bed.

A couple named Whitlock—Adam Whitlock and his young wife, Martha—were in their second year of Caprock homesteading. A week before the sandstorm struck, Adam rode away with a Nine-Bar herd that was bound north to Kansas. He told Martha he had hired as a rider as far as the Red River, and would make the wage of a trail hand for seven days. At the river, he would draw his pay and strike back for home. The fifteen dollars, federal, was important money.

It was five days later when a rider came to the Whitlock house

153

in the dust-laden early morning, just as the sandstorm was settling down to blow. When Martha came out, he took off his hat,
despite the wind. He stayed on his horse and she stood on the
porch, the wind tilting her small figure, and they talked until he
replaced his hat and rode away on the Sweetwater trail.

All this was visible to the two men who had lain in the wind
and strangling dust since daylight, watching from the brush for
sign of life in the clearing below. They saw the rider when he
came to the house, saw the woman on the porch—just a dot of
blowing dress at that distance—and finally, saw the rider head
west, leaving the woman standing alone on the porch.

One of the hidden watchers was post-oak straight and youth-
fully muscled, with a hard glint of humor showing in the shrewd,
thoughtful depths of his eyes. The older man was all the ele-
mental roughness of the land shaped into one shaggy human.
He held his right arm bent to nurse the throb of a three-day-old
bullet crease, and his good hand was never long removed from
the worn strap of a small black saddle bag. One horse, drooped
and still saddled, was staked in a shielding mesquite thicket
behind them.

The older man, as they watched the thin curl of smoke shatter
in the gale as it cleared the nester chimney, groaned heavily.

"I'm starved! Let's hit it!"

"Not yet. In a little while, now. You never attack until you
know the terrain and the enemy's strength."

Brazos, with his lean back turned against the sand, looked at
the heavy man sprawled beside him in the cedars. His eyes, deep
blue and old in a young face, made a contemplative study of his
companion. This put the trace of a tight smile at his dust-caked
mouth corners. He was speculating whether Tanner would favor
a sick buffalo less if his matted hair was clipped from his ears
and low forehead.

"Arm feels like it's coming off," Tanner said for the tenth
time since midnight.

"I saw a lot of arms come off," Brazos said above the wind
noise. "Those Yankees put poison on their bullets I always
heard. You suppose you could buy a new right arm, Tanner,
with all that yellow currency?"

Tanner looked bleakly at Brazos. He spat red and the wind
tossed new sand into his mouth.

At mid-day they came out of the brush on the low knoll and

hurried, jogging, toward the house, bodies bent against the sandstorm.

They did not knock. Tanner opened the door with his bum arm and his gun ready.

Brazos crowded in behind him. Everything in the room reacted with a shudder to the wind blast and inrushing sand.

Brazos kicked the door closed with his boot heel. He saw nothing in the room but the woman standing beside the stove with a white hand pressed to her throat.

The two men were coated with red dirt that left only slits for their eyes and mouths. Tanner's voice sounded in a dry rattle.

"Where's your man?"

She did not speak, but only stared at them. Tanner stalked to her. He grabbed her wrist.

"Any men around here? Speak up!"

Her fear had only been late in coming. It spread, now, a shadow sweeping her face, the special dread of a woman alone.

She shook her head, straining back from Tanner's grasp.

"You think she's lyin'? What you think, Brazos?"

Brazos thought she was only scared to death. She was too young, too white of face, too clean and new for the country in that ironed gingham. He couldn't figure her in this God-forgotten nester house. A region more considerate than the Texas Caprock had shaped her face and put the intelligence into her dark brown eyes. She was almost too proud to be scared, but she was scared, just the same. He continued to look at her while he slapped some of the dust out of his hat.

Young. Pretty as a seashell. Lips beginning to tremble a little now.

She had turned to him, away from Tanner. Their eyes met.

"No men, Tanner." He watched her closely. "No horses in the pen. One plate, one cup, one knife and fork on the table. Make yourself at home."

He moved about nervously, now that the first tension of the break-in was over. It might have been a nester with five grown sons in the shack. If they had known it was like this, they could have come in out of the sandstorm hours ago.

Martha Whitlock stared at the place on her wrist where Tanner's heavy hand had held her.

"What do you want?" She spoke with a dignity too contrived. "My husband will be here in a little while. Just any minute, now. He's—he went—"

"He ought to stay at home." Brazos wiped his face with a sleeve. "What could he possibly ride away to that would offset what he rode away *from*?"

Tanner was squirming out of his coat with awkward movement of wounded arm. Brazos strode to the bed in the corner by the door. He sat, testing his weight to the springs.

"He was a fool to leave this."

The wind howled an ascending series of high shrieks and the whole house vibrated.

"Watch her!" Tanner growled. "You better take a look out the windows, too."

Brazos leaned back, pulling his holster and gun around out of the way, and lifted his worn boots to stretch full length on the clean patch quilt. He grinned tightly at the woman at the stove, his muscles breaking the dirt caulking of face lines.

He saw her eyes shift, and followed her glance downward to the red splotches of dirt his boots made on the quilt.

"That's blood. The Caprock's bleeding to death. . . . You got something cooking there? *Frijoles?*"

Tanner mumbled, "You got any beef to go with 'em? We're starved." He kept peering nervously about the room as if he expected to sight steel traps set at every piece of furniture. The furniture was scanty and cheap, the floor bare, but other than the gritty pink sand layers, everything was clean and orderly. A good housekeeper, Brazos thought. But why not—what else would there be for her to do? He sucked in the smell from the bean kettle, clear down to his famished stomach.

Tanner said, "Lady, I asked you, you got any beef to go with those beans?"

She shook her head. The wind's howling almost drowned out her words.

"Just cornbread."

Brazos was drowsy. Tanner, he thought, looked feverish. Three days on the run. Only three? Well, they had done a right fair job of dodging. Then that howling sandstorm! But if it hadn't been the wind, and Tanner, it would have been a dull ride. Why would the Federals want to occupy a state that blew right out from under you? Looked like whoever won Texas was the one who had lost the war.

He would have to work on Tanner's arm. Tanner dead on his hands from blood poisoning would be more trouble than Tanner alive. *God!*—Imagine trying to shovel out a hole in this blow, deep enough to bury a man in.

"She might have a hired hand," Tanner grumbled. "I ain't satisfied. Go look around the barn."

"And leave this?" Brazos propped the pillow under his head. "How long till the beans and cornbread are done?"

He caught the movement of her eyes. He turned quickly. The small closet in the corner was hung with a long burlap drape.

"Look in the closet, Tanner, behind the burlap, and unload the family .30-30."

As Tanner lumbered across the floor, she met Brazos's shrewd gaze and he saw her face slowly color. Her lips pulled tight.

Brazos laughed. There were sounds of Tanner working the rifle lever.

He swung his boots to the floor and stood tall to face her.

"Madam, we've been in the weather a bit. As you might guess by looking at us. We need food and sleep. That's all we want. We'd be mighty grateful if you would oblige us with your hospitality."

"I want my arm doctored." Tanner was drinking in the girl. "Then I'll feel better."

Brazos turned back. Carefully, he brushed at the red sand circles his boots had left on the quilt.

"You got some hot water and ointment?" he asked. "Some worm salve, maybe?"

She said, "If he's hurt, I'll find something to doctor him with."

Brazos walked close to her, until the frightened eyes were only a few inches away.

"Your husband's gone for quite a spell, hasn't he?"

Her face showed the truth, and he laughed shortly.

"Just don't try anything reckless. We're fed up with brave people. We've gone too far to let a little woman like you, a nice, sensible. . . ." He stopped. He had to pull his glance away from the eyes that held so much anxiety and fear of him.

"Please—I'll doctor him. I'll give you some food. Then—please just go away."

Tanner was trying to examine his arm, puffing from the exertion. Brazos untied the wad of bandana. Tanner grunted and flinched as the crusted old blood pulled loose. The wound was a purplish streak across the fat above his elbow. Fresh blood dots seeped through the crust.

"I think it's all right, Tanner. Put the damn stuff down. You afraid it's going to run away?"

Brazos took the little saddle bag from Tanner's good hand and scooted it across the floor to the wall.

The woman came over with a washed flour sack.

"Hot water." Brazos tore the cloth into strips. He nodded toward the canvas bag. "That's the Bristow Bank, in new quarters. Maybe you better walk wide around it. My friend here's a little touchy about it."

He worked at Tanner's arm, bathing the wound with carbolic water, and then rubbing it with the ointment. She handled the water kettle and medicine, as he called for them.

"Now hold it there, while I tie."

She put her fingers gingerly on the bandage. Brazos's hand rested briefly on hers as he tied, and in the moment of contact her eyes raised to him, and his fingers fumbled. They both cut the glance apart, and he finished and stepped back.

"A nice Irish pennant I tied on you, Tanner. . . . But nobody will see it."

He smiled at the woman. "I don't believe we've been introduced. My name's Brazos and that's the truth. A river was named for me. This *jabalina*, he's Tanner."

She said stiffly, "Mrs. Whitlock—Martha Whitlock."

"You're a long way from home. That talk—where's it from? Louisiana? South Texas?"

"Yes. Matagorda Bay."

The way she said it, the tone, made him think that she must be right proud to be from Matagorda Bay. He looked at her again, with new interest. Small world—unless you had to ride through it in a sandstorm.

"You hear that, Tanner? She's seen big water, miles of water, bigger than the Caprock, and no sand blowing. Clean white sand on the beach, but no red sand blowing in your face. Everything good and wet. The only part of Texas that's got all the water it needs."

He took the rest of the cloth, went to the wash bench in the corner, and opened shirt collar and sleeves.

"Now everything's happened to you, Mrs. Whitlock, hasn't it?" He talked as he scrubbed. "You live on the Caprock where there's sand but no ocean, married to a homesteading husband who goes off somewhere, leaving you alone, and you got me and Tanner for company. By gaddly, wouldn't Matagorda Bay look good *now*!"

He plastered his hair down and combed it with her comb. She was at the stove, stirring the *frijole* pot.

Tanner was sprawled in the one rocking chair, watching her through his burning little eyes, his mouth a dark open hole in the whiskers.

Brazos spoke shortly, "Tanner!"

The shaggy head, like a drowsy buffalo, reluctantly pulled around to Brazos. Tanner stopped rocking and closed his mouth.

Brazos jerked a thumb toward the wash basin.

"Soap and water. Use it—you got one good arm. If I got to bury you I want you washed first."

Tanner growled something. He stood up and dragged seamsplit boots over to the bench. He passed near the woman at the stove. Martha Whitlock drew back from him and Tanner's jaw worked in his whiskers.

Then Tanner turned heavily and stared belligerently at Brazos. The wind momentarily suspended its battering, leaving the three of them frozen in an alien quietness.

"I'm still runnin' this!" Tanner growled. "Don't try to boss me so much. You're too damn smart!"

The strain was unraveling now.

"All right! You're running it. Who was running it when they had you cornered, with your horse played out and that arm losing blood! Why didn't you tell me you were running it then, and I'd have gone on my way?"

"I'm givin' you half!" Tanner snarled. He looked at the saddle bag. "I'm payin' you, all right. Just don't try to run everything."

Brazos turned his back and went to the window. He peered hard out, over the dust-laden range, seeing no sign of life, no movement but the sand gusts and the mesquites bending to the wind. The rounded knoll of brush where he and Tanner had hidden was almost lost in the pinkish fog. In that dust, a posse would break right on top of them without being sighted until it was too late to run.

He had never figured a woman like her. Her mouth looked like she was about to laugh while her eyes looked like she was about to cry. Matagorda Bay. Good wet spume in the breakers, and a salty mist in the air of mornings, and always the lacy wavelets slapping soft white sand that stayed where it was meant to stay and didn't get thrown into your eyes by the handfuls.

The posse could break right in on them. But how would the chase know to come toward this needle in a haystack? Unless they were better trackers than they had any right to be, they'd still be stumbling around in Bird's Nest Canyon, hunting sign on that rocky floor. That was three days away. Well, he and Tanner had come as far as they could go. One horse between them, and it played out. One or the other walking half the time—mostly Brazos walking, with Tanner the shape he was in.

The nester house, with the man gone—this was where they had to get second wind, and it was perfect. He smiled inside, sourly, because it was something, the way he had helped Tanner get away from those federals. They had to eat the same sand he and Tanner had eaten. It was just as slow going for them as it was for Tanner and him.

Tanner, crude and ugly as he was, had given him a means to keep fighting them. Maybe it was just what he wanted, meeting up with Tanner. Tanner had some ideas, some good plans. He would take Brazos in with him, and if they had any luck at all, one day they would be rich. Like Tanner had said, Bristow wasn't the only bank, and that stuff in the saddle bag wasn't the only federal payroll.

He whirled at the sound behind him, but she was only putting a stick of split mesquite into the stove. She took a cloth and opened the oven door. He smelled the hot fragrance of corn-bread.

Tanner was back in the rocker, watching her.

She smoothed a wisp of hair from her face. There were three enameled plates on the table now, three knives and three forks.

She put the beans and bread on the table.

Brazos' mouth pulled tight. How in hell did they *live*? He looked at her, almost angrily.

"When my husband comes back," she said, as if defending herself from what Brazos was thinking, "we'll buy what we need."

"He could have killed a beef!" Tanner complained.

"How far's that settlement to the west?" Brazos asked her, an idea forming.

"Sweetwater's about an hour, in the wagon. We—the store doesn't have much."

Including no credit for nesters, Brazos guessed silently.

He and Tanner ate wolfishly. The *frijoles* with the meager trace of salt pork, and the cornbread, quickly vanished. Disclaiming hunger, Martha Whitlock did not eat with them, and worked silently at the kitchen counter.

Tanner wiped a hand across his mouth and mumbled, "I could have et three times that."

"We'll eat better than this tonight!"

"Where?" Tanner demanded, instantly suspicious.

Brazos asked abruptly. "How does the arm feel? Can you sleep, now?"

"I could sleep a week."

"Listen. I figure we're safe through tonight, maybe another day. Even if they picked up our trail at Bitter Creek. But how they going to travel through that stuff out there? They don't want you that bad, Tanner."

"You don't take no chances in this business. Don't ever figure the other side's not smart as you are and you'll live to spend your money."

But the idea had formed stubbornly in Brazos's mind. He said bluntly, "Anyhow, I'm going in to that settlement store. We've got to have grub. I'm going after it."

Tanner snarled. "You crazy?"

"I can go in there and be back in two-three hours," Brazos argued. "There's a wagon out there. Damn it, we got to have rations, to keep going. Way I figure it, this'll be our best chance. You want to hit that trail again with nothing but *frijoles* and corn meal?"

"I want to hit it as a live man and not a corpse."

"Well, I don't. I'd just as soon be shot as starve to death. I'm going to forage that settlement and stock up."

"You'll have the law on our backs, they see you in there. You ain't goin'!"

"Listen, it's just a little town! We sighted it. Probably they don't even have a law man. This country's starved out, nobody around. Probably nobody but the store man will even see me."

Tanner pondered that. In a few moments, as Brazos watched,

Tanner shifted his gaze from the table top to Martha Whitlock, now washing the plates, her back to them.

"All right." Tanner's tone changed. "You have a try at it."

"I'll make it, don't you worry!" Brazos stood up and took his hat from the bed. "I'll go get the horse and bring him down to the pen. Maybe they got some feed. They got two mules out there—I'll hitch to that wagon and be back by sundown."

Martha Whitlock was facing them. From her expression, Brazos knew she had heard their talk, even with the wind yammering against the walls. Her eyes had widened and she looked at Brazos with an anxious message but he failed to understand it.

"I'm going to borrow your wagon and team, Mrs. Whitlock. You get ready to cook tonight!"

He walked over to the saddle bag. Squatting on his heels, he looked around at Tanner, then opened the bag.

"I got to have some of this stuff."

At first he thought Tanner did not hear. Tanner was drowsily slumped in the chair at the table, but his reddish eyes worked on the woman. He spoke without turning. "Get what you need, Brazos. You go ahead to town."

Digging into the bag, Brazos took out a thick package of currency, flipped quickly through it, and thrust a sheaf of the bills into his coat. He stood, set his hat, hitched up gunbelt, and his hard bootheels clomped over to the door. He pulled a bandana from pocket and tied it about his face to keep some of the sand out of his nose.

Then he stopped. His sleep-dulled senses tried to tell him that they were not thinking this out very well. It was the trail tiredness, the awful sleepiness, and those miles of hard travel since Bird's Nest and Bitter Creek.

"Tanner, now listen. I'll be back by dark. If anything happens, in town, and I don't show up—you better get out of here by midnight. Take the horse and get as far as you can and hole up. We'll meet—" He glanced at the woman. "You know where we said—if we got separated."

He did not catch Tanner's growled reply because Martha Whitlock hurried wide around Tanner's chair. She placed a hand imploringly on Brazos's arm.

"I'm going with you!"

He felt her fingers dig into his sleeve. The dark eyes were pleading.

"Please—don't leave me here!"

With the back of his mind he heard the wind moaning like a hundred dying animals, and with the front of it he dully soaked in the new trouble.

He looked at her, undecided, seeing her fear, then slowly turned to look at Tanner.

The fever, of one kind or another, burned in Tanner's head, showing like pinpoints of live coals in his dogged stare.

Then Tanner was on his feet, lumbering over to them at the door.

He shot out a hairy fist, catching her wrist, and pulled roughly.

"She stays here! Damn it—we can't risk *her* goin' in to that store!"

She tried to pull free. Tanner laughed harshly and jerked at her arm, almost throwing her off her feet. Her back was to the bed, and Tanner suddenly released his grip, slapped his open palm against her bosom and shoved. With a startled cry she tumbled backward, sprawling on the bed with feet flying up, wildly fighting her skirts down with her hands.

Brazos sprang to the corner and grabbed up a stick of stove wood, intending to club Tanner. Tension, hunger and the hours of battling the storm, all rolled up into his brain, to explode in wild and murderous intent.

Tanner retreated, head lowered, hand on gun-butt, backing off from Brazos.

The wind screamed in maniacal frenzy.

After a long moment in which he and Tanner stared at each other in malevolence, he shifted his glance to see her sitting rigidly, hands to her face.

He threw the stove wood into the corner.

"If you can sit that wagon seat two hours in the wind, get your coat on. Tie something over your face."

She rushed quickly to reach into the closet. Tanner plowed the back of his hand across his mouth. He dragged over to the rocker.

"Don't get sore, Brazos."

"All right." He opened the door a crack and the wind flung sand into his eyes. "If a neighbor or somebody happens along, make up some kind of story."

Martha squeezed past him, and outside.

He slammed the door. She crowded beside him, the wind whipping her long thin coat of faded brown, and the sand immediately coated the gray wool shawl' wrapped about her face and head.

"First we got to bring my horse down here," he said, raising his voice above the wind howl. He pointed toward the brushy mound. "You want to wait at the barn?"

"I'll go with you!"

She was enough afraid of Tanner to make the long walk. Well, it was up to her. He could lead the horse back to the pen, with her in the saddle. Then he would hitch those two scrub mules to the sway-back wagon and head for Sweetwater.

He slowed his stride when he noticed how she had to trot to stay up with him. Talking was too much effort. The sand almost forced his eyes to stay closed. He guessed it almost blinded his mind, too—the way he was taking extra trouble like this. A wounded bank robber on his hands would have been plenty, without a woman, a young nester wife.

He searched back in his mind, wondering whether he had ever known a girl like her before. He laughed to himself, under the sandy taste of bandana covering, thinking of how the fair skin behind that old shawl had once felt the sea spray and misty damp air of Matagorda Bay, where the sand stayed on the beach, soaked down twice in twenty-four hours by the good blue-white tide. . . .

2

THE first two miles on the high dry flat, where the wind really went to work with a vengeance, was the Caprock's special brand of torture. Brazos had a mind to turn back, doubting that either man or mules could last out an hour of it.

Only the hunger, and the stubbornness of not wanting to give in while the woman was not audibly complaining, kept him fighting the mules. He held the wagon to the dim sign of old ruts when he was all but blinded, and cursed the cutting slashes of the sand. Cold gusts tore up his words.

Conversation was too much trouble, even if he had wanted to talk to her. His mind was dulled from sleeplessness, his thoughts working numbly on what might lay ahead of him in the settlement.

One word from the woman, maybe just one sign behind his back, could be his downfall in that town. He admitted that he was crazy to be going in, and crazier to be taking her.

His big mistake had been the cocksure idea that he could go to the settlement, spend some of that pretty money of Tanner's, and get away with it. Damnation—a tramp looking like he did, with that much money on him in the middle of a drought in the starved-out Caprock, would be cause enough for suspicion. Much less having a nester's good-looking wife along. And what if the posse was still on their trail? Chances were, if they got this far, they would angle off when they sighted the settlement, to get out of the weather and pick up some grub, same as he was doing.

That would be trouble by the barrel full—to walk into the posse, maybe right in the middle of the store!

Good afternoon, you yellow-bellied Yankee sons—looks like we all decided to do our shopping at the same time, eh?

That struck him as funny in a sour way, and he grinned thinly under the flapping handkerchief. It must have done something bad to his eyes, however, for he noticed her sidewise glance at him pull back. She huddled tight to her edge of the tossing wagon seat.

After two miles the wagon trail, as if seeking cover, unexpectedly angled south. Then he saw that it would skirt a high brushy shelf. There the wind was staved off by a sandstone cliff that stretched ahead for considerable distance, with its upper ridge fringed by the gaunt straining forms of cedars, like a procession of twisted old men.

Now he could open his eyes without feeling shotgun pellets blasting into them. The mules quit fighting the lines and settled to a smoother gait. The wagon jolted and rattled over the rocky floor of the shallow canyon, jostling together the two of them on the seat, one small and huddled, the other erect and watchful.

For the first time, Martha Whitlock looked squarely at him as she pulled the wool shawl back from her lips.

"Thank you." she said stiffly, "for letting me come in with you."

"I reckon I owed you that." He tugged the bandana down

under his chin. "Now listen—you going to make trouble when we get there?"

"Trouble?"

He shot a look at her so hard that she recoiled.

She looked surprised, honestly surprised—or else she knew how to play innocent. He tried to see into the back of her head, to see what notions she might have there about what she would do when they got to the store.

"I reckon you bothered Tanner. Maybe he's not exactly accustomed to running up on somebody that—well, somebody that looks like you. So now I've made Tanner sore, and as soon as you get to this village you think you're going to start yelling that I'm a bank robber or something. Well, don't do it."

"I'm not going to start yelling," she said quietly.

"Why not?" he demanded. "You'd like to see them capture us, wouldn't you? You got an idea what we are, don't you?"

"I—I guess you're bad men. I know that. You stole some money, and the other man—somebody shot him. You're running away, and you had to go somewhere to get out of the sandstorm and eat, and you broke into my house."

"Yeah. Exactly. And you don't want to go back there, so you'll fix us up proper when we get in here? Is that what you're thinking? Well—let me tell you right now, if you want to see somebody get killed, you just start blabbing."

She was silent, and he added viciously, "I ought to turn around right now and take you back. Tanner thinks he's quite a lady's man."

"I'm not going to do anything!" she said pleadingly. "I don't want to see anybody get shot. I won't say a word."

"How do I know that?"

"Because you brought me. I'm not afraid with you, like with *him*! I promise—I asked to come with you, so I guess that's like giving my word I wouldn't make trouble."

She said it like she meant it, and he supposed he was not in his right senses for believing her. But somehow he did, and he jogged up the mules, feeling better.

He said, more to himself than to her, "If somebody had told me a month ago that I'd ever be here, teamed up with a bad man and loaded with money and driving into a strange town with a pretty woman, maybe about to get shot or locked up in the next hour—"

When his voice trailed off, she asked timidly, "Why do you do this? You don't *look* like that other man, you don't *have* to be afraid of getting shot everywhere you go. . . ."

"That is such a long story," Brazos drawled, "that it would take seventeen trips like this to tell you." His grin went off and he frowned hard at her. "Can you think of anything better to do in this dried-up state of Texas? Maybe crawl like a dog around the carpetbagging occupation crowd and pick up the bread crusts they drop? Or maybe I should homestead here on the Caprock and starve lawfully. Not for all the sand on Matagorda beach— not for me!"

She said quickly, "You know Matagorda? You mentioned that before."

"Yeah," he said glumly, slapping the lines hard against the mulehides. "I used to know it. A little."

"When was that?" She spoke with lively interest, bending closer to speak and to hear him. "That was my home. Maybe—"

"You wouldn't have known me," Brazos retorted. He didn't want any more conversation on that. "I was a little kid, and it was a long time ago. . . . How much farther is this blasted place, anyway?"

The canyon road was lifting out, back to the upper flats with its dust-hazy distance of mesquites and cedars broken occasionally by sandstone ridges and shallow gullies.

"It isn't far, two more miles, maybe. Over there."

Soon he could see the windmill, then the drab cluster of frame structures that was Sweetwater. The sun made a pinkish blob half-way down the invisible sky.

There was not much to the place. Just the big frame store building and its windmill and a half-dozen or so houses. He saw with satisfaction that there were no horses at the store, not a living thing in sight.

He caught her arm as she was about to alight from the wagon. "We may have to make up a story in there. How well do they know you? Would they know if you had a brother?"

"I guess not. Yes, I'd like to say you were my brother. It would be better."

He saw color tinge her white face. He hadn't thought of that before. She would want something to say in there, where they knew her. She couldn't just come riding in with a strange man,

with her husband away, and with the strange man flashing a lot
of money around.

"Well, you just keep quiet. You listen to what I say, then you
back me up. I'm taking your word that you won't make any
trouble."

She was off the wagon seat and to the ground before he could
come around and assist her. She walked by his side up the steps,
and stood while he opened the door for her.

He followed closely, with his hand ready at his gun holster.
He looked quickly over her shoulder, taking in the store, feeling
a cold emptiness in his middle.

There were no customers. An old man with fingers laced on
his vest was dozing at the big stove where a skinny yellow cat
napped at his high-laced shoes.

The man got to his feet and peered without pleasure at Brazos,
then at Mrs. Whitlock.

"We want to buy a few groceries."

The gray mustaches waggled and the dim eyes went from one
to the other, suspiciously.

"What with?"

"Money!" Brazos snapped. "And we're in a hurry."

"You got money, you can buy."

The old man looked puzzledly over his specs, from one to
the other, as if trying to clarify their connection. He said gruffly,
"No credit, Mrs. Whitlock. You know that."

"As soon as Adam comes back, Mr. Jensen," she murmured, "we'll try to—"

Brazos heard the painful humiliation in her voice. He said
testily, "How much is the Whitlock bill?"

She put her hand out quickly in a gesture of protest.

"No, I don't want you—"

"Sixty-five dollars and twenty cents," Mr. Jensen said with
crusty emphasis. "And it's over four months old."

Brazos fished out the fold of federal treasury notes. Just the
touch of the money put power into his hands, gave him a pride
that he could feel above all else.

"What's this look like? That's U.S. money, mister, not Confederate firestarter paper. Mark the Whitlock bill paid, and begin loading a box of grub. Coffee first-off."

The old eyes went questioningly from the money to Martha and back to Brazos.

"Didn't know there was that much federal currency in the whole Caprock."

"He's—he's my brother," Martha said. "Ellie Bradford, here visiting us."

The mustaches worked. The proprietor's manner changed to one of calculating friendliness.

"I reckon Adam will be proud to welcome such a guest as him, when he gets back from the trail drive."

"I've been in California," Brazos said boastfully. "Hit it rich out there. Now what about coffee?"

"I might dig up a pound." Mr. Jensen winked. "It's high. Smuggled in from Mexico. Cost you ten dollars."

"Start with a pound of coffee. I want to see there's no gravel in it. Put in some of everything else you've got. Dried beef, hominy, sack of flour. Corn meal. Beans, dried apples, a side of sowbelly, sugar—you got sugar?"

"Nope, the Yankees haven't turned the sugar loose yet. Got some sorghum."

"Well, a gallon of sorghum. Sack of crackers, lard, ham-hock—let's look around and see what you got."

He kept one eye on the door, wishing the old man would hurry. He felt trapped in there.

The storekeeper started scribbling tediously with a stubby pencil. Brazos said, "Include the Whitlock's debt when you add it up."

Martha stood dejectedly by the stove.

"I don't want you to pay our bill," she said listlessly. "We'll manage."

"I'm handling this, sis!" Brazos grinned hard at her. But she raised her chin angrily and walked away, pretending to examine the few odds and ends of apparel in a cracked showcase.

"This will nearly wipe me out," the old man said affably. He tore off the list and put the pad and pencil on the counter. "Ain't done so much cash business in a month as I've done today. First those six birds from the west trailin' the bank robber, now you two. What the posse didn't buy looks like you're taking. Mighty nice kind of brother to have, Mrs. Whitlock, heh-heh!"

Brazos continued his short nervous pace, looking at the

shelves, mostly bare, feeling his mind fighting stubbornly against the echoes of the storekeeper's cracked voice.

When he spoke, the words seemed to scrape his throat. "Posse, you say? When was that?"

" 'Bout noon. They'd lost the trail of this desperado. He robbed the bank out at Bristow. They're just circlin' around now. Camped down at the Bee Branch crossing. . . . You make yourself comfortable here by the fire while I get your stuff collected."

Instead, Brazos followed him, trailing him to the storage room, driven by a mounting urgency to get away.

"That posse—they staying around here?"

"Waitin' for fresh horses, I took it. Right bad humor they were in, too."

"Well, I'd hate to be following a trail in this weather."

"And I'd hate to be the one they're tailin'," the old man allowed. "Hard lookin' bunch."

Finally, the list was filled and Brazos paid, including the Whitlocks' account. The two boxes at the stove were top-heavy with sacks and packages.

"You sure picked a bad day to drive in," Jensen remarked, and headed back to his office to make change from the bills Brazos had handed him.

Martha whispered coldly, "I didn't want you to pay our bill. I don't want help—not with *that* money."

"Well, you can give it back to the posse after the hanging!"

That was a close call. He knew a cold needling in his spine and thought of the bleak miles in the open, back across the windy distance to the Whitlock house. What if they were making a search all around the settlement? What if they were even now at the Whitlocks, with Tanner tied up, waiting for Tanner's sidekick?

Well, he'd soon find out. Impatiently, he waited while the store man brought his change, looking through the front window at the red sand racing over the empty street.

His eyes shifted to the showcase where Mrs. Whitlock had been standing. A little splash of color there—an incongruous bit of yellow daisies and twist of white felt ribbons and blue straw caught his eye. That was what she had been looking at. Good Lord, how would anybody keep a thing like that on in this God-forgotten country of eternal wind?

He pulled the money from his pocket. Jensen was approaching.

"That thing in the case there, mister—that millinery. I'll take that, too."

The old man beamed and hastened around to open the case.

"New spring hat would look mighty pretty on Mrs. Whitlock." He took it out, brushed the red dust off the blue straw and blew it off the daisies. "Drummer talked me into buying this thing," he said, and added confidentially to Brazos, "By dun, thought I was stuck with it. No demand around here, the drought and all. It's five dollars."

Brazos had not looked at Martha Whitlock. In fact, he was unable to even explain his whim to himself. He now glanced inquiringly and was met by fiery anger in her stare.

He shrugged. "You sure need a new spring bonnet, sis. Don't you like it?"

"Not with *your* money!"

Brazos took it from the hands of the storekeeper, thrust out a bill, and stalked to Martha. She looked down at the hat, and barely touched the flowers on it with her fingertips. Then she reluctantly drew her hand back.

"I won't have it."

Brazos laughed, the thing looked so silly and flimsy in his hands. But the little flowers did sort of remind that spring was on the calendar, even if there was nothing but desolation outside. As she stood stiffly before him, he reached and drew the shawl back from her hair. He sat the hat upon her head. Irresistibly, she raised her hand to adjust it.

"Now put that shawl back over it," he said gruffly, "or the blasted thing will blow clean to Del Rio when we mount that wagon."

Mr. Jensen smiled benignly to show his appreciation for the brotherly generosity of the man and the sisterly resistance of the woman. "You two don't favor much," he observed. "Hat becomes you, Mrs. Whitlock. . . . Now you two watch out for that bandit. Lucky you got your brother with you, with Adam gone."

3

THE norther boosted them out of town and the going was not quite so painful, now that the sand gusts were at their backs. The two on the creaking seat rode in silence. Brazos watched constantly, ahead, each side, back toward the settlement in the sandy haze.

Again, the route dropped down into the broken flats and angled left to skirt the shielded stretch of canyon along the meandering sandstone wall.

"Much obliged," Brazos said then. "You did all right back there."

She looked for a long time at hands folded in her lap. Her voice came from far away.

"I've got to tell you something. I—I wrote a note, there in the store. For Mr. Jensen to find."

He pulled up on the lines with wrists gone weak, and shot a hard look at her.

"When was this? What did you say?"

"When you were in the back of the store with him. He left his pad and pencil. I told him—that the bandit was at my house. To send word to the posse."

He peered swiftly back at the trail behind them, as if expecting to see men riding fast to run him down. He searched the empty dust-shrouded country, batted his eyes against vagrant sand flurries, giving his brain time to tie down what she was saying.

When he did not speak for a long time, she turned with an anxious glance. She jostled against him as the wagon bounced, and reached to straighten the hat that perched loosely under the folds of her shawl.

"He—he won't find it," she said meekly, "until he puts wood in the stove. It's folded under the top stick of wood, there in his wood box."

Every dirty gritty fiber in him set up a mocking scream that he should have known of this possibility, that he had been weak and careless. It was anger at himself that he felt. She had double-crossed him, but she had that right. She was in a bad fix, with Tanner and him holed up at her house. And she was just as scared now as she was when they had first broken in. Tanner was smart, after all. Tanner would never have taken such a chance in the first place.

"Why would you write the note, like that, with your brother along? How will Mr. Jensen figure that? How did you say it? Did you say I was one of the bandits, too?"

"No. I didn't say that—Brazos. I said my brother was trying to protect me, that the bandit said he would kill us if. . . . I just said it like that—Mr. Jensen won't exactly understand it, but—"

"But what? Go on!"

"I wanted you to have a chance to get away."

"I ought to put you afoot!" he muttered. "I ought to have left you with Tanner. I ought to start running from here while I *can* run."

Then he asked sharply, "Why did you want me to get away?"

She spoke so quietly he could barely hear her. "I don't know."

He looked back again, feeling an itch between his shoulder blades, the soldier's old uneasiness for an ambush he could feel but not see.

Then he saw it, the sign far behind them, high up on the flats they had left. It was a small dust cloud, a moving trace of color in the haze, different from the sand gusts the wind whipped up.

He said, "You invited trouble, doing what you did. Well, maybe that's it, coming behind us!"

She whirled to look back.

He ran his gaze swiftly over the canyon wall, probing the eroded sandstone face of it, the covering of old cedars and brush. He whipped the mules and the wagon careened around a sentinel boulder, shutting them off from the stretch of canyon at their backs. He pulled savagely on the lines, heading the obstinate mules to the left and up the rocky ridge-cut rise.

He continued to search the broken boulders and cuts in the wall, until he sighted what he was looking for. He worked the team upward, and they dug in, pulling hard, fighting the slope toward the canyon face. They scrambled in the rocks and shale, through the brush and over the rocky cuts. Finally they were far off the canyon floor. He halted them behind head-high cedars when they had gone as far as they could go.

Here he was shielded by the brush and boulders from the trail below. A split in the rocky wall directly ahead formed a narrow shallow cave with an opening between split boulders.

"Get down! We'll wait here until we see whose dust that is."

He stumbled over the rocks to tie the mules. Martha struggled upward to the boulders that formed the low overhang. Brazos quickly caught up paper sacks from the grub boxes and the wagon canteen.

There was not much space within the opening. He followed her through the rock split and peered back. As far as he could tell from there, the wagon and team were hidden from view, if the coming riders stayed on the wagon road.

In the dim light inside the crevice she selected a spot in the sandy cave floor and sat down, smoothing her coat about her ankles. He saw her then as fragile and feminine, incongruously small for the rough land about them. She unwound the shawl and dropped it over her shoulders. She took off the blue hat that was shaped like a miniature poke bonnet and held it in her hands, looking at it. Her lips set in a resigned smile. She tried to straighten the crushed little clump of cloth flowers.

Brazos sat with his back against the sandstone wall, where he could look out between the split rocks and see the brush tops that cut off direct view of the canyon floor. He tore into the sacks and brought out dried beef and big soda crackers. He began to eat. It was choking dry to his throat but he washed it down with water from the canteen. Once he drew his revolver, took a look at the load, and replaced it.

"Want some?" He thrust the sacks and canteen toward her. She hesitated, and then took them, and fashioned a sandwich.

After a while she said, "It's sort of like a picnic, isn't it?"

"Yeah. Just like a picnic. Like on the beach at Matagorda Bay. Just look at those pretty white-caps out there!"

She laughed softly, with a catch in the sound of it. "And the gulls—see how they dip and circle! So gracefully!"

"Personally, I'm watching for the sharks trailing me!"

She raised her eyes quickly at the scowl in his tone.

"I don't suppose you'll believe me now, but I am sorry. I wish I hadn't written that note. I was scared. I was afraid to go back."

"Don't apologize!" He tore off a huge bite and talked as he hungrily chewed. "You're on one side. Tanner and I are on the other. You're law-abiding." He studied her. "I'm just learning this business. First thing I've learned is not to trust a woman. I should have known that."

"You could get away. They would just find Tanner."

"Get away from this lovely Caprock?" He saw how the pink-ish light came through the opening to play a colored glint in her hair and touch up the whiteness of her cheeks. Something—the nearness of her, the sound of her voice, was making him feel soft inside. To fight against that, he tried to put harshness in his words.

"You Caprock people really know how to live! You sit there in that sand-buried shack year in and year out and starve to death. That's what you do. You eat this cursed sand, you work in it, you sleep in it. Too weak to fight and too proud to run! Bunch of fools out here!"

"Maybe there's no place to run to."

"Well, the country's not going to do to me what it's doing to the rest of you. Instead of sitting there, why weren't you doing something about it? You—everybody out here—all the people in Texas. They didn't have to give up."

They were words of defensive attack, something to fight with, against the high-keyed knowledge that she was a woman, a nester's wife, and that he liked her.

"Your husband's gone off to earn a few measly dollars. The sandstorm holds you like a prisoner, and you don't even try to fight back. You could have squawled bloody murder in that store, or just started running. What happened to everybody during the war—did it take all the backbone out of 'em? Did Texas just quit? Now the damn carpetbaggers are piling in and you people keep edging west out to this no-good dried-up country. All the while they're stealing the rest of the state right out from under us."

He squirmed for a more comfortable position. He saw no sign of dust below. He could sleep for a week, he thought. Right here. Soft sandy floor. No wind. Quiet.

She smoothed her coat, holding the hat in her lap. The hem of the coat brushed his knee as he stretched with elbow propping his head, eating and watching the canyon down there.

"Brazos—" she began, and paused, as if trying to find words. "You talk about what the country has done to me. What has it done to you? An outlaw. A—a—robber. You're on the run. You'll always be running."

"Oh, that?" He grinned one-sidedly. "You think I robbed the bank, I guess."

"Well, didn't you?"

"No use claiming I'm not a bank robber, because I certainly intend to be one. I'm just getting started."

"How do you mean?" Her voice was huskily urgent.

"I was just helping Tanner." He thought back to the past three days, to the beginning. It was a crazy, mad whirl. Hazy, like the nagging sandstorm weather.

"There he was," he said slowly, visualizing it again, "that old grizzly cornered in Bird's Nest Canyon, his horse played out and his arm bleeding. And the men that were after him not far off. I was coming from the other way, and when I sighted him I saw what a fix he was in. He tried to get the drop on me but he was too slow. I guess I got a little pleasure, then, in helping him get away from them. Maybe I'm a little different about a thing like that—but he was the underdog there and I figured they'd be a bunch of Yankees trying to get their payroll back. So I said, 'Well, let's give 'em a good chase, old-timer—make 'em earn it.' So we got out of there on one horse. It took some doing."

"You didn't rob the bank? Just Tanner did that?"

"That's right."

She said simply, "I'm glad."

"Well, don't be glad so fast." He was thinking of the plans he and Tanner had made. "There're some other banks and Tanner knows the easy ones. We're going to get us a pile of money, then they can have this hell-hole country. I'll be taking it easy a mighty long way from here."

He took the hat out of her lap, sniffed absently at the yellow daisies, and tossed it back. She quickly straightened it in her lap and held it gently, fingers on the brim. He faced the opening, watching for dust above the cedar tops.

"So you're throwing in with him!" she said fiercely. "You're going to be like him. Another Tanner!"

Well, what if he was? The way she made it sound, it wasn't very good. But the way he and Tanner had planned it, the idea was all right. What was any better? Working all your life at starvation wages?

Tanner knew some easy ones, some hold-ups where they couldn't miss. Very little risk and maybe some really big money. Tanner had already promised him half of what was in that saddle bag, if he helped Tanner to get away from that Bristow trouble.

Two thousand. How long would it take a cowhand to save two thousand at forty a month?

And that was only the beginning.

The idea of bank robbing didn't bother him, either. Drowsily, he assured himself of that. Not like it seemed to bother *her*. God, he'd fought the yellowbellied Yankees and killed them when he could. It had been all right then for soldiers to forage, to steal anything they could get their hands on. It was the way the Confederate armies had lived. Now the Yankees were running everything down here, so what was the worry about taking their bank money, if a man was smart enough to do it. He could enjoy that without a qualm. It was like he was still fighting them.

As if she read his sleepy thoughts, she murmured, "The war is over, Brazos."

"Who says?"

"It's time to change. You have to live a different way."

"Who says it's over?" He came awake with a jerk of belligerence. "Some generals signed a lot of papers. What difference does that make? *I* didn't sign anything."

"But Brazos—"

"You don't just chop it off, whatever you've been doing day and night for three years."

"But I tell you, that's over!"

"War—fighting the other man, trying to kill him before he kills you—that's something you don't just turn off and on inside yourself. I was a part of the war. They didn't consult me."

Her hand touched his shoulder. Under its softness he settled back, but his elbow was tired and numb. He could not resist placing his head flat on his arm, like a pillow, and closing his eyes.

"What do they expect us to do?" he said. "Shake hands with the dirty. . . . Make up and come home and live on jackrabbits and mesquite beans while they lord it over us during this reconstruction business?"

"Tanner taught you to say that!"

He almost admitted that those were Tanner's words. But he resolutely held to them as his own belief, too. She didn't know what she was talking about. Just a girl, almost. Younger than he was. A starving nester's wife, trying to preach to him on something she could know nothing about.

"You stay here!"

He was conscious of her eyes following him as he crawled through the opening. When he cast a quick glance back, her features were almost lost in the ghostly pink twilight of the cave. Her eyes were anxiously raised, and she tried to smile.

"I'll see where our friends have got to by now."

He moved past the wagon at a crouch, keeping cover, until he could see the dusty stretch of the wagon route where it angled from the prairie down into the canyon.

He found them at once. Six riders, moving slowly within their own hoof-raised fog of dirt.

The fog diminished as the riders reached the rocky canyon floor. Soon he could make out the blue uniform. Time sped backward. Blood hammered his ears and he smelled the smoke of old battlefields.

There was just one soldier. He rode third in the single file. They were all slumped in their saddles. Brazos watched tensely, thinking of Tanner alone in the cabin.

As he watched, the soldiers moved his horse up to the lead rider and said something. Then the whole procession turned southward, down the canyon's side, crossed a gulley, and headed for the broken flats in that direction.

Puzzledly, he watched until the riders were lost in the patches of mesquite.

He came back to the cave. It was darker now. Just a dirty gloom, as the whole outside world would be soon. Martha was where he had left her, her glance raised in questioning.

"What would be south?" he asked. "Who lives down there?"

"The first place is the Burgess homestead. It's five miles south of us. Then east of there is the Frasers. Those are the nearest people down there. Some tame Kiowas have a village somewhere beyond that."

"The cavalry detachment at Bristow wants its payroll back. They've got a trooper and five hired trackers looking for Tanner. I expect they're after the cut of the loot they'll get if they bring Tanner in dead to the Yankee boss at Bristow. Rough customers."

"You have time to get away. Will we be going now?"

"Right soon. Give them time to put a few miles between us. They'll search those places out, down there, I think. And circle back east and north, inquiring at the nester houses. Maybe not till morning, though.''

They had lost the trail, he thought. Now it was just random looking. How long would it be before the store man found the note and got moving? The old man might try to send word to the posse, or he might turn the problem over to whatever men were in Sweetwater. Either way, he had better figure that the hired posse or Sweetwater heroes with nervous triggers would be riding down on the Whitlock place by midnight. To stretch the gamble any later than that would be foolhardy.

He could hardly find her features, now, in the gloom of the cave. She was just an outline, only two feet away from him, a still softness in the shadows. The white of her face showed, and he could see the hands holding the little hat.

Fighting against sleep was a constant effort. Almost unconscious that he did so, not knowing why, he reached and placed his hand on hers where she held the brim of the hat.

''You did all right. You'll be rid of us before long.''

He knew she turned her head, but she did not draw her hand away from beneath his fingers. It felt smooth and clean to his touch.

''The East Cove,'' he murmured. His mind was sleep heavy. She was Matagorda Bay, a link to something far back across the hills and gullies of his life. The touch of her brought it over the great distance. ''The waves down there were always the bluest,'' he said. ''And that sand the cleanest.''

She leaned slightly closer to him, as if trying to see his face.

''You know East Cove? Brazos—when did you live in Matagorda Bay? Did you know,'' she spoke in a warm rush of words, ''you are the first person I've seen from there in—since we came out here. Talk to me about it!''

''East Cove was where the rich people had their picnics,'' he said drowsily. ''I used to hide and watch them from up on a bluff. Servants and carriages and such food baskets as I never even dreamed about. I was a ragged-pants kid, maybe twelve, along there.''

''Brazos, we used to go on picnics at East Cove!'' Impulsively, her hand pulled out and closed on his. There was an eagerness in her tone, the excited youthful remembering, the starved finding of someone who linked with her happier years.

''The big people in the town,'' he said, remembering. ''The

Worthams and Finletters and Bradfords, and Judge Leyton who did a big slave business, and—'' He stopped, cutting the words off with his teeth. "The Bradfords," he repeated slowly. He opened his eyes and turned to try to see her. She was leaning toward him, and their eyes searched hard for each other in the gloom.

"You said your brother was Ellie Bradford.'' He laughed shortly. "Don't tell me you were one of *the* Bradfords!"

"Yes," she whispered. "I guess—if that's what you mean. The big house above the bay. . . ."

"Good God!" He sat up straight. The pressure of her hand upon his collapsed the crown of the straw. "You were that little girl—the time I took the washing back, and you rode down to the beach in my cart!"

"Yes! Oh, *yes*—it *must* have been you!" Her voice was a low vibrant excitement. "I remember, Brazos, that night—everything! I know, the name was—you were—wasn't it Mrs. McGuire, the wash—?"

She stopped. But she strained, frozen close to him, staring up, trying to see him.

"The washwoman's son," he finished. "That's right. Señora Rosita McGuire's boy."

His mind was pleasurably back to that summer dusk on the beach, with only the gulls about, and stars like a million new nuggets in the folds of the night above. The small waves of the bay tide were running with sounds like the happy music of concertinas, and the sand was soft and moist to their bare feet. And he was there with the girl from the rich house on the hill.

She whispered, "He was—*you*! The first boy—wh—who ever kissed me. You were Juan McGuire! I remember your father was the Irishman who drowned when the ship went down in the storm. Everybody talked about the Irishman who married the Mexican girl. They said the son would surely be a tempest! And your mother was sweet and beautiful, and you came sometimes with the cart, to get our washing and bring it back. Oh, that seems so long ago!"

He had almost forgotten Tanner, the posse who searched for them with guns notched for money, the distant nagging of the wind.

He said, "I would make believe, sometimes. That we were married and lived in a house like yours." He smiled at the absurdity. "That was before my mother died. Then I never had time to think much about the people in Matagorda again."

"Where *did* you go, Brazos? What became of you?"

"Everywhere. I worked for first one family then another, cattle outfits, and on the docks in Galveston. Finally, the war."

"My father died before the war," she said. "Then we lost everything. Then I married Adam. He was—he didn't go to war."

Something warm dropped on the back of his hand. It was wet, a warm wet tear that dried itself quickly in the sand on his hand.

"After the war, he—he was unpopular with the people in Matagorda," she said quietly. "He was a sympathizer. We moved, and kept moving. Finally he wanted to try ranching. But he had lost everything by then, both friends and money."

He thought again of the rich people of the Texas shipping town before secession, and of the smiling Mexican woman who was his mother, and the strapping, hearty Irishman who had loved her and married her, and whose son he was.

"My mother," he said gently, "died over a washboard, a grubby back-breaking washboard. Rubbing her life out a little every day for the people who could afford to pay a widow for what was beneath them to do themselves."

She said, her head close to his, "That's not the only kind of washboard, Brazos. The Caprock is like that. You can get your life rubbed away a little at a time."

She stopped, and he heard her labored breathing.

Shrewdly, he said what had been in the back of his mind.

"Your husband. Mind if I ask what manner of a man it is that lets his wife starve, and goes off on a trail drive without even killing a beef for her, leaving her alone in this kind of country? When he comes back, you ought to have a little straight talk with him."

She was a long time replying. Then, when she spoke, it was with a dignity that did not quite hide the tremulous edge of her words. He could feel her groping for control of something that ate deep within her being.

"He's not coming back. The trail drive—that was just the excuse. He—I guess he's just tired of all this country, me— everything. It never was right, for either of us. We—the war was just too much, I guess. The war and all that happened to Texas, and the struggle and hard times. Nothing was any good, for anybody—there wasn't enough love there to stand up to it."

He pictured that, knowing how it would have been in this mortally hurt part of the world, through the dragging years while the South slowly bled itself to death.

"You—did you say he was not coming back? You mean he's left you?"

"The rider, this morning. He came to the house. He told me."

Brazos remembered. He saw them again, the rider sitting his horse in the morning wind, the woman's skirts blowing as she stood bareheaded on the porch of the house down in the clearing, as he and Tanner had watched.

"This man had left the drive," she was saying, "and he brought word back from Adam. Just that he was going on to Kansas City, and maybe to California. That—that he wouldn't be back—ever. For me to go back to Matagorda, anywhere I wanted to go. To get a divorce."

Then she said huskily, "I was *glad*! It was what he should have done! There was no love between us, there never was. He was not fit for a life like this, a homesteader's life. He hated it— hated me, I think. When you came this morning—almost the moment you came in, I was planning to pack, to leave this awful Caprock."

"Where were you going?"

"I was going to take the wagon and load what I wanted and just drive south. Toward the coast. Anywhere away from the sand, the horrible wind and sand. Somewhere on the gulf, where there were trees and water and no red sand to cover me day and night. I would work somewhere. I—"

"So you were going to run away!" he said. "You said that was what I was doing. Well, maybe the country and the war whipped me for anything you'd call decent. But I'm going to fight back. I'm going to make somebody pay for it. You weren't even going to fight back!"

"How would I do that? What could a woman do alone? Everybody in the settlement knew that Adam was no good. They felt sorry for me. I guess it was pride. This is rock bottom for a woman—no matter how you might feel about him, it is hard to face people when your man has just gone off, knowing he'll be looking for—for fancy women in Kansas City or San Francisco, everywhere. But that's all right. Just so I don't have to stay here.''

Brazos said from far back in his memory, "There used to be a blue inlet jutting off east from the Bay. I named it Pirate Sound. The water was so clear you could see the fish down there, and a bottom white as a bed sheet. A thousand palm trees, I bet, growing on the shore. A pretty place in the moonlight. I used to dream about it when we were freezing in Virginia and the wounded men were crying all night. One time when my feet froze I went out of my head a little, I think. Imagined I was walking barefooted in the sand along Pirate Sound, in the hot summer, with the sun dazzling on the water and the sand warm and good to my feet. I would like to see that again, some day.''

He did not know when her head had first rested on his shoulder. It was there now, unmoving, with wisps of her hair touching his cheek. He felt a moistness mixed with grit between the clasp of their hands. Her breathing was warm to his throat, and the softness of her dress against him was warm and strangely comforting. He thought that he would like to sleep just where he sat, for hours, all night, and as long as the storm blew. . . .

He must have gone completely asleep. Her hand gently shook his shoulder.

"Brazos!" she whispered. "Hadn't we better go?"

"What?" He came awake violently. Instinctively, his hand jerked roughly away from her hand and clasped his gun holster.

"Tanner," she said. "They'll find him, won't they? If we don't get there? I hated to wake you—"

He was on his feet, dashing the sleep off his mind in alerted tension. Outside the opening he took a quick squint at the dark heavens, trying to estimate the time. But the haze made all the world a dirty blackness.

She followed him, clutching the hat and paper sacks. In a hurry, now, his thoughts working ahead, he guided her through the brush, across the rocky cuts, and to the wagon.

He managed to work the mules around, getting the wagon turned. Driving down the rough slope and onto the canyon trail was an ordeal. But at last they were headed east again, bouncing with the sway and toss of the wagon.

4

THE wind renewed its howling attack when they pulled once more up to the mesquite prairie. Now the night added its cold edge to the discomfort of flying sand. Martha's face was swathed in her shawl, her head turned against his shoulder, and when they were jostled together he could feel the tremors go through her body.

The last three miles were a crawling eternity of cold and suffocated breathing. But when the mules picked up, he gave them the lines, and saw the dark form of the house and then the corral fence loom ahead.

She waited, shivering, while he unhitched and penned the mules. He found hay in the shed and pulled it out for them, and saw that the water trough was filled from the windmill pipe. She helped him to carry the boxes, and they hurried to the door.

"Tanner!"

Brazos rapped heavily, then called again. "Tanner. It's us!" He didn't want Tanner to be half awake and trigger fast.

He heard movements inside. Now they'd have hot food, and real coffee.

Tanner gruffly called out, "All right!"

Balancing the heavy box, Brazos freed a hand and turned the knob. He edged aside for Martha, following her in, and kicking the door closed.

"Light the lamp, Tanner. Dark as pitch in here."

He heard the scratch of a match, but in the split second before that sound his brain told him the room did not feel right.

Then he knew everything, before the light revealed it. His scalp pulled tight. There was the rush of hot knowledge, and his knees drained out their strength. *What a fool!*

The tiny flame moved up to touch the wick of the lamp on the back wall.

He clutched the box that seemed to swell to monstrous size. It pressed so hard into his chest that his ribs tried to cut off his breathing. As if it were a fragment from the sobbing wind outside, he heard the low startled moan from Martha's lips.

The six of them faced him, strained and triumphant in their moment, with the yellow light playing on the guns in their hands.

He blinked at them, from one set of hard and purposeful features to the next, around to the last one. He was a chunky man in the brush-snagged trooper's uniform. The slit of his mouth worked in his red boiled face. The sergeant said, "Take his gun, Nesbitt."

With the gun muzzles following him, Brazos warily stooped to place his box on the floor. He took Martha's load from her and put it down, and straightened with his hands carefully out. The man called Nesbitt, gaunt and sharp-eyed, circled and took the gun.

Tanner slumped on the edge of the bed. His chin dug down into his chest. Sleep-reddened eyes clung appealingly to Brazos, like a dog slinking up for its whipping.

"They jumped me," Tanner mumbled. "I was dead asleep."

Nesbitt said, "Punch up the fire in the stove, Jess."

Martha Whitlock drew herself erect and stoutly raised her chin.

"What are you doing in my house! Who are you—who is this man?" She gestured to Tanner.

The sergeant holstered his revolver. He looked at Martha arrogantly, up and down. He said aside, "Keep your guns on 'em. . . . Is this your house, lady?"

"It certainly is!" she said with dignity. "We've been to town. Now we return to find this—this intrusion. Will you please explain what this means?"

Nesbitt and the trooper exchanged questioning glances.

"I thought you were in town with your brother!" Nesbitt said sharply. "The man at the store sent word you'd written a note, that you were in with your brother and that your husband was away. Just how was it, lady?"

Brazos felt numb appreciation for the effort she made. But it floundered under their hard stares and trickled out to nothing.

"He called from outside," one of the men spoke up. "He said, 'Light the lamp, Tanner.' They're side-kicks, all right."

Tanner stared at Martha, as if fascinated by her effort to shield Brazos. He peered wonderingly at the hat she held in her hand, and then at the sandstone smears on her coat, and the many wrinkles.

"Search him, one of you," Nesbitt ordered.

A man came behind Brazos and went through his pockets. He drew out wrinkled yellow bills.

Brazos saw Tanner's saddle bag, open on the table. So this was the end of the road.

"This matches up with what's in the bag." The man showed the bills around. "This is his partner, all right."

Nesbitt said, "I don't understand, Mrs. Whitlock. I thought you was scared this pair would kill you, way the store man reported it. You wrote the note—are you trying to cover up for this one?"

"We had her buffaloed," Brazos laughed easily. "Told 'er if she didn't act just right we'd come back some day and settle things in a way she wouldn't like."

The sergeant's sharp eyes worked from one to another. Before he could develop whatever thought was forming in his mind, Brazos laughed mockingly at them and doubled fists on his hips.

"Well, you guys are damn smart, for a bunch of yellow-bellies. How you like trackin' in a sandstorm?"

Nesbitt said, "We like it all right. How you like it?"

"The way you circled south from the canyon, that was right smart."

"Yeah, we thought so. Of course we didn't have a gal to take our minds off our business."

Brazos winked broadly at him. "You figured I was hid out there, watching, didn't you? They played it right all the way, Tanner." There was nothing left now except to get Martha cleared, and he was working on that. Then they'd move on to the sorry business that awaited them at Bristow.

His racing brain told him of one little try he could make.

"They out-smarted us, Tanner. If we hadn't stopped up there a while at Aransas Rock we might have made it."

He tossed the words out, craftily watching them, keeping his smile set. No face changed expression.

His mind cried out to her. *Aransas Rock! The lighthouse, Martha! Don't you remember?*

As he swept the circle of their unsmiling faces, he let his eyes travel last over the lamp on the wall. If she was looking at him, perhaps she would see his glance drag across it, pausing ever so slightly, then come back to the sergeant.

The trooper nodded grimly. "When we got word from the store, you hadn't been gone very long. So we headed here, right off, but we circled to come in from the south, in case you had a lookout."

"She tricked us!" Brazos turned with such a hard scowl that Martha looked genuinely startled. He had to make it strong.

"We broke in on her this morning. Made her go to town with me after this grub. I guess if there's any reward, she'll get a part of it. Lady, you plain out-foxed us."

They'd never split with her. When they rode away with him and Tanner, tied up like mummies, back to a drumhead trial and the scaffold at Bristow, she'd never see a penny of that money.

The new wood popped and crackled in the stove. The whine of the wind played up and down, and sand rained lightly against the clapboards.

The sergeant fingered his jaw. "What'd you say, Nesbitt? You boys want to start with 'em tonight, or wait till morning? What'd you think?"

"What I think, Sergeant Eckart," one of the men cut in, "is that wind's awful mean to ride in. I'm fagged out, myself."

Nesbitt pondered that. Brazos was conscious of the small shivering body beside him. Glancing at her, he saw the moistness in her eyes.

"I guess you were right," Brazos mumbled. "I picked the wrong road."

They would not know what he meant. But she would. She would know that he had just been riding through the country, going nowhere or anywhere, an article of backwash from the war, ready for anything that looked interesting—except what he would wind up with at Bristow. Maybe she would know, too, that he was glad about one little part of it.

Nesbitt said roughly, "You sit on the bed, by him, mister. Jess, go get a rope off your horse. I don't like the looks of this young one. Tie 'em up. I think maybe we ought to take that wagon and pack 'em in to Sweetwater tonight."

Brazos moved over and sat beside Tanner.

"How's the arm, old-timer?"

"Don't guess it makes any difference now," Tanner mumbled. "It's my neck that's beginning to hurt."

The guns were back in holsters. The men stood warming at the stove, talking and watching the two on the bed.

Martha turned her back and carefully hung the new hat, then her shawl, on a nail in the wall. She slipped out of her sand-smeared brown coat, with every eye following her body movements.

"We have coffee here," she said. "Would you gentlemen like some?"

"Coffee!"

"Good gosh, yes, lady!"

"I'd give this bag of money for a mug of real coffee!" one laughed.

She carried her coat to the draped closet door, reaching her arm inside to hang it. With eyes veiled, Brazos followed her, seeing that the men alertly watched Tanner and him again. Jess stalked to the door on his way out to get the rope. Martha's eyes flashed to Brazos, sharp and commanding. He tensed, setting the muscles in his legs.

The lamp on the wall bracket was just above her shoulder, at the side of the closet opening. As Jess opened the front door a gust of wind blasted in. In the same moment, Martha turned, arm still upraised. Her arm struck the lamp bracket.

Brazos held his breath. The glass chimney tottered undecidedly, and then reluctantly pitched over.

The wind gust struck and wiped out the naked flame as Martha exclaimed, "Oh, heavens, I've—!"

The chimney crashed to the floor. Darkness swathed the room and Brazos had Tanner's arm, pulling him, and they were at the door.

Someone cursed, and then there was a full torrent of words and confused movements.

He located Jess with his hands. Jess's back was still turned at the open door, and Brazos's fingers closed on Jess's gun handle. He swung the Colt up and down and Jess went limp. He flung the man aside.

"Damn it, strike a light, somebody!"

"The door—they're—!"

"Lady, get out of the way!"

"Don't shoot, damn it—Jess is over there!"

The night was a cavern of blackness and Brazos hit it running. Tanner plowed beside him, guiding on Brazos. When the first shots finally thundered from the doorway, the slugs whined wide and lost in the storm. The scrape of running boots made elusive targets in the wind. The black night absorbed them, then the wind laid its impartial howling protection over their sounds. The bullets blasted again, searching the night, but with no direction from the frustrated hands that sent them.

The horses should be south of the house, hidden away from the corral side. Brazos ran harder, shoving at Tanner to change course to the right. They made the first mesquites. He stopped, straining to listen. Faintly, he heard the horses moving.

They hurried toward the sounds and found them—six mounts, tied to sapling trees, all saddled. His quickly exploring hands touched saddle bags, bed rolls and canteens.

"Hurry it, Tanner! Get the reins of two more—we got to lead two apiece!"

"I got 'em!" Tanner puffed. "Let's go!"

The rest of it was fumbling desperation and hard riding, oblivious to thorns, brush, pain.

He fought for distance, fighting it all as living enemies, the wind, the cold, the slap of mesquite branches, the tugging reins of the horses that tried to hold back.

But the sandstorm, even the biting wind, made great gulps of freedom to be tasted. He took exhilarating swallows of it, sand and all, and laughed soundlessly.

After a long time, when his hands were exhausted beyond strength to lead the spare horses farther, he pulled up.

"Let's tie the other horses here." Brazos swung down. "We'll make better time and they sure can't find 'em before daylight."

As they worked at that, Tanner puffed words at him.

"She did it a-purpose, Brazos, when that galoot opened the door. By gaddly, she knocked that lamp chimney off a-purpose! I *saw* her! But they won't know that—it looked like an accident. Now why would she help us get away, I wonder?"

"I don't know," Brazos said tightly. "Let's ride."

He wanted to praise her to Tanner, to tell him about Aransas Rock. He wanted—but the words swelling inside would be torn to shreds by the wind.

The night wore on, miserable and long. But exhilaration of escape helped to repel drowsiness, made him superior to hunger and cold. Twice they stopped to rest the horses.

When the wind lessened at dawn, as if exhausted by its own night of tumult, they were in the Capitan roughs and he knew their escape was complete. The posse could do little but try to outfit itself with new mounts, take the recovered money, and ride back west. From the Capitans on, a man could be as lost from his pursuers as if he had vanished from the earth.

In the first pink shadows of the new day, they found a sink hole in the rocks. Men and horses drank of the scummy water, the canteens having been near empty at the outset and long since drained.

They unsaddled in a rocky cut where the renewed wind was diverted by a ridge to the north. The last that Brazos heard was Tanner's chuckling mumble, "We sure whupped 'em, Brazos. By the skin of our teeth—but we whupped 'em! I swear she knocked that lamp off'n the wall *a-purpose*!"

The sun glow in the overhead dust haze showed mid-afternoon when Brazos awoke. He got up with muscles knotted, groggy from the hard sleep. He was famished. He aroused Tanner. They saddled and rode back to the sink hole for water.

Brazos stood up from the red mud remaining in the hole. He wiped his brow with sleeve, smearing the red caking of dust. In the far recesses of memory, his mind made his eyes see in the sinkhole a white beach, washed white sand and blue waves leaping with spatters of lacy bubbles, and a soft white face with dark eyes uplifted confidently to him.

He smiled in his heart and raised his head to look back north to the ugly country they had crossed.

A man had to cross the ugly countries of his life—the ugly land that was war, and reckless wanderlust, and the equivalent of the Capitan roughs in his own soul. Sometimes a man could be trapped there for a lifetime, in his own badlands. A man had to choose, and the choosing made him what he was.

He turned to Tanner who was watching him with hard probing pinpoints of speculation within the dirt-matted hair.

"So long, old-timer."

Brazos thrust out his hand.

Tanner grunted and shook with him.

Brazos said, "Here's the sixgun. You take it. You'll be cutting east, I guess. I'm going another way. Good luck."

"I reckon I knew it all the time." Tanner wagged his buffalo head. "You'd made a good side-kick, Brazos."

Tanner puckered his mouth and worked his tongue in the side of his cheek. He fumbled down into his shirt front. When he brought out his fist, he clutched a fold of yellow currency.

"I got about a hundred here. Ratholed a little they didn't

find.'' He chuckled uncomfortably. ''Didn't mean to hold out on you, boy. Half's yours.''

Brazos looked at the money held before him. A grubstake there, and maybe a fresh horse at the next Indian village, and a gun. A man was mighty helpless out here without those things.

I don't want help—not with that money!

They were her words, spoken proudly in the store, there in the midst of bad trouble and abandonment and no credit.

The difference, he thought, was in quality—in humans, just as in anything else. Inside, there was a difference between him and Tanner that could never be reconciled, and the woman's quality had showed the difference in her, from him. But a man could try to raise his quality, if he could ever get his sights set right. It never had been the money he wanted. He guessed that whatever it was, he had found it. His share. A kind of currency there was no way to split with Tanner.

''You keep it, old-timer.'' Brazos swung into the saddle. ''I'll manage. So long. Take care of that arm.''

The cold sun worked twice across the hazy spring skies, and on the third day the wind subsided and the sun came up a healthy red over a land relieved at last of its sandstorm ordeal. The gaunt man came down from a high ridge where he had watched northward through the morning. In the far north distance, a crawling dot of movement enlarged itself as it came southward.

He met her on the trail. The loaded wagon creaked to a halt and the mules sagged to a rest in their harness.

She looked down at him from the wagon seat, to where he stood waiting. He met her eyes, her level, honest scrutiny, and saw the lips that looked about to laugh and the eyes that looked about to cry, and the miraculously clean and crisp dress showing beneath the brown coat, and the soft hands that held the lines, and the rifle on the seat beside her. Those things. . . . And the hat with its limp cloth daisies.

He went around to tie the horse at the wagon gate, then climbed to the seat beside her.

He took the lines gently from her hands and started up the mules.

The old ruts stretched endlessly southward, but the creaking wheels beneath him were the faraway fifes and drums of the Gulf waves. The badlands turned into a serene expanse of white-capped blue water.

The wagon rolled on, a lonely dot of life in the vast brooding solitude. The spokes of the wheels and the hoofs of the team left diminishing little trickles of red dust to hover in their trackless passing until a warming breeze blew it away.

Elmer Kelton is widely considered to be one of today's finest writers of contemporary and historical fiction set in his native state. He has won three WWA Best Novel Spurs, a feat unequaled by any other author: Buffalo Wagons *(1956),* The Day the Cowboys Quit *(1970), and* The Time It Never Rained *(1972). He is equally adept in the short-story form. The best of his early tales can be found in* The Big Brand *(1986); ''The Last Indian Fight in Kerr County'' is outstanding among his recent efforts.*

The Last Indian Fight in Kerr County

★★★★★★★★★★★★★★★

Elmer Kelton

I N later times, Burkett Wayland liked to say he was in the last great Indian battle of Kerr County, Texas. It happened before he was born.

It started one day while his father, Matthew Wayland, then not much past twenty, was breaking a new field for fall wheat planting, just east of a small log cabin on one of the creeks tributary to the Guadalupe River. The quiet of autumn morning was broken by a fluttering of wings as a covey of quail flushed beyond a heavy stand of oak timber past the field. Startled, Matthew jerked on the reins and quickly laid his plow over on its side in the newly broken sod. His bay horse raised its head and pointed its ears toward the sound.

Matthew caught a deep breath and held it. He thought he heard a crackling of brush. He reached back for the rifle slung over his shoulder and quickly unhitched the horse. Standing behind it for protection, he watched and listened another moment or two, then jumped up bareback and beat his heels against the horse's ribs, moving in a long trot for the cabin in the clearing below.

He wanted to believe ragged old Burk Kennemer was coming for a visit from his little place three miles down the creek, but the trapper usually rode in the open where Matthew could see him coming, not through the brush.

Matthew had not been marking the calendar in his almanac, but he had not needed to. The cooling nights, the curing of the grass to a rich brown, had told him all too well that this was September, the month of the Comanche moon. This was the time of year—their ponies strong from the summer grass—that the warrior Comanches could be expected to ride down from the high plains. Before winter they liked to make a final grand raid through the rough limestone hills of old hunting grounds west of San Antonio, then retire with stolen horses and mules—and sometimes captives and scalps—back to sanctuary far to the north. They had done it every year since the first settlers had pushed into the broken hill country. Though the military was beginning to press in upon their hideaways, all the old settlers had been warning Matthew to expect them again as the September moon went full, aiding the Comanches in their nighttime prowling.

Rachal opened the roughhewn cabin door and looked at her young husband in surprise, for normally he would plow until she called him in for dinner at noon. He was trying to finish breaking ground and dry-sow the wheat before fall rains began.

She looked as if she should still be in school somewhere instead of trying to make a home in the wilderness; she was barely eighteen. "What is it, Matthew?"

"I don't know," he said tightly. "Get back inside."

He slid from the horse and turned it sideways to shield him. He held the rifle ready. It was always loaded.

A horseman broke out of the timber and moved toward the cabin. Matthew let go a long-held breath as he recognized Burk Kennemer. Relief turned to anger for the scare. He walked out to meet the trapper, trying to keep the edginess from his voice, but he cold not control the flush of color that warmed his face.

He noted that the old man brought no meat with him. It was Kennemer's habit, when he came visiting, to fetch along a freshly killed deer, or sometimes a wild turkey, or occasionally a ham out of his smokehouse, and stay to eat some of it cooked by Rachal's skillful hands. He ran a lot of hogs in the timber, fattening them on the oak mast. He was much more of a hogman and trapper than a farmer. Plow handles did not fit his hands, Kennemer claimed. He was of the restless breed that moved westward ahead of the farmers, and left when they crowded him.

Kennemer had a tentative half smile. "Glad I wasn't a Comanche. You'd've shot me dead."

"I'd've tried," Matthew said, his heart still thumping. He lifted a shaky hand to show what Kennemer had done to him. "What did you come sneaking in like an Indian for?"

Kennemer's smile was gone. "For good reason. That little girl inside the cabin?"

Matthew nodded. Kennemer said, "You'd better keep her there."

As if she heard the conversation, Rachal Wayland opened the door and stepped outside, shading her eyes with one hand. Kennemer's gray-bearded face lighted at sight of her. Matthew did not know if Burk had ever had a wife of his own; he had never mentioned one. Rachal shouted, "Come on up, Mr. Kennemer. I'll be fixing us some dinner."

He took off his excuse of a hat and shouted back, for he was still at some distance from the cabin. "Can't right now, girl. Got to be traveling. Next time maybe." He cut his gaze to Matthew's little log shed and corrals. "Where's your other horse?"

"Grazing out yonder someplace. Him and the milk cow both."

"Better fetch him in," Kennemer said grimly. "Better put him and this one in the pen closest to the cabin if you don't want to lose them. And stay close to the cabin yourself, or you may lose more than the horses."

Matthew felt the dread chill him again. "Comanches?"

"Don't know. Could be. Fritz Dieterle come by my place while ago and told me he found tracks where a bunch of horses crossed the Guadalupe during the night. Could've been cowboys, or a bunch of hunters looking to lay in some winter meat. But it could've been Comanches. The horses wasn't shod."

Matthew could read the trapper's thoughts. Kennemer was reasonably sure it had not been cowboys or hunters. Kennemer said, "I come to warn you, and now I'm going west to warn that bunch of German farmers out on the forks. They may want to fort-up at the best house."

Matthew's thoughts were racing ahead. He had been over to the German settlement twice since he and Rachal had arrived here late last winter, in time to break out their first field for spring planting. Burk Kennemer had told him the Germans—come west from the older settlements around Neu Braunfels and Fredericksburg—had been here long enough to give him sound advice about farming this shallow-soil land. And perhaps they might, if he could have understood them. They had seemed friendly enough, but they spoke no English, and he knew nothing of German. Efforts at communication had led him nowhere but back here, his shoulders slumped in frustration. He had counted Burk Kennemer as his only neighbor—the only one he could talk with.

"Maybe I ought to send Rachal with you," Matthew said. "It would be safer for her there, all those folks around her."

Kennemer considered that for only a moment. "Too risky traveling by daylight, one man and one girl. Even if you was to come along, two men and a girl wouldn't be no match if they jumped us."

"You're even less of a match, traveling by yourself."

Kennemer patted the shoulder of his long-legged brown horse. "No offense, boy, but old Deercatcher here can run circles around them two of yours, and anything them Indians is liable to have. He'll take care of me, long as I'm by myself. You've got a good strong cabin there. You and that girl'll be better off inside it than out in the open with me." He frowned. "If it'll make you feel safer, I'll be back before dark. I'll stay here with you, and we can fort-up together."

That helped, but it was not enough. Matthew looked at the cabin, which he and Kennemer and the broken-English-speaking German named Dieterle had put up after he finished planting his spring crops. Until then, he and Rachal had lived in their wagon, or around and beneath it. "I wish she wasn't here, Burk. All of a sudden, I wish I'd never brought her here."

The trapper frowned. "Neither one of you belongs here.

You're both just shirttail young'uns, not old enough to take care of yourselves.''

Matthew remembered that the old man had told him as much, several times. A pretty little girl like Rachal should not be out here in a place like this, working like a mule, exposed to the dangers of the thinly settled frontier. But Matthew had never heard a word of complaint from her, not since they had started west from the pineywoods country in the biting cold of a wet winter, barely a month married. She always spoke of this as *our* place, *our* home.

He said, ''It seemed all right, till now. All of a sudden I realize what I've brought her to. I want to get her out of here, Burk.''

The trapper slowly filled an evil black pipe while he pondered and twisted his furrowed face. ''Then we'll go tonight. It'll be safer traveling in the dark because I've been here long enough to know this country better than them Indians do. We'll make Fredericksburg by daylight. But one thing you've got to make up your mind to, Matthew. You've got to leave her there, or go back to the old home with her yourself. You've got no business bringing her here again to this kind of danger.''

''She's got no home back yonder to go to. This is the only home she's got, or me either.''

Kennemer's face went almost angry. ''I buried a woman once in a place just about like this. I wouldn't want to help bury that girl of yours. *Adiós*, Matthew. See you before dark.'' He circled Deercatcher around the cabin and disappeared in a motte of live-oak timber.

Rachal stood in the doorway, puzzled. She had not intruded on the conversation. Now she came out onto the foot-packed open ground. ''What was the matter with Mr. Kennemer? Why couldn't he stay?''

He wished he could keep it from her. ''Horsetracks on the Guadalupe. He thinks it was Indians.''

Matthew watched her closely, seeing the sudden clutch of fear in her eyes before she firmly put it away. ''What does he think we ought to do?'' she asked, seeming calmer than he thought she should.

''Slip away from here tonight, go to Fredericksburg.''

''For how long, Matthew?''

He did not answer her. She said, "We can't go far. There's the milk cow, for one thing. She's got to be milked."

The cow had not entered his mind. "Forget her. The main thing is to have you safe."

"We're going to need that milk cow."

Impatiently he exploded, "Will you grow up, and forget the damned cow? I'm taking you out of here."

She shrank back in surprise at his sharpness, a little of hurt in her eyes. They had not once quarreled, not until now. "I'm sorry, Rachal. I didn't go to blow up at you that way."

She hid her eyes from him. "You're thinking we might just give up this place and never come back . . ." She wasn't asking him; she was telling him what was in his mind.

"That's what Burk thinks we ought to do."

"He's an old man, and we're young. And this isn't his home. He hasn't even got a home, just that old rough cabin, and those dogs and hogs . . . He's probably moved twenty times in his life. But we're not like that, Matthew. We're the kind of people who put down roots and grow where we are."

Matthew looked away. "I'll go fetch the dun horse. You bolt the door."

Riding away, he kept looking back at the cabin in regret. He knew he loved this place where they had started their lives together. Rachal loved it too, though he found it difficult to understand why. Life had its shortcomings back in east Texas, but her upbringing there had been easy compared to the privations she endured here. When she needed water she carried it in a heavy oaken bucket from the creek, fully seventy-five yards. He would have built the cabin nearer the water, but Burk had advised that once in a while heavy rains made that creek rise up on its hind legs and roar like an angry bear.

She worked her garden with a heavy-handled hoe, and when Matthew was busy in the field from dawn to dark she chopped her own wood from the pile of dead oak behind the cabin. She cooked over an ill-designed open fireplace that did not draw as well as it should. And, as much as anything, she put up with a deadening loneliness. Offhand, he could not remember that she had seen another woman since late in spring, except for a German girl who stopped by once on her way to the forks. They had been unable to talk to each other. Even so, Rachal had glowed for a couple of days, refreshed by seeing someone besides her husband and the unwashed Burk Kennemer.

The cabin was as yet small, just a single room which was kitchen, sleeping quarters and sitting room combined. It had been in Matthew's mind, when he had nothing else to do this coming winter, to start work on a second section that would become a bedroom. He would build a roof and an open dog run between that part and the original, in keeping with Texas pioneer tradition, with a sleeping area over the dog run for the children who were sure to come with God's own time and blessings. He and Rachal had talked much of their plans, of the additional land he would break out to augment the potential income from their dozen or so beef critters scattered along the creek. He had forcefully put the dangers out of his mind, knowing they were there but choosing not to dwell upon them.

He remembered now the warnings from Rachal's uncle and aunt, who had brought her up after her own father was killed by a falling tree and her mother taken by one of the periodic fever epidemics. They had warned of the many perils a couple would face on the edge of the settled lands, perils which youth and love and enthusiasm had made to appear small, far away in distance and time, until today. Now, his eyes nervously searching the edge of the oak timber for anything amiss, fear rose up in him. It was a primeval, choking fear of a kind he had never known, and a sense of shame for having so thoughtlessly brought Rachal to this sort of jeopardy.

He found the dun horse grazing by the creek, near a few of the speckled beef cows which a farmer at the old home had given him in lieu of wages for two years of backbreaking work. He had bartered for the old wagon and the plow and a few other necessary tools. Whatever else he had, he and Rachal had built with their hands. For Texans, cash money was still in short supply.

He thought about rounding up the cows and corraling them by the cabin, but they were scattered. He saw too much risk in the time it might take him to find them all, as well as the exposure to any Comanches hidden in the timber. From what he had heard, the Indians were much less interested in cattle than in horses. Cows were slow. Once the raiders were ready to start north, they would want speed to carry them to sanctuary. Matthew pitched a rawhide *reata* loop around the dun's neck and led the animal back in a long trot. He had been beyond sight of the cabin for a while, and he prickled with anxiety. He breathed a sigh of relief when he broke into the open. The smoke from the chimney was a welcome sight.

He turned the horses into the pole corral and closed the gate, then poured shelled corn into a crude wooden trough. They eagerly set to crunching the grain with their strong teeth, a sound he had always enjoyed when he could restrain himself from thinking how much that corn would be worth in the settlements. The horses were blissfully unaware of the problems that beset their owners. Matthew wondered how content they would be if they fell into Indian hands and were driven or ridden the many long, hard days north into that mysterious hidden country. It would serve them right!

Still he realized how helpless he and Rachal would be without them. He could not afford to lose the horses.

Rachal slid the heavy oak bar from the door and let him into the cabin. He immediately replaced the bolt while she went back to stirring a pot of stew hanging on an iron rod inside the fireplace. He avoided her eyes, for the tension stretched tightly between them.

"See anything?" she asked, knowing he would have come running.

He shook his head. "Not apt to, until night. If they're here, that's when they'll come for the horses."

"And find us gone?" Her voice almost accused him.

He nodded. "Burk said he'll be back before dark. He'll help us find our way to Fredericksburg."

Firelight touched her face. He saw a reflection of tears. She said, "They'll destroy this place."

"Better this place than *you*. I've known it from the start, I guess, and just wouldn't admit it. I shouldn't have brought you here."

"I came willingly. I've been happy here. So have you."

"We just kept dancing and forgot that the piper had to be paid."

A silence fell between them, heavy and unbridgeable. When the stew was done they sat at the roughhewn table and ate without talking. Matthew got up restlessly from time to time to look out the front and back windows. These had no glass. They were like small doors in the walls. They could be closed and bolted shut. Each had a loophole which he could see out of, or fire through. Those, he remembered, had been cut at Burk Kennemer's insistence. From the first, Matthew realized now, Burk had been trying to sober him, even to scare him away. Matthew had always put him off with a shrug or a laugh. Now he remembered what Burk had said today about having buried a woman in a place like this. He thought he understood the trapper, and the man's fears, in a way he had not before.

The heavy silence went unrelieved. After eating what he could of the stew, his stomach knotted, he went outside and took a long look around, cradling the rifle. He fetched a shovel and began to throw dirt onto the roof to make it more difficult for the Indians to set afire. It occurred to him how futile this labor was if they were going to abandon the place anyway, but he kept swinging the shovel, trying to work off the tension.

The afternoon dragged. He spent most of it outside, pacing, watching. In particular he kept looking to the west, anticipating Burk Kennemer's return. Now that he had made up his mind to it, he could hardly wait for darkness, to give them a chance to escape this place. The only thing which came from that direction—or any other—was the brindle milk cow, drifting toward the shed at her own slow pace and in her own good time for the evening milking and the grain she knew awaited her. Matthew owned no watch, but he doubted that a watch kept better time than that cow, her udder swinging in rhythm with her slow and measured steps. Like the horses, she had no awareness of anything except her daily routine, of feeding and milking and grazing. Observing her patient pace, Matthew could almost assure himself that this day was like all others, that he had no reason for fear.

He milked the cow, though he intended to leave the milk unused in the cabin, for it was habit with him as well as with the cow. The sun was dropping rapidly when he carried the bucket of milk to Rachal. Her eyes asked him, though she did not speak.

He shook his head. "No sign of anything out there. Not of Burk, either."

Before sundown he saddled the dun horse for Rachal, making ready. He would ride the plow horse bareback. He climbed up onto his pole fence, trying to shade his eyes from the sinking sun while he studied the hills and the open valley to the west. All his earlier fears were with him, and a new one as well.

Where is he? He wouldn't just have left us here. Not old Burk.

Once he thought he heard a sound in the edge of the timber. He turned quickly and saw a flash of movement, nothing more. It was a feeling as much as something actually seen. It could have been anything, a deer, perhaps, or even one of his cows. It *could* have been.

He remained outside until the sun was gone, and until the last golden remnant faded into twilight over timbered hills that stretched into the distance like a succession of blue monuments. The autumn chill set him to shivering, but he held out against going for his coat. When the night was full dark, he knew it was time.

He called softly at the cabin door. Rachal lifted the bar. He said, "The moon'll rise directly. We'd better get started."

"Without Burk? Are you really sure, Matthew?"

"If they're around, they'll be here. Out yonder, in the dark, we've got a chance."

She came out, wrapped for the night chill, carrying his second rifle, handing him his coat. Quietly they walked to the corral, where he opened the gate, untied the horses and gave her a lift up into the saddle. The stirrups were too long for her, and her skirts were in the way, but he knew she could ride. He threw himself up onto the plow horse, and they moved away from the cabin in a walk, keeping to the grass as much as possible to muffle the sound of the hoofs. As quickly as he could, he pulled into the timber, where the darkness was even more complete. For the first miles, at least, he felt that he knew the way better than any Indian who might not come here once in several years.

It was his thought to swing first by Burk's cabin. There was always a chance the old man had changed his mind about things . . .

He had held on to this thought since late afternoon. Maybe Burk had found the tracks were not made by Indians after all, and he had chosen to let the young folks have the benefit of a good, healthy scare.

Deep inside, Matthew knew that was a vain hope. It was not Burk's way. He might have let Matthew sweat blood, but he would not do this to Rachal.

They both saw the fire at the same time, and heard the distant barking of the dogs. Rachal made a tiny gasp and clutched his arm.

Burk's cabin was burning.

They reined up and huddled together for a minute, both coming dangerously close to giving in to their fears and riding away in a blind run. Matthew gripped the rawhide reins so tightly that they seemed to cut into his hands. "Easy, Rachal," he whispered.

Then he could hear horses moving through the timber, and the crisp night air carried voices to him.

"They're coming at us, Matthew," Rachal said tightly. "They'll catch us out here."

He had no way of knowing if they had been seen, or heard. A night bird called to the left of him. Another answered, somewhere to the right. At least, they sounded like night birds.

"We've got to run for it, Rachal!"

"We can't run all the way to Fredericksburg. Even if we could find it. They'll catch us."

He saw only one answer. "Back to the cabin! If we can get inside, they'll have to come in there to get us."

He had no spurs; a farmer did not need them. He beat his heels against the horse's sides and led the way through the timber in a run. He did not have to look behind him to know Rachal was keeping up with him. Somehow the horses had caught the fever of their fear.

"Keep low, Rachal," he said. "Don't let the low limbs knock you down." He found a trail that he knew and shortly burst into the open. He saw no reason for remaining in the timber now, for the Indians surely knew where they were. The timber would only slow their running. He leaned out over the horse's neck and kept thumping his heels against its ribs. He glanced back to be sure he was not outpacing Rachal.

Off to the right he thought he saw figures moving, vague shapes against the blackness. The moon was just beginning to rise, and he could not be sure. Ahead, sensed more than seen, was the clearing. Evidently the Indians had not been there yet, or the place would be in flames as Burk's cabin had been.

He could see the shape of the cabin now. "Right up to the door, Rachal!"

He jumped to the ground, letting his eyes sweep the yard and what he could see of the corrals. "Don't get down," he shouted. "Let me look inside first."

The door was closed, as they had left it. He pushed it open and stepped quickly inside, the rifle ready. The dying embers in the fireplace showed him he was alone. "It's all right, Rachal. Get down quick, and into the cabin!"

She slid down and fell, and he helped her to her feet. She pointed and gave a cry. Several figures were moving rapidly toward the shed. Matthew fired the rifle in their direction and gave Rachal a push toward the door. She resisted stubbornly. "The horses," she said. "Let's get the horses into the cabin."

She led her dun through the door, though it did not much want to go into that dark and unaccustomed place.

Matthew would have to admit later—though now he had no time for such thoughts—that she was keeping her head better than he was. He would have let the horses go, and the Indians would surely have taken them. The plow horse was gentler and entered the cabin with less resistance, though it made a nervous sound in its nose at sight of the glowing coals.

Matthew heard something *plunk* into the logs as he pushed the door shut behind him and dropped the bar solidly into place. He heard a horse race up to the cabin and felt the jarring weight of a man's body against the door, trying to break through. Matthew pushed his own strength upon the bar, bracing it. A chill ran through him, and he shuddered at the realization that only the meager thickness of that door lay between him and an intruder who intended to kill him. He heard the grunting of a man in strain, and he imagined he could feel the hot breath. His hair bristled.

Rachal opened the front-window loophole and fired her rifle.

Thunder seemed to rock the cabin. It threw the horses into a panic that made them more dangerous, for the moment, than those Indians outside. One of them slammed against Matthew and pressed him to the wall so hard that he thought all his ribs were crushed. But that was the last time an Indian tried the door. Matthew could hear the man running, getting clear of Rachal's rifle.

A gunshot sounded from out in the night. A bullet struck the wall but did not break through between the logs. Periodically Matthew would hear a shot, first from one direction, then from another. After the first three or four, he was sure.

"They've just got one gun. We've got two."

The horses calmed, after a time. So did Matthew. He threw ashes over the coals to dim their glow, which had made it difficult for him to see out into the night. The moon was up, throwing a silvery light across the yard.

"I'll watch out front," he said. "You watch the back."

All his life he had heard that Indians did not like to fight at night because of a fear that their souls would wander lost if they died in the darkness. He had no idea if the stories held any truth. He knew that Indians were skillful horsethieves, in darkness or light, and that he and Rachal had frustrated these by bringing their mounts into the cabin.

Burk had said the Indians on these September raids were more intent on acquiring horses than on taking scalps, though they had no prejudice against the latter. He had said Indians did not like to take heavy risks in going against a well-fortified position, that they were likely to probe the defenses and, if they found them strong, withdraw in search of an easier target.

But they had a strong incentive for breaking into this cabin.

He suggested, "They might leave if we turn the horses out."

"And what do we do afoot?" she demanded. Her voice was not a schoolgirl's. It was strong, defiant. "If they want these horses, let them come through that door and pay for them. These horses are *ours!*"

Her determination surprised him, and shamed him a little. He held silent a while, listening, watching for movement. "I suppose those Indians feel like they've got a right here. They figure this land belongs to them."

"Not if they just come once a year. We've come here to stay."

"I wish we hadn't. I wish I hadn't brought you."

"Don't say that. I've always been glad that you did. I've loved this place from the time we first got here and lived in the wagon, because it was ours. It *is* ours. When this trouble is over it will *stay* ours. We've earned the right to it.''

He fired seldom, and only when he thought he had a good target, for shots inside the cabin set the horses to plunging and threshing.

He heard a cow bawl in fear and agony. Later, far beyond the shed, he could see a fire building. Eventually he caught the aroma of meat, roasting.

''They've killed the milk cow,'' he declared.

Rachal said, ''We'll need another one, then. For the baby.''

That was the first she had spoken of it, though he had had reason lately to suspect. ''I shouldn't have put you through that ride tonight.''

''That didn't hurt me. I'm not so far along yet. That's one reason we've got to keep the horses. We may need to trade the dun for a milk cow.''

They watched through the long hours, he at the front window, she at the rear. The Indians had satisfied their hunger, and they were quiet, sleeping perhaps, waiting for dawn to storm the cabin without danger to their immortal souls. Matthew was tired, and his legs were cramped from the long vigil, but he felt no sleepiness. He thought once that Rachal had fallen asleep, and he made no move to awaken her. If trouble came from that side, he thought he would probably hear it.

She was not asleep. She said, ''I hear a rooster way off somewhere. Burk's, I suppose. Be daylight soon.''

''They'll hit us then. They'll want to overrun us in a hurry.''

''It's up to us to fool them. You and me together, Matthew, we've always been able to do whatever we set our minds to.''

They came as he expected, charging horseback out of the rising sun, relying on the blazing light to blind the eyes of the defenders. But with Rachal's determined shouts ringing in his ears, he triggered the rifle at darting figures dimly seen through the golden haze. Rachal fired rapidly at those horsemen who ran past the cabin and came into her field of view on the back side. The two horses just trembled and leaned against one another.

One bold, quick charge and the attack was over. The Comanches swept on around, having tested the defense and

found it unyielding. They pulled away, regrouping to the east
as if considering another try.

"We done it, Rachal!" Matthew shouted. "We held them
off."

He could see her now in the growing daylight, her hair
stringing down, her face smudged with black, her eyes wa-
tering from the sting of the gunpowder. He had never seen
her look so good.

She said triumphantly, "I tried to tell you we could do it,
Matthew. You and me, we can do anything."

He thought the Indians might try again, but they began
pulling away. He could see now that they had a considerable
number of horses and mules, taken from other settlers. They
drove these before them, splashing across the creek and moving north in a run.

"They're leaving," he said, not quite believing.

"Some more on this side," Rachal warned. "You'd better
come over here and look."

Through the loophole in her window, out of the west, he
saw a dozen or more horsemen loping toward the cabin. For
a minute he thought he and Rachal would have to fight again.
Strangely, the thought brought him no particular fear.

We can handle it. Together, we can do anything.

Rachal said, "Those are white men."

They threw their arms around each other and cried.

They were outside the cabin, the two of them, when the
horsemen circled warily around it, rifles ready for a fight.
The men were strangers, except the leader. Matthew remembered him from up at the forks. Excitedly the man spoke in
a language Matthew knew was German. Then half the men
were talking at once. They looked Rachal and Matthew over
carefully, making sure neither was hurt.

The words were strange, but the expressions were univer-
sal. They were of relief and joy at finding the young couple
alive and on their feet.

The door was open. The bay plow horse stuck its head out
experimentally, nervously surveying the crowd, then breaking
into a run to get clear of the oppressive cabin. The dun horse
followed, pitching in relief to be outdoors. The German res-
cuers stared in puzzlement for a moment, then laughed as
they realized how the Waylands had saved their horses.

One of them made a sweeping motion, as if holding a broom, and Rachal laughed with him. It was going to take a lot of work to clean up that cabin.

The spokesman said something to Matthew, and Matthew caught the name Burk Kennemer. The man made a motion of drawing a bow, and of an arrow striking him in the shoulder.

"Dead?" Matthew asked worriedly.

The man shook his head. "*Nein, nicht tod.* Not dead." By the motions, Matthew perceived that the wounded Burk had made it to the German settlement to give warning, and that the men had ridden through the night to get here.

Rachal came up and put her arm around Matthew, leaning against him. She said, "Matthew, do you think we killed any of those Indians?"

"I don't know that we did."

"I hope we didn't. I'd hate to know all my life that there is blood on this ground."

Some of the men seemed to be thinking about leaving. Matthew said, "You-all pen your horses, and we'll have breakfast directly." He realized they did not understand his words, so he pantomimed and put the idea across. He made a circle, shaking hands with each man individually, telling him *thanks*, knowing each followed his meaning whether the words were understood or not.

"Rachal," he said, "these people are our neighbors. Somehow we've got to learn to understand each other."

She nodded. "At least enough so you can trade one of them out of another milk cow. For the baby."

When the baby came, late the following spring, they named it Burkett Kennemer Wayland, after the man who had brought them warning, and had sent them help.

That was the last time the Comanches ever penetrated so deeply into the hill country, for the military pressure was growing stronger.

And all of his life Burkett Kennemer Wayland was able to say, without taking sinful advantage of the truth, that he had been present at the last great Indian fight in Kerr County.

This amusing and entertaining novelette is one of many notable yarns to carry Bob Obets's byline in such Western periodicals of the forties and fifties as Dime Western, Western Story, .44 Western, *and* Zane Grey's Western Magazine. *A native Texan who spent much of his life in the Gulf Coast region of the state, Obets published only two novels, both in the later stages of his career:* Blood-Moon Range *(1957) and* Rails to the Rio *(1965).*

The Girl Who Invaded Texas

★★★★★★★★★★★★★★★

Bob Obets

CHAPTER ONE

Hell in Her Heart

S HE was lovely; sensuous, perhaps, but not immoral, not a "loose" woman. She was only determined. She knew what she wanted and she went after it. Specifically, she went after a young, reckless no-good, a gambler named Chauncey Delafew Ramsay, from good family and—she thought—from a rich family. She wasn't too particular how she went after him or where she went to get him.

She chased him down to Texas, in those days part of the State of Coahuila, in Mexico. She chased him and she roped him, as securely as if she'd used a rawhide *reata*. Old Sam Houston, who had his own sharp eye for a well-turned filly, shook his head at her tactics, the while he thought, *More power to you, Ma'am!*

Her name was Louise, though her friends—most of them men—called her "Lou." Lou DuSang, of the Fausse Rivière DuSangs, came by her willful ways quite honestly. Her mother, until the day she died, had been a queenly woman whose rich beauty and velvet voice ruled Chevalier Plantation's dusky servants and charmed its guests; and not one of them ever guessed the secret of her flame-red hair and blue eyes.

For Madame DuSang was Irish. Brawling, back-of-the-hand Irish, from Killarney. While her husband, Jacques René, that slender and polished blade, could trace his blood lines back through the courts of the Louis. His own father, Lou's Grandpère Hippolyte, had quit France a skip and a jump ahead of the guillotine, taking what he could grab of the family fortune along with him.

Lou's hair was red, too, her eyes deep blue. For men she held a fascination that could be fatal. The day she turned eighteen the brothers Legendre had fought over her and she had watched them from the willows, held her breath as steel rang on steel, tasted blood from her own lip at sight of the blade tip, a dark crimson tongue, licking through the back of Jean's sword sash, just above the kidney.

Then, with the victor, his face anguished, on his knees beside his brother, she realized she did not want either of them. She would go away for a while, visit Aunt Cleo, in New Orleans, meet some new people, some new young men. She ran through the willows, through the gray dawn, with never a backward glance for the Legendre boys. It was this day that tragedy struck, when part of her world came to an end.

Looking for her father, eager to tell him of her plans for the trip, she came to the sugar house, found her father there. Syrup was bubbling in the vats, machinery clanking.

Later, it all seemed like a dream, a horrible nightmare. Her father crying out with pain, his hand, part of his sleeved arm disappearing before her eyes, gone into those grinding, metallic jaws like a stalk of cane. He grabbed up a broad-bladed knife, used for chopping cane, thrust it into the hands of a frightened black boy. "Chop! Chop it off!"

The boy could only gibber. It was Lou who did the chopping. Two days later gangrene set in and her father died.

Some part of Lou DuSang died with handsome Jacques, some part of her hardened, crystallized. Until this point in her life money had been something she took for granted, something she asked her father for. Now, with the settlement of the estate, she found that if she was going to continue living the rich life, money was something she was going to have to get hold of; for she was worse than broke: she was in debt. Chevalier Plantation, the furnishings in it, the slaves on it, even her jewels, went to her creditors.

Eh, bon Dieu! She would get money. She would get it the best way she knew how—grab herself a man who had plenty of it! In New Orleans, at a dance, she met one Chauncey Delafew Ramsay. He not only had money, he was handsome, dashing, reckless. He would do—and more than that, he fascinated her. That first night, the feel of his lips against hers—well, she knew; her mind was made up. Mr. Chance Ramsay hit her like swamp fever, and come tomorrow night—

She heard the sad news next morning. Chance Ramsay—a little matter of a misunderstanding over cards. Chance, after seeing her home, had sat in on a poker game. It was thought that the man he had shot, young Tom Gid Paisley, would not die—but Chance hadn't waited for Tom Gid's friends to think it over, come looking for him; Chance had pulled out for Texas.

Lou's first thought, when he came up missing, was a violent thought. Her next: *Le bon Dieu willing, I'll go get him!*

She left New Orleans that night, wearing pants, a short heavy coat, and other accoutrements, riding a fine three-gaited mare she had borrowed without consent or knowledge of her Aunt Cleo, with approximately thirty dollars in one pocket, a double-barreled derringer in another.

With determination in her soul and hell in her heart, she headed the mare for Texas, on the trail of Chance Ramsay. She wasn't sure whether she'd marry him or shoot him, but she was going to find him!

Chance Ramsay, gay blade and gambler—altogether the Southern gentleman, seh—knew nothing about this, the woman on his trail. Mr. Chauncey Delafew Ramsay was from New Orleans—or, to be more exact, from the rich plantation country upriver from New Orleans. Mr. Chance Ramsay, heading for Texas, was in a hurry—so much so that he kept looking over his shoulder, breathed a sigh of relief when he sighted the Sabine, though it was bank-full, roiled, ugly-looking.

He looked across the silty water and saw Texas and for him it was the promised land. What it promised was safety from the law and from the friends of Tom Gid Paisley, who no doubt were following him. Other than that, so far as Chance Ramsay was concerned, Texas could go back to the Indians, or to the Frenchmen—to anybody else who wanted the damned place.

But Chance Ramsay was a rich man's son. Young Tucker Bright, tow-haired and impudent, going on eighteen, came from poor folks, from the Smoky Mountain country of Tennessee. So to Tuck Bright, Texas was more than a land of promise. It was what he had dreamed about, it was a new life, it was a lump in his throat.

Tuck Bright and Chance Ramsay happened to meet simply because they both were bound for Texas and reached the Sabine on the same September afternoon. A raw rain was falling, bringing night on early.

Ramsay reached the river first. He took another quick look back over his shoulder and gave thanks for the good sorrel under him. The sorrel still had some bottom left, and in his money belt he had enough gold double eagles to buy land, cattle, almost anything else in Texas a man might want.

He stared through the rain; across swirling silt-red water he saw the gloom of live oaks on the Texas bank. His dark eyes took on a bitter shine, and he shut them.

Immediately blue segar smoke seemed to curl around him; he could almost taste it—and hear the susurrus of cards, the tinkle of glasses. "Here, boy. Brandy"—and a rivulet of rain water slid down his spine.

Damn Tom Gid Paisley's sharp eyes! That last brandy had made his hands clumsy, else the loud-squawking rooster never would have seen that card come off the bottom. And just when things were going so good, too. That False River woman, Lou DuSang, shining up to him— Ah, well, the pot was a fat one. Time enough to grab it before he shot Tom Gid, thank God, and maybe Lou would wait. If not, there would be other women.

Against the far bank he made out some sort of ferry. He stood in the stirrups and shouted, "You, ferryman!" Then shrugged. Tom Gid might not die. Someday that business would be forgotten. He could go back to New Orleans and good brandy and that golden-skinned octoroon on Rampart Street. . . .

They were on the ferry, almost across to Texas—Chance and the gallant sorrel that had carried him from New Orleans—when young Tucker Bright, in coon cap and buckskins, proud in saddle of a swaybacked mule, pulled up on the Louisiana bank.

"Look yonder, Beulah! Condemn yo' spiny hips an' sorry hide—Texas!"

Both boy and mule gazed across the swollen water. Beulah made a bugling sound, maybe meaning that up beside Tennessee that foreign place didn't stand hip-high. But the boy was seeing far beyond the gloomy live oaks, and his eyes brightened with something close to glory.

He saw long-horned cattle as fleet as deer—forests filled with game—plains of grass so high it tickled the bellies of the wild mustangs that grazed on it—broad rivers so full of fish they jumped right into a man's skillet. And land! It stretched yonder until it met the sky, and any Texas man could own a big chunk of it. If he had a wife, those Mexicans would give him more land—and there must be one of those black-eyed señoritas just honing to make a strong, good provider a fine wife!

No, not merely the dreaming of a mountain lad who never in his life had owned much of anything. Texas, for Tuck Bright, had been the Promised Land ever since he could remember. He'd talked to Tennessee folks who'd been there, slowly made his own plans. And that day he'd gone squirrel hunting instead of grubbing brush off the tobacco patch—well, that was the last time his uncle would try to larrup him! He'd left a note.

> Deer Uncle puce—take this in hand & i will be on way to texas & wisheing to thank you for vitls & all—also for horse pistil & Beulah—your loving nepew tuck.

Tuck had got a mite of schooling under the Widow Flannigan, down on Coon Creek, and if it hadn't been for that skunk he'd found in his trap, that morning on the way to school— But he intended to keep on learning, aimed to write up his experiences in a kind of journal—*Señor Tucker Bright in Texas.* Use the back part of Uncle Puce's tobacco-and-pelt book, to start with. Thing now was to get in Texas. He wondered if he'd run across Davy Crockett, the big bear hunter from Tennessee. . . .

Tuck didn't have a copper in his pocket, so no use to yell for the ferryman. Had an ax he'd build him a raft, because Beulah purely wasn't much swimmer and himself, he'd never learned how to. But get to Texas the best he could.

They almost made it. Tuck's head kept going under, while Tuck kept hoping his buckskins and stuff, tied on the saddle,

wouldn't get soaked—especially his powder horn. He must have
swallowed ten jugs of river water. Just got his head up, was
looking at Texas, when that damned log came along, knocked
him loose from his tall hold on Beulah. Then he guessed he
swallowed the whole river.

Next thing he knew, a wet stranger with the maddest, blackest
eyes he ever saw, face like a hawk's, was pumping water out of
him. He wrote about it that night in his journal.

> *Febry dog if i no—first nite in texas & in shed of Captan
> gaines with beulah—man puled me out of sabbine name of
> ramsay but to mad for proper aqantanse wet as hen—come
> out with powdr dri & if Captan & ramsay keep argyn politiks
> in ther one be out in rane—not me! hed for san felipe come
> sun up—hastie you veestie as us meskins say.*

Chance Ramsay, next morning, thanked the captain for his
hospitality. He'd thought, for a minute, there, the old boy was
going to chase him out in the rain with that poker!

He saddled the sorrel and headed on down a pair of wretched
ruts which, so Captain Gaines had assured him, was the King's
Highway. Go on to San Felipe, he guessed; that was Stephen
Austin's town. Gaines claimed it was right lively, and, that far
from San Antonio, a man wasn't apt to see any of the fight that
was looming with the Mexicans.

Anyway, nothing could disappoint a gambler in this Godforsaken wilderness! About now, back in New Orleans, be taking
his coffee laced with bourbon. Belle Marie bringing it to him.
Bless her golden skin! And maybe, if he talked real pretty, Lou
DuSang—well, he wouldn't marry her, but maybe an arrange-
ment, a bed-and-board agreement. That woman sure wanted
finery and foofarraws, a man to go along with all the good
things!

Lou DuSang thought he was a rich man, at least the son of a
rich man. And so he was—or had been. The trouble was, a few
seasons of reckless spending and careless planting, poor crops
and worse markets, had taken the Ramsay fortune, ruined them.
But someday—ah, someday he would marry a rich girl—like
Lou DuSang. . . .

Ramsay sneezed. As if that were a signal, from somewhere

close ahead of him a gun—a hand gun, he thought—popped spitefully.

This King's Highway here twisted through dismal trees, bearded with Spanish moss, interlaced with vines. A man riding it could not see past the next bend—and Ramsay's first thought was *Indians*! His next, *Horse, take me away from here!*

Came another spiteful pop from the hand gun, and the sorrel took the bit in his teeth and bolted straight ahead. Ramsay was still trying to curb the fool beast when, rounding a sharp bend, the sorrel stopped, apparently as surprised as was Ramsay.

On his back in the tall grass lay a man, and standing over the man, holding a derringer that still trailed smoke, was a slender figure in checked pants and a short coat—a figure that scowled down fiercely and said, "Now, Mr. Rowdy Ben Brashears, what was it you had in mind? Pawing me, putting your hands—I ought to—"

A pair of eyes so deep blue that they looked black, stormy black, came snapping up and stared at Ramsay. The scowl disappeared, the mobile face registered incredulity, recognition, pure delight.

"Chance! You! I thought I'd have to hunt all over—that is, imagine seeing you here!"

A few strands of flame-red hair had escaped from beneath the man's hat—and then those eyes, and the ivory skin with the pulsing glow beneath it!

Ramsay said, "Lou! By all that's holy—Lou DuSang!"

He was more surprised, almost shocked, to see her here in this Godforsaken wilderness. But he was too much of a gambler to let her read his thoughts. He grinned sardonically.

"Who's your friend, Lou? An old dancing partner, perhaps?"

The blue-black eyes went stormy again. "I crossed the Sabine last night, ran into a bull-train freight outfit. This—this Rowdy Brashears was with the freighters. He recognized me for a woman and followed me. His intentions were strictly dishonorable. Damn such a country, anyway! Well, he caught up with me, said he was going to Nacogdoches, but what he wanted was to get me to himself in this wilderness. We wrestled and fought and I had this derringer. I used both barrels, finally, and if I'd had another round in it—"

"I heard the shots," Ramsay said, and stepped down. "See if he's dead."

Mr. Rowdy Ben Brashears groaned, tried to sit up. Lou planted a foot against his chest and shoved him back down.

"It looks like," she said, "a poor defenseless woman has no business traveling by herself, in Texas! Which way are you heading, Chance?"

CHAPTER TWO

Fightin' Man

They traveled southward in a direction that should take them to Steve Austin's town, San Felipe, on the Brazos. After they reached it—who knew, who cared?

Chance didn't even know what had brought Lou DuSang to Texas. He questioned her and she made vague reference to friends in Gonzales. After her father died, she told him, she had been filled with melancholia, with lonesomeness. A wildness had come over her, she said, and she had left Chevalier Plantation in the hands of a business manager.

Land, money—poof! Those things meant nothing to her. But this friend in Gonzales—his name was Franchot Villars, and she was tired of fighting him, of living alone; guessed she would marry him. Ah, the burden, the responsibility of having money!

And Chance thought, *Yes, and the inconvenience of not having any!* Maybe, he thought, he would marry her yet. But, *Don't rush into this thing, boy, don't rush! Something here smells of shrimp. Why did she come to Texas?*

Yes, Lord, and still raining! After that wetting, when he'd pulled that fool kid out of the Sabine, Captain Gaines's jug was probably all that saved him from the bastard pleurisy. That lariat the captain tossed to him was probably all that saved him and the kid both from drowning.

Mighty fine man, the captain—but that kid! First thing the young idiot wanted to know was, "Stranger, is this sure enough Texas?" Seemed really concerned! If he never set eyes on the kid again, be soon enough!

It rained on Chance and the girl constantly; all the creeks were flooded. They got wet from both ends, rain down their necks, creek water in their boots. When they reached the Neches it was bank-full and swimming; the sorrel went clear under with Chance.

That night a settler put them up. His name was Jenkins, and not a drop of whisky in the cabin. Ramsay found the man poor company, but when the settler's wife set out the side meat and corn pone, Ramsay heaped his plate, added a covering of black-strap molasses, and went after it like a starved timber wolf—while Lou DuSang smiled at him in a mocking, wicked way.

In Texas, those days, a guest in the house was something of an occasion. The settler wanted to talk.

"You mark my words, son," he said earnestly. "It's either whip them Meskins now, or some other time. Put Steve Austin in a dungeon down in Mexico, try to take our arms away! They's a bunch of militia from New Orleans already here to he'p us, an' more a-coming. Look like some of a fighter, yo' ownse'f.''

Ramsay grunted and reached for another corn pone. Lou kicked him under the table.

"Allus did admire to see a fightin' man eat," the settler said, and went on to speak of crops and weather and religion—was a Blue Light Presbyterian, himself. What might Ramsay's faith be?

"Hard Shell," Ramsay said, and the settler chuckled. Thinking that here was a good stiff-necked brother, he proceeded with a mild joke; whereupon the three youngsters grinned like possums.

When the settler's wife, herself a staunch Baptist, began to purse her lips, he put an arm around her and squeezed with such affection that her ribs popped. All of them laughed heartily.

"Rufe, you old fool," the woman said.

And in a poor cabin miles from any neighbor, not a musical instrument or even a book in it that Ramsay would see, drinking creek water, watching out for Indians—how could people live like this, be content, be happy? Didn't know any better, he guessed. Well, tomorrow, before he pulled out—

"Pa," the settler's wife said, "we could all sleep on a Baptist pallet—on the floor in a ring around pillows. But these young folks are tired. Mr. Ramsay, you and your wife take our bed; Pa and me and the kids will take the shucks in the shed."

"I—the fact is—" Ramsay was not so much embarrassed; he

simply was at a loss for words. "Mrs. Jenkins, this young woman and I are not man and—"

"Oh, hush," Lou said. "Mrs. Jenkins, you take your own bed. Chance—my husband and I—we'll take the shucks. You see, we've been married only a week. It was what you call an agreement wedding. As soon as we get located, get our crops in, and—and everything, we're going to have Padre Muldoon say the church words."

"Pa," Mrs. Jenkins said, "isn't that fine? Married only a week, and come to Texas to fight and work and make their home!"

"Young man—Ramsay," Pa Jenkins said, "Texas can use fightin' men. Fixin' to enlist in Sam Houston's army my own-self. Whereabouts did you say you was headed for?"

"Anywhere the Mexicans—"

Before he could finish with "are not," Lou rose from her chair and said, "We better hit the shucks. Chance, he's all worked up about this Mexican affair. We'll see you good folks in the morning."

The corn shucks on the floor in the shed were dry and scratchy and when a man rolled on them they made a hell of a noise. It was cold in the shed even under the big comforter Mrs. Jenkins had given them for cover. Pretty soon, after Ramsay had blown out the tallow dip, he got to thinking and wishing.

Lou's voice came softly in the darkness: "I thought you were a fighting man—a man, anyway. What are you thinking about— husband?"

She was under the comforter, too—under the edge of it. Man couldn't get any warmth from her! Ramsay said wickedly, "Why, I was thinking about a certain golden-skinned woman on Rampart Street. Wishing, by God, I was back there—or she was here."

Silence, then a taunting chuckle from Lou. "And on our wedding night, too! But I could make you forget her, your— what is the word?—paramour? If you were like our host, Jenkins—going to join up with Sam Houston's army, shed your blood for Texas, perhaps—why, I could make you forget a lot of things. Every woman loves a hero."

"Let the Mexicans keep Texas," Ramsay said. "I'd rather be a live coward. I might add that I still don't know why you're here, in this Godfor—'' He sneezed, guessed he still hadn't escaped the bastard pleurisy. Probably die with it in this wilderness, coyotes howl over him, buzzards pick his bones.

''You with all your money,'' he said. ''The hell with you, Lou DuSang.''

''Let's go back,'' she said. ''You and I, Chance. Let's get out of here, go back to God's country, to New Orleans.'' She rolled over and the corn shucks crackled. ''You've got plenty of money. You've got a way with—you could have any woman. Good food, music, brandy, segars—ah, Chance, I'm as sick of this place as you are.''

''But you haven't got Tom Gid Paisley to face—granting the sorry rooster's still able to flap and crow, is still alive. He's got friends, too, and—damn you, woman, quit tempting me! You're worse than that snake in old Adam's garden.'' He sneezed again; his teeth chattered.

She got up and pattered around in her bare feet. Their saddles were against the wall yonder, and he heard her fumbling in the darkness, heard her swear softly. Then she moved toward him; the shucks crackled as she sat down on the edge of their rude pallet.

''Here, take a good pull. It came all the way from New Orleans.''

It was brandy, good brandy. Ramsay swallowed, sighed. The warmth reached clear to his toes.

''I take it back, Lou. That golden-skinned woman is growing dimmer by the moment. Another slug of that stuff and I'll be braver than lions. Mexicans, Indians, wild bears—Lou, you really want me to be a hero? You can't fool me, you came here, clear to Texas, looking for old Chance. S'funny thing, Lou. I wanted you, thought about you all way from N' Orleans. But now, you come chasing me—t'hell with you, Lou. You and your money.''

There was a gurgling sound. Ramsay said, ''Ahaa!''

Lou grabbed the bottle. She shook it. She took a long swallow.

''Rahh!'' she said. ''If you—your old daddy—or is it uncle?—was without money, what would you be, Chance Ramsay? I wouldn't spit on you if your—insides were on fire! In the morning, you go your way and I'll go mine!''

She tilted the bottle again. ''But I love you, Chance Ramsay.

I always will. If I can't have you, nobody else will. And if you think I want you to get yourself wounded, shot all to doll rags—the devil can take Texas! Chance, I'm cold. Put your arms around me, Chance.''

"Can't seem to move," Ramsay said.

"Why, damn your sorry soul!" She slid under the comforter and grabbed him. She bit his ear and put a knee in his belly. "Damn you, Chance—"

They were two miles on their way next morning when Rufe Jenkins overtook them. The settler shoved a gold coin into Ramsay's hand. "You must of forgot this at breakfas','' and he jerked his nag around and was gone. Ramsay shook his head.

"They're so poor, got nothing," he told Lou. "I just thought—I slipped that goldpiece under my plate. These Texans!"

Late of an afternoon they rode beneath the ancient live oaks that bordered the Trinity. Ramsay cut a far different figure from the handsome, well-turned-out young man who, short days ago, had put New Orleans, all that gay and indolent world, behind him.

Thorns had ripped his coat, laid scratches across his face; his boots might never have felt a black boy's cloth, his once-fine shirt was ready for the rag bag; he was taking on a gaunt, alert look peculiar to wild woods animals and Texas men.

Miss Lou DuSang, of the Fausse Rivière DuSangs, was, if anything, in worse shape than Ramsay. She was beginning to hate Texas with a passion almost as intense as her feeling for Chance Ramsay—but she wasn't going to leave the damned place without him.

Ramsay was down, the sorrel sucking water from a fingerling stream, when he heard a sound that brought him instantly alert. It was a twanging sound, and something went whispering past him.

Suddenly, across the stream, the underbrush began to bristle with feathers. Ramsay saw a copper-hued face rise into view, and whirled, and Lou, still in saddle, lifted a high, thin yell.

"Indians!"

Ramsay was back in saddle, not knowing how he got there. His scalp, the back of his neck, seemed to come alive, tingling and twitching; he yelled, "Lou, come on!" and the sorrel leaped beneath him.

They headed upstream with the Indians behind them setting up a lively caterwauling. Ramsay led the way, forgetting to be gallant. The sorrel carried him through a screen of saplings and thorny vines, and in a patch partially cleared of brush he saw a cabin.

He looked back, saw Lou, and yelled, "Come on!"

A young girl, not as old as Lou, lay across the cabin doorway, her arms reaching toward an elderly man who lay a few feet from her, the feathered haft of an arrow bristling from his chest. Ramsay leaped down beside the girl, saw that her eyes were open. Wonderful blue eyes, filled with pain, with sadness. Her hair, he thought, must have been yellow, like sunflowers.

He said gently, "Girl, you'll be all right. We're here. We're friends."

Her lips smiled at him, a brave smile that made him feel foolish. "Those red boogers have killed me. Me and Pa. It—it don't matter so much. But my brothers, Big Jim and Little Jim— they're in Gonzales settlement—somewhere—gone to fight with Sam Houston's army."

"We—Pa and me—just come back from San Felipe when the plagued Indians jumped us. We went there to see if there was news of our two Jims. All we heard was—going to be a fight at Gonzales—about a cannon. Mexicans going to take it away from the settlers. Pa and me, we were going to get our belongings together and head for Gonzales—try to help—when—when—"

"There," Ramsay said, "there, girl."

But she did not hear him. He looked up and saw Lou, from her saddle, watching him. Her eyes were mocking.

"You and I, maybe we're the ones wrong, Chance. What is this fascination Texas holds for these people? They not only want to fight for it. They seem to glory in dying for the miserable place! She's dead, Chance, so—"

But he had the girl in his arms, was carrying her inside the cabin.

"In here," he told Lou roughly, over his shoulder. "Jump, damn you! Get some hot water. For once in your pampered, worthless existence, be a woman. Be a human being."

"Listen at the pot," Lou said, "calling the kettle black."

The girl at Ramsay's arms made a faint sound. Her eyes,

staring up at him, were filled with wonderment. She murmured, "I've dreamed about you, a man like you, fine and brave and handsome. Here in Texas—and then you come along—too late."

She sighed and Chance Ramsay, sophisticate, cynic, sporting man, gambling man, bent his head and kissed her on the lips, tenderly, as if she were a little child.

"Now, I don't want to die," she said. "But I know I'm going to. Find my brothers, Big and Little Jim—Hawkins. Tell them—tell them to keep fighting. Tell them—Texas—"

Ramsay held her in his arms a moment longer, feeling anger lace through him, anger and frustration and something close to guilt. It all seemed so useless, so pointless. This young girl was dead. Her last thought was of Texas. But why? This barbaric land had taken her life, her father's life; probably her brothers, Little Jim and Big Jim, would die for Texas. But it was wrong! It was fanatical! Texas, nothing in the place, nothing about it, was worth dying for.

Ramsay laid the girl on a wall bunk. He turned and saw Lou watching him, surprised to see tears in her eyes.

"Sniffle, damn you," he said roughly. "It's better, I guess, than dying for money."

"You've got me wrong," Lou said. "I might live for money; I sure don't want to die for it. See if you can find a spade, something to dig with. You start the graves while I put the horses in the corral I saw tacked onto the back of the cabin. Those red boys are still skulking around here. How are you at Indian-fighting, Chance my lad?"

CHAPTER THREE

Her Hero

Sun should be up, but you couldn't be sure. It was so gray and dismal that young Mr. Tucker Bright, the Texas Traveler, could barely see Beulah's ears. Having trouble with that mule! Nearly to the Trinity, and she kept fiddle-footing, craning her neck this way and that. She went through a stand of young pecan trees, danced through sideways, abruptly planted her feet and snorted.

Her ears went forward, and past them, in a patch cleared of brush, Tuck made out a clapboarded cabin surrounded by dead, girdled live oaks. Thin smoke curled from the cabin's stone chimney. All seemed peaceful—but Beulah refused to budge. His heels wouldn't budge her, so maybe a good cussin'—!

"Now, listen, you mis'able cross-bred—"

He saw them then, like shadows in the brush. A big bronzed buck, feather stuck in his hair, grinned at him.

"Please, Beulah, any direction! Move!" The buck put hand to mouth, raised a horrible whoop.

Beulah lined out in the direction she was pointed, straight for the cabin. She would have crashed into it head-on had not the door swung open. Dogwood switches were whipping past Tuck, all that screeching hullabaloo behind him. He ducked his head and rode Beulah right on inside the cabin.

For several minutes afterward, it was touch and go—looked like those red boogers were going to come in after him! Then Tuck got in a good lick with the old rifle that had been his pappy's—flattened the big buck with the lone feather in his top-knot—and the rest of the red brothers withdrew for a powwow, taking the wounded buck with them.

Tuck was ramming a fresh load down old Bess's throat, feeling a little dizzy, when the girl—throatiest voice he'd ever heard— spoke up at his shoulder.

"Let's take a look before you bleed all over that buckskin shirt. Skin out now."

Tuck, for the first time, took a good look at her—and his heart turned flipflops. He didn't know her name, but she was wonderful. No black-eyed señorita for him! Why, with his own land and cattle, nice cabin, a wife like this to love and work for—of course, he might have to fight some first: those Mexicans. But soon get that trouble tended to, and then—

"You going to moon all day? Don't think those Indians won't be back!"

She skinned the buckskin shirt off over his head, wasn't too gentle about it. There was a groove below his shortribs she could have laid a finger in, and she shook her head.

"You were lucky!" She doctored the wound with whisky and bear grease, while Tuck went red to the ears and Ramsay, of the black eyes, stood watch at a window, his thin lips showing a sardonic amusement.

"This is Texas, Tuck—and here they come again!"

It went like that all day, the Indians making feints, showering the windows with arrows, but always halting in the edge of the brush.

"Aim to make us use up our powder," Tuck decided. "Then, come mornin'—"

But that night, by candlelight, he wrote some more in his journal.

> *In cabbin near trinitie & wild indins all around us to blame neer!—will put my palet at west door & ramsay at east with gerl in midle—protect her with my life!—dont no if live till moarning but miss lou onlie girl for me—real texan doktored my wound & purty as pictur! Her & ramsay dont git along much but i will marrie her if have me.*

So wrote Tucker Bright, taken in by Lou DuSang, the adventuress who had chased her gambling man down to Texas—Lou, who had borrowed the rough homespun clothing of a girl named Dessie Hawkins who would not need the clothes anymore. Dessie lay outside in a shallow grave beside her father; Dessie, whose last words had been "Find my brothers, Big and Little Jim Hawkins. Tell them to keep fighting. Tell them—Texas—"

Dessie Hawkins would have made a fine wife for Señor Tucker Bright, the Texas Traveler—but Lou DuSang was not for him. . . .

They made down their pallets, and after a time Lou spoke with mocking softness in the chill darkness: "Where to from here—if we go anywhere from here—my brave fighting man? Remember your promise, Mister Ramsay. Remember Big Jim and Little Jim and that cannon, at Gonzales. We can't let the Mexicans take that cannon away from the settlers, can we?"

Ramsay muttered something about "to hell with the settlers and the cannon both." Ramsay was cold, bone-tired, disgusted, and hungry enough to eat his own boots. All they'd found to eat in this miserable cabin was a few corn pones, some jerked venison, and ten hickory nuts. Those damn' red boys were prowling around somewhere outside, there was barely a hornful of gunpowder in the cabin, and not a drop of whisky.

All of this to plague a man, and now Lou snugging up to him in the dark, rubbing it in with her soft, sarcastic damned tongue! A good thing for her that that fool kid was over there, too bashful, too much the young gentleman even to warm her back, else he, Chance Ramsay, would give her something to talk smart about! He had a good mind to give her her needings, anyhow.

Then young Tuck, the boy hero, had to speak up: "Come mornin', if we see the mornin', let's all make a break for it. Head for Gonzales and he'p them settlers whup the Meskins. You and me can do it, Mr. Ramsay—Chance. You and me and Miss Lou. Can't we, Miss Lou?"

"Ask Ramsay," Lou said wickedly. "My husb—Chance is the big fighting man. They tell me that, up in Louisiana, he used to hunt bears with a switch, catch big alligators with a noosed rope, then ride the beasts just for sport. Your friend Ramsay's quite a *caballero*, Tuck—as we say down here in Texas."

"Now, you're pokin' fun at Ramsay," Tuck said stoutly. "Well, let me tell you, Miss Lou! He might dress sort of—of fancy, but he's got more guts—he's sure not no coward. Hadn't been for him I wouldn't be here. I'd still be in the ol' Sabine, drowned deader than—"

"Shut up and let a man sleep," Ramsay growled. Then another thought hit him and he murmured, "But go ahead, if you want to. Tell Texas Lou, here, what a brave lad I am. Partner, when we get to Gonzales, the Mexicans had better start a-running, that's certain sure!"

"Chance Ramsay, if you think I'm going to Gonzales—!" Lou said. "San Felipe is too close to those Mexicans, but—"

"My mind's made up," Ramsay said. "I'm going to Gonzales. You go where you damn' please." And in the darkness he caught the tip of her ear between his teeth, breathed into the ear with short, sharp breaths.

"Stop it," Lou whispered fiercely, "or there's going to be a mighty dead hero in this cabin. I've got my derringer under this corn-shuck pillow, my hand on it, and it's pointed right at you, Ramsay."

"Say," young Tuck spoke up, "what's all the whisperin' about? You folks keepin' ary secrets from me? Because if you are, I can tell you right now—"

"Why, Tuck, the idea!" Lou said in a voice that could have melted butter. And added to herself, *You young whipper—not dry behind the ears yet!*

The Indians struck again at dawn. They hit from two sides, one group of screeching devils driving arrows through the west windows and against the door, so that Tuck and Ramsay were hard-pressed to stand them off. The other group—Lou saw them coming, and screamed, just as the heavy log they were using for a battering ram crashed against the east door and it gave inward with a splintering sound, the butt end of the log and a couple of greasy, bronzed bucks coming on in with the door.

Immediately more whooping savages jammed the doorway, and Lou snarled, "Damn you'" and let drive with her derringer. She missed and grabbed an iron skillet from the cold fireplace.

Ramsay was down on his back, a grinning buck sitting on his chest; he kept on grinning after Lou had brought the skillet down on his topknotted head.

Mr. Chauncey Delafew Ramsay, with that buck astraddle of him, scalping knife in hand, lived a lifetime while his heart struck a couple of beats. He saw Lou swing the skillet, felt the buck's dead, smothering weight slump across him, and he heaved the greasy body aside and thought, *Rampart Street, good-by; good-by, Belle Marie of the golden skin. If Lou wants me, I'm bought and paid for!*

He sat up and Lou, wild-eyed, yelling words no lady should have, banged *him* over the head with the skillet.

"Murdering red-skinned sons of—Chance! Chance, why didn't you stop me? Have I knocked your poor brains out?"

She dropped to her knees beside him, stroked his pale cheek, then rose and stood over him, the skillet handle grasped in both hands as she cast about wrathfully for another target.

Tuck Bright saw the last of this. Tuck had put a ball through the belly of the other buck who had come spilling into the cabin; and when he whirled, ready to use old Bess for a club, he saw Lou's skillet descend upon Ramsay's black-haired head.

Tuck didn't understand what it was all about, but inside him something grinned. So she wasn't so stuck on Ramsay! She was open game for any man to court, make love to! He saw a passel of red boys crowding through the doorway, and leaped toward them with a wild exultation surging up in him.

Tuck never saw the three travel-weary men who came riding boldly into the clearing. Tuck, at that moment, was down beneath a bunch of grunting, rank-smelling savages, fighting desperately to save both his topknot and his life. But later he wrote in his journal.

*Goeing toard gonzales on the warloope—was near to lose
my cow lik maw so proud of when Steve austin & partie come
on scene—Steve on way to politicl meating at washington on
brasos & he is called litle padre of texas the litle father—a
litle man but look big when you see his eyes & verrie pale
becaus just out of Mexico citie dunjun—Says setlers must
whup meskins war only recorse—says i can join up with ar-
mie & we will whup meskins prontoe & i plan to marrie Lou
& becom big texas ransher—this a wonderfull plase! Lou
wonderfull gerl hit ramsay with skilet but ramsay good
friend—wish uncle Puce see me now!*

The business of talking the Cherokees out of lifting such easy
scalps had certain drawbacks, even for so fluent a speaker as
Stephen Austin. He refused to give them Lou's fine three-gaited
mare, so they took Ramsay's sorrel and Beulah. A bit later, the
soul of hospitality, the Indians' leader invited Austin and his
friends to partake of a spot of lunch. Ramsay ate like a starved
wolf.

They were headed on toward the Brazos, Ramsay and Tuck
walking, the rest riding, when Ramsay voiced an uneasy question.

"That stew—I've been trying to place the flavor of it. Not
beef or venison—"

"No," Austin said gravely, "nor not dog meat, such as my
friend, Sam Houston, praises so highly. Mr. Ramsay, you have
been introduced to a new delicacy. Call it—stew *à la* Beulah."

Lou's laugh ended in a gagging sound. They had to stop for
several minutes while Ramsay was sick.

The little group of travelers split at the Brazos, Austin and his
companions going on toward Washington; Miss Lou, Tuck, and
Ramsay holding to the ruts that would take them to Gonzales
settlement. Here it was, at the Brazos, that Tuck Bright spoke
to Austin of what was in his heart.

"Mr. Austin, suh—how would a man go about joining up
with the Texas army? I come here to find a wife, to make my
home—but I'm a pretty fair fighter, Mr. Austin. Was raised to
believe that anything wuth having is wuth fighting for"—and
here he looked at Lou, his whole soul in his eyes.

Stephen Austin looked at the boy, and something like glory
touched his pale, worn face. His voice came husky with emo-
tion.

"God bless you, son, God bless you. There have been many times—when I was in that damp, lonesome dungeon—when from letters I received, it seemed that men I had trusted, Houston, Wharton, and others, had all forsaken me—those times I doubted if the game, the Texas game, was worth the candle. But boys, young men like you, coming here to make their start in life, ready to fight for that start—Tuck, you see Johnny Moore, in Gonzales. Tell him I sent you. He'll have good use for a young man who's a fighter."

And he put a slender hand on Tuck's shoulder and looked long at him and said, "God bless you, Tucker Bright."

Ramsay became conscious of Lou's mocking gaze upon him, heard her say, "Ramsay's a right good fighter, Mr. Austin. He's just—too modest to say as much. But he sees the light, Mr. Austin. Give him a commission and he'll follow you as if you were leading him to the Promised Land. Ramsay, speak up! Talk for yourself, hero mine!"

Ramsay's feet were blistered, his wallet was missing. Sometime, during the set-to with those Indians, he had lost it.

He said, "Give me a good horse—any horse—and I'll get the hell out of this damned place!"

They all looked at him, and young Tuck's face showed shock, Austin's something like sadness.

"I take it, sir, you did not come here looking for a home, a place to make a start. So, without being cruel, I will have to say this: Texas has no place for you. Texas, as young Tuck, here, put it, is worth fighting for. Unless a man is willing, ready to fight—and to work and endure the struggle—Mr. Ramsay, my advice to you is, go back to New Orleans, the easy life, the life of luxury.

"But remember, sir, that if all Americans had been like you, there would not be any nation, any United States. There could not be any free Republic of Texas. I bid you good-by, sir, and you"—to Tuck—"you see Johnny Moore. *You* will find your place here."

CHAPTER FOUR

Come and Take It?

Gonzales settlement consisted of a handful of clapboarded cabins strung along the east bank of the Guadalupe. The trio of weary travelers reached there with dark coming on, and young Tuck immediately went in search of Captain Johnny Moore.

Lou looked back at Chance and Chance looked back at her; after tramping across Texas for what seemed a thousand miles, while she rode her fine three-gaited mare, Chance hated the sight of her.

"Well, my husb—my hero," she said. "What now? Maybe Captain Moore would make you a sergeant in the Gonzales Rifles."

"And maybe," Ramsay growled, "I could go over yonder to that store and bar I see and forget Johnny Moore and Texas—maybe even forget you. I found a gold double eagle in my watch pocket, and that ought to buy a lot of whisky in this place."

He bowed to her mockingly, said, "Later, my dear wife. Perhaps," and went limping across to where yellow lamplight spilled across the legs of a man who sat, half in, half out of a doorway, nursing a bottle that surely held something stronger than water.

Texas! Ramsay was thinking. *Gonzales—the damned cannon the Mexicans want back! Let them have it! Let them have the whole country! Before God—*

He stepped across the legs of the drunken man, glancing down as he did so. Fellow looked vaguely familiar. He headed for the bar, which was an unpainted pine board supported by a packing-case, a whisky barrel, and a carpenter's sawhorse. Ramsay shoved in between a bearded man in buckskins—there were, he noted, quite a few bearded, buckskinned men in the place, and all of them talking loud—and a slender-shouldered man who wore the remnants of a black broadcloth suit and a beaver hat.

Ramsay said, "Whisky. The best!" and his solitary goldpiece rang with authority on the bar.

The slender man in the beaver hat turned, said, "Chance! Chance, you old dog!" and cuffed Ramsay lightly on the cheek and showed him some proud white teeth. "Fancy meeting you here! I thought, after that shindig with Tom Gid, you wouldn't stop till you reached Mexico. Or—my God!—maybe we're in Mexico!''

He was Luis Ravenow, from New Orleans, and he told Ramsay that Tom Gid Paisley, the gay blade Ramsay had shot, was indeed dead. It gave Ramsay quite a shock until Ravenow, shaking his head in alcoholic sadness, explained.

''Why in hell else would I be down here in this uncouth, primitive, God-forgotten place? Chance old friend, that slug of yours cut a little blood from his comb, but mine took him center through the gizzard. My fuss with him was over a woman—and damn my eyes, but the sorry son has friends—*had* friends. I'm an exile, Chance; I'm stuck down here; you can go home, back to your Belle Marie, back to living; but me—'' and he put his face against Ramsay's shoulder and cried.

''Luis, old friend,'' Ramsay said, and was thinking of New Orleans with a nostalgic longing rising in him so strong that it choked him. He mentioned a small loan, say a miserly hundred dollars—and perhaps the loan of a horse. ''Look, Luis, I'll pay you back. First time I see you in New Orleans, at Claro's—''

Luis pulled himself together; he looked at his old friend with sadness, with resignation. ''I was thinking of touching you for a loan, perhaps a horse. Rode two until they were windbroke getting down here. Haven't pocket change enough, or any other kind, to pay for these drinks.''

And Luis smiled a white-toothed smile; he grinned. ''Old friend, I think I'll join this Texas army. How about you?''

''I,'' said Ramsay, ''think I'll shoot myself. Through the head.''

He turned away from the bar, and his friend, and made light-footed way toward the door. His belly was as empty of food as his pockets were of coins. The whisky had hit him hard. If it hadn't been for the whisky, perhaps he would have paid more attention to the loud, fierce talk of the Texas men in this place—perhaps he would have recognized the red-whiskered man nursing his bottle in the doorway.

The loud talk was about the Mexicans as a group, and about one Lieutenant Castañeda in particular; for he was the officer who had come, with a hundred dragoons, to take the settlers' little four-pounder cannon back to San Antonio. These men of Gonzales had buried the cannon in settler George Davis's peach orchard; they had impounded all boats from up and down the river and secured them on the east bank, so that Castañeda and his lads, if they came across at all, must swim the river. But these strategic moves, to the warlike Texans' way of thinking, were not bold enough or emphatic enough.

Now, as Ramsay crossed to the doorway, one barrel-chested man shouted, "I-God, they give us thet cannon to fight Injuns with; now they want it back and all our small arms as well! Boys, I move, I-God, we dig up that cannon, pound us out some chain shot, and use it on them dragoons! Castañeda's Gen'l Santa Anna's man, and if we don't all pitch in now, show 'em what's what, they'll make slaves out of us or run us all out'n the country!"

That speech drew ringing cheers, and then Mr. John Sowell, the blacksmith, said, "I'll pound out the chain shot, you boys dig up the cannon! We'll put 'er on wheels, by damn, and send them dragoons lopin' back to Béjar!"

There were lusty cries of "Hear! Hear!"—and Miss Lou DuSang, of the Fausse Rivière DuSangs, stepped past Ramsay and in the middle of the room held up a commanding hand.

"We women are making up a flag, with a cannon on it and a motto, a challenge! That challenge, gentlemen, is *Come and Take It!* All of you who are willing to fight for that flag—for Texas—step past me to yonder side of the room!"

And something about Lou, her husky voice, the blazing blue of her eyes, caught on with these rough men, thrilled them like the keening blast of a war trumpet. Mr. John Sowell started the move, and then they were shoving, jostling one another as they lined up along the wall to Lou's left.

Then Ramsay, who had paused near the door and was watching Lou, wondering what she was up to, became aware that the Texas men were eyeing him in a questioning, threatening way. Of a sudden Ramsay felt lonesome. All he wanted was out of here—until Mr. John Sowell spoke up.

"Well, what's holdin' you, stranger? Don't you aim to fight? I'll tell you now, you'd better aim to!"

Maybe it was that challenge, or the whisky; maybe it was the mocking look in Lou's eyes. But suddenly Ramsay drew himself up straight and tall; in a clear voice that sounded loud he said:

"Fight for Texas? I see nothing here worth fighting for! A two-bit cannon with the touch hole spiked; a lot of sorry land inhabited by Indians, wolves, and rattlesnakes! No, no, gentle-men, I never came to Texas to fight. I came because it was the only place in God's world I could go to!''

And he gave them a mocking bow. The Texas men, the entire bunch of them, were closing in, slowly, with purpose. Ramsay stepped backward toward the door.

''Chance! Look—''

Lou's warning was a bit late. The red-whiskered man in the doorway, behind Ramsay, might have been drunk, but he swung a mean bottle. It caught Ramsay across the ear; then the Texans were upon him.

They gave Ramsay the beating of his life, but through most of it he was swimming in blackness. When he came to he was lying on the ground outside the saloon. He tried to sit up, set his teeth and tried again. Those Texas sons must have cracked several ribs!

He thought of Lou with bitterness. So she was going to play the patriot, help make a Texas flag! Why, the lying two-faced wench! And where was she now, leaving him out here like a dog in a gutter?

He heard a clanging as of iron upon iron, got up and moved painfully toward the sound. He reached the corner of the building and a hand clamped his arm, drew him off of the packed-clay walk.

''Chance, you damn' fool, where do you think you're going?''

Ramsay stood in pale moonlight and stared at her, stared at Lou DuSang out of bitter eyes. For sprawled against the building was the red-whiskered man who had clubbed him with the whisky bottle. And now Ramsay recognized the man. Rowdy Ben Brashears, the same Rowdy who had tried to force himself upon Lou. The man she had creased with a slug from her der-ringer.

''I might ask you some questions too, Miss DuSang,'' Ramsay said. ''Like what you're doing here playing pattycake, in the dark, with that fellow. Like what you meant by that big show you put on inside the saloon. Going to make a flag, fight for Texas! Why, blast your sorry soul—''

''I was going to get you a horse—I have got you a horse—but I don't think I'll ride out of this miserable land with you,'' Lou told him with angry bitterness. ''I was at the door, fixing to come in after you, when you told Luis Ravenow you were stony-broke. Well, I see through you now! It's not only you who's broke; your whole family is bankrupt! You're nothing but an out-at-the-cuffs gambler. You tricked me into thinking you had money, and why I waste time on you now only God knows!''

"Then why did you put on that big act for those Texans?" Ramsay shook her roughly, his fingers biting into her arms. "And where is that horse? With a horse, I can go back to New Orleans, and that's where I'm going!"

"The horse is around in front, with my mare—Rowdy Brashears's horse," she said, her voice suddenly weary. "I had to let him paw me some before I hit him with that rock, but he won't be needing his horse anytime soon. As for the act I put on—those Texans think I'm quite a woman. They'll let me ride with them, at daybreak, when they cross the river to fight those dragoons.

"I had it in mind, before Rowdy Brashears came into the picture, to get in with these men, maybe borrow a horse for you. I thought we could cross the river with them and keep on riding—clear to the coast, where maybe we could catch a boat to New Orleans. We're broke, worn out. We never could get out of Texas, reach the Sabine, the way we came. But it's not far to the coast. So I thought—but what difference? My man has got to have money. Luis Ravenow might be broke now, but he's got money. A lot of it. So—well—''

"It suits me," Ramsay said harshly. "You greedy little Jezebel—you go your way, I'll go mine. And I thought *you* had money! Well, you're right about one thing. Luis Ravenow's got plenty of the stuff. My advice to you is to marry him, quick, before some Mexican puts a bullet through him!"

He turned and lurched away, saying, "Anyhow, it was nice to have been—married to you. *Adios*, as we Texans say. Happy hunting.''

"Chance! Where are you going? I told those men you were my husband, that you were a real fighter but half-crazy from Texas fever. Chance, that clanging—John Sowell and Mr. Chisholm are in the blacksmith shop, beating out chain shot. Go see them, Chance. Apologize. Go across the river with us in the morning—any maybe you and I and Luis will ride on to the coast together. But by yourself—Indians, maybe Mexican dragoons— Chance, you'll never make it!"

"Who cares?" Ramsay said. "I sure as hell don't. Much. But that one night was nice, something to remember. You kept me almost as warm as Belle Marie used to."

He went on around the corner, smiling sardonically at her, choked, "Ah, damn you! I hope—"

The horse was a leggy dun. Probably Rowdy Brashears had stolen the beast. But what was the theft of a horse in this iniquitous land?

Ramsay climbed on the dun and rode downriver, with his head aching, his belly growling from hunger, and little devils dancing around inside his skull and screeching, *To hell with Lou DuSang, Lou DuSang. New Orleans, Belle Marie, brandy juleps, brandy juleps—*

The easy-gaited dun carried Ramsay perhaps two miles through gloom of the bottomland. An owl hooted down at Ramsay and his nerves quivered, and he thought of Lou—Lou and Luis Ravenow; he had no doubt but what she would rope him in, for Luis was always a pushover for a beautiful woman. Yonder in the darkness of live oaks a coyote wailed mournfully; Ramsay shut his eyes and saw Lou and Luis, in some lonesome cabin.

"Devil take that woman," he muttered, and again an owl hooted. His eyes popped open and then he saw them, or thought he saw them, shadowy figures there in the underbrush. Lord, it was lonesome—

Lord, I don't want that woman, but I'd like to keep my hair!

And he wheeled the dun and his heels drummed the beast's flanks. They headed back for Gonzales at a faster clip than had brought them away from that settlement.

CHAPTER FIVE

"Call It 'Love' "

Ramsay got back to Gonzales just in time to cross the river with the Texas men. He had to do some tall talking—eat crow, as Texans put it. To save his soul, he told Captain Johnny Moore, he didn't know what had come over him; the fever, he guessed, had gone to his head. Why, he had come here to make his home, he loved Texas, was more than willing to fight for Texas.

The captain of the Gonzales Rifles said gruffly, "God knows we can use fighting men—but if you're fooling us, seh, if you're fooling us—"

Lou, sitting her mare between young Tucker Bright and Luis Ravenow—Tuck worshipping her with his eyes—gave Ramsay a mocking smile.

Some fifty of them were mounted; these staunch ones led the way across the river. The rest of them, perhaps a hundred strong, crossed over in boats. They were armed with bowie knives, a few rifles and pistols, and with lances they had made from sharpened files stuck into poles. Their spirits were high, for they had the six-pounder cannon and they had their flag: *Come and Take It!*

On the Guadalupe's west bank they held a council of war; Reverend Smith, from Rutersville, made a stirring address. Fog had descended thick and clammy, so that when, about midnight, they took up the line of march, it was in high hopes of surprising the enemy.

Ramsay, jogging along in the fog on the jug-headed dun, kept thinking about Lou.

He remembered her in New Orleans, the belle of the ball with every dandy rushing her, wanting to dance with her; and later, the full yielding warmth of her lips. He remembered her standing over Rowdy Brashears, the bully boy, beneath the gloomy trees on that miserable road called the King's Highway. He remembered her on the shucks, in the settler's cabin. . . .

And now she was riding into battle. Lou and a lad named Tuck Bright; Lou and Luis Ravenow, with all his cash and his rich arpents of sugarland.

Damn her, he thought, *it's a shame the DuSangs lost all their money. We could have fun, enjoy the good things. Lou, your flame-bright hair, your satin skin—*

Somewhere in the fog ahead a dog was barking. Came a rattle of musketry; then, beside Ramsay, a growled oath.

"There goes our surprise. That's the dragoons' picket line, I'll bet a pretty."

Johnny Moore lifted a bronze-lunged shout: "Hold yo' places. Save yo' powder for daylight. Artillerymen! Haul the cannon for'rd to position."

The sun came up and burned the fog away. There on a hillside were the dragoons, their bright armament glittering in the sunlight. Surely there were more than a hundred of them! Ramsay, who had an eye for color, for beauty, felt a tingle run up his spine.

Johnny Moore rode back from a parley with Lieutenant Castañeda, and the captain's face was grim. He took position a little to the right of the cannon, looked once to see if the two artillerymen were ready, then raised his hand smartly.

With no more to it than that, the first shot was fired in the Texas Revolution. For at the captain's signal, a match was applied to the touch hole. The four-pounder belched flame and chain shot. She reared back on her clumsy cart wheels and the whistling, shrieking sound she made was weird and terrible to hear.

Texans' horses plunged away from the cannon. Ramsay's dun, surprising him mightily, put a hump in his back and tried to toss him into a mesquite bush. Rattle of gunfire and triumphant Texas yells smote Ramsay's ears. He dug his heels into the dun's flanks, and the next think Ramsay knew, a hundred Mexican dragoons were heading out across the prairie, and Ramsay and the dun were hard on their heels, Ramsay sawing futilely on the reins, the damned dun refusing to stop.

So ended the Battle of Gonzales, the skirmish over the cannon—but yet to come was the siege of that old fortress called the Alamo, the massacre at Goliad, the Runaway Scrape, the final curtain, the victory, at San Jacinto. Loud was the bragging in Gonzales that night, long the drinking.

But there was a climax, an epilogue, to this little affray. An insignificant event not mentioned in any history. Leading up to this, it might be mentioned, was young Tucker Bright's last entry in his journal.

> *Gonzales on the Warloope—Reeched here laste nite & joined up with Col. moore—some call him onlie captan—anyhow we will whup Meskins & never let them take cannon or nothing ellse—feer i have loste Lou for she crasie about friend ramsay—Texas men threw ramsay out of saloon laste nite as i was goeing in—to git leemonade—Lou was in there & cussed about ramsay & cried about him & i could not savvy it—She said he was broke & no dam good & i said he*

*is to—She kissed me!—Anyhow i never go bak on a friend &
will not on ramsay & think he is fine brave man spoil by to
much monie—will try to bring him out of that!—yes & find
me a new girl—this a fine plase!*

> *Tucker Bright the texas traveler*

So Ramsay, the "no dam good," still trying to curb the runaway dun, saw a swag of switch mesquite and retama ahead of
him. The dun went plunging into it—and a half-dozen dragoons
were waiting there.

The dun, as he hit the bottom of the dry creek bed, stumbled.
Ramsay sailed past the dun's ears. He struck the sandy creek
bottom with such force that breath left his lungs; when again he
was able to breathe, several dragoons were standing over him,
scowling.

A dragoon held a musket against Ramsay's head. The fluted
end of the thing reminded him, though he was not an especially
religious man, of Saint Gabriel's trumpet. The dragoon said,
"Ah, pobrecito," and Ramsay drew in a great breath of Texas
air, thought it surely the sweetest air he would ever breathe. He
shut his eyes and said, "Shoot!" and heard a yell, a banging
explosion.

Surprised to find himself still alive, Ramsay flopped onto his
belly, pushed up on his hands and knees and was facing in the
direction he had come from when he started to roll. The sorrowful dragoon who, moments ago, had been about to annihilate
him was down, not moving. In his place stood a scowling brown-
faced buddy, this one, too, holding a musket.

For perhaps two heartbeats Ramsay stared, musket and mustached face above it staring back at him. Then Ramsay yelled
and sprang up from the ground, knowing that he was too slow,
far too slow. Strangely enough, thought of Lou touched his mind
and a great longing, a great regret overwhelmed him. The next
moment, young Tucker Bright had charged past him, was square
between Ramsay and the fluted snout of the musket.

Tuck's rifle was empty so he used it for a club. He swung it
lustily and yelled at the dragoon, while Ramsay, driving in from
an angle, slammed his shoulder into Tuck's ribs. The dragoon's
musket belched sound and smoke and flame. It scorched Tuck's
buckskin shirt; its round ball, at that close range, tore a great
hole in the boy's side.

Ramsay stood above Tuck, staring across the boy at the dragoon with the smoking musket in his hands. So fast had all this happened that Ramsay could scarcely believe it had happened. He began to shake. Rage surged up in him so bitter, so intense that he felt dizzy. He grabbed up Tuck's rifle and swung it at the dragoon's head just as that unfortunate one was taking to his heels.

Ramsay had the rifle by the barrel, so it was the stock and part of the breech that caught the dragoon above his ear. The rifle stock splintered. There was a sound as of a squashing gourd, and the dragoon was down, already dead.

There were three more of the buckos, dancing around now, cursing Mexican curses, trying to catch Ramsay in line with their muskets. He charged them, swinging the rifle with its splintered stock as if it were a scythe. Something about him, something in his eyes perhaps, was too much for the soldier boys. They scattered before him like squandering quail, heading for their tethered horses.

Ramsay dropped to one knee beside Tuck Bright, saw that the lad's eyes were open. Death already was touching his face, graying his lips, laying a wonder in his eyes.

"Saw your horse—stompede, Ramsay. But them dragoons was—surprise. Be happy—you an' Miss Lou. With her for wife—get you league and labor of land—think of it, Ramsay! This—wonderful—place."

Tucker Bright, the Texas Traveler, had ridden his last Texas mile. Ramsay stared down at him for a long moment, the bitterness in him growing, sharpening until it was a pain in his chest.

"A wonderful place," he said. "Yes, Tuck—a wonderful place."

Ramsay laid the boy in a shallow ravine, covered him with rocks, and rammed the barrel of the old squirrel rifle into the ground for a marker. Anywhere in Texas, he guessed, would do for young Tuck. Strange, he thought. This boy, this bright-eyed kid, had given his life for the life of Chance Ramsay, who wasn't worth the powder to blow him to kingdom come.

Back in Gonzales, he looked for Lou. She was last seen, he was told, riding eastward, toward the coast, with Luis Ravenow. Quite a few of the weaker-hearted settlers already were pulling out, heading back for the States.

Ramsay took up quarters in a deserted cabin in the edge of the settlement. A queer lethargy had come over him, sapping ambition and desire. His first impulse had been to ride after Lou. But something, pride perhaps, had held him back, and finally he told himself he didn't care where she went, or what man she went with, slept with, mocked, or married.

He didn't even want to go back to New Orleans. Belle Marie seemed a dim and shadowy figure, like remembered perfume, on the fringes of his mind.

A couple of evenings he went down to the river, where the Texans, the companies of Johnny Moore, Jim Fannin, and Tom Alley, were drilling and making plans to march onto San Antonio and whip the Mexicans who then held that place.

He was down at the river the afternoon Lou and Luis came riding back. With them were three young blades from New Orleans, young wastrels with whom Ramsay was slightly acquainted. Sam Houston, it seemed, had put a notice in a New Orleans newspaper:

Volunteers from the United States will . . . receive liberal bounties of land . . . Come with a good rifle . . . Liberty or Death!

The drama was unfolding. Fighting men, lured by the promise of rich land, by the love of adventure, were hurrying to Texas by wagon, by boat, and on horseback. Some were outlaws, some were statesmen; some of them, like Jim Bowie, were to die in the Alamo, some were to die at Goliad, their blood to secure Texas for the Union. One thing they held in common: a heart that beat strong.

Chance Ramsay watched while the New Orleans men became Texas soldiers. They joined the Gonzales Rifles. No papers to sign, not much to it.

Johnny Moore said, "You men willin' to take my orders, to fight till the last ditch if it maybe means dyin'? . . . Fine and dandy! Consider yourselves privates in the Gonzales Rifles."

And he swung around and put a sharp stare on Chance Ramsay. "What about you?"

"I don't know," Ramsay said. "I guess I'm not much of a fighter."

He turned and walked away. He heard Lou call, "Chance! Chance, wait!" But he did not stop.

His mind was confused. He thought of his father, of Belle

Marie with the golden skin; memory came back to him of all the money he had spent when the Ramsays were in the money, when by a crook of his finger he could order a brandy, have a black boy bring it to him, when with a flirt of a pencil he could sign an I. O. U. for more money than he was ever apt to see again.

And once more, in his mind, he saw a girl with yellow hair, a girl named Hawkins who thought he was a fighting man, a girl who had died in his arms with an arrow in her breast. Big Jim and Little Jim, her brothers. *"Tell them—tell them to keep fighting. Tell them—Texas—"*

Chance Ramsay could not understand it—but one thing he knew: behind all of these people, Big Jim and Little Jim Hawkins, their sister with the yellow hair; behind Steve Austin and behind young Tuck Bright, the Texas Traveler, there was a driving force, a vital belief in something that was bigger than life itself.

What, he asked himself, was his reason for being? Why had Tucker Bright died for him? In this whole world, that he, Chance Ramsay, had thought was so shining, what was really worthwhile?

It came to Ramsay, finally, that he was worth no more than a grain of sand. Tuck Bright had not died for him; Tuck had died, actually, for a principle, for something he believed in. He had believed that anything worth having was worth fighting for. His boyish mind had reached even further than that. He had fought so that others, even so sorry a one as Chance Ramsay, might live to enjoy the bounty of Texas.

Ramsay, still a young man, had been educated in the finest of schools, brought up on silver and silk. To him Tuck's reasoning was a little pathetic. Still, now, he believed that he could understand that reasoning.

The Mexicans, who owned this land, had an arguing point; the settlers who had come to Texas, following Steve and Moses Austin, had an arguing point. Which side was right? *Quien sabe?* But each side, Mexican and Gringo, was willing to fight until the last ditch. In the final analysis, Ramsay guessed, no man was too important; it was only what that man stood for, was willing to fight for, that was important.

Ramsay went back to the cabin and sat on the edge of the bunk. He was, he had thought, a sophisticated man, but tears came into his eyes and he felt lost, lost, no good, forsaken. He did not think of Lou, her flame-red hair, her supple body, her blaze-blue eyes. Instead, strangely enough, he thought of his father.

The "old man," as he thought of him, had fought in the Battle of New Orleans, and before that he had fought against the Seminoles, with Andrew Jackson. His old man, his father, had fought and worked and built a place for himself, gained title to many arpents of sugarland above New Orleans, furnished his son with a purse that, for many years, had no bottom. The old man had never harped at him for the wastrel years; the old man, in all his life, had never said, "I can't. I quit."

Chance Ramsay, the gambler, the no-good, put his head in his hands and said aloud, "Papa, I cannot quit. I won't quit. Papa, I don't know where I'm heading, but I'm going to fight."

"You're a little late, Chance," a husky voice said. "Your—papa is dead."

Ramsay looked up and saw her standing there—Lou with the flame-red hair, the blaze-blue eyes.

"Those boys—the tall, blond one—told me," she said. "Your father died a month ago. A fever. I'm—sorry, Chance. Now, do you want to go back to New Orleans?"

"Why," he asked, "didn't you keep going? You were headed home—you and Luis. What made you change your mind?"

She shrugged, sighed. "It goes that way. We met these three buckaloos from home. They were hell-bent to reach the frontier, maybe give out with blood for the cause, for Texas. Luis, the damn fool, wants to be a hero too. Let him be one. I quit."

"E-yeah," Ramsay said, "and I am going to bed." He sat down on the edge of the bunk, began pulling off his boots. He was thinking of his father, that spirited not-too-old man, and somehow he resented Lou's being there.

"Good night, Lou," he said, and pulled his one blanket over him. Then he had to say, "I hope that you and Luis make a happy go of—"

"Chance, you—you—why, you—" and she was on her knees beside the bunk. There were tears, he was almost certain there were tears—or maybe it was the candlelight shining in her eyes.

"Good night," he said. "Blow out the candle, Lou."

"Luis!" she said. "Chance, don't you know? Don't you know

anything? Luis—we rode a hundred miles and we came back. I
had to come back, Chance. I came to Texas to find you. I know
I'm a—a mercenary, sorry, no-account woman, but, Chance—
Chance, I—don't you love me a little? Chance, remember that
night at the settler's shack? Remember—Chance—''

She got no further because Mr. Chauncey Delafew Ramsay,
sitting up in the bunk, had grabbed her. He caught her in a grip
that would have strangled a Texas steer.

He said, in a choked, queer voice, "Lou—Lou—''

Later, he thought of his father. The old man, he guessed, had
given him a good enough start in life, an education, money, a
good name. If the money was gone now, he still had the education, still had the name, and with Lou he could whip lions,
nothing could stop him. Go back to New Orleans, be a big sugar
man; stay in Texas, raise cattle—what was the difference? He
had his health, he had Lou—no limit to a man's future!

Next morning Ramsay and Lou rode out of Gonzales. They
followed the Texans, who with their flag and their "Flying Artillery," the four-pounder cannon, were hell-bent to capture San
Antonio and run General Cos, who had a thousand well-armed
men, clear back across the Rio Grande.

But, somehow, with his father dead, New Orleans no longer
appealed to Ramsay. He put the question up to Lou: Go back,
or stay in Texas?

"New Orleans," Lou said. "That's where you belong, where
we belong. With money—I mean, we can ride to the coast, catch
a steamer, any boat—''

They tagged along after the Texas "army." Dark came on.
Ramsay was fretful, vaguely dissatisfied. He had Lou, he was
heading for home, he ought to be happy. But somehow he wasn't.
Liquor, segars, gambling, seductive women—he guessed he
could have all those things, forget this raw barbaric place. But
somehow he felt cheated; something was missing, something
was wrong.

"Lou, are you sure you want to go back? Are you sure you
love me? Suppose—?''

"Suppose what?" she asked a little sharply. "Chance, are
you going noble on me? I've told you I love you. I've—proved
that. What else, in God's name, do you want?''

"Don't know," Ramsay said glumly. "But one thing I do

know. We're lost. Which way from here is the coast? Where have those Texans we've been following got to?''

"My God," Lou said, "can't you even find the coast of Texas when it stretched for over a thousand miles?" She added something that sounded like "To hell with the Texans we've been following!"

They came upon the Texans quite suddenly. They dropped down into a brushy draw, so shallow that their heads were in bright moonlight, and the voice of Luis Ravenow said, "Ramsay! Down, man, get down! You're skylighted."

They fell off their horses, saw the shadow shapes of ten or twelve men. Ravenow said, "Johnny Moore sent us out to reconnoiter—Mexicans ahead. What in hell you doing here, Chance? With all that money waiting for you in New Orleans, I thought you'd be burning the breeze—''

"Money?" Ramsay said sharply. "What money?"

"Didn't Jules tell you? Jules—he's the tall, blond chap, father a judge. Seems that some years ago your father set up a sort of trust fund for you. The judge handled it. Fifty thousand dollars. Chance, old chappo, you're rich! Why else," he added ruefully, "do you suppose your sweet Lou, there, decided on you instead of a handsome, gay dog like me? When we ran into Jules and them and Lou heard about—''

The look Ramsay gave her was black and bitter. "I might have known! So that's what brought you back. You mercenary, cozening wench!"

"Chance, Chance," Ravenow chided mockingly. "Don't be hard on a woman that beautiful. Don't let a little spending money come between you. Lou, honey, I'm not exactly broke. I'll take you back."

"You!" Lou spat. "You couldn't wait to tell him!"

She turned and caught Ramsay's arms. "Well, I guess that tore it—didn't it, Chance?"

"We're through," Ramsay said through his teeth. "All I want from you is the feel of your neck between my hands."

The tall, lean shape of Jim Bowie loomed up. "Ravenow, take Gus Jones and go ahead a piece, see if you can locate those Mexicans. But keep to cover, keep down."

Bowie, who had joined the group in Gonzales, turned and made his way to the top of the ravine, crawling the last few feet, then motioning for the others to join him. Ravenow and the kid named Gus crawled up the slope and kept going.

Minutes of silence and then Bowie's low, almost agonized cry: "Down, man, I told you to keep—"

There was the rattle of musketry. Bowie was up and charging forward, rifle at the ready, calling, "Come on, men! I see them now—dozen dragoons, maybe. They got one of the boys, sure!"

The Texans were over the bank with a yell, and Ramsay, not realizing he was moving, was hard after them. Bowie and his men ran on past Luis Ravenow; Ramsay stopped, dropped to a knee beside his friend. Luis Ravenow, the gay blade, the woman lover. The life was spurting out of him with each beat of his heart.

He looked up, saw Ramsay, tried to grin. "And it would—been the great adventure. Man like me, never worth a damn, thought for once I'd see how it felt to—fight for something—worthwhile." Luis died that way, mocking himself, faintly smiling.

In the brush ahead rifles and muskets were banging away, men were cursing, shouting, probably dying. Ramsay heard a sound like a sob, turned and saw Lou.

"And this is only the start of it," she said. "A lot of men like Luis will die. Do you suppose Texas is worth it?"

"I don't know," Ramsay said, "but I intend to find out. I've never really worked for anything, fought for anything, but— What's it to you, anyway?"

"Just this," she said, and she caught him to her and kissed him fiercely, then shoved him away. "You can't get rid of me, Chance. You can't run me away. I'm going to go wherever you go, stay wherever you stay. I thought money was the biggest thing in the world. But I've decided there *is* something bigger—call it 'love,' if you want to be poetic."

"And when the fighting's over?" Ramsay said. "Suppose I decide to stay in Texas—be a farmer, a rancher? Suppose I'm a poor man, flat broke? My father warned me to have money—I guess, because he thought I'd never be able to make any for myself. But, fifty thousand in trust, or not, he left a lot of debts. When I pay them, Lou, I'll be—a tramp again."

"You'll be a soldier," she said. "But not just fighting for Texas. Fighting for yourself—for me—for our future."

He kissed her then, crushed her against him. All the uncertainty, all doubts, were gone. He was happier than he'd ever been in his life.

"Go back to Gonzales, Lou," he said finally. "I'm going to find Johnny Moore. I'm going to help his Gonzales Rifles lick hell out of somebody; I don't much care who!"

They walked back to their horses. From the rising triumph of the Texans' yells, it sounded as if they were getting the best of this little skirmish. Lou, on her horse, looked down at Ramsay and reined the mare around.

"Fight good, husband!" she said. Then her last words came back to him: "Who'd ever thought I'd be such a damn' fool!"

About the Editors

Bill Pronzini has written numerous Western short stories and such novels of the Old West as *Starvation Camp* and *The Gallows Land*. He lives in Sonoma, California.

Martin H. Greenberg has compiled over 200 anthologies, including westerns, science fiction, and mysteries. He lives in Green Bay, Wisconsin.